The
Midnight
Dancers

RANDOM HOUSE   NEW YORK

Anne Maybury

The Midnight Dancers

The
Midnight
Dancers

I

I CLIMBED the narrow stepped street in the old city of Bou Hammagan toward a house I had never seen, to meet a woman I did not know.

The burning blaze of the afternoon sun was made bearable by my own excitement. The three of us—a man, a woman and a child—walked as closely as we could in the purplish shades of the ancient clay walls and the tree branches that spread over them from hidden gardens. And as we moved between those merciful shadows, the African sun struck us, sharp as a blade.

The world of Bou Hammagan was stirring from its siesta as we climbed from the Kabenès Gate where we had to leave the car. Men uncurled themselves from under fig trees or the shades of jutting balconies, their djellabahs swinging as they rolled up their mats or put on the shoes which had served as head rests.

There was mystery in the gaping blackness behind the iron-grilled windows of the houses. I had a feeling that we—white skinned and briefly dressed—were watched secretly and with curiosity as we walked in a town which had not yet been opened to tourists.

To our right, the view was of the flat roofs of houses; to our left a three-arched minaret rose skyward near a blue dome and a cluster of cypress trees was a dusky cloud in the glittering light.

But the excitement I felt at being in a strange city was superficial. Beneath it was a whisper of fear that I had made a mistake in coming, and yet that it was too late to turn back.

The longing to join Mark, my husband, who was working with a television film crew in North Africa, together with the lure of an art commission that was the most exciting of my career, had proved irresistible. I had not really paused to question the wisdom of what I was doing. Only as I walked up the ancient stepped street to Beit el Faskieh—the House of the Fountains—where Mark was already staying and where I was to join him for the next few weeks, did the full realization of what I had done hit me. Realization—and a memory . . .

Mark saying soon after our marriage, "I can't be possessed, Cathy. I can only exist if I feel free in my work and my life."

"Of course. Of course," I said, impatient at his attempt to explain himself. I told myself that I understood him. A television reporter must come and go as his work demanded. Foreign assignments had become a specialty with Mark and, as he once put it to me, "I've been East of the Sun and West of the Moon." Although the work was exacting and at times exhausting, Mark loved it all, and it was no real hardship for me because, loving him, I was happy. Also, while he was away, I had my own two engrossing occupations. There was my much loved eight-year-old stepdaughter—my enchanting waif, Pippa—to care for and my own career as a stained-glass artist to keep me busy and stimulated. This meant that when Mark returned from his foreign journeys, I had something of my own to talk to him about. I had a career and Mark liked that because he said independence should be a mutual thing.

As we climbed the long, worn steps to the house where we were to stay, my own thoughts were interspersed with Pippa's constant need for reassurance. She kept touching my hand with fingers as damp with heat and the effort of climbing as mine, and I tried to make my replies to her questions as bright and comforting as I could.

Yes, those houses we passed must be very dark inside . . . No, I didn't think the ginger dog that slunk past us was starving—it was just that animals living in hot countries were usually thin.

Behind us we could hear the steady clip-clop of the little gray donkey's hooves pulling the cart on which our luggage had been piled for the journey up the steps to the House of the Fountains.

"I'm tired," Pippa said. "Won't the donkey be tired, too, with all our luggage?" She dragged her feet, looking over her shoulder.

"He's used to the heat, darling, and he wouldn't be trotting so lightly if he were tired." Knowing himself to be home, I thought; food at the end of his journey and the smell of the Sahara in his soft nostrils. While I? I was over a thousand miles from home and in an alien place where I was still uncertain of Mark's wholehearted welcome.

The back of my neck tingled and tiny red-hot needles pricked the soles of my feet. But Mark's brother, Justin, who had met us at the airport in Algiers, seemed impervious to discomfort, nor had the long drive to Bou Hammagan tired him. He strode ahead wearing a sky-blue T-shirt and beige shorts, his fair hair only slightly ruffled. Occasionally he remembered us and checked the stride of his long, sun-tanned legs to our shorter steps, waving an arm toward landmarks.

There, seen through a gap in a crumbling wall, was the Casbah, which was thirteenth century. "Marvelously crenelated walls, aren't they? . . . There's Isakila Square, the chief meeting place for everyone. Of course, it's really the *medina,* only they call it a square out of gratitude to an English government who did them a favor, in the shape of a big monetary loan, a hundred years ago." Justin flicked at Pippa's long hair. "If you go to that corner, you can see the mosque quite clearly. The dome is made of a precious stone called lapis lazuli."

She let the jewel name pass. "Can I go and see inside?"

"If you tried, the Bou Hammagarbs would chase you out."

"That's a funny name—Hammagarb."

"The natives of Bou Hammagan, sweetie," Justin said.

"People here pray a lot, don't they?"

"Yes. And the children learn at a very early age to recite the Koran. You'll probably hear them chanting. In the big cities in North Africa they now use mechanical devices to call people to prayer. In Bou Hammagan they still have the muezzin who climbs the minaret and chants. Here, if you've got good sight—and you have, haven't you?— you'll see a man standing high up in the minaret making his peculiar call. And, wherever they are, the faithful will pray. After all, they've got something to thank heaven for. Oil. 'Allah has chosen us to reap this great benefit. Allah be praised.'" Justin turned to me. "Oil is going to make this state rich, though it is only a pocket-handkerchief country at the moment."

Pippa let go of my hand, forgetting that she was hot and tired, and ran across the step to peer through the gap in the pinkish clay wall. I hadn't the energy to follow her. There were plenty of days in which I could stand and look out over Bou Hammagan. At this moment, after a plane journey and a long car drive, I felt like someone shut in a baker's oven and too hot for sightseeing.

I watched Justin standing behind Pippa with his hands on her shoulders, looking down on the city, and wondered how he liked living in Bou Hammagan. Mark had told me that he had left England reluctantly because his small private income wouldn't stretch to a comfortable existence there.

Justin didn't like work, but he hated discomfort even more and so he had accepted an offer made to him by a British tourist agency to act as a guide for rich customers who wanted personally conducted tours along the North African coast. His earnings were spasmodic, but he was invariably fortunate in receiving big tips from those to whom he acted as guide. He was paid not only for his considerable knowledge of the history and languages of North Africa but also because of his easy, almost throwaway charm.

His type of existence, pleasant enough to anyone whose main enjoyment was sun-drenched days with cheap living conditions thrown in, infuriated his wife, Harriet. She had been at art school with me and had shown great promise as a landscape artist. When she went out to Africa to join Justin, she had plans to show her paintings in the large hotels in Algiers and Tunis and sell to tourists. But in this she had only been partially successful for, as ambitious as Justin was idle, she priced her work too high.

Harriet and I were opposites in so many ways that had she not become my sister-in-law, I doubt that our friendship would have lasted after art school. As it was, we accepted one another, met very seldom, agreed to differ on most things and nursed a friendship too casual to matter much to either of us.

The idea of sending a television team to North Africa had already been discussed at what Mark called "Round Table" level when Justin arrived in London several months ago. He was on his routine visit to the tourist agency which employed him, and at such times he stayed with us.

"The idea of the New City, as they call it, is marvelous," Justin said. "It will attract people who want to live in some Western-dominated corner of North Africa where they can exist together in a luxury community. Already a lot of Europeans are building villas there and they say the streets will be avenues of flowers—you know the sort of thing: bougainvillaea and palms and oleander. As the state has no architects and very few technicians, they're paying foreigners very high prices to plan their city."

I broke into the conversation, telling Justin that Chris Lanyard, the artist in stained glass for whom I worked, had an architect friend who was in Bou Hammagan with plans to build two villas and a church there.

Justin said, laughing, "I met your boss, Lanyard, once. I thought he looked like a cross between Hemingway and an African lion. All that beard the color of sand . . . All right, I'm not trying to belittle him—in fact, he seemed to me rather larger than life."

Two months after that conversation, Mark left with a film crew to cover the story of the building of a new city, from the oil wells which gave it birth to the planning of the city itself. It would be no second Brasilia, but the government had optimistic dreams that it would rival the Costa Esmeralda where the rich build their villas and spend their fortunes.

Mark's first letter to me which began by giving me practical facts ended by being almost lyrical.

We have found a small house near the Casbah for our headquarters. It's a bit cramped, especially as Stuart, our cameraman, takes up the space of two, but we usually spend our leisure at the hotel here. There's only one and it's not particularly exciting, though it does have a swimming pool.

I have seen the architects' plans for the enormous building project here. A white city is to rise out of clouds of oleander and palms and lianas; the villas themselves are being designed by architects who dare also to be poets.

It's strange, isn't it, that something as unmagical as oil flowing from ugly wells way out in the desert will pay for such beauty? After which the rich Europeans will take over and multiply the city's wealth.

This is the biggest assignment I've had and it's going to take some time, since nothing out here moves beyond the pace of a tortoise. But our biggest headache is the invasion of onlookers. Even when we're in the desert the villagers seem to collect from miles around. The mobile cameras fascinate them. We've had to employ three men and post them to keep the people back while the cameras are running. But it's all in a wonderful cause, Cathy dear, and one of these days I'll buy you diamond earrings.

Bless you.

No letter I had received from him during his assignments abroad had ever included the words that I would have loved to hear: "I wish you were here with me." I tried to be realistic about it. Mark and his team were working under pressure and there was little time or solitude for him. But that was something with which I comforted myself in order not to admit what, deep down, I knew. Mark never laid his thoughts and feelings entirely bare. He was a very detached, contained man. I loved him, but I didn't fully understand him.

All our friends commented on his courage, his great humanity. He drove himself into the danger of violent coups d'état; into countries where blood boiled easily; to the stricken site of a volcanic eruption.

Mark was thirty-three, seven years older than I. We had met at a party given in a very beautiful new office building to celebrate the final fixing in place of one of Chris Lanyard's finest stained-glass windows. It was a great wall of glowing, living color.

Although I had often watched Mark Mountavon's programs on television, I had never longed to meet him. His way of life and mine were poles apart and all I had ever felt was a vague envy because his work took him to marvelous places which I longed to visit.

I was introduced to him as I stood with a small group of people below Chris's vast window. We talked, drank champagne and then he took me out to dinner. He had very few illusions about his work. "They pay me royally, but it's tough. I can be in favor today and out of favor tomorrow." He had shrugged and laughed. A few months after that first meeting we were married and I discovered how much dedicated work went into each program: the planning, the discussions, the mountains of notes. I admired the stamina necessary for those hour-long programs.

"He drives himself hard," said one of his friends, "and shows himself no mercy."

But that was Mark . . .

Leaning against the old shaded wall, I waited for Justin to tire of playing guide to Pippa. It was a relief to pause for breath along that hot, stepped street.

In those moments when I was alone, I knew that my first objective would be to convince everyone that I was not playing the suspicious wife nor in any way coming between Mark and his assignment. I was in North Africa on a commission of my own and that fact was neither coincidence nor the result of design on my part. All over Europe sudden interest in the New City had sprung up, and I was in Bou Hammagan because a friend of Chris Lanyard's had come to see him one afternoon at his studio and workshops in Fulham.

David Sullavan, short, fair, stocky and thirtyish, had called to ask Chris if he would take on a commission to design a stained-glass window for the church for which he had been the architect. He explained that the idea was for an interdenominational building—rather a hall than a church, since it was to serve more than one sect. On the face of it, David explained to Chris, the idea did not seem practical and he had a suspicion that, in the end, the plan would fail and the building would become a church for one particular Christian group. That didn't concern him. What did, was the fact that there was to be a stained-glass window and that as yet those who met in Algiers to discuss it had not been able to agree on size or theme. One sect wanted a window that would dominate. Another, which scorned ornamentation, would agree only to the compromise of a small window.

"The point being," David had explained, "available land for the New City is not that extensive and it would be impossible for individual churches to be built. Hence the compromise. So, will you come out and look the building over—it's fairly well advanced—and work out some designs?"

Chris would not. He was busy designing a huge wall of stained glass to be set in a new London building, and I knew perfectly well that he was too single-minded to want to divide his attention. One job at a time had always been his motto.

He said, absently, more interested in watching the cutting of a tall symbolic figure in flashed glass, "Take Cathy."

I had been at work at the glazing bench at the far end of the studio and I would have been out of earshot had the men in the adjoining workshop not, at that moment, stopped soldering the joints of a smaller work which one of Chris's students was doing. As it was, I heard him repeat his words. "Take Cathy."

David began a protest. "But—"

Chris gave him no time to finish. "She's my assistant; she has a marvelous eye for color and an entirely modern approach to stained glass. After all, the authorities over there will see the designs she submits. If they don't like them, she can do others. She'll work with you out in Africa until the cartoon stage and then when she brings the O.K.'d design to the workshops, I shall oversee the final stages. That is," he added, "if there are any. Because I really can't see the idea working."

The tapping and the hammering began again in the workshop and

I heard no more. But two days later David came again and I was asked if I would go out to Bou Hammagan, see the site of the church and make some on-the-spot drawings.

Before I gave my final answer, I knew I had to tell Mark. I put through a call to his office in Bou Hammagan, and after a long and irritating wait while the little African exchange kept making contact and then cutting me off, I heard Mark's voice clearly. I told him that I had this opportunity to design a church window, but wondered how he felt about my being in Bou Hammagan while he was there.

"I'm coming out to work," I said. "I won't be running after you. I won't be a camp follower."

I heard him laugh. "No, Cathy, I can't picture you as that. Of course, come out. You understand, though, that I'll be away in the desert a great deal of the time."

"I'll keep away from you. I'll even go into hiding if we find ourselves in the same street." My voice was light with the heady joy I felt that he didn't protest that I must have engineered the whole thing. "David Sullavan, the architect I'll be working with, is already out there with a number of architects and landscape gardeners, so I'll have them to talk to. There's also Pippa, who has started her school holiday and will certainly want to come with me."

"The one and only hotel here isn't particularly luxurious," he warned.

I didn't care. I would have camped in the desert if that was the only way. "But you're quite happy about my coming?"

"Darling, this commission means you're really making a place for yourself in the art of stained glass. That's fine and I'm delighted for you."

"Thank you," I said wryly, and wished he had told me that his delight would be to see me. I tried to convince myself that he meant that too, and that he was looking forward to my coming.

I told an enthusiastic Pippa the news that we were going to North Africa. We got out the atlas and the huge geography book someone had given her for her birthday and read everything we could about the tiny state of Bou Hammagan. From that moment until Justin met us at the Algiers airport, explaining that Mark was filming in the desert, I had not let myself doubt the wisdom of what I had done.

Now the doubt was fretting inside me. Across the stepped street, Pippa was laughing at something Justin said. Ahead of us, the donkey man was plodding on by the side of the rattling cart.

Standing still wasn't cooling me much. I called to Justin and he came over, saying, "You've rescued me. Pippa asks too many questions. She's exhausting."

"But I want to know." She swung her dark hair as she looked up from one to the other of us, and her eyes were bright sea-green.

Justin said, "I have no more energy to talk. I know—let's have a competition." He walked by my side up the steps. "Let's see who can keep silent the longest. Starting . . . *now*."

Pippa giggled and put her hand over her mouth.

The man, the donkey and the luggage were now far ahead of us. Dogs lay panting in the shade of an occasional tree, and when I put my hand out to steady myself on a broken step, the clay wall I touched was burning to my fingers. Under a fig tree a beautiful little dark boy still lay asleep, his face on his arm.

The news that we were not, after all, to stay at the hotel had only reached me two days before leaving London. Among the many people attracted to the idea of living part of the year in a new and beautiful city set on the outskirts of the ancient and romantic one was an old friend of Mark's.

Alexandra Sorel was a rich widow who, since the death of her husband, had wandered from place to place, resting nowhere. According to Mark's last letter to me, they had met twice recently. The first time was in Paris when the newspapers had reported that Alexandra Sorel had been in a car accident and Mark, who was in the city, had gone to visit her in the hospital. The other time was when the papers reported that a British television company was in Greece covering a find of archaeological importance and Alexandra, who was in Athens staying with friends, had gone to see Mark on the site of the dig.

"News of the arrival of foreign residents," Mark wrote to me, "travels quickly in small places. So, when I heard that Alexandra was one of those building a villa at the New City, I got in touch with her. She was interested that you and Pippa were coming out and we have all been asked to stay with her. She has rented a lovely old house while waiting for her villa to be built. You'll like her, Cathy."

I sincerely hoped so and I hoped, equally, that she would like us. It could be an ordeal for us all—strangers living together in a house where one was hostess, three were guests and one of those, a child.

II

THE HIGH WALLS HEMMED us in interminably until at last Justin paused on a step.

"Now you'll be able to get your breath back. That door, you see"—he pointed—"leads to the House of the Fountains."

Set in a high grayish-white wall, the door was made of blackened wood braced with iron. It was so formidable that I felt that if ever one were locked out, a battering ram would be needed to break it down. Medieval England could surely not have had anything more secure.

The donkey driver was pointing and gesticulating happily. Justin went forward and pulled an old-fashioned bell. The sound jangled in the distance and almost immediately a small grille opened and a dark face peered out at us, broke into a wide grin of recognition at seeing Justin and swung the door open.

We walked into a large courtyard shaded by orange trees rich with full golden fruit. As the door closed behind us, I looked around for the man who had let us in, but he had vanished into a little stone hut partially screened from the courtyard by a bougainvillaea so thickly flowering that it was like a fountain of purple. The whole courtyard was sweet with the scent of roses.

"The man who let us in was Yussef, Alexandra's doorman," Justin said. "He inspects all callers, lets you in or refuses you, and then disappears into his hut."

A fountain splashed sunlit sequins of water into a green mosaic basin. A Moorish archway leading to a second garden was covered with morning-glory, its turquoise petals folded protectingly against the heat of the day.

Pippa said, "I'd like to take my clothes off and sit under that fountain. Could I? I'm so hot."

"You're no mermaid, darling, and this isn't our house. It's kind of Mrs. Sorel to ask us, but you are a guest. Remember that."

The house, dazzlingly white, occupied three sides of the courtyard. The flat roof, on three levels to conform with the steep slant of the street, was reached by an outside staircase and rose to the terrace that ran along the second floor. Urns of geraniums and marigolds stood on low pedestals at intervals up the curved flight of steps.

A servant had appeared at a far door. Pippa's small, hot hand caught hold of mine and I felt her awe. The man was huge and splendid and mahogany-dark. He wore a crimson headband which matched the cummerbund on his immaculate white uniform.

Justin greeted him in English. "Good afternoon, Ahmed."

The inclined head possessed a touch of regality as he made the slight gesture of welcome, his arm across his breast. "Madame is waiting for you, monsieur."

"He was trained in France," Justin whispered as we walked through the arched doorway. "But the only French thing about him is his form of address. In every other way, he's wholly Hammagarb."

Pippa let go of my hand. "Oh . . ."

Her single, awed exclamation was sufficient. We were used to our small Regency house in London, which had been built for exiled Huguenots. It was going to be difficult to adapt to this Oriental house with its suffocating silken luxury. Pippa would spill something on the cream leather hassocks or scuff her feet along the mosaic floor. This was no place for a child. The great hall into which we had walked was filled with small, scattered tables of exquisite marquetry intricately worked in silver, mother-of-pearl and ebony. On them were carved malachite urns, cloisonné boxes and bowls that, because of the deep unusual yellow glaze, I guessed were Chinese. Pippa, rushing across the floor, could easily knock something flying, and I had visions of the two of us creeping out of the house, hushed and shaken by the sight of broken pieces of porcelain.

I looked down at the child by my side and saw that she had no such qualms. With all her sensitivity and imagination, she had no conception of what might happen in one impulsive moment in that house. But then children can adapt more swiftly and easily to luxury than adults. For them the accidents of tomorrow are nothing.

"Isn't it w-wonderful!" She spoke in a dreaming voice and put out her hand and touched one of the marble columns that made a kind of royal arcade down the length of the dark hall. They glowed softly pink in the relieving cool twilight and they were unlike any columns I had ever seen before, not rounded and bearing classical capitals, but slim and angular.

Justin urged us forward. "Go on, the rooms are at the end."

We walked in silence under the high carved wood ceiling from which elaborate bronze lamps hung on heavy chains. The walls of the hall were covered in tiles patterned in green and gold and pink and there were low divans covered with cushions along one wall. Although I walked as softly as I could and Pippa, watching me, exaggerated her steps to a tiptoe, we couldn't stop the sharp echoes of our heels.

As we approached the far end of the hall I heard the rustle of silk and I knew, as soon as she appeared, that this was Alexandra Sorel.

Only someone who lived among such magnificence could walk with that contradictory combination of imperiousness and welcome. By her side, held by a strong chain, was a cheetah. His eyes in a broad magnificent face, watched us. There was a snowy-white ruff around his neck and his short, tilted-back ears twitched. There was intelligence on his splendid golden mask, and in spite of his obvious tameness there was an alertness in the way his body curved around the long flowing folds of Mrs. Sorel's sapphire caftan as if he were protecting her, or needed protection himself, against us who were strangers.

Justin drew me forward.

"I'm Catherine," I said. "But most people call me Cathy."

"I shall call you Cathy," she said and turned to Pippa. "You don't remember me, do you?"

13

Pippa frowned, her eyes on Mrs. Sorel's face. "Daddy said in a letter to Cathy that you knew him and Mummy, but—"

"Of course you couldn't possibly remember one isolated visit. You were a very little girl when I stopped for a night on my way from Paris to New York. You were just going to bed and very sleepy. I'm afraid I didn't come to England again, so that was our only meeting."

Pippa's polite interest in the past had waned. She turned fascinated eyes on the cheetah.

Mrs. Sorel stroked her golden pet. "You don't have to be afraid of him."

Pippa answered Alexandra's amused comment with her straight, grave look and, obviously mistaking it for nervousness, Alexandra Sorel bent and put her hand below the cheetah's eyes. "This is always the way to approach such animals. Let them see your fingers; move slowly and gently. Swift movement from above—out of their vision, as it were—startles them. His name is Durandal, and I don't let him off his chain unless he's with me, although he's perfectly safe. You can stroke him."

Pippa did so, crouching by his side. I recognized the signs of instant love as she looked up at us, and I dreaded the moment in London when she would ask for a cheetah instead of a dog. The sheen of magic was on her.

"I call him Dura for short," Alexandra said. "But come along. You can talk to him later."

We were led into a room where the shutters over the high windows were pulled close and three-tiered lamps, similar to those in the hall, hung from the ceiling. Low, cushioned divans stood against the walls, which were covered in carvings of arabesques, and in a corner was an enormous mantelpiece shaped like a bishop's miter.

"You'll find the house very dim, but that's intentional; it helps toward a sensation of coolness."

"It's very beautiful," I said.

She nodded. "If you like ornate decor, yes. It happens to amuse me. This is the living room—although it doesn't look very lived-in. That's because I had a screened patio built in the garden so that I can be out of doors in the shade and untroubled by flies. I have my own sitting room upstairs which I use when I have friends to stay —it's good for both guests and hostess to be able to relax from one another sometimes."

I could see a garden beyond the open door where a second fountain played.

Mrs. Sorel pointed to it. "That's where we'll meet for tea. It's called the Women's Garden. This house, you see, was built and owned by a Turkish merchant who is making a very good thing out of renting it to foreigners. Most of the small things, the cloisonné vases and the Chinese bowls, are mine because—although I'm only here until my villa in the New City is built—I like to have my own possessions around me. But you must be longing to go to your rooms and freshen up. We'll talk later."

Ahmed appeared without apparently being summoned and took the cheetah. Mrs. Sorel led us to a narrow marble stairway hidden in the corner of the hall. "Will you and Harriet come back for dinner?" she called to Justin, who had been standing back, watching our reaction to the villa with amusement.

"That would be lovely. Harriet said you'd probably ask us." He tossed a dancing look my way and then grinned at Mrs. Sorel.

I thought as we followed her up the stairs that the combined charm of eyes and voice and expression was Justin's "enchanter's wand." He could not have known Mrs. Sorel very long, yet he was totally at ease with her.

"You must have had a very hot and dusty drive from the airport."

"We did," I admitted.

"It's such a boringly long way away, but everything will be easier when the little airport is built here. At the moment there's nothing particularly modern about Bou Hammagan except electricity and piped water." She paused at the top of the stairs. "And the walk up those interminable steps isn't exactly a heavenly journey, is it?"

Shuttered windows along the passage obviously led to the three levels of flat roofs. Below us I could hear voices and the thud of our luggage being brought into the house.

"I have put you in a room that looks out over the courtyard. The rooms on the other side are directly overlooked by people on the roofs above us on the hill, so the windows there have to be very high up and they give visitors from the West a sense of claustrophobia. But from your room you can see right up the street to the Phoenician Arch. They say that it really was built by the Phoenicians when they came to North Africa and founded Carthage."

She fascinated me, not by her looks—for she was not in the least beautiful—but by the power of her face. It was entirely without sensuality, and she gave no hint of ever having lost herself in an emotional affair. I could not see her in love. Her features were arresting, her nose strong, her mouth long and full, her forehead out of proportion to the rest of her face, so that, except for her eyes, it dominated.

Then, as she led us into a room and the half-light shone through the slats of a shuttered window, I saw that her coloring was glorious. Her eyes were a startling blue, her skin very pale tan, as though she had been careful with her sunbathing; her hair, upswept and swathed on top of her head, was a rich bronze. She made me think, as she opened the shutters and stood for a moment in the sunlight, of a pheasant haloed in brilliance. She was slim and tall and I guessed her age to be around forty, but it had always been a joke with my friends that I could quite happily miscalculate ages by twenty years. I did not know; neither did I care. Just before she pulled the shutters across the window and turned toward the twilit room, I saw that her sapphire-blue caftan was shot through with green, so that it shimmered like birds' feathers.

"I was very interested," she said, "when Harriet told me that you were an expert in stained glass."

"Harriet exaggerates, I'm afraid. I've worked for some years with Chris Lanyard, who does mostly secular work. But I'm no expert."

"Mark tells me you have a commission to design the stained-glass window in the church here."

"I hope so. It depends on whether they approve the designs I submit."

She smiled at me. "I hope they do, and then you'll be staying here a long time."

I shook my head. "I shall work here with the architect on the planning and size of the window and, of course, the actual design. But most of the work will have to be done by the craftsmen in Chris's workshops in London. I may be here a week—I don't know."

"You must make it longer. I enjoy having people, and until the villas are built, the place has precious few Europeans. There are Harriet and Justin and a family called Mitchell—Frances and Clive—who are staying at the hotel, and we all cling together."

Pippa whispered to anyone likely to answer her, "Are we *really* going to live here?"

"Why? Don't you like it?" Alexandra asked.

"It's *wonderful*. It's . . . it's like walking into Christmas time."

Fairy lights and glimmering wrapping paper and flimsy, glowing baubles . . . Oh, darling, if you only knew, just one of the things you see would keep us in comfort for a year . . . A snatch of music and verse ran through my mind:

For lust of knowing what should not be known,
We take the Golden Road to Samarkand.

". . . dispense with formalities," Mrs. Sorel was saying. "Will you please call me Alexandra? Pippa . . ." She looked down at her. "Do you like your name?"

"No. It's horrible. It's as if I was one of those pomegranate things I hate—"

"Full of pips," I said unnecessarily.

Alexandra smiled and glanced around the room into which she had shown us. "I do hope you'll be comfortable here. My apartments are at the other end of the house. I believe this was the bedroom for VIP guests and Pippa's adjoining room a dressing room."

The luggage was being brought in by Yussef. A slightly hatchet-faced, unsmiling woman, obviously European, hovered behind, asking in English with a strong foreign accent if she could unpack for us.

Alexandra said, "This is Lisette. I brought her with me from Paris. I don't think I could exist without her."

"Thank you, Lisette," I said. "But we can manage very well. I'm afraid our haphazard packing would shock you, anyway." I laughed as I spoke. Her lips curved into a faint, polite smile and she shrugged her shoulders, not understanding those who chose to do things that others had offered to do for them.

Alexandra said kindly, "Take your time and rest for a while if you like. When you come down we'll have tea—I hope you like mint tea. Out here it's more refreshing than Indian, but you can have that if you like."

"We'd love to try mint tea," I said.

Pippa was running a finger down a cloisonné jar, and Alexandra called to her. "Come and see your room."

I watched them go through a door in the far wall and thought how like her own cheetah Alexandra was: supple, glossy, graceful.

I could hear their voices in the second room, but I didn't follow them. I wanted them to get acquainted. I couldn't think of them as already known to one another, since a very small Pippa had years ago merely opened a sleepy eye to her parents' guest. I remained, wandering around my room—mine and Mark's . . . We would sleep under an arched ceiling, walk on a tiled floor, be surrounded by the richness of silk in the colors of vermilion and jade. The double bed was very low, so that one would almost plunge down to it, and so enormous that we could both lie in it and yet be isolated by its width.

Mark's imprint was in the room already. His brushes lay on the carved table, his clothes hung in a cupboard that had a fretwork door. Folders of notes on programs already completed were piled on a small ebony table.

I glanced in the mirror and saw my reflection, strained with tiredness. I had done running repairs to my face before we left the plane because I had wanted to look as immaculate as I could when I met Justin. But during the drive from the airport the color I had smoothed on my cheeks had gone. My face was pale and my hair hung limply around my shoulders.

Mark had once said, "Never cut your hair short, Cathy. I love it as it is." He had let it drift through his fingers. "It's the color of sparrow's wings," he had said and we had both laughed at his touch of poetry.

I had drawn his head down so that we both looked into the mirror. "Do you realize that our eyes are the same color?"

"Oh, no. Mine are just gray; yours have silver lights in them."

The memory of that evening was there as I stood and saw myself in the mirror in Alexandra's guest room. I ran my hands over my high cheekbones and traced the line to my chin. I looked tired; I *was* tired. But behind it was excitement and wonder.

I turned to the window, pushed open the shutters and looked out on to the rich green branches of trees, and through the leaves I saw the fountain in the courtyard.

A vista of roofs stretched away and I could see women crouched over some work they were doing—I saw laundry and sheepskins drying on lines. Although the house was cheek by jowl with its neighbors, it seemed by contrast with their cheerful shabbiness to stand in splendid isolation. The House of the Fountains was like a medieval king surrounded by his subjects.

Beyond the roofs I could see the Phoenician Arch, and away to the horizon lay the Sahara. The desert was not hidden by vast Westernized hotels and concrete blocks of apartments; it was here on Alexandra's doorstep.

III

"CATHY, come and look. I c-can sleep in here?" Pippa sometimes stammered when she was excited.

I tore myself away from my window and went into her small adjoining room through a door which was covered with a thin sheet of beaten bronze.

Alexandra had left us, and Pippa stood quite still, her toes turned in, her long dark hair falling about her shoulders. "It's funny," she said, "the ceiling goes into points like the tents we make when we go camping—only m-much more gorgeous."

I slid an arm around her shoulders and looked about me at the small room allotted to her. It was like a stage setting for a pantomime scene. Folds of dark gold silk swept from the walls and were gathered in a single dark star in the center of the ceiling. There, as in our room, the bed was a low divan with orange cushions scattered over it. Elaborate latticework covered the two shuttered windows. It was a claustrophobic room, hung too lavishly with silk; Oriental in conception, yet, of its type, beautiful.

Pippa darted from under my arm and ran to the bed. On it was a parcel. "Look . . . it's got my name on it."

"Then open it."

Small, strong hands tore at the string and wrapping paper. Inside was a box and in it lay about a dozen slender silver bangles. Pippa slid them on and held up her arm, jangling them. Then, having admired them, she glanced at the accompanying note. "They're from Daddy, with love." She raised her head and her small heart-shaped face was radiant. "Didn't Daddy give *you* something, too?" She dashed ahead of me, looking on the low table by our bed, and held up a parcel addressed to me.

Inside my package was a necklace of slim gold links set with topaz. The note said:

Bless you,

Mark.

"Oh, Cathy, he *is* w-wonderful, isn't he?" Pippa's love for her father ran like a quivering thread through her life. I watched her shake her bangles, making tuneless music, and thought: *One day it must change. She'll find the world—other people.* But for the moment Mark contained her whole world.

I gave Pippa the keys to her suitcase and left her to enjoy her silk tent of a room and the black marble handbasin where, with the sheer enjoyment of such luxury rather than a desire to be clean, she was washing her hands.

The dressing table drew me. Four panels of glass framed in gilded wood quadrupled my reflection—a kind of composition of me full face, two side faces and half the back, multiplying me as I was multiplied inside myself. A woman with a husband she loved and a stepdaughter she adored. Yet, although I was aware that they loved me, I was uncertain of their depth of feeling. I had told myself many times that the fault lay in myself, that I must not expect to have from those I loved more than they were able to give.

My standard had been set by my parents, who had adored each other. My two brothers and I had accepted that none of us had ever come first in the lives of our mother and father. Still, we had had a close and happy relationship among ourselves until the three of us had married and my elder brother had gone to farm in Cumberland

and my younger brother had married a Canadian girl and lived in Vancouver.

I was the only artistic one in the family. My father, who had been an airline pilot, had had no interest in art—more than once he had been known to hold an abstract painting of mine upside down.

My mother, who had before her marriage worked on a fashion magazine, had protested. "But, darling, stained glass? For churches, you mean? Oh, but why don't you do fashion designing?"

I had explained that I hoped to work mostly on secular windows, but she wasn't quite convinced as to the wisdom of my choice of a career until she had met Chris Lanyard. Then she had said, "If you work with a personality like that, darling, you'll never find life dull."

They had seen me begin my career, but neither my mother nor my father had lived to see me married. They had been killed together in an air crash over the Dolomites.

One night eighteen months ago a tragedy had also happened in Mark's family. His wife, Louise, had been killed while crossing the road outside their house. Friends of Mark's told me that when they had broken the news to Pippa, she had just looked at them out of blank green eyes. The storm of tears they had expected, or the alternative brooding, had not come. She had accepted her mother's death with a calm Louise's friends had called unnatural.

The story of the sudden death of the wife of one of television's well-known reporters had made minor headlines. Reading about it, I had never dreamed that some months later I would take Louise's place.

At the inquest one of the two witnesses to the accident had said that Louise had rushed out of the drive and into the road without pausing to look for traffic. The other witness had insisted that Louise had hesitated but that the car had driven straight at her.

Pippa had been questioned, gently and tactfully. Before she went to bed, she told the coroner, she had seen her mother crying—but she often cried. When she was in bed, she had heard voices downstairs and thought her father had returned. But when she had got up and gone halfway down the stairs, she had seen her mother running through the open door. She was shouting to someone and Pippa had been frightened and had crept back to bed. She was asked if she had actually heard her father's voice. No. All she knew was that there were two people in the house and that her mother sounded very angry.

Pippa's evidence did not help at all. She thought . . . she supposed. She was a child and they stopped questioning her.

One witness had said that a woman had passed Louise at the moment when she had stumbled into the road and had been knocked down. She had slipped away into the darkness, probably because she hated being at the scene of an accident. The other witness was certain that the driver had deliberately swerved toward Louise. But the car was not traced and the case had never been closed.

Mark did not talk to me about it, and I heard arguments about Louise's death from acquaintances who had known them both. Perhaps Louise had indeed flung herself at the car, not to commit suicide but to scare Mark. To brush a wing tip, to be grazed by a wheel . . . "I will make you feel guilty of neglect, Mark . . . of too little love . . ." How did anyone know how Louise had felt that night?

When Harriet had talked to me about it, she had said, "If you take Louise on a superficial level—and that's all you *could* do with her—then she had a lot to live for—looks, money, comparative youth. But these are the people who crumple if they can't get the ultimate in what they want—they can't compromise like the rest of us. I think she wanted more of Mark than Mark was prepared to give her. He'll never belong entirely to any one woman—but then you know that, don't you?"

"So you think she deliberately walked in front of the car. If so, the driver should have stopped. Why didn't he?"

"That, my dear, is another question altogether and turns on still another possibility."

"What do you mean?"

"The car could have been waiting for her."

"But that's . . . monstrous. Who . . . ?"

"Yes, who?" Harriet said.

Out of all the questioning and the conflicting evidence, only two things were indisputable. Louise was dead and the car had not stopped.

Ours was not a great, romantic affair. We saw each other at gradually shortening intervals, and then one day Mark took me to see Pippa at the boarding school to which he had sent her. Mark's little daughter was gregarious, but the confinement of the school in the country bored her. She wanted to come home and be with her father and go to day school. When she heard I was going to marry Mark, her comment was entirely matter-of-fact. "Now I can come home, can't I?"

Louise had possessed a considerable fortune and the large Thames-side house had been hers. In her will she left everything to her daughter, with Mark inheriting should Pippa predecease him. Everything, including the beautiful furniture, the pictures and the porcelain, was left to Mark's discretion to sell or keep for Pippa when she came of age.

"The child didn't know a Hepplewhite from a piece of Victoriana," Mark once told me, "and she still doesn't. But she has a feeling for beauty, so, when I took her around the house, she pointed to the things she wanted to keep. They weren't the most expensive, but they were undoubtedly the loveliest. I sold the rest and a great deal of money is in trust for her."

Mark and I were married eight months after Louise had died.

I had stood in the office of highly glossed wood in front of an unctuous man in a dark suit and become Mrs. Mark Mountavon. I had no wedding bouquet and no one threw silver horseshoes or rice over us after the brief, practical ceremony. It was how we wanted it, without fuss and with just a few friends to drink champagne with us afterwards. I even flouted superstition and wore green for my wedding. That same night we flew to Carcassonne for a week.

Mark's mother was dead. His father lived in Peru, where he was absorbed in the study of the ancient Inca civilization which was more real to him than his two sons.

Harriet had told me something of the history of the Mountavon family at the time of her marriage to Justin. "I'm marrying into a family whose ancestors came to England with William the Conqueror. That's funny for me, who's a nobody, isn't it? The Mountavons had rich lands in Northumberland and masses of noble ancestors. Then, when Bonnie Prince Charlie tried to take the throne of England, they gave generously to his cause. The last of the Lords of Mountavon died in the Prince's defeat at Culloden and only a woman remained, Sophia Charlotte. When she married, she insisted that her husband take her name, and that is the only reason the name exists today. But I'm afraid their wealth was finally eaten up by the wild gamblings of Sophia's grandchildren during the reign of the Georges. So, no money now and no lands. Justin has a tiny income from a relative on his mother's side. Mark is all right; he's doing well on television."

Mark and I moved into a small Regency house in Chelsea where, instead of the lavishly appointed playroom in Louise's tree-ringed house, Pippa had to be content with an attic looking out over a London square, and instead of grounds stretching down to the river where a boat was moored, she had a very small garden to play in.

The change from luxury to ordinary comfort did not seem to affect her at all. She never talked about her mother. Friends told me, "Pippa has a great deal of Mark's self-sufficiency." But during the months I came to know her, I learned differently. Pippa possessed powerful emotions, and there must have been no room for her mother in her needs and her longings. Mark had every inch of her love.

I understood even more when Harriet told me, during one of her rare visits to London, that Pippa had been an unwanted child. "Louise never loved her," she said, her bare legs hanging over the arm of a chair. "In a way, I can understand. I don't know that I want children, either—they demand too much. But I would never have said what Louise did once when she introduced Pippa to some friends who had come to dinner. 'Do meet the major mistake of my life. Thank God she's at least physically presentable.' I think Louise never dreamed that Pippa would understand, but she did. In some ways she's very young, in others she's too intelligent."

It was a warning to me, and I planned to go gently with her. But Pippa set the pace and eased my nervousness by a warmth and a response to my affection that made me mock my own fears.

Mark went away soon after our brief honeymoon, and I made a great mistake when we sat together on his first evening back home. I gave him his coffee after dinner and then ruffled his hair. "Hi, stranger, I'm looking for any gray hairs that might have sprouted since our last meeting. At least you haven't grown a beard."

As soon as I had spoken, I realized that the thing I must never do was to comment on his absences. He had suffered from too many tears and complaints from Louise, and the fact that I spoke lightly, making a joke of it, did not ease his sudden withdrawal from me.

"Cathy," his voice was steady, "I want you to understand. I shall never say to you, 'What a damned nuisance this job is, I don't want to go,' because whether it's Hong Kong, Timbuktu or the Seychelles, I shall always want to be there. It won't mean that I am tired of my home, but the job I do is, to me, as natural as breathing."

"I understand, Mark . . . I do . . ."

"I'm a selfish man, Cathy."

"Who cares?" I cried. "We are all selfish."

"But whatever happens, promise me one thing. Never be my doormat. But no, don't promise, because I know you won't, and promises are damnable things."

After that conversation I never again said "Hi, stranger!" when he came home from abroad.

I listened to the praises of our friends. "That talk Mark gave last night on the new excavations near Troy was fascinating, and the pictures were superb." . . . "It was quite terrifying when we watched those scenes of the volcanic eruption. Mark seemed to be standing just where the lava was coming down red-hot—like a sort of burning river. I held my breath, didn't you, Cathy? Don't you ever wonder if one day he'll get too close to danger?"

I did, but I never admitted it to anyone. Sometimes I had an incredulous suspicion that Mark was deliberately defying fate, reporting from too near a dangerous precipice; walking into a burning building almost as if there was something that he wanted to exorcise by daring fate to destroy him. The dreaded thought crept into my mind more than once that this feeling could be guilt over Louise. Perhaps she had threatened suicide, and he had not taken her seriously and was now suffering a deep unspoken remorse. Perhaps . . . If it were so, Mark had no intention of talking about it.

I had been staring, without really seeing my face, into the center panel of the mirror where I met myself eye to eye. Something flashed across my reflection with a swift, dark sweep. I swung around, my hands stretched out with an instinct to ward it off. But there was nothing and no one behind me. I had left one of the shutters open, and the shadow must have been an eagle or a vulture flying across the face of the sun.

The flight of a bird. Yet such was my belated doubt as to the wisdom of this journey that I saw the shadow as an ill omen. Then I laughed at my reflection for its ridiculous superstition.

A thud from the next room made me start. "Pippa, what are you doing?" I held my breath, visualizing the first breakage.

Her voice came back calmly. "I dropped my diary."

"Oh, darling, you didn't bring that heavy thing." I crossed the room and stood in the doorway.

In brown shorts and white sleeveless top, she looked too natural to exist in the exotic background of the bedroom allotted to her. She was hugging a book. "It's all right, Cathy. You *know* my luggage didn't weigh too much at the airport. I left out a pair of shoes—

I didn't cheat, honestly I didn't." Her eyes watched me, willing under-standing.

I understood. Every Christmas one of her presents from Mark was a very special diary an imaginative publisher brought out. It contained two pages to a day and was bound in simulated dark-red leather. There were always four beautiful illustrations in it, one at the begin-ning of each season, and these varied in subject year by year. The one for the current year had scenes from Shakespeare's plays *The Tempest, Romeo and Juliet, A Midsummer Night's Dream* and *Twelfth Night*. The illustrations were made by fine artists, and they were marvelous milestones for a child's life . . . . A magic island, Ju-liet's balcony, Titania enchanted by the ass's head and a city in Illyria.

I had protested that the book was too heavy to bring with her. "Airline baggage has to be light. If you take that diary you'll prob-ably find that the plane flies lopsidedly all the way to North Africa."

Pippa was naturally obedient about most things, and I had thought no more about it. But I realized now that her first adventure abroad would be nothing without the diary into which she could pour her excitement and her impressions. She was, in interests and aptitude, her father's daughter.

I went back to my bedroom, and, as I cleared my suitcases, ten-tacles of memory reached out and linked things I touched with inci-dents in the past. My wedding day when Mark had given me the beautiful little bedside clock in gold, set with rose diamonds and Bur-mese rubies; the night he had slipped the crimson and white Dior silk scarf around my neck and said, "Straight from Paris, darling. After a night spent with five kittens in a hayloft because our car broke down in the depths of the Cevennes and the trucks were miles ahead."

I ran the scarf through my fingers, and the thought of it around my neck in the heat of Africa made my skin prickle. I folded it and put it away in one of the cedar-wood drawers, and I hung up my robe, which was little more than folds of dark-blue chiffon. Mark had seen it in a shopwindow in Rome.

Pippa was so quiet in her room that, with only shoes left to unpack, I went to see what she was doing. I found that she had crawled into a thick embrasure in the wall and, face pressed against the grille over the window, was peering down at something that riveted her attention.

"You'll get your nose stuck in the bars if you're not careful, and then we'll have to get the firemen to come and release you—always providing there is a fire department here . . . Darling, what *are* you looking at?"

"There's a woman on that roof and she's beating carpets. Isn't it funny? We don't, do we? Come and see."

"How can I when you're taking up all the space?" I pulled gently at her bare feet. "Come down and let me look."

She crawled out of the embrasure and then laughed at my own difficulty in fitting myself into the window space between the enormously thick walls. Peering through the grille, I saw that Pippa's window looked directly onto roofs of different levels. The walls of the next house were cracked and pitted. Perhaps, a very long time ago, it could have been almost as splendid as the House of the Fountains, but the neglect was only too obvious. The pots on the broken parapet were chipped and discolored and empty of plants. Junk littered the roof and chickens clucked and scrabbled among the rubbish. So, in Bou Hammagan wealth and poverty lived side by side without any of the definite divisions usually found in the West. The woman continued to beat the carpet, using such energy under the blistering sun that I felt the outside heat crawl over me at the sight of her.

I withdrew my head and jumped down onto the floor. "We're snooping. That roof is private, just as ours is to the people above us on the hill."

Pippa had lost interest. "She had awfully big feet," she said and sat on the bed and opened her diary, her long hair falling like a scarf of shining brown silk about her shoulders.

I felt better after washing in the black marble bathroom; the edges of the gilt taps, shaped like half-moons, dug uncomfortably into my hands as I turned them on. When I had changed my dress and my shoes, Pippa and I went down to join Alexandra. Our sandals clattered on the stairs, but below us in the darkened hall there was swift, silent movement as Ahmed came out of the shadows. I would have to get used to hearing no footsteps before servants appeared, since they walked on slippered Oriental feet.

Without a word he led us past a screen of exquisitely patterned rosewood and toward the Women's Garden.

I recognized Harriet's voice at once, because it had an edge to it as if she were always on the point of anger. ". . . and that new hotel at Bizerte will take two paintings, but they insist on desert scenes. So I thought I'd go out to Kourifia. Justin is delighted with the idea—he says the more hotels that display my work the better—more lovely money for us. That's right, isn't it, *my—dear* . . . ?"

"*My dear*" italicized, stressed with more dislike than affection.

So they had been quarreling again, and of course it had been about money. Justin was too idle to answer her, and I knew this infuriated Harriet. The wonder was that they had ever been attracted to each other—Justin, the elegant idler, and Harriet with her longing for the good life.

Alexandra was in the patio. The chairs, set haphazardly among stone urns of marigolds and stocks, were white with yellow cushions, all of them rather thin—I supposed because our great soft English ones would be too hot in the desert climate. Durandal lay at Alexandra's feet, and I had a swift memory of a childhood book in which a dragon guarded the gates of an enchanter's palace. Durandal guarded his mistress like that recumbent legend.

Harriet got up to greet me with a peck on my cheek. "It's such ages since we met, isn't it, Cathy? But then I so seldom get to London. The agency pays for Justin's capers back and forth but I—" she let the rest of what she was going to say sink resentfully on the air.

Justin, untroubled by Harriet's scarcely muted bitterness, asked lightly, "News, Cathy, that's what we want. All the news; all the gossip about people we know."

As I answered, mentioning our few mutual friends, I noted that Harriet had changed the color of her hair. It was naturally a dark brown, but she had dyed it to a pale fawn, and as Bou Hammagan lacked even tourists as yet, I supposed that she had had to do it herself. Although the color went strangely with her sun-tanned skin, I liked it. And the way she wore it, tied back with a thin red ribbon, somehow suited her high cheekbones and slanting Magyar eyes.

Pippa wandered in a kind of dream toward the banks of flowers, cautiously touching a thorned rose and running her fingers through the oleander bushes. "They're so lovely, I could *eat* them."

"I shouldn't," Alexandra said. "The leaves are very poisonous. But, Cathy, come and see my roses. I'm very proud of them. The man who looks after them is half French, half Arab, and is working as a landscape gardener in the New City. He has introduced these special roses to my garden."

"They're lovely."

She touched the petals lightly as we walked past them. "That one is called Apricot Silk, and we had difficulty getting it started out here. And that's Diorama, and there is Royal Tan—I love copper and golden roses."

They grew in profusion, vermilion and tangerine and flame as well as her favorite golden colors.

"Now, come and let's sit down. Pippa, this hassock is very comfortable for small people."

Pippa stared at it with awe. "It shines . . ."

"Gold thread. There are dozens in the house. They were probably embroidered by the women of the harem many, many years ago while they sat and fattened themselves on Turkish delight."

When Pippa was happy she gave a series of small quick sighs. Mark said it was the nearest thing she could get to purring like a little cat. She sat down on the cream-and-gold hassock near Alexandra and clasped her hands around her knees, watching the supine, spotted cheetah with fascinated eyes.

I leaned back and relaxed. The water from the fountain that fell in silver droplets turned to transparent jade as it reached the basin. Apricots hung ripe on one wall and below, in long stone troughs, canna lilies rose like flames.

IV

IT WAS ALL so beautiful, so unexpectedly exotic, and yet even as I thought that, my serenity left me. I was back again with my nervous doubts at coming and, with them, a quiver of homesickness for our small house with its may tree outside the French windows and our cat called Augustus.

And when Mark comes, what? Before I could answer, Ahmed appeared with a fair, stocky man whose glance encompassed the room and rested on me.

I gave a cry of pleasure. "David!"

Alexandra laughed. "I hoped it would be a surprise, but when you've been out here a week or two you'll know that it is inevitable for the Europeans to meet. We're less than a minority, and so we have to keep together. We eat up any Westerner who sets foot in

Bou Hammagan, and from that moment they haven't a hope of avoiding us.

"You'll stay for tea?" she asked David.

"Thank you, but I'm afraid I haven't time—"

"Time?" Alexandra demanded with mockery. "Oh, but surely living among the people here has taught you that time is nothing. Do stay."

He laughed and hesitated. "Perhaps, after all, I'm too British to say 'No' to that habit. Thank you."

Alexandra spread her arms, indicating a chair, and the wide sleeves of the embroidered caftan fell back. I looked at her hands and thought how someone had told me hands were important; how they had to have character. Alexandra's were full of it; broad and only lightly tanned, with the veins showing faintly blue, thumbs sloping back, nails short and pink.

I had no idea what signal she had given—perhaps the very fact that Pippa and I had appeared was enough—but Ahmed came out of the house carrying a silver teapot on a cloisonné tray and six little drinking glasses.

"It's green China tea," Alexandra explained, "and Lisette just dips some mint into it. Do you take sugar? Usually this tea is drunk terribly sweet, but perhaps you'd rather have it as it is."

I said I didn't take sugar.

"There's also some rose water in it," Alexandra said, pouring the tea. "The particular brand I use is brought over from the rose gardens of Isfahan."

The tea was refreshing after the long journey, and I was grateful for the low key of the conversation. Traveling with an excited child and sitting through an eighty-mile journey during the heat of an African afternoon were not exactly a rest cure.

"If you had come here earlier in the year," Harriet said, hands behind her head, fawn hair melting into the pale cushion she leaned against, "you'd have seen that wall over there covered with jasmine— it's the lucky flower out here." She stretched. "The first time I met Ahmed, he had two jasmine flowers stuck behind his ear."

Beyond the flow of conversation I could hear distant sounds. Children's voices and dogs barking, people roused from their high-noon sleep, revived and calling to one another. The clop of a donkey's slender hooves up or down the stepped street; strange wailing flute music; the cry of a street seller—all mingled and so muted by the thick, high wall.

My meandering thoughts were brought up sharply by the mention of the church window.

"There's still argument between the various denominations," David said. "One group is holding out for a small, unobtrusive window, the other insisting that it must be large and dominating."

"They could have settled the argument before I came, surely," I said in dismay. "I hate delay."

"Chris told me you were inclined to be impatient." He laughed. "But never mind, I'll take you to see the church so that you can get an idea of the size of the building. It's not large and it's very streamlined—but then a Gothic building would look ridiculous standing among white tropical villas."

Somewhere outside the high walls there was a sound like the cracking of a whip. Durandal's head shot up and I saw his back muscles ripple. Alexandra leaned down and stroked him. "It's only children playing on the steps, Dura." She spoke soothingly and the golden blaze faded from his eyes. He blinked sleepily at us and laid his head sideways under the massed blooms of the miniature roses that grew in stone urns.

"If you like, we could go tomorrow morning to look over the church," David continued.

"To subdue my impatience?" I asked. "Yes, I'd like that."

"Can I come with you?" Pippa asked.

Alexandra answered, "I think you'd be rather bored. I'll take you with me to see the *souks,* and Cathy and David, if he's free, can meet us at—" She considered the point. "Not at the hotel, but somewhere more exciting—at Hashim's."

So, when Mark arrived, I would be able to say, "I'm starting work on the window tomorrow." And by that piece of news let him know that I had not come out with Pippa to watch him. Tonight would be ours; tomorrow he would go his way and I would go mine.

"Tomorrow," Justin was saying, "I take around the town two Brazilian millionaires and their wives who are staying in Algiers. Not that they're interested in the architecture or the atmosphere, but they're looking for unusual things to take back to their Rio de Janeiro home. If they think Bou Hammagan is an Aladdin's cave ripe for the picking, they've got disappointment in store. Never mind, Harriet will like their lovely money." He shot her a laughing glance. His behavior toward her was—unlike hers toward him—entirely without malice.

*   *   *

I might have known that Pippa would see Mark first. Although Justin had told us that he wouldn't arrive until late afternoon, she had been waiting and watching for him from the moment we came to the house. When the bell at the heavily studded door rang she leaped up. "It's Daddy. I know it's Daddy . . ."

"Pippa, sit down." My voice faded into a helpless silence. Yet I envied her the freedom of her extreme youth to be impetuous.

"Let her be, Cathy," Alexandra said. "Go on, Pippa. Go and see who it is."

Her small, sandaled feet were making a clatter over the tiles, her leap through the archway which led from the Women's Garden to the front courtyard was a thud that made Justin shiver.

"Why *do* children run on every inch of their feet instead of on their toes? Pippa's like a young elephant."

I heard voices, laughter. Then Mark was there. He had a way of registering everything without seeming to notice. I knew he saw all of us in that first moment of arrival—Alexandra, Harriet, Justin and David. But his eyes looked straight at me as his hands disengaged from Pippa's ecstatic clamoring fingers and reached to me. I went to him in what felt like a single flowing movement, past the canna lilies and an old fig tree.

"Cathy." My name was almost inaudible against the murmuring of the fountain, but Mark's smile warmed me. Like a child I kept crying silently to some deity, "Thank you . . . thank you . . . thank you . . ." because at least Mark wasn't hating my arrival.

"And how are you going to enjoy sleeping in the kind of luxury the old sultans' wives knew?" he asked.

"I shall probably dream exotic dreams and clap my hands for the eunuchs to appear."

"Daddy . . ."

He reached down, swung Pippa around and gave her a smacking kiss. "Well, my darling daughter, I hope you're going to enjoy Africa."

"Do *you* like it? Do you like it a bit better because I'm here?"

"Of course." His glance greeted everyone in the group and I felt their immediate interest in him. I had noticed so many times at gatherings that Mark had only to enter a room for eyes to turn and attention to focus sharply upon him.

It was a magnetism that had nothing to do with looks, for he was not handsome. His face was too stern, too lean, too withdrawn. But when he smiled a light came into his eyes and gentleness softened his mouth. Just as he loved my hair, so I loved his. It was nearly black and gleamed in lamplight as if it were wet and, in strong winds, it curled up like small feathers.

Watching him as he turned from me, I thought, *How beautifully he walks . . . with a litheness and a quiet grace . . .*

He was saying to David, "I hear the hotel is going to be enlarged."

David laughed. "It needs improvement, though I can't complain. Because I'm an architect, I'm treated like a prince. They're afraid I might have a few adverse things to say about the place, otherwise. But this"—he looked up at the house—"is real Oriental architecture, solid, practical and yet with a kind of stark beauty outside. I like it."

"There's nothing stark about the inside," Justin said. "Alexandra, you have shown David around, haven't you?"

David said, "The structure of the house has a formal beauty inside as well—it's the Oriental interior decorating that changes it into something out of *The Thousand and One Nights*." He glanced at his watch and rose.

At the same time Harriet jerked Justin to his feet. "Come on, we must be going too."

During the small commotion of their leaving, a feather of fear that had clung to me ever since I knew that Alexandra and Mark were old friends, disappeared completely. My first assessment of her was obviously correct. She wasn't interested in playing the role of charmer to Mark. He was a friend, but a casual one, and although she was obviously pleased that he was there, she had made it quite clear that she was equally pleased that Pippa and I had come to stay. Perhaps we gave an aim to her empty hours, we transformed her from a woman with little to occupy her into a hostess.

"You're all coming back to dinner," Alexandra was saying. "And I'm including you, David."

There was a murmur of thanks, and as they went through the arch, Alexandra turned to Pippa. "I want you to get to know Lisette. She makes the most wonderful nougat with honey and nuts."

Pippa politely allowed herself to be led away, but she kept looking over her shoulder at Mark.

Your turn will come, darling, I said silently. *Presently Mark will sit with you and talk to you and you can write down every word he utters in your diary. But for now, Mark must be mine.*

They had all gone. I heard their voices retreating—Pippa's asking her interminable questions of Alexandra; David laughing at something Justin said; Harriet's sharp admonition. Mark and I stood alone.

"Come," he said, and took my hand.

The bedroom with the peacock silk spread on the divan might have been our London room for all the notice we took of our surroundings.

Mark closed the elaborate carved doors, and came to me. Before he could touch me, I asked, "Do you mind?"

"Mind what?"

"That I've come out here?"

He put his hands on my shoulders and drew me to him. "You have the strength of gentleness," he said.

"I don't think that's an answer."

"Oh, yes, it is." He ran his hands up and down my bare arms. "If I had said 'Don't come' you wouldn't be here now, and you would never have held it against me that I hadn't wanted you. In those circumstances I'd have felt the meanest heel this side of Paradise. That's how you're strong, Cathy—by your very acceptance of me as I am."

"I don't know that even that is an answer."

"Then will this do?" He kissed me and his hands touched my face and moved slowly over my body. To be needed was all I asked in those moments, and I existed in a state of suspended joy.

"Catherine . . ." In moments of love he would say my full name with a slow enjoyment that was a caress in itself. I lay on the great divan and felt the weight of his body and the softness of his breath on my face.

"We have a long time before dinner," he said, and while life went by quietly inside the house and distant music vibrated on the air, I had Mark's love.

Time was a charmed circle shutting out all past and all future. Mark's arm lay around my shoulder, my face was turned to him so that my lips touched his throat as we lay closely and quietly. The sound of footsteps beyond the room didn't belong to our world and, hearing them, I moved my head drowsily, not really fearing intrusion.

The door of the room burst open and Pippa rushed in. Her glance flew to the bed and she jerked to a stop in the middle of the room. Her face changed in a flash from joy to blank incredulousness. She said "Oh . . ." just once, and before I could move out of Mark's arms, she turned and ran.

I leaped out of bed and flung my robe around me. "Pippa . . . Pippa . . ."

There was no one in the hall. She had fled from us and I had no way of knowing down which wide stone passage she had gone. Then, as I stood in the doorway tying the sash of the blue robe, I heard the click of a door closing. The house was as strange to Pippa as it was to me, and I was alarmed at this trespass into an unknown room only a few hours after we had arrived. I knew I had to give her time to escape from whichever room she had taken refuge in, and the only way to do that was to let her hear the closing of our door. I did that loudly and firmly.

Mark lay on his face. I sat on the edge of the bed and he reached blindly for me.

"We must be careful," I said. "Pippa's room leads out of ours, so she could run in on us at any time."

He asked, his voice muffled by the pillow, "What's so wrong about her seeing us together?"

"We hurt her, Mark. She doesn't understand."

"Nonsense, of course she does. She's an intelligent child."

"We were lying very close when she came in."

He rolled over and looked at me. Then he reached for a strand of my hair which hung over my shoulder and ran it through his fingers. "Come here, I haven't finished with you."

But I drew away and, crossing the room between the bed and the dressing table, picked up the necklace of topaz. "It is a lovely present, Mark. And thank you." I held the stones in the palm of my hand.

"Darling." Mark was behind me. "Stop being sensitive about Pippa. Children see their parents in bed together."

"But I'm not her parent. And Harriet told me that after her mother died, Pippa said, 'Now I'll have him all to myself.' Meaning you, Mark."

"Harriet exaggerates. And, if Pippa did say that, then she'll have to be taught, oh, gradually and kindly, that no one has the exclusive right to another's love."

"That could sound hard to a child."

"I don't mean it to be." He put his hands around my face and his expression was gentle. "But I'm right, am I not? Love . . . I suppose I love Justin a bit and I love my job. And so do you love yours. Perhaps I wouldn't love you so much if you didn't."

Yet Pippa's face haunted me. It was difficult to understand the sudden look of pain and stricken loneliness. She had seen us together so often, greeting one another when Mark returned from abroad, kissing, hugging, close and laughing. But Pippa was eight, and in the past few years there had been a vast change in the age in which childhood became aware of sexual matters.

It was possible that for the first time, without understanding, she had sensed the sensual undertones of our closeness. She had burst into our room shining with excitement and then, as if a lance had been thrust in front of her, forbidding her to come closer, she had felt herself an outsider.

Mark now opened the cupboard and tossed his favorite dress at me. "Wear that tonight. You're the color expert, but I think the topaz necklace will look well with it." The dress was lime-green chiffon.

Perhaps with all the excitement of being in North Africa Pippa has already forgotten . . . Perhaps I'm making too much of it, anyway. Pippa knows that she is loved and that is all that matters. I began to sing softly to myself.

V

As soon as we opened our door and went into the corridor I saw Pippa, whose hearing reached out like antennae, racing between the high columns of the hall below. She sped up the stairs, past me and into her father's arms.

He gave a theatrical grunt as she plunged at him, hugged her and said, "In spite of your smallness, you're an Amazon."

"What's that?"

"Never mind now. This isn't the time for a history—or is it a geography?—lesson."

I walked on down the stairs. The swift darkness had fallen and fine wire screens had been drawn across the flowering patio, beyond which the fountain danced in the lights from the house. The moths began their fluttering suicide dance, and the stars were so low they looked like small silver eyes watching us.

Harriet and Justin sat in the same chairs they had occupied earlier.

They might never have gone home except that, glancing at my watch, I saw that two hours had passed since Pippa and I had drunk mint tea, and Harriet had changed from slacks into a dress. It was a mixture of North African caftan and Chinese cheongsam, loose and wide-sleeved and slit up to her thighs to show her lean brown legs. Her hair, freed from the ribbon she had worn during the day, softened the bones of her face.

Alexandra was not with them, and I could hear Pippa talking excitedly to Mark. I guessed that she had dragged him into her bedroom while she changed into something prettier. At eight years old she had stopped being disinterested in what she wore.

Harriet said, "Sit down, Cathy. You'd better start feeling at home here. Alexandra has gone to the kitchen to see Lisette. And you'll have to get used to Justin and me suddenly appearing—Alexandra loves people around her, and we have a kind of permanent invitation to use the garden. Ours isn't—a garden, I mean. It's a backyard with a tree in it."

Justin stretched. "That child," he said, "has been sitting down here, filling her diary with such tiny handwriting that nobody will ever be able to read it."

"Nobody ever will," I said. "She'll not only record all her adventures today, but she'll also tell that book her secret thoughts." I sat down in one of the chairs grouped in a semicircle around a table on which were drinks.

"As soon as she heard you and Mark come out of your room, she was like a tigress clamoring to join her family. You've made an impact there, sweetie."

But I knew Mark was the young tigress's happy target, not I . . .

Justin struck a match and lit a cigarette. The scented smoke, blowing my way, mingled with the perfume of the oleanders.

Harriet asked, "Does she ever mention her mother?"

"No. And I think I've done right in not asking her—I hope I have. It's as if she wants to close that chapter."

"Louise was beautiful," Justin said, "which is more than can be said for her daughter. She's got a little crooked face, hasn't she? Her eyes are gorgeous, but tilted; her mouth is tilted too. Thank God in the right direction—upward. But you should have seen Louise—"

Harriet lifted her hand and fanned away the cigarette smoke that was blowing in her direction. "Oh, for heaven's sake, don't go nostalgic about her. She was as two-faced as a reflection in a mirror." She closed her eyes and her lips curled around her next words. "You know, and I know, there was a man—"

It was the first time I had seen Justin really roused from his lethargy. "Damn you, Harriet."

She opened her eyes and her glance was too bright, too alert. "Isn't it time to stop glossing over our private history? We're 'family,' the three of us, and Alexandra isn't here. Oh, God, I'm bored with this secrecy about Louise. Why shouldn't Cathy know? It can't hurt her; in fact it might make her feel a little bit more understanding of Mark's dilemma at the time of the—er—accident."

Justin leaned forward and stubbed out his cigarette in the ashtray. "Shut up, do you hear? Just shut up."

"One of these days someone will tell Cathy much less kindly than we will."

Before Justin could speak again, I said, "Tell me—what?"

Harriet turned her bright, predatory eyes my way. "*We* knew—Justin and I and a few of Louise's so-called friends—that she had a lover." She waited. "Mark has never told you that, has he? But I'm sure he knows."

"It's past." I spoke sharply, wanting to defend myself against hearing something I would rather not know. But I recognized the look on Harriet's face. She was all set for a moment of truth.

"Whether you like it or not, the past always encroaches on the present. Louise is certainly dead; but she's not forgotten. Not with all that lovely money of hers floating around."

"You," Justin said very quietly, "are a bitch."

"I'm a realist," she retorted, "and it's high time we, as a family, played the truth game." She closed her eyes in simulated dreaminess. "I sometimes wonder how much Pippa knew; if she sometimes saw them together—Louise and her secret lover, I mean. If she did, it's probably that which has given her this obsessive love for her father—a subconscious desire to give him something that Louise denied them both. You'd better watch it, Cathy."

"Shut—up," Justin said softly.

The silence was hard and heavy, like stones weighing us down. I looked at my nails and wished I had done something about them before I came downstairs. But I didn't want to go back to the bedroom while Mark was with Pippa. If I appeared, it would seem that I was resenting her moments with her father. So I stayed where I was, wishing that I could hate Harriet for bringing Louise into the peace and beauty of Alexandra's garden. I couldn't hate her, though,

41

because it was typical of her to throw a wrench at contentment. The French had a word for her—*"malicieuse."*

Harriet began to speak again. "Louise left Pippa to the mercy of nannies," she said, "and, with Mark away so much, I wonder that child felt she had anyone really belonging to her."

"She'll find her level of emotions as she gets older," I said. "And, so far as I'm concerned, I want to forget all about Louise and the past before I knew Mark."

"You can't, Cathy. You'll never be able to," Harriet said. "There's a marvelous Persian saying: *Ana iza takalamtu bil kalimah malakatni wa iza lam atakalam biha malaktuha.* It means, 'If I utter a word, I am its slave and if I don't, I am its master.' That applies as much to the listener as to the speaker. You have heard and you can't forget. Anyway, it always helps to be forewarned, so just accept it."

"We should have had a heart-to-heart before I married Mark," I said dryly, "though there would still have been a wedding."

"You're weak, dear. The Mountavon charm does that to people. It ensnares, though if you try to analyze it, you can't."

"You talk too much," Justin said. "And now, having got all that off your chest, perhaps you'll do what I say, and shut up. Here's Alexandra."

She came, bringing Durandal. Her sapphire silk caftan had a gauze overdress of pale gold, and her only jewelry except for her two rings was an emerald on a chain at her throat. Behind her came Mark with Pippa, who had chosen to wear a scanty little dress of blue cotton. Her nut-brown hair was in a thick ponytail which she kept flicking from one shoulder to the other.

"When I leave school"—she seated herself on the gold-embroidered hassock near Alexandra—"I'm going to have a house like this—perhaps I could have *this* house."

"When you leave school, my darling daughter," Mark said lightly, "you're going to learn to be useful. You can choose what you'll do, but do *something* you most certainly will!"

"I'll be rich . . . everyone says so and I won't need to earn—"

"Then you can own a flower shop or one of those fancy restaurants; I don't care what you do."

"Then I'll write. *You* wrote," she reminded him, "before you did all this television stuff, because you told me. It was before I was born."

He laughed. "And one day, when I grow too old and ugly to be

42

seen on television, I'll write again. It's in my blood far more strongly than facing a camera."

I sensed the interest of the three people who were silently watching us, three who had all known Mark longer than I had. I supposed they were wondering what our life was like in London; whether I minded Mark's journeys abroad and what my relationship with Pippa was.

"I write a lot," Pippa said. "Every day I put down in my diary what I see and feel and the things I do."

"And perhaps one day," Alexandra said, "a hundred or so years from now, your diaries will be famous—a kind of account of a little girl's thoughts and doings so long ago."

"I shall never let anyone read my diaries. Never . . ." Her small face became dark with violent feeling. "No one will, will they?" She turned to Mark. "They won't . . ."

"If you don't want anyone to read your diary, then no one will."

There was relief on her face for, as always, she trusted Mark's word.

Ahmed served drinks, handing Pippa a glass of fresh fruit juice. By the time David arrived we were having our second drink. He apologized for his lateness and explained. "A worker has been taken ill. A girl who is in love with him gave him some kind of fungus in mistake for truffles. She is actually from one of the desert tribes who believe these truffles to be a love potion. Fortunately for the girl, his life isn't in danger."

Justin said, waving a slender brown hand, "That's Bou Hammagan for you."

Some time later, while I relaxed in one of the white chairs and listened to the arguments for and against living in Bou Hammagan, the sounding of the gong startled me. The single note began like the crashing of the sea and rose to a crescendo. Instinctively I looked at the cheetah. He had lifted his head and his short ears twitched, but the sound was obviously very familiar to him for he relaxed and again stared ahead of him into the massed pink oleanders.

"Shall we go in to dinner?" Alexandra said. As she leaned forward to put her cocktail glass on the table, the green jewel on the chain at her throat glittered, catching the sudden gleam of the lamps in the room behind her.

Pippa's eyes, missing nothing, reached up and tentatively touched the jewel. "It's like green fire."

Alexandra shot Mark a swift glance over Pippa's head and said vaguely, "Yes, and that's what they sometimes called these stones in Brazil, where they are mined. Green fire . . ."

Pippa's greater interest was in Durandal and as she hung back, crouching to stroke him, Alexandra said softly to Mark, "I'm sorry about that. I didn't know whether to tell her or not."

"Oh, she wouldn't mind," he said and explained to me, "Alexandra's emerald once belonged to Louise. She left her friends certain of her jewels in her will."

A hand from behind me caught my wrist and held me back. Harriet whispered, "Louise had a morbid pastime which drove her lawyer nearly mad. She was always putting codicils to her will, leaving her friends various possessions. Do you know what she left me?" She hissed the last words as we walked down the long, lamplit hall. "An old Victorian necklace that was quite hideous. She didn't like me, you see. Not that all that fuss over her will meant anything. She believed herself to be immortal."

Alexandra asked, laughing, as we entered the dining room, "Who is immortal?"

"Louise thought she was."

"Only she wasn't," Alexandra said quietly. "Cathy, will you sit next to David?"

The dining room was in Western style. As if reading my thoughts as I scanned the long yew table and the chairs with their orange brocade seats, Alexandra said, "I imported the furniture for this room from Paris. I really couldn't bear the idea of crouching on hassocks at a table so low that my guests had to sit cross-legged to eat, and then probably get indigestion. Pippa, come and sit by me and I'll tell you what is in the various dishes."

We had iced soup, chicken flavored with almonds, and stuffed vine leaves. The wine was imported from France and Ahmed served us little pastries that tasted of oranges and were delicious.

Pippa cast awed eyes around the candle-lit table, but I saw that she was fighting tiredness and made a mental note to see that she had a much lighter meal in the evenings so that she could go to bed soon afterward.

When dinner was over, we went back to the patio for coffee. The luxuries on the small white table before us had the allure of forbidden fruit for Pippa.

Alexandra waved her hand. "Do all help yourselves."

Immediately Pippa's fingers made swift, hovering movements over the glacé cherries.

Mark leaned forward and plucked her hand away. "If you eat any more, you little glutton, you won't sleep tonight."

Alexandra and Mark drifted into talk about mutual friends she had lost touch with. "It's all so long ago," she said ruefully, "and the few times I've been to England since my marriages, I've felt almost alien."

"But you and I have never quite lost touch."

She laughed. "That's not thanks to your letter-writing. It's merely because we found ourselves in the same country on occasion."

"I left correspondence to Louise—"

Whether or not he intended to mention her I had no idea. The words could have slipped out involuntarily. But a little silence fell awkwardly, as if an unwelcome stranger had crept between us.

"I don't blame you," Alexandra said. "I'm no letter-writer either."

"Oh, look . . ." Pippa's voice merged with Alexandra's.

We followed her fascinated eyes and saw a moth with green, translucent wings fluttering against the screen.

"That," Justin said, "is something you'll see nowhere else in the world. It's rare even here. The Hammagarb name for it, translated, means 'the midnight dancer.'"

"Why 'midnight'?"

"Because that is the time when that moth is usually seen—if it's seen at all—as though it has a built-in clock mechanism."

Pippa got up to watch it more closely. "It's lovely. It has a little fringe to its wings."

"There's a legend about them," Justin said. "There has to be, since the only other sort of moth you see in North Africa is the one that eats clothes. The story is that an eccentric Englishman came out here in 1900 and brought with him matchboxes lined with lettuce leaves that made little cradles for the moths which he had carefully bred in England. Whether it's true or not, I don't know. But certainly this species is only seen in Bou Hammagan, and it isn't a lavish breeder."

"You'll be able to write about that in your diary, won't you?" Alexandra said. "The midnight dancers . . ." She shrugged her shoulders. "I suppose soon, now, some entomologist will be out here peering and studying them."

As the little moth whirled before the screen, I saw the web-thin, emerald veins of its double wings catch the light from the hanging

45

lamp over the patio. Pippa, torn between watching the cheetah with adoring eyes and the moth with wonder, was having the time of her life.

The telephone bell rang as Mark was telling Alexandra about the crash of a past mutual friend's political career.

She was saying, "I read something about it in the Paris newspapers," and then looked up.

Ahmed was at her side. "There is a telephone call for Monsieur."

"And *now* what do they want me for?" Mark got up looking faintly irritated and went into the house.

When he returned he said, "I'm sorry, I'm afraid I have to go out."

"Oh, Mark, not on Cathy's first night, surely."

"Today's film has to be flown to London for processing, but we were late getting back and the post office—God forgive them for calling it that—is closed. The parcel will now have to be delivered direct to the airport at Algiers and strings pulled to get it on the night plane. It's one hell of a drive into Algeria, but I know the road and I'll take it fast."

Justin said, "Surely one of the crew could go?"

"None of them know this part of Africa as I do. I shan't take any wrong turnings or end up halfway in the desert as they might."

"Shall I come with you?" I asked.

"No. No, you stay here. It's dark and so there'll be nothing to see and it's a dusty, tiring journey." He turned away from me. "I'm sorry, Alexandra, but you do understand, don't you?"

"Of course." Her smile was cool and friendly, with the ease of someone who knew the man to whom she spoke extremely well, yet felt no emotion toward him. In that moment I realized how much more Alexandra must know of Mark than I did.

When Mark had gone, Harriet said, "I know there isn't a full moon, but there's enough for you to have seen a bit of the country around if you'd gone with Mark. I think he might have taken you."

"I'll get him to take me some other time." I called to Pippa, who was edging toward the patio door, trying to make herself small so that I wouldn't see her and send her to bed. "Oh, no, you don't!" I pounced and caught her. "One of these days someone is going to use cave-man techniques on you."

"What's that?"

"This," I said and tugged her hair gently.

I hung about my room while she undressed and washed, calling out to me that she was quite certain the taps were real gold. I was as certain that they were not and privately thought them hideously ornate. But I let her hold on to her gilded imaginings, and when she was in bed I tucked the sheet and blanket around her. Her breath was scented from the crystallized rose she had eaten when Mark had forbidden her the cherries. I wondered to myself how much toothpaste she had used, but tonight was an exception—she could keep her rose taste.

She had, with a little regal tilting of her head, allowed me to kiss her goodnight. Whatever she had felt that afternoon when she had rushed in on us was, if not forgotten, at least forgiven.

I remained for a while longer in my room, tidying my first casual unpacking, glancing through drawers where Mark kept his things, not in the least surprised to find that I had no need to tidy them.

My love for him was in everything I saw. In the clothes hanging in the great carved wardrobe; in my hairbrush which he liked to use on me himself, drawing it deeply, sensuously through my hair; in the very atmosphere of the room that was ours for a little while. I saw the light under the door to Pippa's room and knew that she was writing her daily report in her diary. I wondered if I would have loved her so much had she not been Mark's child.

VI

THE GROUP in the screened patio lit by the single bronze lamp had something almost theatrical about it. Durandal sat with his paws stretched before him, a still, spotted Sphinx with glittering eyes. Alexandra sat laughing and playing with her rings. Harriet was leaning her head slightly sideways and listening to David and Justin, who were discussing Bou Hammagan's involved politics.

Alexandra saw me first. "Oh, Cathy, it isn't your birthday, is it?"

"No."

"Then someone has sent you a 'welcome' present or else Mark has had a surprise gift delivered to you." She reached out and picked up a parcel from the table before her. Ahmed, who had been standing by her, brought scissors. He was like a sorcerer's apprentice, producing the props at the right moment.

I tore off the brown-paper wrapping and found inside a large silver box. The lid was intricately chased with a classic design of Pandora opening the box out of which rushed the evils that affected the world. On the side panel I recognized Hippomenes dropping the golden apple and Atalanta bending to retrieve it. The other sides of the box also had scenes from Greek myths. Cupid and Psyche; Narcissus adoring his reflection in the pool; and Orpheus looking back on a fleeing Eurydice.

"It's—beautiful. But who on earth would send me anything so valuable?"

Alexandra leaned forward. "I wonder where Mark found it? Bou Hammagan is entirely poor in silversmiths and this is the work of a master craftsman."

I was searching among the wrapping paper for a note. Justin said, "It's probably inside the box."

I lifted the lid and found a piece of folded paper. A verse was written on it in illuminated script which was not easy to read.

"What does it say?"

I had no idea who had asked the question for as the group watched me, I read the lines to myself.

> Brightness falls from the air
> Queens have died young and fair.
> Dust hath closed dark Catherine's eye.

"Well, what does it say? Come on, give . . ."

I left the lid open with the note lying in it unfolded. The box was heavy and I gave it to Justin with both my hands. My fingers burned as though the silver were molten.

"Good God." Justin held it as if it were something supernatural which would bewitch him through touch. "It can't possibly be . . . it's too crazy . . ." I had never before seen him look stunned.

"It can't possibly be—*what?*" My voice came thinly across the puzzled quiet of the patio. The only sound was Durandal purring dreamily to himself.

"This—bloody—box"—the elegant indifference had gone—"belonged to Louise. It disappeared after her death."

Harriet snatched at it. "Of course it can't be hers. It's too ridiculous—" She broke off, turning it sideways and peering into a corner of the Orpheus design. Then she lifted her head and made a small stammering noise, rather like Pippa did when she was excited or dismayed. "B-b-but you're right; it *is*. It's the box Louise used to keep on that table near her bedroom window. No one knew who gave it to her, it just appeared, and she always said, 'Oh, I've had it packed away for ages and forgot it. Then one day, turning out an old trunk of my grandmother's, I found it. That's all.' Personally, I didn't believe her. Louise never had anything tucked away—all her possessions were on show. Justin, look, here are her initials: 'L. M.' That's another reason why I knew her tale of grandmother's old trunk was a lie. Her maiden name was Charlton and that *doesn't* begin with an 'M.'" She turned a stunned face to me. "What does the note say?"

I nodded to Justin, who had taken it out of the box. He passed it over to Harriet, who frowned at the difficult script. "I don't understand. What is this—some sick joke?"

"I don't know about that. It's just a verse obviously written for Cathy."

"Just a verse? Then you'd better read it again," Harriet retorted. "It's horrible, using her name with a threat."

"I suppose it's a quotation," Justin said. "Or, of course, it could be original. Poetry was never my strong point."

"But the coincidence," Harriet protested. "Louise's box here, in Bou Hammagan. It doesn't make sense."

"It does to the one who sent it," Justin said dryly and looked across at Alexandra. "You're not understanding a word of this, are you?"

"As I knew Louise, yes, I am. I only once saw the house where she and Mark lived when they were married and I don't remember the things in it. But if Louise owned the box, I suppose Mark or Pippa inherited it. Of course, that's merely a guess since I was in South America at the time of her death."

"It was odd, but after Louise died, the box disappeared," Harriet said. "I remember Mark asked us if we knew if she had left it privately to someone without specifying it in her will—someone who perhaps took it. You've no idea how Louise's so-called friends swarmed to her house with condolences after she died. One of them, we thought, could have just walked off with the box because the promise of it might have been only a verbal one. But Mark decided that it had got caught up in one of the many 'lots' sold by auction."

"But it hadn't. Or perhaps whoever bought it has sent it to Cathy because she is Mark's wife," Alexandra said. "Yet, I don't know. It doesn't really make sense, does it? The first thing to do is to find out who delivered it. Justin, ring for Yussef, will you? Whoever brought it must have handed it to him at the gate. We'll soon see—"

"If only Mark were here," Harriet said, "he could probably give us a lead."

"Since he couldn't find a lead himself at the time of Louise's death when the box disappeared, and everyone searched for it, I really can't see that he'll be much help now," Justin said.

Alexandra rose with a rustle of silk as Yussef appeared. "A parcel was delivered just now. Who brought it?"

"Someone ring the bell, madame. Then, when I look, I see no one. I open door and there is the parcel."

"And no one on the steps?"

He hesitated, then shook his head. "No one, but—"

"But—?"

"I see Ahmed's daughter. She come here tonight and she just standing"—he pointed—"little way down steps and she crying."

"You asked her if she had left the parcel or if she had seen anyone?"

"I call to her, but she do not speak because she is crying. But she make me understand she do not leave parcel." Yussef burst into swift Hammagarb.

Alexandra looked at Justin. "What does he say?"

Justin lit a cigarette carefully and exhaled a circle of smoke. "Just that Ahmed is angry with his daughter. But that's their affair and has nothing to do with us."

Alexandra turned to Yussef. "Will you take Durandal for his walk and tell Ahmed I want to speak to him?"

The cheetah had been so still that I had forgotten him. Alexandra reached for his great chain which hung over the arm of an empty chair and handed it to Yussef. When they had disappeared through the arch, Harriet said to Justin, "I understand a certain amount of Hammagarb. Though Yussef talks too quickly, I did hear one thing. Why did he mention your name?"

"If you heard that, you must have noticed that he only said 'Mountavon,' and then clammed up."

"Yes. Why? What was he afraid of?"

"Nothing that I can think of. He was probably going to refer to Mark, and then decided not to."

"How did he—and how do *you*—think Mark comes into this?"

"Well, he might have thought Mark had—er—dropped the box."

"And that's a damned silly remark," Harriet said. "You don't 'drop' a valuable silver casket and even Yussef, who is certainly not bright, couldn't think that." She eyed Justin with suspicion.

52

"Then," said Justin, unabashed, "perhaps you know what Yussef so nearly said and didn't quite."

Alexandra stopped the sharp interchange. "All this isn't really helping Cathy, is it?"

"Sorry," Justin said, "but Harriet thinks she understands far more than she does. All Yussef was obviously going to say was that he saw Mark arriving or leaving here." He turned his head toward the door leading into the house.

Ahmed had come into the patio and was standing quite still waiting for Alexandra to speak, his face like a carving in polished wood.

"I understand your daughter called on you tonight, Ahmed."

"That is right, madame."

"Is there anything worrying her?"

"Nothing, madame, that cannot be put right by me, her father."

"But something is wrong?"

He inclined his head. "A family matter. I have told her she must not come here. She will not come again."

"A parcel was found lying outside the door tonight, addressed to Mrs. Mountavon. Do you know anything about it?"

"It is Yussef who would know that, madame."

"He doesn't, and that is why I am asking you."

Ahmed's expression was impassive. "When my daughter left, madame, I did not go with her to the door, and so if there was a parcel there, I would not have seen it."

It was a stalemate and we knew it.

When Ahmed left us, Alexandra's hand hovered over the porcelain pot. "Would anyone like some more coffee?"

None of us did. We sat, the silver box between us, and the note somehow in my hands. I realized only dimly that Harriet had passed it back to me while Alexandra was questioning Ahmed.

I must have been gripping the small, thick piece of paper very tightly, for the long scar on my thumb began to throb. I had cut myself badly at Chris Lanyard's studio when, picking up a piece of paper from a bench, I had also grasped a sliver of stained glass that had lain unnoticed underneath it. The glass had been as crimson as the blood that flowed from my wound. The studio and Chris and the jewel-tinted glass with which we worked were in a world far removed from this one where I sat, slowly starting to tear up the elaborately illuminated verse. I had a feeling that perhaps if I destroyed it, I could exorcise the evil at which it hinted.

Justin's hand shot out and took the half-torn paper from me. "We'll show this to Mark."

Harriet said, "Who, though—*who* could have done this? And why, after all this time, return the box? Most certainly not because someone has a conscience—*that* possibility can be wiped out by the note."

"I suggest we forget it until Mark comes back," Justin said. "He's the one . . ."

But he wasn't. *I* was. The note was for me because Louise had died strangely and I was alive and I was Mark's wife. A hatred of me—which had left me in peace in England—had caught up with me in Bou Hammagan. Or perhaps had followed me, knowing that I was more vulnerable in a place where the police service was probably little more than a name and a uniform.

David, who had been sitting quietly in the shadows, rose. "I have to be up early in the morning." He looked across at me. "I'll call for you about ten o'clock and take you to the church. Don't worry." He glanced at the silver box. "I'm sure that Mark will find out—well, what it's all about." I knew from his tone that he was embarrassed by the tension around him. He was a man who couldn't deal with emotions.

"I'll see you to the gate." Justin jumped up and waited, lighting a cigarette and then stubbing it out, while David bade us goodnight.

When they had gone, Harriet said thoughtfully, "Justin is jumpy tonight. Did you notice? And what does he want to see David off for? He usually just waves a languid hand."

"I think the delivery of the box has shaken us all," Alexandra said.

"Oh, Justin never really cared for Louise. So resurrecting her ghost wouldn't trouble him."

"It's a long drive from the airport. He could be tired."

"He could be," Harriet said without conviction.

Justin was gone some time, and when he returned, he sat down quietly and took no part in Alexandra and Harriet's light, running conversation, part gossip, part friendly argument and none of it important.

I knew they were trying to ease the tension. But in the African garden with the fountain playing, we were a bewildered group playing at being social and waiting for Mark.

"It's absurd," Harriet said at last. "Mark could be hours. I think we'd better go."

"I'll wait for him in my room. I'm sorry, Alexandra, it *is* rather late . . ."

Distant footsteps merged with my last words. I stopped speaking and listened.

Mark came through the archway from the courtyard, pushed open the screen door and joined us.

Harriet raised her eyebrows. "Oh, no, not Algiers and back in an hour!"

"I used a little gentle persuasion on the crew and reminded them that my wife had just arrived from England. When that didn't bring forth a rush of offers to go in my stead, I hung a carrot before Geoff Lyne's nose. We can well do without him tomorrow, and I know he has a weakness for the nightspots. So I painted a splendid picture of the gaiety of Algiers after dark. I also got John to promise him that, since he wouldn't know the road as well as I and therefore would take longer to get there, we'd pay his hotel bill just in case it turned out that, after all, it would be impossible to get the film through to London tonight."

"All of which," said Harriet in a bored tone, "is another waste of good English money, since in that case it could have been posted here in the morning. But never mind that now. We've got something far more important to discuss." Harriet indicated the silver box, which I had picked up and held out for Mark to see. "You didn't notice this on the table, did you?" she asked him.

The silence seemed to shudder. I couldn't take my eyes off Mark's face. It was set in an expression I was unable to read, but when he spoke his voice had a forced control. He was either very angry or very shocked. "*Where* did you get this?" He took the box from me and held it in his hands.

"*We* didn't get it from anywhere," Harriet said. "It was left outside the door. A present for Cathy. There's a rather horrible note with it. It is—or—or rather *was*—Louise's, wasn't it?" She waited for an answer, but none came.

I held my breath as she continued. "It disappeared, didn't it, after her death? And now it's turned up here." Her tilted eyes watched him.

"The note you said came with the box." Mark held out his hand, flicking his fingers impatiently.

Justin gave it to him. "Cathy started to tear it up, but I rescued it. I thought you ought to see it."

Mark fitted the two torn pieces together, read it and then put it in his pocket. He tucked the box under his arm as if it were an unimportant parcel. "I'm going out," he said quietly. "And when I come back, please no one mention this."

"For God's sake," Harriet exploded. "Someone does this extraordinary thing and all *you* do is to walk off with the box and tell us not to talk about it. You can, at least, explain. Cathy should know what you know—it's she who's menaced—if I've interpreted that verse correctly."

"Damn it all!" Mark reacted violently. "How can I explain what I don't understand? I'm sorry." Tenderness softened his expression. "But the best thing for everyone is for me to get this thing out of the house. I doubt if anyone here wants to see it again."

Harriet said softly, "You forget. If it was once Louise's, then it now belongs to Pippa."

Their eyes met, cold, unaffectionate. "Pippa has probably forgotten all about it, and since it was sent with an ugly message to Cathy, I think we'll ignore this particular small inheritance."

"What are you going to do? Bury it in the sands of the desert? *That's* an easy way out."

Mark refused the challenge and went to the screen door. His hand was on the latch when Justin called, "Aren't you even going to try and find out who sent it?"

"The first thing to be done is to try and find out who, in this town, can write in illuminated script."

"And the best of luck to you," Justin murmured. "Are you going to the police?"

"No," said Mark, and was gone.

Harriet said, "You know my brother-in-law, don't you, Alexandra? He was always secretive. But this is odd behavior even for him."

"If you can't talk about something else and leave Mark to cope, then shut up, darling Harriet," Justin said softly.

"You did your share of questioning," Harriet retorted.

We sat upright, regarding one another as sudden enemies, fighting over Mark's integrity.

Then Harriet laughed. "Oh, take no notice, Cathy. I'm always on the side of suspicion. All right, so Mark is as shaken and puzzled as we, and he has gone into the town. For what? To try and clear up the oddness of the box turning up here in this benighted town, or to bury the damn thing? Justin, we must go home."

Alexandra said, "In spite of saying that he wouldn't go to the police, I'm sure Mark will do that."

"To tell them what?" Harriet demanded. "That his wife has received a present? There's nothing criminal about that—nor in writing some obscure verse in illuminated script. And even if Mark went to them to have the sender traced, they'd be useless. They wouldn't be able to find their own police station if it were lost. Goodbye, Alexandra, and thank you for our gorgeous dinner, and this heavenly garden to sit in."

"One thing." Justin paused on his way across the patio. "There was a lock on the box, but where is the key?"

"That's right." Harriet's bright glance fastened on Justin. "Well, do you think Mark noticed? I mean, that there was a lock. Heaven knows, he must have seen the box enough times on Louise's table." She looked around the patio at our half-shadowed faces. "And now what happens? Or perhaps the rest is silence and we'll never know."

VII

THAT NIGHT, propped up against pillows, I listened vaguely to distant music, thin and plaintive as a sea bird's call. The fine wire window screens that kept out the possible invading armies of insects did not keep out the scent of Bou Hammagan; the mixture of incense and spices and camel. Somewhere beyond the high wall I heard shouting and then laughter—a quarrel and a making-up. Three times, as I lay listening, I looked at my bedside clock, and an hour passed slowly. Then Mark came.

He crossed the room and sat by my side. His face was so gaunt and the dark lines under his eyes so much deeper that I reached across the divan and turned on the other lamp to give his features less shadow.

"What have you done with the box?"

"It's locked up at the office."

"And—that's all?"

He laid a hand over mine. "Not entirely. But any investigations take time. Surreptitious acts—and that is what this is—need surreptitious handling. But let me do the worrying, Cathy."

"Perhaps if you showed the note to the police, they could trace it?"

"What in the world do you think they'd make of illuminated script here?" Amusement lightened his voice. "Oh, Cathy . . . Besides the impossibility of the Bou Hammagan police being able to trace something so alien, the whole of the North African coast is alive with pauper artists living cheaply and trying to exist on what they can make out of the tourists."

"Mark, I'm afraid."

He leaned over and put his hands around my face, smoothing back my hair. "Leave it to me, Cathy, please."

"There's one thing I want to tell you. While you were out, I had a sudden thought that perhaps Louise did have a visitor on that last night and that she gave him . . . her . . . the box as a present."

"I'm afraid it wasn't in character for her to give during her lifetime, particularly not something as valuable as that piece of silver."

"But if she knew she was going to—"

"She didn't," he said sharply. "Cathy, don't start suppositions about something that is over and must be forgotten. I knew Louise."

"How can you be so certain? Do we really understand the people we live with? How do you know how anyone would behave in a sudden emotional crisis? I don't know how *I'd* behave, so how could anyone else say for certain that I wouldn't do something desperate? I can't imagine it, but on the other hand, I won't be categorical about it. And I'm sure you can't be about Louise. Oh, Mark, why are we arguing?"

"*We* aren't. *You* are. And since none of us was there at the time of Louise's death and the two witnesses didn't agree, how can we ever know now?"

He had risen and walked away from me. I saw his reflection in the mirror on the ebony table. The silence was tight with anger.

Mark said, "And now, suppose we stop playing this macabre guessing game?"

"It could help—"

"It can help nothing," he burst in furiously. "Nothing at all. That bloody box arrived here and somehow I'll find out how and why. But stop talking about Louise." He reached over the bed and gripped my arms. His gray eyes had golden spots of anger where the lamplight caught them. "Stop it now—and forever."

I tensed under his grasp. "If the past can help the present, can help to throw a light on something that threatens me, I have no intention of shutting it out. It's I who received that note, Mark. Not you."

"All right. Then I'll tell you what I believe. Someone could be trying to harm me through you. Whoever it is probably realizes that it would take a lot to alarm me about my own safety, so they are using you. Fundamentally, I don't believe you are involved."

"But I am. You've just said so. Someone trying to harm you through *me*. In other words I am the target."

"Cathy, stop it, for God's sake."

"Daddy!"

He wheeled around. Pippa stood in the doorway staring at us. She said, "You're shouting."

"Go back to bed, Pippa. I'm sorry if I woke you."

I swung my legs over the side of the bed and reached for my robe. "It's cold at night, darling, and you're barefoot. I'll come and tuck you in."

"I don't want you to. I want Daddy."

He went to her, put an arm around her shoulders and disappeared with her into her little silk-hung room. The door closed between us.

I turned out one of the two lamps and lay in the half shadow, my eyes closed. So he wanted me to behave calmly, as if I were uninvolved . . . Damn brave men who could not understand the fear of those less courageous! Oh, Mark, what am I thinking of to condemn you for a courage I haven't got?

I heard Pippa laugh and I thought, *Behind that closed door are the two people I love.* But when I questioned, *Do they love me?* I gave myself only the dusty answer, *There are degrees of loving. How do I know how much or how little someone else loves me?*

The bed swung gently as Mark got in beside me. He lay quite still for a moment or two and then said quietly, "I'm sorry, Cathy. I didn't mean to shout at you just now. I've had a long demanding day, and when I'm tired I'm not in control of my temper. Forgive me."

I reached for his hand, and we lay each on the far side of the great bed, our arms extended so that we could just touch with our fingers. I forgave him; I would always forgive Mark anything. But there was still a barrier of shock inside me that stopped me from going into his arms.

I said, "Do you think I should go back to London?"

"Is that what you want?"

"If this is the beginning of some plan to scare me, yes. I'm not so brave that I can take threats."

He let go of my hand and covered his eyes with his arm. "Stay, Cathy. This commission of yours for a window in the church is a wonderful step forward in your career. I think you would always regret it if you turned your back on such a challenge. Besides which, I'm here; whereas in London, you'd be on your own."

"I wasn't threatened at home."

"Whoever is here with his mind full of sick ideas can catch a plane to London as easily as you or I."

Mark was right, of course. He moved toward me. "I'd like you to stay so that I can keep an eye on you, and, when I'm not around, Harriet and Justin can do it for me."

The sounds of the night circled around the house, musical and discordant, subtle and raucous—men's voices, dogs, someone shouting from a rooftop; then, when the rest had quieted, I heard thin, Oriental music from a house nearby.

Mark's anger was spent, but the repercussions still lay between us. I knew that the wise thing would be to leave the subject alone, but it still nagged at me so much that I asked, "What did you do with the note that came in Louise's box?"

"Suppose we stop calling it that. Unless it was left to anyone specifically, it's Pippa's."

"The note . . ."

"It's in my wallet where I can get hold of it quickly if I find a lead on who sent it."

I lay and stared at the silver stripes made by the moonlight through the slatted shutters.

Mark moved and was lying over me lightly, resting his arms on either side of my shoulders. "Trust me, Cathy. Please trust me for, whatever happens, I'll never be far away from you."

His voice, his words broke the barrier between us. I put up my arms and drew his head down. "And I make you a promise. This journey to North Africa was an exception. I'll never try to follow you or be a hanger-on."

"And having settled that," he said softly, "shall we sleep? Negative emotion is exhausting—and we've both suffered that during the past hour." He kissed me quietly, without passion. "Goodnight, darling."

Whatever the strains and anxieties that troubled Mark, he had the ability to brush them aside and fall asleep immediately. I had never had that marvelous gift, for marvelous it was.

Half asleep, Mark had turned from me, but I lay on my back, my mind too stimulated by the recent stresses. With an effort I switched my thoughts and began to play with ideas for the church window. It had to be beautiful and contemporary, and it must not quarrel with any of the denominations that used it. Chris had reminded me before I left London that I must work closely with David if I wanted to achieve a sense of unity between the window and the church itself.

As I lay beside the sleeping Mark, other things took command of my mind. I went back, in memory, to the day four and a half years ago when the principal of the Farringdon School of Art had called me in to discuss my future.

I had said tentatively, "I would like to be a dress designer."

The principal was tall and thin and balding. "Is this your burning ambition? Think, Miss Fareham, before you answer. Is dress designing the thing above all else you wish to do when you leave here?"

I had to admit that it wasn't.

"Then I suggest, since nothing burns in you to be done over above everything else, that you try to find something more original. Too many have gone into that branch of design, and so many have failed. Go away and think about it."

It was at the end of a term and I went away. I went to France for a vacation, and it was Chartres Cathedral that revealed, in the glory of the crimson and purple and emerald of its stained glass, what I wanted above all else to do.

On my return to Paris I stopped at the Forest of Rambouillet and walked across the glade where Henry IV had encamped after Ivry. I scarcely saw the turrets and the towers and the green woods. Instead, the sumptuous windows at Chartres haunted me.

When the next—and my last—term at art school began, I went to see the principal again. "I know now that I want to work in stained glass."

He was delighted. Chris Lanyard was a personal friend of his, and he knew that no apprentice could have had a finer start. I joined Lanyard's studio and got to know not only that dedicated artist but also the craftsmen who worked for him. Chartres had been my first real sight of stained glass. Before that, if during vacations I had visited a cathedral, my eyes had appreciated color and design and had flicked away without a second glance. Lanyard had made me study the twelfth-century windows at York Minster, the marvelous translucency of fifteenth-century glass. I traveled through England—Gloucester, Fairford, Winchester. I had found a world of magic color and glorious design.

Chris's studio was completely self-contained, with workshops where everything was done from the milling of the leads to the final cementing and waterproofing of the completed panels.

I would spend hours watching the craftsmen glazing a window after it had been fired, but I was not allowed to touch glass until I had served my apprenticeship in each of the complicated processes. Chris spared me nothing, and at the end of my apprenticeship I had practical experience in every technique. Stained glass was called the most elusive of all the arts, and a window created in a studio could look quite out of place when set in the building for which it was designed. That was why I had been sent to Bou Hammagan where the light was strong. I had to find a harmony in both color and atmosphere in that harsh African brilliance.

My great ambition was to be individual, to allow no stained-glass artist to influence me. But when I saw some of the wonderful secular work that had been done, I knew that, because I was most certainly no genius, great artists must guide me. Hard work and long study, plus broken nails and bruised fingers, had tempered my extravagant belief in my own gifts. I had lost my soaring ambition, but beneath it my dream was untarnished. Perhaps, hundreds of years hence, people would look at a secular window and say, "Catherine Fareham designed that." And nobody would remember that I had become Catherine Mountavon . . .

VIII

WHEN I opened my eyes, dawn was filtering flamingo-pink through the screens. I lay thinking of the gentler spun-gold of an English dawn, but the long-drawn singsong of a muezzin's call dispelled the English memory. Cocks were crowing and the faithful were being called to prayer.

Mark lay on his side away from me, and I got up carefully, sliding out of the low bed onto the cool tiles, and crossed to the window. Venus, the morning star, which the Egyptians had called the Queen of Heaven, still shone. I took a few long breaths of air and smelled apricots. Somewhere a donkey brayed.

Hands touched my shoulders, fondled my throat, drew me back into enfolding arms. "Come back to bed, darling," Mark said, and bent and lifted me up. "You're so little." He put me gently down on the bed and spread himself by my side. "Your face is dyed pink with the dawn."

In the morning brightness, the previous night lost some of its menace. I lay curled up close to Mark, deciding that cowards who wrote anonymously would not resort to violence. Mark or Harriet or Justin, all of them knowing a great deal more of Africa than I did, would eventually find whoever hated me, or Mark, or both of us.

I raised my head, listening to a new sound that was like a small tinkling trumpet.

"The garbage collector," Mark said, and moved away from me, flinging back the light blanket. "I'm going to have a bath, and then I'm going out. I've got into the habit, while I've been here, of wanting some activity before the sun gets too high. We can't start the cameras at dawn, unfortunately, because the men won't stir until half past seven. We go to Gharb Acho this morning. John is meeting me at the Kabenès Gate at half past eight—I shan't be wanted until then, and I must have my quota of silence."

In other words, he wanted to go alone. I listened to him splashing in the bath. Half of him coped easily with people; the other half was like Kipling's cat that walked by himself. But I wouldn't change Mark for an easier man.

He dressed quickly in green shirt and beige slacks. "I never wear shorts in the desert," he said. "The sand occasionally whips around my legs, and just when I'm facing the camera I want to scratch."

I told him that, to viewers, that would be a nice, homey note. But he said homeyness wasn't written into his contract.

When Mark left me, I went to the window and watched him go past the fountain in the courtyard to the door in the high wall. I could just see him climb the shallow steps to the top of the street where the city ended and the desert began. I looked beyond him to the distant mountains like legendary towers bathed in dawn light. Elbows on the window sill, chin on my hands, I would have given much for Mark to have said, "Come with me."

Pippa was dancing barefoot with delight on the lovely silk rugs laid out on the flat roof. Urns of geraniums and stocks stood at intervals along the low wall.

"Can I come up here whenever I like?" Pippa asked.

"I don't know," I said. "It might be a place which Alexandra keeps for herself when she wants to be quiet."

"But *you* came up here."

"Because I saw you prancing about like a ballerina."

I began idly to count the steps that led up from the courtyard to the roof.

"So that's where you've got to." Mark arrived by the inside staircase.

Pippa leaped across the rugs, hair flying. "Can we all go somewhere together this morning? Please, oh, *please* . . ."

"I have to go to Gharb Acho today," he told her. "It's where they are drilling for the oil that will pay for the New City. But I'll be home this evening and as hungry as an ox, so mind you don't eat up everything before I get back." He flipped Pippa's cloud of hair away from her shoulders. "Why don't you tie back that mane of yours? In another hour or so you'll be complaining how hot it is around your shoulders."

"Will you tie it for me, Daddy?"

"Are you turning me into a lady's maid? Go and find a hair ribbon."

"Come with me. Please . . ." She hugged him around the waist.

"My young clinging vine," he said with tender mocking and pushed her away from him. "Run along and tie your hair back."

I watched them together, both intent on having their own way. In spite of Pippa's immaturity, their profiles were very alike: features proud, straight and clear-cut. I leaned against the low wall, my hands pressed back onto the warm stone, and as I watched, I wondered how much Mark loved me for myself, and how deep was his need of me for Pippa's sake. Had she never been born, would I have become Mark's wife? Out of the recent past I recalled something a friend of his had said to me. "I'll make a bet with you that Pippa chose you for her father. He took you down to her school to meet her, didn't he? Ah, I thought so. And that's when she gave her seal of approval."

As if it mattered now. The months of our marriage had assured me that I was important to them both.

After Mark had freed himself from Pippa's little clawing hands, she had vanished, I supposed in search of a hair ribbon.

I said, leaning over the parapet and watching the cheetah, whose eyes were following the skirmishing of flies, "Durandal . . . that's an odd name."

"It was the magic sword Charlemagne gave to Roland for saving his life at Aspremont. And don't think I'm being very clever knowing that," Mark added. "Alexandra told me." He moved behind me toward the outside stairs.

"I'm not going to be popular this morning. I'm late."

"Good shooting," I called after him.

"You're tempting the gods," he warned me. "I'd rather you prayed for a few clouds to cross the sky while I'm working in the desert—not that such a prayer at this time of year would do any good at all—but I'm not keen on being roasted, and I only hope that the peculiar cooling-gadgets they've got on the trucks work. One let us down that time in Syria, but so far they have behaved themselves here."

I said, "How does John Mayne enjoy North Africa?"

"He doesn't. He loathes the heat. But he's too good a director to refuse such an assignment. You'll have to come and meet the crew."

"Oh, no," I protested too quickly. "I don't want them thinking I'm a wife who chases her husband across the world."

He threw back his head and laughed. "That one's been disproved, so don't be so sensitive."

"But I am. And there's nothing you can do about it, Mark. Tell me." I changed the subject. "What is the government going to do with all the money the oil will bring?"

"Build the New City and play the foreign stock markets. Great fun if you have millions."

I looked away to where the minaret rose, like a slender carved wand, into the burning blue. "Bou Hammagan is fascinating and strange and Oriental. But I don't think I'd like to live here. I wonder if Alexandra will be bored?"

"The people who are taking villas will only be here for a few months of the year. They'll arrange among themselves to meet in Bou Hammagan at the same time, open their villas to parties and bridge and the rest of the social clip-clap, and agree unanimously on the date when they'll all depart again until the following year."

The tone in which he spoke amused me. "It wouldn't be your life, Mark, would it?"

"I'd loathe it."

"Don't worry. I'd never wish that kind of existence on you."

"I'd divorce you if you tried. And now let me go, woman, will you? I have to get to Gharb Acho before the sun rises much higher." He raised his hand in a light salute and left.

I was still standing by the parapet when Alexandra came up the inner staircase. "I was thinking, Cathy. You don't want to take Pippa with you this morning, do you?"

"I shan't be there very long, and it won't hurt her to spend an hour or so with me. I want to get the feel of the place and discuss the window with David."

"I'll take Pippa. I want to go to the bazaars. There's a man who embroiders the most beautiful caftans, and I want to order one. They are wonderful to wear out here. I've talked to Harriet and David on the telephone, and, as David has to go on to some other villa after you have looked over the church, she will call for you there and drive you to the Kabenès Gate. You can have coffee in Isakila Square. I'll meet you there and then leave Pippa with you because I'm going to have drinks with the Mitchells at the hotel."

I glanced at Pippa jumping about on the rugs as if she were on a trampoline. "Did you mind us coming onto the roof?"

"Of course not. But I warn you it's very hot and much nicer down in the shade of the garden. I have a covered terrace outside my own rooms—I must show them to you—and I can lie there and look right down through a gap in the houses over the old city. It's quite lovely in the early morning, especially with the palms and the orange trees."

Pippa left off her rather violent exercises and joined us. "What are we going to do now, Cathy?"

Alexandra said, "You're coming to the bazaars with me while Cathy goes to see the church. Then you'll meet her later with Harriet, and I expect you'll have a sherbet while they have coffee at Hashim's."

"Can we take Durandal?"

"He'd hate it and so would everyone else. He has his morning and evening walk with Yussef—a long one right up the stepped street to the great empty spaces beyond, where there's nothing but a few palms between him and the desert. I've given Yussef a bicycle which he keeps up there, and he rides it while Durandal runs—like the wind. You'll have to go and watch them one day, though you'll never be able to keep up with them."

"And Durandal doesn't run off?"

"Good heavens, no. He's like a well-trained dog, and after his violent exercise he's perfectly happy to lie in my garden during the hottest time of the day and be fussed over and fed and watch everyone."

"I wonder what he thinks about?" Pippa said, chin on her hands, gazing down.

In the vivid morning sunlight Alexandra's face had great dramatic power, but as she laughed, the features softened. "We'll never know what Dura is thinking. But we'd better be going. It will be far too hot later in the bazaars."

I was grateful to her for taking Pippa because I knew that the technical talk I would have with David would be boring for a child. At the same time it amused me—although it didn't surprise me—that Alexandra had taken such complete charge of the first part of the morning. While I had been idling up on the roof, she had been making arrangements for us with Harriet and David. It was kind of her, but I would have to make it clear that I had no intention of shelving responsibility. After today Pippa must always come with me.

When they were gone, I went and sat by the fountain and waited for David. It was a quarter to ten when he rang the bell. Yussef let him in, and he came over to me and said, "You should be spending your first morning enjoying the sights of the city—not that there are many. It has little history, or, to be accurate, its history has been neglected and so, forgotten and buried. Do you really want to bother with the window this morning?"

I reached over the fountain and felt the cool drops of water sprinkle my palm. "My fingers are itching for paper and a pencil."

"All right, then, let's go."

As we walked down the stepped street, David said, "I'm afraid my car is down at the Kabenès Gate. It's just off Isakila Square. Do you mind walking?"

"And the alternative if I did? To ride a donkey?"

"I suppose I could carry you." He looked at me speculatively.

"I like walking, and Justin left his car there yesterday afternoon, so I know how far it is."

The stimulation of being in an African town swept away the tiredness I felt from not having slept well. Knowing that Louise's silver box was locked somewhere in the television crew's office and that the note was in Mark's wallet seemed to lift a load from me. I had a job to do and the morning was hot and golden and I liked the man walking by my side.

The steps stretched down through lines of huddled houses, but the view of the Casbah with its crenelated towers was clear and marvelous against the vivid sky.

"The New City," David said, "is being built beyond the existing old one." He pointed. "Over there, right on the horizon. From the top windows of Alexandra's new villa, she will just be able to see the Mediterranean."

70

"And blocks of high-rise apartments," I murmured, "spoiling the skyline."

"There won't be any apartment buildings. Millions of—all right, let's talk in sterling—millions of pounds are being poured into the development of a kind of sculptured dream—villas inhabited by the sort of people who appreciate beauty. That sounds ridiculously idealistic in this day and age, doesn't it, but I hope it's true. I'm told that there will be nothing that obtrudes—just gracious, expensive white villas standing among trees and flowered walks and fountains. Since a number of rich Moslems will also be coming to live here, a fine new mosque is being built. No architect working in this city will feel himself caught up in an economy drive. Everything will be geared to make a beautiful city. The only economy I know of, so far, is in the building of the church to accommodate the differing denominations. But once they all agreed to my plans, there was no argument over costs." He stared ahead of him. "It could quite easily be the last of the dream cities. It's possible that from now on it will be the industrial designers who will build for tomorrow, not the architects who are creators and have dreams."

"And all this because oil has been found in the desert."

"Yes. There's one good thing, though, from the point of view of those who live here. Although the government has imported European experts, they have refused to let in foreign speculators. There are some fabulously rich people in Bou Hammagan, and they are bearing the initial costs of the whole project, for which they will receive an enormous return."

I watched some young men coming toward us, their ankle-length djellabahs as voluminous as the robes of monks. "I thought North Africa was now clothed in jeans and T-shirts."

"Not here. Not yet, though that may come with the sophistication that the New City will bring."

I stumbled on a broken step and David steadied me. "You chose a strange branch of art for a woman."

"I love it. I want most of all to design secular windows for new buildings."

"Chris thinks a lot of you, so you probably will be doing just that one of these days."

"This is my first big chance, thanks to you, and I've *got* to succeed."

"Are you very ambitious?"

I didn't echo his hint of laughter. "I don't know. I suppose I always wanted to be successful, but since I married Mark I'm more anxious than ever because he is ambitious for me."

"Then he's an unusual husband," David said dryly.

I didn't tell him that Mark must have had his fill of living with someone who had no real interests, no aim of her own in life. I said lightly, "Oh, Mark conforms to no Victorian rules."

The sun was hot on our backs. A pistachio seller tried to sell me some nuts; a little girl with matted hair sucked at an orange and then held it out to me. I smiled at her and because she was so ragged began to open my purse.

David laid a hand over mine. "Don't start that or you'll end up always having a trail of beggars after you. And, to ease your conscience, let me tell you that most of them aren't in need. With the New City being built, there's work for all."

I asked David if he was longing to get back home to his house in Windsor. "Chris told me," I said, "that it's lovely."

"It has a beech forest and as I know I'll always return to it, I don't really mind being away. You must come and see it one day."

I said we'd love to, inferring that the visit would include Mark. David was a bachelor and lived comfortably with a manservant. Chris had told me that there had never been even the vaguest rumor of marriage. He was a partner in a well-established London firm of architects and, although he was only in his late thirties, was in constant demand because his ideas were neither too outrageous nor functional to the point of sterility. Nobody could look up at a new building designed by Sullavan and say with distaste, "The architect for that huge pile of masonry which looks like an elongated lump of sugar was David Sullavan." He had designed a few high-rise buildings, but he had used vision, breaking their line by interesting window spaces and set-backs.

As we walked down the steps that were so wide that I had to take two paces to David's one I asked him if it was easy dealing with Hammagarb workmen.

He said, "The natural Hammagarb attitude toward building is that, for every stone they put into place, they need to pause for breath. I suspect they believe that if they wait long enough, Allah will finish the building for them. They believe in miracles. But the foremen, who are mostly Italian out at the oil wells, have a harder job because the Hammagarbs don't expect mechanical things to work. If a tractor fails, they just spread their hands, sit down and curl up in its shade. I've seen it happen on the building sites in the New City. It's almost as if they're saying, 'Allah didn't make this monster, how can anyone expect it to work?' I suppose it's the only really unmodernized state in the whole of North Africa."

We had reached the last step and immediately were caught up in the crowds that milled around like some slow and ill-formed ballet. There was a maze of narrow streets where craftsmen hammered at brass pots and cut intricate designs in leather. Their stalls were so small that they could reach everything they needed without rising.

"In the larger towns," David said, "the trades are usually localized, but here everything just crowds in together."

The shadows of the buildings and the matting stretched across poles kept the growing intensity of the sun off us. The smells were myriad, leather and thyme and verbena among them. Water sellers hesitated, looking hopefully at us, and a man with a tray of fruit stood before us, eyeing my purse as though willing money to jump out of it.

"Prickly pears, an acquired taste," David said, and waved the man away.

In the courtyard of the mosque were lines of slippers. I looked up at the dome. "Justin told me that it is covered with lapis lazuli," I said. "How could the people of such a little state afford it?"

"In the old days Bou Hammagan was an important trading center. It was on one of the spice routes from the south to the sea. But that was more than three hundred years ago. I'd make a fair guess the house you're staying in was built then."

I smelled hot bread and, turning to the cavelike place where it was being baked, nearly fell over some clucking hens.

David laughed. "In Bou Hammagan you watch your step because there are no nice safe pedestrian paths, and the donkeys and the camels have as much right as we to walk here."

We turned into a small square with orange trees and worn mosaic paving. "Isakila Square," David said. "And there's the Kabenès Gate. The shed where you saw Justin park his car is the best that can be managed by way of a garage."

It was ramshackle and open and there were about half a dozen dusty Fiats and Land Rovers standing close together in one corner as if the garage owner were clearing a space for a great invasion of vehicles.

"Does Alexandra keep a car here?" I asked.

"I think so but I'm not sure. I've only met her three times. The first was when I was having drinks with the Mitchells at the hotel and she joined us. Then she invited me to her house, and the third time was last night."

It had been a long walk down to the Kabenès Gate, and I marveled that someone like Alexandra, used to the easy luxury of Paris and Rio, could be bothered to live so far away from any form of transport. But then, the New City would have roads joining the main artery to Algiers and Sfax and Tripoli. Alexandra was a very temporary tenant in her Turkish merchant's house. Once she was living in her villa, her car could come to her door.

David explained that he had managed to rent a Fiat from a garage in Algiers for the duration of his stay. "It's a bit shabby," he said, opening the passenger door for me, "but I only use it for very short runs around the New City."

We drove north, through the outskirts of the old town and across flat sand-colored earth, past tumble-down groups of huts and small plantations of palms. The roads were appalling, and David had to nurse the car as we drove down slopes and across a dry riverbed. We were well past the noise and commotion of Bou Hammagan, and ahead of me I saw the beginnings of the New City. Huge water pipes were piled at the side of the dirt tracks that would one day become roads, and there were so many cement mixers that I lost count. A few villas were completed except for the laying out of the gardens and the final touches of wrought iron, colored tiles and mosaics which every owner hoped would make their homes individual.

"A city grows slowly," David said. "It can't spring up like a flame. It will take years before this one is in full beauty."

"You love the whole concept, don't you?"

"Yes, because I like individualism."

IX

WE DROVE for about five more minutes and then came to a place where the road crossed another.

"This will be the city center, and a fine small square is going to be built here. Water, of course, is the greatest need, but it will be piped from the sunken wells at Bodaia."

"Whoever chooses to live here," I said, feeling the heat burn through me, "will have to enjoy being baked, boiled or fried."

"Oh, none of them will stay during the hottest season. Over there" —he nodded to the west—"an airstrip is going to be built, and we're only ten miles away from the sea. Now, look a little to your left."

I saw the church standing in a natural arc of palm trees. It was of curved concrete, and the walls were white stucco.

"Le Corbusier," I said softly.

"I admit it. But so many of us are using his ideas. To me he was the greatest architect of his time."

"I like it," I said. "Your design, I mean. It's modern and elegant, and yet it doesn't thrust its function at you."

"Thank you for that," he laughed. "In other words, if the church authorities don't finally agree to share the building, this could be put to other uses. Perhaps a secular one—a hall for meetings, if the rich ever go to meetings, that is. And you could still design your window."

We crossed the threshold and were immediately in deep shadow which cooled my burning shoulders. On one side a cataract of light poured in from a space I knew had been left for the window.

"It's very quiet," I said.

"The men have had to stop working because there are arguments about the way the interior should be finished. One group of the committee wants mosaic columns, the others demand stark wooden ones."

"But they surely couldn't let the whole scheme fall through now that the building is almost completed."

"Why not? They could always get rid of it—everything in the New City is eminently saleable." David waved a hand. "You're facing south at the moment. But we couldn't have a window there"—he pointed ahead of us—"because of the sun's heat. West is also impossible, so I knew it would have to be a north window. That's where you see the gap."

"Just one window? That will look odd, and *that* sounds as if I'm trying to get a better deal—three windows instead of one! I'm not, of course, but—"

"Oh, the ecclesiastical powers-that-be have ideas for the other walls. Personally, although the lines of the building are clear and simple—I'm praising myself, you see—the inside is going to be a hodgepodge."

"You've left a space for a very large window," I said.

"I arranged it that way to be on the safe side in case those on the committee who want a dominating window get their way. If they don't, we can easily fill in the space between the window and the wall."

"Which means I design for both large and small?"

"Yes."

There were heavy footsteps behind me and, since Bou Hammagarbs walked quietly, I wasn't surprised to find a European coming toward us.

"Cathy, this is Mac." David introduced us. "Mac Riven, our invaluable foreman. Mrs. Mountavon is here to submit designs for the stained-glass window."

Mac, red-haired and craggy-faced, threw a glance toward the gap facing us. "Funny thing to have here, I'd 'a thought," he said lugubriously, and it was obvious that to him North Africa and stained glass, whether Gothic or abstract, were doubtful neighbors. I was inclined to agree with him, but I was here to produce a window. Unless those who had commissioned it could not agree and scrapped the whole idea, I was going to use every ounce of imagination and skill I possessed to make it a design I could be proud of. A stained-glass window was not like a picture and I hoped the three denominations which had banded together to produce it understood that.

"Never forget," Chris had once said to me, "that a window is a translucent wall of color that must be in harmony with its surroundings." So, standing with David in the hushed and as yet unhallowed white shell, I felt a rush of excitement. "Let the color sing," Chris had so often said to me. I would let it sing in this white church in Bou Hammagan.

I climbed the ladder Mac had brought me and for a while was busy with my notebook and my six-foot spring rule. David wandered around, occasionally pausing to shoot questions at me. I had to be good at mathematics for the job I was doing, didn't I? I told him that I had never liked the subject much at college and that because I had taken little interest in it there, Chris had made me go to night school for extra study. He had said, "If you can't work things out and know whether to use a one-and-a-half- or a two-inch scale for what is to be done, and if you can't work to one eighth of an inch, you're no good to yourself or to me."

David then asked me about the actual painting of the glass.

"That," I said, "is the part I like best of all." I held up my right hand. "I even have proof that I've been through every process of stained-glass making myself. My battle scar," I said and showed my marked thumb.

When I had finished and my notes were complete for two possible sized windows, I tossed the spring rule and my book of notes to David while I climbed down the ladder. "Now I can go away and start thinking about the designs. I hope they won't go on arguing for long because I want to get to work."

"So do I," David said. "An uncompleted shell of a place isn't a good advertisement for me."

"Cathy? David?" Harriet's voice echoed through the empty space. "Oh." She came with her long swinging stride toward us. "There you are. Have you finished?"

"All I've been able to do initially, yes."

She looked about her. "It's a bit stark, isn't it, and I wonder when all those different religions—"

"Denominations of the same religion," David said.

She gave her sharp, slightly grating laugh. "All right—denominations then. I wonder how soon they'll agree on what is to be done."

"It will be strange working for people I never meet."

"Oh, you'll meet them eventually," David said. "I'll probably have to drive you into Algiers since, to mix our religions a bit, I'm not certain whether Mahomet will come to the mountain or the mountain will have to drive through the dust to Mahomet. But I want the design O.K.'d first because, when they meet you, they could think you're rather young to be given such a commission. So, the window design agreed on first, and then the meeting."

"Which means *you* think I'm too young."

He laughed. "I go by talent, not age." He gave a surreptitious glance at his watch, and immediately I said that we must go.

I tucked the notebook into my purse, and David said, "I hope you enjoy looking around the *souks*. They're not as elaborate here as in the larger cities, and besides food, they sell silks and pottery, but they're interesting. I have to go over to a villa a mile or so away. I've designed it for some people who are staying in Algiers, and they're going to meet me to discuss a glass dome they want. I've got to persuade them to forget about it. The glass will attract the heat. It's extraordinary the lengths to which some rich people will go to outdo their neighbors in grandeur." He came out with us to Harriet's small car.

"I'm sorry Justin isn't with us," she said as we drove away. "He's showing those four Brazilians around the town and then putting their chauffeur on the right road for Tunis. We had an argument before he left this morning over Alexandra, of all people, and I bitched a bit—I always do when I think of rich women." We shot, with a jerk, over a hump in the baked earth. "Justin, as usual, shut his ears, smoothed down his hair and left. He'll spend the rest of the day delighting the tourists with the Mountavon charm. But you know all about that from Mark, don't you?"

I said with amusement, "I wouldn't have said that Mark exudes charm." The car dipped into a pothole and I shot forward, righted myself and looked at Harriet.

"Mark's kind of charm," she said, "is the most insidious, and don't tell me you don't know that, too, because you're no babe in arms, sweetie. Mark's quiet, his reserve, the way he implies to everyone he meets that he'll never be an open book, is enough to make every woman want to try and read him. He's a challenge to them. But no woman will ever understand him."

I said evasively, "Oh, neither Mark nor Justin shows his emotions."

"I've never quite known," Harriet said thoughtfully, "whether Mark likes Justin, though I do know that Justin has that 'my brother, right or wrong' feeling toward Mark."

I had no idea how either of them felt because neither was given to confidences concerning the other.

"We quarreled about—of all things—Louise's silver box," Harriet said. "I suggested that, as he knew the people here, he try and find out who delivered it at the door. Someone must have been paid to do it. But he merely said, 'Leave things alone and let Mark sort it out.' That's when I flew at him. I told him that he, more than any of us, could help. But I might have known that he was too damned idle." She waited for me to comment, and when she saw I had nothing to say, she asked, "Has Mark talked to you about it?"

"Just to tell me he's going to do all he can to find out who sent the box. Do *you* know any artist who can do illuminated script?"

"No. There's so little call for it anyway—and certainly none out here."

But someone who could write it had been in Bou Hammagan . . .

"You know," Harriet said thoughtfully, "I'm sure the box held love letters, and that's why Louise always kept it locked."

Knowing Harriet, I was on my guard. She had a curious insensitivity where any opportunity for scandal was concerned. That I might not want to discuss Mark's first wife did not occur to her, or, if it did, she enjoyed the possibility of a good gossip too much to care how I felt about it. I wanted to drop the subject of Mark, and I made some vague comment about a group of stunted trees that hid the beginnings of a village.

"Dragon trees," Harriet said vaguely, and returned to Louise. "I wonder if the man, her lover, perhaps had a key to the house and let himself in sometime after Louise's death? He could have watched and waited until Mark and that grim old servant he pensioned off were out, and then let himself in and taken the box. There could have been some reason why he was afraid of a scandal if the letters were read by outsiders. Or, he could even suspect that—well—that Louise actually committed suicide because of Mark, and want a sort of revenge. The other possibility I've been thinking about is that Louise was generous with money, and after her death, her lover would enjoy no more of her financial favors. He could believe Mark was the cause of that and hate him for it. The goose no longer laid the golden egg."

"I don't want to talk about it, *or* think about it. Harriet, please stop."

"Sorry. I was only trying to make it easier for you."

"*Easier—for me?*"

"Because you'd obviously hate to consider the fourth alternative."

"There isn't one."

"Isn't there? If one of those witnesses was right, who drove the car at Louise?"

"Witnesses at scenes of accidents—especially at nighttime, and it was dark when Louise was killed—are notoriously inclined to use their imagination."

"Are they? Oh, well, let's leave it like that, shall we?" she said.

X

ORANGE TREES lined Isakila Square, and I was no longer going purposefully with David to a job that had to be done. I had leisure enough to stroll and look about me, and what I saw was fascinating. Between two *souks* one selling babouches, the other lanterns with brass mountings, I watched a man fanning the tiny flames of a fire.

"He's selling honey cakes," Harriet explained. "Hey, be careful!"

She spoke just in time. A train of donkeys, each laden with baskets, was nosing its way past me, and I skipped out of their way.

"If Pippa sees them she'll be miserable all day. She can't bear to see any animal suffering."

"Oh, they aren't. Those baskets are as light as air and empty. They're being brought to the *souks*. Men from the villages bring their stock in to be sold."

I noticed that the goods on display were not of the kind to tempt tourists, but I guessed that this would change as soon as the New City was built. Then there would be elaborate leatherwork and caskets and beautiful silks. But I saw nothing that I found irresistible. I didn't want the rather harshly colored carpets or a leather saddle or even one of the silver sheaths for the daggers the men wore as ornaments. In one *souk* I saw some soapstone bowls that I liked, and Harriet told me they were carved by Berber tribesmen.

I was on the point of buying one when flashes of color caught my eye. Gold and silver embroidered caftans hung under an awning stretched over a booth.

"Now, those—"

Harriet stopped me. "You've got plenty of time to look. And don't pause now—just register what interests you and walk on until you decide that you really want what you saw. Never show a tourist's interest and always, always bargain. Haggling is in their blood, and although there aren't enough hotels here to attract visitors, every Hammagarb knows a stranger when he sees one. Oh, heavens, what did I tell you?"

Hands pressed together in greeting, the owner of the caftan booth was approaching us. He had a splendid head and cunning eyes. "Caftan? Caftan?"

Harriet waved an imperious hand and spoke to him in Hammagarb. He bowed to her and retreated, still smiling.

"I envy you," I said, "being at home in an African town, knowing the language, the people . . . everything."

"Including the reason *why* we're here, which is lack of money. Oh, well. Smell the air."

I sniffed. "Rosemary."

"That's right. You see that wall? A rich Hammagarb family lives in a gorgeous house behind it. They have rosemary hedges and the scent is heaven after so many whiffs of camel."

"I can smell other things, too," I said. "Coffee and spices and people and hot air . . . Harriet, look. Candied fruits."

"You'll find a storehouse of them at Alexandra's, so you don't need to buy any." She strode past the little crowded cafés and the hooded groups squatting on the ground. Catching sight of us, they held out their hands, begging.

"Take no notice," Harriet said. "They probably live quite comfortably."

"That's what David told me just now."

"This state was forced to look after its poor before the men would agree to work on the New City. They copied our Western idea of striking for what they wanted and, believe me, they struck with daggers and knives and even a few old-fashioned muskets their forefathers had brought from Morocco. So, the state gave in and the poor are pensioned—little enough by our standards—but it keeps them in tobacco and mint tea and dates."

Through the crowds I caught sight of Alexandra, elegant in pale blue, making her way toward us.

"How beautifully she walks." I watched her with envy. At a party in a crowded room all eyes would turn from a beautiful face, drawn by her magnetism of authority and pride.

Harriet put it in her own abrupt way. "That's what the arrogance of money does for you." She paused and laughed. "Oh, don't mind me, I'm just jealous."

Alexandra came up to us, the sun on her bright head, her skin the color of apricots. "Pippa is tireless. She has skipped almost the whole way and her head is never still. I have a feeling she has seen more in an hour than I have seen all the time I've been here."

"I think she was born with printer's ink on her fingers. Mark was once a journalist, as you know."

Pippa herself wasn't listening. Her profile was clear-cut and sweet against the moving background of people. She was frowning into the distance. "Isn't it funny? The buildings over there are all colored like the coffee Cathy gives me, with lots of milk in it. And look"—she pointed to the square towers of the Casbah—"they've got carvings on them like the Tudor roses we had to draw in art class at school."

"Introduce her to Hashim and his coffee," Alexandra said. "Or you could go back and sit in far more comfort in my garden. Just do what you want. I'm off to the hotel to see the Mitchells. Here, Pippa, you can take your parcel."

The little girl drew back. *"My* parcel? But . . ."

"Of course. You didn't think I was buying these babouches for myself, did you? They're far too small for grown-up feet. And you chose those because you thought they had the prettiest gold pattern."

"Mine!" She hugged the parcel.

Alexandra laughed and left us. Pippa, carrying the slippers like a coveted school prize, walked between us singing a little meandering song which, merging with the noises about her, seemed to have neither tune nor audible words. She was watching children far smaller than herself twisting the skeins of silk for embroidery. Men sat in the shade drinking Turkish coffee and reading newspapers. Native women passed us and only their eyes moved, swiveling around to watch us—bare-legged, bare-armed, crazy Westerners who worshiped the sun from which they carefully covered their bodies. Outside a canopied booth, folds of wet colored wool hung from bamboo poles.

A small boy, untidily sucking a pomegranate and intrigued by us, wandered away from his voluminously clad mother and walked toward Pippa.

"What's your name?" she asked.

The woman, hearing a strange tongue, turned, flashed black, suspicious eyes at us and dragged her child away, shouting angrily. The boy scuffed his slippered feet, letting out a soft, despairing wail.

"Why is she cross?" Pippa asked. "I wasn't going to hurt him."

"You're a stranger, that's why," I said. "You mustn't mind. Their habits are different from ours."

Her eyes followed a lean, ginger dog, then a dirty little white kitten. "Oh, look." She darted toward it.

Harriet clamped a hand on her shoulder. "No, you don't. He's probably mangy and full of fleas."

Pippa wrenched herself away, her eyes defiant. "I mustn't speak to anyone; I mustn't touch kittens. There doesn't seem to be anything I *can* do here."

"There's plenty," Harriet said. "But keep away from animals—"

"Because you don't like them and *I* do."

"Because, my child," Harriet said with exaggerated patience, "you don't happen to be in Europe."

Pippa stood quite still, staring at the kitten, which was sitting under a bench in a *souk*, watching us.

"We don't mean to be unkind," I said, "but the kitten belongs to someone, and I'm quite certain he doesn't mind being dirty."

She hunched her shoulders against my touch and my hand fell to my side.

Harriet called from a few yards ahead of us, "Oh, do come on."

Pippa scuffed in front of me, complaining, "I only wanted to take him home and wash him. I wasn't going to *steal* him."

"You wouldn't get him past Ahmed," said Harriet, who had overheard.

There was a strong new smell of roasting meat, and I saw a stall where it was being cooked on wooden skewers. It made me think of the lovely food we ate at the House of the Fountains, and I asked Harriet if she had ever seen Alexandra's kitchen. Was it modern or traditional Turkish?—whatever I meant by that.

84

"I've only been in it once," Harriet said, "and I doubt if you'll ever be invited. Everything domestic at that house is behind the scenes. Even the laundry—which the Hammagarbs put out to dry on the roofs —is taken by Lisette to someone else's house to be done."

"She is the housekeeper, isn't she?"

"Oh, no. She 'maids' Alexandra and cooks. Ahmed is the boss. He's always around, and sometimes he makes me nervous the way he suddenly seems to be in the background, watching. Justin hates it too. He says it makes him feel that he's suspected of planning to steal Alexandra's jewels."

I thought as I listened that the friendship between Alexandra and Harriet was curious. But it seemed obvious that the isolation of Bou Hammagan had drawn them together. I doubted that any chance meeting between them would have grown into friendship had they lived in New York or London or Paris.

A sudden wild cry made me start. A Hammagarb in a dirty djellabah lay on the ground, and a donkey stood by his side, lifting delicate hooves to avoid him. The yells of the man joined the shouts of the crowd.

Harriet put a hand on my arm. "Don't waste your sympathy. It's an old trick. They don't see many tourists here and so when they do, they try that ruse. He is a poor man, and has been knocked down. You are a European and you have money and pity. You will give him the first—he cares nothing for the second. In larger cities more frequented by tourists, the man will choose a car to knock him down."

"For just a few dollars?"

"Here, yes. In the bigger towns, he'll demand compensation from the car owner. Oh, not because he's starving, but so that he can pay for his daughter to have a big wedding."

Pippa cried, "Look, there's Daddy. Cathy—l-look."

The man had picked himself up, glanced across at us and, finding his effort wasted, began to shout at the owner of the lean, indifferent donkey.

Pippa was hemmed in by a group of men arguing about a dead chicken. *Daddy—*

I followed her fiercely focused eyes and could not see Mark. "He's gone into the desert where they're drilling for oil," I said.

"He *hasn't*. He's *here*—" She streaked through the crowds, running toward a café.

"Pippa . . ." I shouted and pushed my way after her. Harriet followed, complaining that Pippa had better stop seeing her father in every harmless male who happened to have a pale skin.

As I caught up with her, Pippa stopped dead. "He's gone." She turned, eyes large and tragic. "Cathy, he *saw* me and he just went."

"You imagined him, darling."

"I *didn't*. He was at that table where that lady is sitting, the one in the orange dress. There are two glasses, so she *did* have someone with her and it *was* Daddy. Only there were all those people in the way and when I looked again, he wasn't there."

I put an arm around her and felt the thin body tense.

"The lady said something to him and he looked right at me—Cathy," her voice wailed, "he really d-did . . ."

The girl was very beautiful. Her skin was too dark for her to be a European and not dark enough for a pure Hammagarb. She wore a dress with sleeves reaching to her wrist and her arms were folded, relaxed and patient, on the table. Her profile was perfect, as straight and classic as a Persian painting. As I watched her, she turned slightly and I saw that she wore a huge silver medallion on a chain between her breasts.

"That is Hashim's café," Harriet said, "and it's crowded. There just aren't any tables. We'll go back to Alexandra's and have coffee in the garden."

"Wait a minute. There is a table, over in that corner by the orange tree."

"No, there isn't. Those three men are going to it." Harriet dragged at my arm.

Pippa stood quite still. "I want to go in there." She pointed to the dark interior of the little café. "That's where Daddy went."

"Darling." I reached for her. "Everyone has a double, and you've just seen your father's."

"He knew me! He d-did know me—but he didn't want to."

"Tonight," I said, "when you see him, you'd better tell him that you nearly accosted a strange man, thinking it was he."

"What's 'accosted'?"

"What you nearly did."

I was the only one who laughed. Pippa's eyes were disquieted, suspecting my truthfulness. You did not lie to a sensitive child, but she believed we had. We were tottering on our pedestals of trust, and somehow I had to try to put myself right with her. "Perhaps he hasn't yet left for that place he told us he was going to in the desert, Gharb Acho, and he was just waiting for whoever was going with him."

86

Harriet said impatiently, "Cathy, do come on. It's getting too hot to breathe in this crowd." She seized Pippa and pushed her forward, saying with too much emphasis, *"Of course it wasn't your father."*

"But I know—"

Harriet pointed. "That corner of the Square, by the wall—look, Pippa. That's where Muhammed ben Kader, the astrologer, tells the people's fates by the position of Mars and Venus and the rest. All guesswork, of course, but the crowd never seems to get tired of hearing the things he tells them are in store for them."

Pippa listened with a kind of dull obedience and then turned away. I felt her hurt at what she must be thinking was her father's rejection of her. For I had little doubt that it had been Mark. Pippa was too strongly observant to make a mistake, and I was angry for her sake. Hurt and the experiences of betrayal, which were at the end of childhood, shouldn't come through Mark. He was, until I had proved myself to her as a strength she could also trust, the only anchor she had.

"Down there"—Harriet caught my arm—"is where we live. The third door on the right—the only one with a lamp over it. You'll have to come and see it, though it's not particularly attractive except for that tree you can just see over the wall. It's a myrtle."

"Daddy *did* see me."

Harriet gave an exasperated groan.

"I'm not *blind,* Aunt Harriet," Pippa said angrily. "Daddy always used to want to see me. It's only—"

"Only what?" I asked as gently as I could.

She didn't answer me and pushed between three men standing immediately in front of us. They sprang back when they saw Pippa, and the swiftness with which they moved made me wonder if perhaps we, the infidels, must not touch their robes. We had most certainly been jostled wherever we went, but never after the crowds had seen that we were white-skinned.

Pippa, who was usually so observant, noticed nothing of the men's swift withdrawal, but that was something she would not understand. "Daddy did see me," she said in a small sad voice to no one in particular.

"Oh, God," Harriet said under her breath. "How that child does keep on!"

Conversation became a stilted dialogue between Harriet and me. Without giving any impression of sulking, Pippa remained silent.

As we climbed the long stepped street, I said, "Suppose Justin goes to Hashim's thinking we're there?"

"Then he'll have to come and look for us," Harriet said abruptly. "By the way, has Mark said anything to you about giving Justin money?"

"No."

"If he did, would you mind?"

"Why should I?"

"Well, you might think 'There's the price of an evening dress gone west.'"

"Oh, Harriet, how stupid . . ." I began to laugh, and then said soberly, "I'm so sorry if things are rather tough with you."

"Oh, *I* didn't think they were—in fact I thought we were better off than we've been for ages. Justin had a fat present from his last rich South African customers. But I saw money pass between Mark and him the other day, though I wasn't supposed to be looking. I'll make a guess that Justin immediately wrote off to Paris for some silk shirts, because I'm quite certain we're not on the bread line."

"Perhaps Justin has a few debts to pay off. And Mark is generous. I'm glad he is."

"Oh, from the side view that I saw of them, Mark looked anything but pleased as he handed the money over. But I didn't interfere— I'm afraid I never do where money's concerned."

Pippa was walking just a step ahead, Harriet's toes almost touching her heels. I knew she had been listening to us talking, and she suddenly whipped around and almost overbalanced on the edge of a step. I steadied her.

"*I* saw Daddy give Uncle Justin money, too. It was late last night but I couldn't sleep and I looked out to watch Yussef take Durandal for a walk. I heard Uncle Justin say, 'No, I don't find it funny, either.' But Daddy wasn't laughing; he looked very cross."

Harriet said edgily, "We're standing right in the sun. Let's get to the garden."

XI

ALEXANDRA'S GARDEN was an oasis of peace. Her gardener was just leaving, carrying a basketful of overblown roses, and his eyes, as he turned to look at us, caught the sunlight and were like tiny flames.

The white chairs were set out in the shade and we sank into them, stretching our arms, letting the air circulate around us. I looked in my little purse mirror and said, "I'm getting tanned."

As if it had been hubble-bubbling on the stove waiting for us, coffee came almost immediately. I glanced up as Ahmed set the tray down, and caught his gaze, steady and seemingly merely questioning, in silence, if there was anything else I wanted. Yet, behind the patient look I sensed a faint insolence, a mockery. I looked quickly away, murmuring thanks.

Pippa had unwrapped her parcel, and the yellow slippers with their gold embroidery glimmered in the strong light. Durandal lay with his head against an oleander bush.

"The slippers are lovely," I said. "Put them on."

But Pippa chose not to hear me. She got up, ducked under my outstretched arm and ran into the house.

I didn't call her back, but I could hear the clink of the thin silver bracelets, and I guessed she was going to tell her diary all the hurt feelings at Mark's rejection which Harriet and I had refused to understand.

The sun glinted on the spray from the fountain, on the crimson lilies, on Harriet's legs as she stretched them out. I sat in the chair next to her. "It can't have been Mark."

"So what if it was?" She glanced sideways at me. "You should let sleeping dogs lie. Stir up trouble and you're in for complications that would never happen if you just stayed quiet. Even if it *was* Mark and he was having coffee with a pretty girl, so what? Of course, as soon as he knew that Pippa had seen him, he should have remained and introduced you. But perhaps he thought you—"

"I what?"

"Oh, would have made a scene about it later. After all, if he had the time to spare, he should have taken you around the *souks,* not met some girl—"

I picked up my coffee cup. "It might or it might not have been Mark. Whichever way it is, let's not talk about it. I hate keeping tabs on people."

Durandal rose, stretching himself, and I went and knelt by his side. He bent his head, rubbing against my arm, and his purr was like the distant throbbing of drums.

I was still crouched by Durandal's side when Harriet stirred. "I'd better get home. I've got to think out one or two ideas for paintings which the hotel said they will show for me. But we're meeting tonight, did you know?"

I said I didn't, and she reached out and lifted the head of a crimson rose. "We've been invited to dinner again. I'm afraid you're going to get bored at the sight of us, but Alexandra adores company. And Justin and I like good food. So, I'll be seeing you."

I went to the door with her and Yussef let her out. Then I wandered back and sat on the rim of the courtyard fountain and watched the light stab the spray. Time seemed to have become petrified by the dry blazing heat, so that I had no idea how long I sat there. The children who lived in the houses along the stepped street were at school, the dogs were quiet, and I heard only the faint sound of the water seller's bell and the distant clucking of hens from one of the flat roofs.

During a lull, when everything became quiet and the only sound was the singing of the water as it struck the green mosaic basin, I heard Pippa's voice and then Alexandra's. She must have returned while we were in the Women's Garden having coffee and gone straight into the house. Pippa's voice rose and fell in the breathless, nonstop way she had when telling a story. I wondered how Alexandra felt about being bombarded by an excited child in her own house, and I knew that I would have to keep watch over Pippa. Children, to someone like Alexandra who had none, and was not the maternal type, could be tiresome.

Their voices came from somewhere in the house, and I got up and went back into the Women's Garden. The coffee cups had been cleared away as if Ahmed had a secret spy-hole from which he watched us, and as I opened the screen door, Alexandra and Pippa came out of the house together.

"Oh, Cathy, there you are. Where's Harriet?" Alexandra asked.

"She went home. I think she had some painting to do."

Alexandra sat down in one of the long chairs. "It's horribly hot. Sit down and relax. I've got something to suggest to you. I've already told Pippa and she's thrilled, aren't you?"

She stretched her broad hands with their beautiful nails before her and looked at them. "You know that when I left you I went to the hotel and joined the Mitchells. They're charming and fairly young and I enjoy their company. I didn't tell you beforehand in case my idea wouldn't work, but I knew their two children, who are on holiday from school, had flown out to be with them. I went quite frankly to look the children over and to sound them out." She smiled at herself. "They're nice—high-spirited and friendly and they're about Pippa's age. I thought it would be a good idea if Pippa could spend her days at the hotel swimming pool. John and Clarissa would be company for her. The Mitchells are delighted with the idea and so are the children."

"Cathy, I can go, can't I?" The eager voice came from the embroidered hassock where Pippa sat hugging her knees.

"It's a wonderful idea, but do the Mitchells really mean it? I don't know them."

"Oh, it won't worry them at all. They'll go their own way. They have a maid with them and she'll keep a watchful eye on the children, though they're old enough not to need it. But she'll see, for instance, that they get their lunch."

"I'll give you money for yours," I said to Pippa.

"So I *can* go?" Pippa turned to Alexandra and put out both hands in a small characteristic gesture of gratitude that I had come to know so well. "It's wonderful. You mean I can swim *every* day?"

"Of course."

She sat and looked up at the strong face. "I'm going to love living here."

"Oh, you'll soon get bored."

"Never. Never. *Never.*" She got up and rushed into the house.

"She has gone to write that piece of excitement down in her diary," I said, laughing. "But it really is kind of people who don't even know me—"

"They will. I've asked them to dinner tonight, and anyway, Mark has met them. Don't feel awkward about it, Cathy, or you'll spoil both the Mitchell children's pleasure in having someone to break the monotony of a twosome, and your own peace of mind. I'm sure Mark will be delighted."

"All right, then, so will I. And thank you for arranging it."

She waved aside my gratitude. "Another young couple have arrived at the hotel," Alexandra said. "They're looking for land here and they joined us on the terrace. I thought I might as well get to know my neighbors across the oleander bushes as soon as possible, so I've asked them to dinner tonight, too." She lay back watching me. "How did your morning go?"

I told her that I had measured for different-sized windows in the church. "I hope they won't be too long arguing about it."

"It would be nice for me if they did. I enjoy having you. I'm afraid I'm a woman who is very easily bored." She reached back and pressed a bell on the wall and when Ahmed appeared, asked for figs. "I have a weakness for them and they are really lovely here."

They came, glowing with a purple sheen in the cloisonné dish Ahmed set on the table. He hesitated, and as Alexandra glanced at him, he said, "My daughter, madame—"

"What about her?"

"I think she is being bad. Bad, madame—"

"Yes, I understand. Willful, naughty. Well—?"

"My wife is upset and she cannot scold her. It is for me, I must go and see her and be angry with her."

"You mean now?"

He nodded. "Before she does something more foolish, madame."

"Of course, then, go. It isn't far to your house."

"I will not take long. I whip her, perhaps, and then I come back."

"You must not beat your daughter, Ahmed."

"Here, if a daughter is unmarried, madame, she must obey her father. It is the law." He stood very upright and darkly splendid, looking first at Alexandra and then at me. I had a feeling he would have liked to say more, but thought better of it.

When he had gone, Alexandra said, "Ahmed married a Turkish woman. They have two daughters, one of whom is married, and four sons. I believe the unmarried girl is quite a problem to them with their strict Mohammedan principles." She leaned forward. "Oh, well, it's their affair. Come, Cathy, try these figs."

They were sweet and succulent, crimson-purple inside and luscious as no fig I had ever tasted in England had been. We wiped our fingers on tiny green napkins and Alexandra said, "Tell me about yourself, Cathy. All I know is that you're an artist in stained glass, that you married Mark almost a year ago and that you live in Chelsea."

I told her that I had two brothers and that my parents had died in the Dolomite air disaster. She asked me if I had ever been engaged to anyone else before I married Mark.

"It never reached that stage," I said, laughing. "I met men and learned that I was perfectly happy to do without them. You see, I loved my work . . . And then, I met Mark."

Alexandra was a good listener and never once gave the impression that she thought my life spent either in a small London house or in Chris's busy workshops, dull. Durandal lay at our feet, the muscles of his body occasionally rippling as if he were dreaming of a jungle.

"You have a career. How does being Mark's wife fit in with that?"

"Perfectly."

"I wish I had been trained for some interesting career," Alexandra said, "but I'm not gifted. I was very young when I married my first husband, and when he died nine years ago, I married again. Both my husbands were more than twenty years older than I. The second one was French, hence my surname. He was amusing, and we married without any illusions about one another. After he died I sold our house in Rio de Janeiro and wandered. I shall probably buy an apartment in Paris and live part of my life there and part here in Bou Hammagan. I realize that I must have roots." She ate another fig. "And now tell me more about you. How do you spend your time when you're not working? Do you play tennis, swim, go to theaters?"

"A little of all those things. Swimming when we are on vacation; tennis, very badly, when we spend weekends with friends who have a rather battered court. And we read books and argue about them—that's fun, though Mark is much more of an intellectual than I am. And we entertain—quite simply, but that's fun, too."

"You really do love him, don't you?"

"I think I'm only completely alive when I'm with him."

Alexandra flicked over the pages of the French *Vogue* she had picked up from the table. "It must be wonderful to feel like that. I never have. I didn't marry either of my husbands because I loved them; I married for money and social position—does that shock you?" She laughed as I shook my head. "But I feel I'm exonerated because they both married me because they saw in me a good hostess. They entertained largely, and it was amusing how they both tried me out socially before they asked me to marry them. Neither of them wanted an awkward wife who didn't know how to cope with dinner-table conversation and menus."

"But you were happy with them?"

"Happy? Oh, yes, I suppose so." She brushed the question aside, leaned forward and ran her hand lightly across Durandal's back. "You know, Louise once told me that we were two of a kind—do you mind me talking about her?"

"No," I said not quite truthfully.

"Neither of us wanted children and Louise envied me because I had none." She lifted her shoulders in a slight, dismissing gesture. "But then Louise was possessive where Mark was concerned and she felt Pippa came between them. She used to pour out her resentment in her letters to me. Quite often she found excuses not to take Pippa on vacation with them—either she arranged for her to go to some youth camp or stay with relatives, her reason being that Pippa would be happier with other children—anything to get Mark to herself. Only months before she died, though, the three of them went to the Isle of Wight. That time Mark was home and insisted on a family vacation."

"Of course." I sat up. "The sand . . ."

"What sand?"

"Pippa has a bottle with various colored sands in layers. They come from Alum Bay on the island and she treasures that little phial; but she never talks about the holiday—or even any others."

At the moment of talking about her, Pippa came out into the garden and sat down on the hassock at Alexandra's feet, stretching out her hand to Durandal. "I saw Daddy this morning. He was sitting at a table with a dark lady. Cathy and Harriet said he wasn't there, but he *was*. And he didn't want to see me."

"Now, why on earth should you think that?" Alexandra demanded. "You're very intelligent, and such a thing just couldn't be true."

"It was, and I *did* see him, I mean. Nobody believes me."

I laid my hand over hers. "We've been around a good many years longer than you, darling. So just believe us this time, will you? Everyone has a double somewhere."

She looked straight into my eyes and I realized that she believed I had seen Mark too and was lying. I turned away from her, defeated, neither knowing how to reassure her or convince myself that she was wrong.

XII

THE DAY moved slowly. I had come to Bou Hammagan anxious to work on the window and I was fretting to start. In the world of stained glass, big opportunities didn't pour into artists' laps, and I couldn't bear to lose my chance.

That evening I was in the patio with Alexandra and, hearing the clack of heels on stone, looked up and saw Harriet coming toward us. There was a swinging self-confidence in her walk that was quite different from the half-defiant, "whether-you-like-it-or-not-I'm-here" attitude which she used to adopt at art school. In those days she was perfectly aware that, in spite of her undoubted artistic gift, she was not popular, either with teachers or students. Her sardonic tongue made easy enemies. This off-putting manner of hers had partially disappeared, and I wondered if marriage to Justin had changed her, or if the difference in her were even more recent. It could be because the rich and potentially influential Alexandra had come to Bou Hammagan and given her her friendship. Whatever it was, the fact remained that Harriet was different, and although her relationship with Justin was by no means perfect, there was a grudging acceptance of compromise which she would never have conceded in the old days.

She said as she came toward us, "Justin will be coming later. I left him busy writing a letter to Paramount Tours, more or less saying 'Remember me? I'm the man whom your clients find irresistible. So, what about sending more?' You have to keep on at these people who have valuable clients on their books or someone else cuts in."

As we sat talking, I realized how little went on in the small, enclosed state of Bou Hammagan; how far away was the hectic world of politics and fret and hustle. But I knew too that I could never live in such a confined place. I needed the stimulus of big cities: the challenge of competition.

The rest of Alexandra's guests arrived in relays. First the Mitchells —sleek, groomed people. Frances with a rich overlay of warmth and impulse that made me like her immediately, and Clive, her husband, with dark, cautious eyes and an aura of inherited wealth. David Sullavan came later with the Averys, the young couple who were in Bou Hammagan to choose a site for their villa. Benedict Avery was an expert in antique furniture, and I discovered that he and Marian, his wife, lived near us on the Chelsea Embankment.

Frances Mitchell was saying to Alexandra in her clear carrying voice, "Our villa is going to be fairly unglamorous. With two children racketing around, we can't very well have lush hangings and cloisonné and all those delicate and lovely things you have."

Alexandra laughed and looked down at Pippa. "Then I must be extremely fortunate. Pippa is the perfect small guest. So far she hasn't even broken a kitchen plate, have you?"

"I don't break things," Pippa said, not entirely truthfully, and lifted her head, swiftly alert to a sound beyond the arch. Then, without a word, she sprang to her feet and raced away from us.

"It's an easy guess that that's Mark," Harriet said.

He came, ducking his head under the tendrils of morning glory, and joined us, explaining to Alexandra, "I hoped to be back much earlier, but the day has been full of complications."

Pippa waited, standing first on one foot and then the other, while introductions were made. Then she said, "I saw you this morning in that place—"

"Isakila Square," Harriet said. "You should be able to remember place names."

Pippa ignored her. "And you looked right at me and then you went away. Daddy, you hid from me. Why didn't you want to see me?"

This was not the moment for a showdown, and I said quickly, "Later, Pippa . . ."

"I *saw* you." She didn't take her eyes from her father's face. "You were with a dark lady in an orange dress and—"

"And didn't know my own daughter when I looked at her? Or, as you accuse me, ran away? Shame on me!" He hugged her, and turned to Alexandra. "Am I very late, or have I got time for a bath before dinner?"

"Of course, take your bath. Food should always be eaten with a feeling of well-being."

He glanced around the group. "You'll excuse me while I get the dust off my skin?"

Pippa was poised, ready to follow him.

"No," I said, "you can talk all you want later."

To stop argument, I turned my attention to Marian Avery, who sat by my side, asking her if she had lived in Chelsea long. She answered that they had had to move from an apartment to a house with a garden because they had a huge Pyrenean mountain dog which needed a garden.

There were ten of us at dinner that night, and once, toward the end of the elaborate meal, I glanced at my watch. It was as if an outside force urged me to make that surreptitious movement, for it had been at that time on the previous night that Louise's silver box had been handed to me. Only twenty-four hours, yet in that large room lit by elaborate brass lamps, I felt a shiver run through me and, glancing up, saw Mark's eyes on me as if he guessed my thoughts.

Occasionally someone asked me for some news of England. Like Alexandra, the Mitchells had been abroad for a long time, in Portugal and Sardinia searching for a place to build a vacation home, but they had decided against both. I sensed the carefully controlled longing of the exiles for news. At the same time, they seemed happy with their final choice. Bou Hammagan was full of the sunshine they adored and, once the little airport was built, would be easily accessible from London.

The Mitchells and the Averys looked at me with interest when Alexandra explained my reason for being in North Africa. I felt that they thought stained glass was for churches, with Madonnas and haloed saints, and that they had never seen some of the lovely abstract windows in modern secular buildings.

I saw a shooting star in the west and sent my wish down the sky on its back. A wish for all things to be made clear, for good or ill— but at least clarified. Standing alone in the courtyard long after the guests had gone, I heard a clock strike one. A light went out somewhere in the house and, feeling the great weight of aloneness, I turned and went upstairs to the bedroom. Mark had not started to undress and was standing by one of the screened windows, his back to me.

I went first into Pippa's room. Her light was out and she was sleeping, her dark cloud of hair loose on the pillow and one hand hanging over the side of the bed. I laid it gently under the light blanket and then went back and began combing my hair. I had chosen to wear a sleeveless dress of cream chiffon and the lamplight gleamed on the plain gold band I wore around my neck.

I asked, "Were you in Isakila Square this morning, Mark?"

"Yes."

"So Pippa did see you."

"I have no idea. I was sitting at Hashim's drinking coffee while John was having something done to his car."

"It was eleven o'clock when we were there. You surely didn't film in the heat of the day?"

"We didn't go to Gharb Acho. When I reached the office they told me there was a spot of trouble at the wells and if we went, we'd be in the way. So the whole thing had to be postponed. Later, John and I went down to the New City and looked around for something that was interesting enough to shoot when the cameras had a spare day. But the work there isn't sufficiently advanced. We'll have to fit shots of the New City in later."

I went on combing my hair slowly, watching my reflection. "Pippa must really have seen you, then. And you didn't see us."

"Do you think I'd play hide-and-seek with my family?"

I wanted to ask: Who was the girl? But I didn't. The café had been crowded and it was possible that Mark had found one of the few vacant seats. At the moment when Pippa saw him, John could have arrived and Mark had probably just got up to join him. That was, of course, what had happened.

*   *   *

Several days later, I returned to the patio raging with impatience after having spoken to David on the telephone. Alexandra was sitting reading the English and French newspapers.

"They still haven't agreed about details of the window, and this delay is infuriating."

Alexandra laughed. "It's much too hot for strong emotions. Don't worry."

"But I do. After all, I work with Chris and he has to know how long I intend to be here and what's happening. The men in the workshop have to plan the time to set aside for the cutting and firing of the glass. I'll have to write to Chris and ask if I should come home. Probably the whole thing will fall flat. The idea of denominations sharing a church is too idealistic."

"It has been done in Central Italy," she said. "I read about it some time ago. So, suppose you just wait and see?"

"In the meantime, I'm idling."

"You sound a little like Pippa, anxious always to be doing something. But then, young people today are so full of energy and the need for action." She held her hands before her and her face was thoughtful. After a few moments' silence, she looked at me. "Suppose I ask you to design a stained-glass window for my villa?"

It was like an answer to a prayer. *At least let me have something to keep me here until a decision is made, one way or the other, about the window* . . . Alexandra sat watching me with amusement, her eyebrows curving upward like slim, russet wings.

I asked, "Are you suggesting this out of kindness, because if you are—"

"Oh, Cathy, don't be so cautious. Any kindness I possess has a selfish intent. I think it would be amusing to have something in my villa that no one else has, to my knowledge, thought of."

There was a strong reason why I should not remain in Bou Hammagan. A beautifully illuminated script had contained a devious threat. But Mark had said, "Stay. This is a wonderful step forward for you." And now there was another reason why I should not go back to England. A window for Alexandra's villa.

"If you really mean you would like me to do some designs—" I began, still a little in doubt.

"Of course I mean it."

"Then I'd love to."

"That's fine. Of course, you'll have to see the villa first. But we can talk about that later. Didn't I hear that you and Pippa were going out this morning?"

"Mark wants to show us the Kourifia Caves somewhere in the desert."

She nodded. "I've heard about them, but I haven't been to see them myself. I'm not very interested in sightseeing. But I'm glad Mark can be with you for a while."

"He has to go away tonight."

"Yes, he told me. For three days' filming in the desert. From what I hear of them, you'll find the Caves interesting. They will be a great attraction when Bou Hammagan supports a tourist trade, which it can't at the moment."

The car Mark used to take us to the Caves was one of those hired from Algiers by the film crew. It was dusty and unpolished and looked very much the worse for wear.

"It will get us there," he reassured me, seeing my obvious doubt, "and it's the best I can do—in fact, it's the car I always use, so I know it quite well. I'm not needed this morning. They're working on the tapes and may do some retakes down at the New City. My commentary is O.K., though. I refused to be needed. I told them I was entitled to some rest before we begin our three days at Bodaia tomorrow. We shall have to start work just after dawn."

"Oh, no!" Pippa, climbing into the back, nearly toppled over as she turned her dismayed face toward her father. "Three—whole—days. Oh, Daddy, and we came all this way to see you."

"You came here with Cathy because she has work to do and I have my job. Stop looking like that. It's not the end of the world and I'll be back on Thursday. Now, get in." He gave her a brisk slap on her bottom.

The car had been shut up and locked all night, as much against dust as against vandalism, so that the scent of sandalwood, although not strong, was distinct. A woman's scent, heavy and subtle and Eastern. I didn't comment on it. Any one of the crew could have had a date the night before and used the car.

Mark drove carefully through the crowds, taking side streets so narrow that even a donkey cart would not have been able to pass. But the town was small and we were soon clear of it and onto a rough road where dust whorls swept up in our wake. We passed a large shed, rather like the garage, where camels knelt to be loaded and unloaded, their skins ridged into dun-colored folds. Chickens missed us by a hair's breadth and Pippa, bouncing about, saw a bird riding on a cow's back. Palms fringed a line of sand dunes and a small camel caravan passed us.

"Here," Mark said, "a man can get a divorce by speaking certain words in the hearing of his camel."

"I hope the women can do the same," I said. "I'd hate to think it was one-sided."

We laughed and slowed down so that the dust our wheels churned up would not choke a group of women standing around a mud-built hut, holding platters of bread to be baked.

Small oases rose up out of the dusty earth: low, brick-red dwellings with their slit windows stood between the palm trees, and groups of men sat in any patch of shade they could find, bargaining over the fruit in their huge woven rope baskets. Cactus hedges sprang harshly against the cinnamon background. This was the real North Africa, far removed from the sophisticated beaches and vast white hotels along the coast.

Mark said, "This road we're taking—"

"Road?"

"Track, then. All right. But once, hundreds of years ago, it was part of the Trik es Soltane—the royal route—that led through the hills and the plains to Alexandria. What you see is all that's left of this particular part of it, but," he said over his shoulder to Pippa, "that's something for your imagination to feed on. Like the old spice-caravan route to China and the golden road to Samarkand, it breathes poetry. One of these days you shall read Flecker's poem about that."

Pippa, uninterested in poetry, remained silent. But I knew Mark's love of rhythm and words; his marvelous memory when I, beginning to quote something I had learned and of which I could remember only the first line, would hear him finish without hesitation. Poetry . . . *verse* . . .

"Dust hath closed dark Catherine's eye . . ." Mark hadn't said he recognized that, but then it could have been original. To us, though, it was the writer of the illuminated script, not the poet, who was important.

"Are we now in the desert?"

"The outskirts. But we're only going a little farther—just as far as the Caves."

Almost immediately I saw them—ridge upon ridge rising out of the arid earth with only an occasional tree—thorn or locust, Mark explained—to break the hot sandstone color of the baked, primeval rocks.

We were alone there, not a man nor a camel was to be seen. Yet as I got out of the car and felt a flame of heat envelop me, I followed the long track going east, and my imagination rose at the thought of the centuries of camel caravans laden with incense and cowhides, peaches and silks, taking this arid road to the sea and Damascus.

Pippa cried, "Oh, look," and reached for the camera I had bought her for her birthday.

Something was moving in the shadow of a nearby rock. A camel rested there, and a man leaned out of the shelter of the rock to watch us.

Pippa lifted her camera.

"Oh, no, you don't." Mark put out his hand and pushed the camera away. "To the Hammagarbs that thing is the evil eye. Camels are very important and you don't cast spells on them."

"I only wanted to take a picture. I could even promise to *give* him one."

"For which he wouldn't thank you. So put that back in the car. There's nothing here for you to photograph, only rocks and sandstone and flat country."

Pippa frowned. "Why don't they ride horses? They look much kinder than camels."

"Because a camel's back is just the right height to prevent a rider from getting scorched by reflected heat waves," Mark said.

"Oh," Pippa said vaguely, not understanding the subtleties of reflected heat.

Mounds of rock rose in shapes like monsters petrified by the arid climate. It was a miniature massif spread across the east, a formidable boundary keeping out marauders.

"The Caves are around the corner," Mark said. "I stopped the car here because this is the finest view of the rock ridge."

It was as if an army had wiped out a small town and left it derelict. Ten thousand years or a million years were nothing in this place. It was timeless.

Pippa ran in front of us, diving in and out of the piled boulders, clambering, sliding, laughing and keeping up a running commentary as her sharp eyes found things that interested her. A group of cactus, a golden rock shaped by age to resemble a cat's face, a blue stone which sand had decorated into a pattern like a star sapphire.

It was a world of light and wide horizons. There was an intense sense of a release from the confines of the cities I was most accustomed to, and as I looked about me, I felt I could understand a little of what the men felt who climbed mountains or crossed the wonderful and terrible places. I was on the fringe of comprehending "aloneness" as contrasted with "loneliness."

Two of the caves had great black openings, but across one of them were two wooden planks in the form of a cross.

Mark said, in surprise, "It must have been blocked up because of a bad rock fall. The authorities should shore the place up inside so that visitors can go in and see them and be safe. But Bou Hammagan hasn't yet woken up to the importance of what is on their doorstep, and unless something is done soon, the historic value of these drawings will probably be lost forever." He put an arm around Pippa and we entered the second cave. "Let's see what the prehistoric men painted in here, shall we?"

It was cold inside, and I had the same sensation as that when I had visited the Cheddar Gorge in England, at once a dislike and a fascination. Mark turned his flashlight around until he found the faint red and blue lines of drawings.

"Stone-Age dancers, I should imagine." He traced them with his finger. "Look, their arms are stretched out touching their neighbors, and they are stamping their feet. Here's an animal—a rhino, I'd say. And a bird—it could be an eagle's wings, or a vulture's beak or something probably now extinct. These were already here thousands of years before Christ. At that time," he said to Pippa, "much of the Sahara was green and fertile."

A little bored by the paintings, she was trying to squeeze through a place where the two walls narrowed. Mark called her back sharply. "This rock is crumbling." He broke a handful off and sprinkled it on the ground. "It won't endure like the Egyptian marvels. Pippa, I told you not to go through there."

She returned reluctantly. "I want to see where it goes."

"You'll have to learn not to let your curiosity run riot, or you could land yourself in trouble." He caught her affectionately by the back of her neck and walked her to the cave entrance.

As we left the shadows, the heat hit us. We wandered along the line of the massif and climbed boulders to reach farther into the depth of cliffs, and found that there were no more cave openings. "I suppose time has sealed the rest," Mark said. "There must have been a great many, for records show that, after the cave dwellers, there were villages and farms here."

The upthrust of rock stretched so far inward that it was impossible to explore to the end. When we returned to the car, Mark paused and pointed to the horizon.

"Do you see that line of mountains? That's Djebel Thamadi. There are beautiful springs up there and almond trees, pomegranates, sweet marjoram and roses everywhere. I'll take you there before you leave, but it will mean a whole day's journey."

"If it's so beautiful, I suppose they'll develop it like Marrakech."

"It's a bit tricky because it's on the fringe of an earthquake area. There is talk about developing it and using some architect's idea of building on soft earth as a precaution against earth tremors, instead of sinking the foundations into rock. You'd better ask David to explain it all, I can't."

I stood looking about me and decided that this place of titanic rock formation could be the mood for Alexandra's window since she seemed to love rich color. But, because of the power of the sun in Bou Hammagan, I hoped the church authorities would want cool colors—green and violet and blue—for their window.

I did not see Mark for the next three days. The television crew was in the desert following the engineers' discovery of water at Bodaia.

On the morning following our visit to Kourifia, I went to see Alexandra's villa in the New City. It was as yet little more than a shell with walls that were to be covered with mosaics and a vaulted ceiling in the hall. David was not her architect, and I suggested that she introduce me to the man who was. "I need to discuss the window with him."

"But I know exactly what I want," she protested and then laughed. "That sounds arrogant, I suppose. But my architect is an obstinate man who tries to browbeat me. And hates me because he fails. I want my window *there*." She pointed.

It was, fortunately, a north wall and the best place she could choose. She left me to measure and study the gap, which was one of three left by the builders for window space. When I had finished, I turned and found her watching me with amusement.

"You look so small and fragile to be doing such masculine work," she said.

"The heavy part is done in the workshops, but believe it or not, I've served my apprenticeship there, too."

"Come, let me show you upstairs."

The inside staircase had not yet been built, and the only way to the upper floor was by a flight of outside steps.

"Take care." She led the way. "They are temporary and a bit shaky. The final steps will be of stone, and I plan to have mosaic treads."

An arched terrace ran around the house, and from one side of it we stood looking out at the empty country. I saw a thin gray line in the far distance.

"The sea," Alexandra said. "It's a very long way away. I'm afraid Bou Hammagan doesn't have a Mediterranean coast."

"But the view is lovely."

She pointed to groups of trees clinging together as if to give each other shade from the raging sun. "Palm, orange, fig and apricot. But come along, let's leave it now. The Mitchells have asked us for drinks at the hotel."

We climbed down and got back into her car, a small, elegant one of French make which Alexandra drove with a kind of indolent ease.

The problem of keeping Pippa amused had been solved, and if I had had any doubts, the laughter and splashing from the children that afternoon at the pool dispelled them.

The Mitchells' pretty maid, Alice, usually came to fetch Pippa and, if she could not, Ahmed took Pippa to the hotel. This left me free all day long to work.

Alexandra had offered me a small room as a studio. One side of it opened onto the columned terrace, heavily shaded with bougainvillaea climbing in purple glory over the ancient stone. The room had been empty, but Alexandra furnished it with tables and chairs. I had pleaded for something very simple and cheap on which to work, terrified of spoiling one of the inlaid tables by scratching it with my drawing board or marking it with paint. She had laughed, and Ahmed had produced from somewhere plain, unpolished tables and two simple, upright chairs.

Harriet told me where I could get paints. "It's a *souk* at the far end of Isakila Square, just where I showed you we turn the corner to our house."

I had brought my brushes with me, and the paints could wait until I had worked on the drawings. I completed one idea using the Caves, and I scrapped some garden designs I thought I might have used for Alexandra's window. I could see that the result would be a muddled conglomeration of color. The window must be like a poem of controlled jeweled light. Since it was to be placed in the smaller space of the hall of a house instead of in a church, the effect of its nearness on those of Alexandra's guests who stopped to look at it would have to be carefully considered.

Alexandra had said, "I want a sunburst of color."

I tempered her enthusiasm. "But you must have it without dazzle, and that's going to be difficult here in Africa. It's lucky that you want it set in the north wall, but we must be careful how we use color."

"I love blue . . ."

"That's one of the most difficult colors of all. It can make a window look too heavy if too much is used."

She suddenly dismissed the whole argument. "I leave it entirely to you, Cathy."

Although she liked the idea of having a stained-glass window in her house, she was obviously not the least bit interested in detail. I had a feeling that the whole suggestion had been an impulse. I decided, therefore, to begin planning her window with my own quiet proviso that I would watch for any sign that she might be becoming bored with us. She was rich enough to indulge her whims, but I had no intention of being the guest of a reluctant hostess.

Although the window might be a secondary consideration, a kind of poor relation compared to the interest she took in her house and the planning of her garden in the New City, her innate good manners made her show an interest in what I was doing for her. She studied the designs I drew, commented on and compared them, and paid me compliments.

The one she liked best was of the titan rocks of Kourifia against which stood a tall, unidentifiable woman with a cheetah. I had described the coloring I had in mind . . . Sapphire horizon; the fanged teeth of the rocks more golden than the originals, and a woman in a green gown . . . Alexandra, with Durandal at her feet.

XIII

I HAD no idea what woke me—a brush of air, the scrape of a piece of furniture on a tiled floor, footsteps. Whatever it was struck across my light sleep and I was suddenly awake. I started up in bed and called out the name most real in my mind. "Mark?"

It could have been, for it was the third night that he had been away. As no one answered me, I could have been dreaming and forgotten the dream. But as I switched on the light and reached for my robe, I had a sensation that someone was near. I swung my legs over the side of the bed and sat quietly listening. Then I thought that something moved, like the noiseless shadow of a bird in flight, across the screened window. But it was so swift that I doubted that it was anything but a trick played on my sleep-filled eyes. I had a sensation that somewhere beyond the room, someone was listening. But that, too, could be imagination.

I had been staring at the tall window leading to the terrace, and I saw that the screen, although pulled closed, was unlatched. It could have been my own carelessness, since there had been no wind to warn me it might blow open.

Alexandra had said once, "The house is very safe. Nobody in Bou Hammagan would dream of breaking in—any lawlessness they have they use among themselves. Besides, no one could get through the door with Yussef sleeping just by it."

But I had never before left the screen of the terrace unlatched for any wandering moth or insect to drift in the gap, and I didn't believe I had inadvertently done it that night.

The tile floor was cold to my feet as I padded across to Pippa's little room. She was fast asleep, and she made no movement as I looked in. Reassured, I closed the door and went onto the terrace. In the silence I heard Durandal growl, a rumbling and lonely sound like something roused in its lair and alert to hidden danger. So I had not been mistaken. Durandal, too, had been disturbed.

I looked down into the courtyard and saw nothing move. The fountain had been switched off and the moon was low behind the far-off hills, so that only a glimmer of its light struck the tips of the plumed palms.

A flying insect brushed across my face, and I darted back into the room, pulling the screen behind me. Then I opened the velvet bag where I kept my few pieces of jewelry, each in its separate compartment, rings, brooch, necklace. Nothing was missing.

But I didn't get straight back into bed. I sat on the edge again, hugging my robe around me. It was possible that the noise which had aroused the cheetah and me had come from beyond the walls of the courtyard and had nothing to do with my unlatched window. I tilted back onto the bed and lay staring at the ceiling, listening to the silence. My eyes grew heavy and I closed them and felt myself drifting back to sleep. But in my unnatural position, spread across the bed, I would probably wake with stiff limbs, and so I got up. Just for my nerves' sake, before I climbed into my huge bed, I would have one more look outside. I unlatched the screen and stepped onto the terrace.

Someone had been near my window in the last few minutes while I had drowsed—the scent of Egyptian tobacco was unmistakable. Justin and Harriet smoked them, and also Mark lit one very occasionally.

I followed the scent of the smoke and found a half-burned-out cigarette lying at the top of the outside flight of steps that led down to the courtyard. So someone had crept across the terrace between the time when I had first gone out to look and this second time when chance had taken me back for a last check.

I could go down and rouse Yussef in his hut. But reason told me that I had disturbed whoever had been on the terrace and he, or she, had tossed the cigarette away in a hurried flight. Whoever it was would be gone by now, and the reason Yussef had not been aroused could be that there was another door in the high wall that surrounded the house. Perhaps one led directly into the inner garden and was at one time used by the women of the harem to come and go without being seen by the men visitors to the house.

I walked the floor of my room, looked at my bedside clock at least three times and, as I passed, peered through the screen. I saw nothing but the darkness of the African night.

I even crept downstairs and went into the various rooms, identifying Alexandra's treasures, finding them still in their niches and on the inlaid tables. Her jewels I knew were in a safe behind her bed. So, nothing seemed to be missing from the house and there was no reason to disturb anyone. They would very likely reassure me that the sound which had disturbed me had come from the street, and would send me back to bed embarrassed that I had roused them from sleep. But for the remainder of the night I was restless and slept fitfully and dreamed impossible dreams of breathless escapes from unknown terrors.

When I opened my eyes to morning, Pippa was sitting on the side of my bed watching me. "You're very late," she said with an adult severity, "and I'm hungry."

"Then go and get your breakfast. I won't be long."

She got up slowly and her eyes, lingering speculatively on me, had lost their usual dancing brightness.

I reached out my hand to her. "Are you all right?"

"Yes, thank you."

"Would you like us to go into the town and do some shopping this morning? It would be a change for you and you could meet Clarissa and John later."

She shook her head. "I'd like to go to the pool as I always do," she said in a small, polite voice. "Can I go now?"

"Darling, of course you can. Since when have you had to ask?"

She didn't answer, and as soon as she had left me I went and ran my bath. I felt as if I hadn't slept at all. My eyes and my head were heavy and I seemed to have acquired a deep depression during sleep.

Except for our morning with Mark at the Kourifia Caves, I had seen little of Pippa, for after her days at the hotel swimming pool, her evenings, until bedtime, were passed seated on her favorite hassock. Her attention was always divided between Alexandra, whose clothes seemed to fascinate her, and the cheetah.

Alexandra always breakfasted on her private secluded terrace, and when I went downstairs Pippa had already eaten and disappeared. The croissants set for me on the table in the patio had been made by Lisette and were always delicious; the honey came from Mount Hymmett in Greece; the butter was cool and crisp in its covered ice container; the coffee was French and fragrant. But I had no appetite.

I ate a little for good manners' sake and drank two cups of coffee. Then I got up and looked for Alexandra. She was in the courtyard with Durandal by her side.

"He was growling last night," I said. "Something disturbed him."

"He was probably dreaming of a fight."

"I don't think so because I was disturbed, too. I thought someone was on the terrace, but when I went out to see, there was no one there."

"Nobody would ever break in here, Cathy. Yussef sleeps lightly."

"But someone had been around. When I went onto the terrace a second time, I found a half-smoked cigarette on the outer staircase."

She said, frowning, "Why didn't you call one of us? Yussef? Me? Just for your own peace of mind?"

"I nearly did. Then I realized that I had let too much time pass and if anyone had been here, he must have escaped by the way he came and it would be too late to find him. Justin once told me that this town is the easiest in the world in which to hide because it's full of narrow alleys. I went downstairs and looked around and nothing was missing."

She laughed. "Oh, I have a wonderful feeling of security in this house. But I'm sorry that you were disturbed. I think I know what must have happened. Yussef always does a round of the house and garden about midnight."

"But it was long after that."

"He could have been late. He's usually very quiet, though. We'll go and ask him if he was smoking when he went around last night. He smokes quite a lot."

"Expensive Egyptian cigarettes?"

She laughed. "There are all qualities and I pay him well. Come, let's go and find him."

Yussef was sitting outside his stone hut, and he sprang up as we approached, giving us his usual grin of pleasure. I wondered if he really enjoyed his job and decided that he must, since Paradise, for such as he, would be sitting in a garden.

Alexandra spoke to him in a mixture of English and Hammagarb, translating for me. "Yes, Yussef was around about midnight and he was smoking. He says he sat for a while with Durandal because he was so restless."

But would a cigarette tossed down at midnight still be burning at one o'clock? Perhaps in this dry air it would last that long. I didn't know. But since Alexandra seemed satisfied, I put the small incident out of my mind.

I wandered by Alexandra's side as she went on an inspection of her garden. The roses, the oleander bushes and the beds of marigolds came under her sharp scrutiny. "When everything is ready, I shall design my own garden in the New City. I know what I want, and Ibrahim, my gardener, has promised to remain with me. There will be much more work to be done there."

Pippa came running toward us, dropping her swimsuit and towel onto one of the wrought-iron chairs drawn up in the shade.

Alexandra said to her, "I'm going to do some shopping in the *souks*. Would you like to come? Or, no, it's much better for you to be with your friends having fun at the pool."

Pippa's wide mouth quivered a little as if she were trying to get words out. Then they came. "B-but I'd *love* to come with you."

"It's very hot down there," Alexandra warned. "You'd be much cooler at the hotel."

The light went out of Pippa's face. "You d-didn't really want me, did you, Alexandra? You only s-said—"

"You silly child, as if I would ask you to come if I didn't want you to. Of course I do, but I felt—"

"Then I will . . . I will . . ."

She started to run to the gate, but Alexandra called her back. "You'd better take your swimsuit because I shall dump you at the hotel at twelve o'clock. I never walk in the heat of the day. And also you'd better just go and telephone Mrs. Mitchell and explain that you'll be late. Ahmed will get the number for you."

We watched her go, and Alexandra said, laughing, "What a child she is in some ways and yet how intelligent in others. I hope you don't mind her coming with me, but I'd love to buy her a small present."

"Please don't spoil her."

"My dear Cathy, I wouldn't dream of it. But you see, I knew Louise, and that child had so little spoiling. She has a lot to be made up to her."

I had my own childish impulse to protest that if anyone should spoil Pippa—and I didn't want too much of that for her—it should be Mark and me.

I also had my private protest that Pippa hadn't wanted to come to the *souks* with me when I had suggested it. I tried to be adult about it. Pippa had a right to her preferences, and Alexandra was a glamorous newcomer in her life.

When Alexandra and Pippa had gone, I went onto the roof. But the blaze and heat of the sun could not dispel the small cloud of depression that settled on me. Africa was changing us—changing Mark and Pippa and me, and I knew that the return to what we had been to one another was something completely out of my hands.

I was still leaning on the hot stone when Ahmed called me. I was wanted on the telephone.

Harriet's sharp, clipped voice said, "Oh, Cathy, I'm going to the Kourifia Caves late this afternoon. The government authorities here want to publicize any special features of Bou Hammagan, and so the hotel has agreed to hang two of my pictures showing the Caves. They are going to be important when the residents and the tourists arrive. I thought I would do one at dawn, if I can get there at that time. The other will be a sunset out there—I've only seen it once, but it was really spectacular. It's a bit of a bore driving all the way by myself and I wondered if, perhaps, you'd like to come with me."

"I'd love it. I want to see them again, too. But I haven't bought any watercolors yet. I'll have to get them this morning."

"Meet me at the bottom of the steps and we'll go and buy paints, and then you can come and see our house. It's time you did, but don't expect much. It's what people call picturesque when they mean poky and bloody uncomfortable."

Harriet's home was as she described it. A small stone house in a street of similar houses, leading out of Isakila Square. The window space was diminutive, so that not too much sun filtered in; the rooms were untidy and cluttered; the courtyard had tubs of tired-looking geraniums and one lovely myrtle tree under which we sat drinking coffee.

I told Harriet that Alexandra had taken Pippa shopping with her, and then, because I had to say it to someone, I added, "She wants to buy Pippa a present. I don't know what, but I do hope she's not going to load her with gifts. She's very generous, but Pippa is at an age to adore indulgence."

"Oh, don't worry about that. You're just new brooms to Alexandra, that is, you and Pippa are, and she's the one who's indulging herself. It's different with Mark, of course. They're old friends. But don't let that worry you, either. There's never been any hint of romance between them."

"No, I didn't imagine there had been."

"That's all right, then. But often a woman meeting an old friend of her husband's, and one as glamorous as Alexandra, might have qualms. As I say, you don't need to. Alexandra isn't attracted to him, or in fact to anyone. She's completely self-absorbed. And she's certainly not Mark's type."

I asked, laughing, "And what is Mark's type?"

"Oh, not strong, dominating women."

It was the way Harriet said it rather than what she said that made me wonder if she really liked Alexandra, or found it expedient in such a place as Bou Hammagan to accept her friendship.

Harriet and I met at six o'clock that night and drove out of the town. I had had many experiences of her driving, which was fast and careless, but on the road to Kourifia there was very little margin for error. The legs of children, the necks of hens, the waving tails of dogs only escaped our wheels by inches as the young and the animals and the birds cavorted and clucked across the streets.

The road along which Mark had driven to the Caves was wider and more comfortable than the one Harriet was now taking.

As if aware of what I must be thinking, she said, "I suppose Mark took you by the more direct route, but this is the most interesting way. Look, over there to your right. That long, low building with the tiers of white arches is Sheikh Sabhir's house. He's what they call a benevolent dictator."

She was forced to stop as she spoke because a string of laden mules stood solid and refused to move until the driver had adjusted a pack that had slipped on the leading animal's back.

But Harriet couldn't wait. "We *must* catch the sunset," she said and snapped an unrepeatable curse under her breath at the grinning mule driver. Her impatient hands swung the wheel sharply, and the car bounced across the rocky side of the track, so that I shot out of my seat and nearly hit the roof.

"If this car were a living thing," I said, "you'd be arrested for cruelty."

She laughed. "It's taken worse and survived. Don't worry. I'll get you there; Mark won't have to send out a search party. Oh, and speaking of Mark, I saw him earlier. I had to go and collect some food for our supper before I fetched you, and he was in a Land Rover following a truck and another car. It was quite a cavalcade in a place that seldom sees even one mechanical thing. We met in a tunnel of a street in the Zizefal quarter. We shouted at one another and I yelled 'Cathy . . . Kourifia Caves' at him as they drove past. He nodded as if he understood, so when he gets home he'll know you're with me."

Because of our different cross-country route, Harriet and I came to the Caves from another angle. The sun had not yet begun to set.

"At least we've got here in time," Harriet said. "And we wouldn't have if we had kept to the main road out of the town. That will be choked with camels and donkeys making for the rest places. Bou Hammagan has its evening traffic problem, but instead of gasoline fumes, read camel."

I recognized on the right the saber-pointed tips of the caves.

"Let's get our stuff out of the car and set up," Harriet said. "I even plan my colors in advance as far as I can so that I shall be ready for the moment when the sun goes down."

Harriet had lent me a spare easel and I had brought my own brushes and paper from London. We climbed out of the car, and, while Harriet knew just the place from which she wanted to work, I needed to get a feeling of the general atmosphere. I had time to kill, and so I said I would wander a bit and wait for the sunset.

"You have about a quarter of an hour, so don't go too far. Those rocks cut deeply into the desert for almost half a mile, and even if you walk around them you could get lost. Keep close to the edge."

"I've quite a strong sense of self-preservation."

Harriet was already at her easel, legs sprawled on either side of its struts, lean, tanned hands squeezing out colors, mixing. She had an absorbed expression and I felt that she had already forgotten me. My easel and rough design were ready for me to rush to work as soon as the sunset touched the distant mountains.

I wandered away toward the curious upflung massif and found a dusty cactus and a few sparse trees growing out of crevices. The rock world of Kourifia was silent, eerie and full of suffocating light. More than once I paused to look across at the distant mountains. Mark had said Djebel Thamadi was cool and beautiful, and I enjoyed my own fantasy of it as a kind of Shangri-la. One day we would go there, he had said.

I tried to keep Harriet's car always in sight, but I also wanted to find the cave where Mark and I had seen the primitive paintings. I climbed higher and saw the tip of a jutting wooden plank and beyond it, around a bend, the rapt figure of Harriet at her easel. I had managed, somehow, to walk three quarters of the way around a circle.

Below me, where the cliffs ended, were wind-swept ripples of sand dotted with stalks of stiff grass and spiky shrubs which, in turn, gave way to a faint pink line of earth.

There was a village not far away with palms and clay huts. Women were kneeling in front of what was possibly a spring. It seemed miraculous that water could force its way through that parched earth.

Then, clambering and jumping from rock to rock, I reached the Caves.

XIV

THE PLANKS were neatly crisscrossed over one cave, and the opening of the other was huge and curiously welcoming, in spite of its yawning blackness, because it promised coolness and relief from the glare.

When we had entered with Mark, he had had a flashlight. I hadn't thought to bring one, but I hoped the light outside would penetrate sufficiently. I was right. The interior was lit up by the low sun for a considerable way.

Inside the cave I found that the ground was a mass of rock and dust piles which I must have been too absorbed to notice on the first occasion. This time I kept stumbling over hazards, and when the cave turned sharply to the right, the vivid daylight seemed to fade into the twilight. I realized then that I had found no paintings. Instead, I could just see rough shallow carvings on the walls, and I traced some with my fingers. Elephant and rhinoceros must once have stormed over Kourifia. It did not seem to me that I had come any farther into the cave than when Mark brought me, and yet we had found no carvings. I looked behind me. Nor did I remember the great corner of rock which was obscuring the intensity of the desert light. In front of me were barely discernible jags of rock framing the depths of the cave, and, annoyed with myself for not having asked Harriet if she had a flashlight I could borrow, I fell headlong over a rock on the uneven floor of the cave. I picked myself up and, looking about me, decided that somehow Mark and I must have missed the carvings because we were too intent on searching for the faded wall paintings.

"Cathy? Cathy? Are you in there?" Harriet's voice came loudly and clearly and, although I couldn't see her, I knew she must have come to look for me because I had wasted too much time.

"I'm here . . ."

"Cathy." Her voice came more urgently. "Answer me if you hear me. I can't find you anywhere."

"I—am—here," I shouted.

"Then come out. It will soon be sunset." Her voice echoed around the cave and, when it died down, there was a faint rumble and a shower of dust.

I coughed and put my hand to my face. Above me came a noise like taffeta rustling and pieces of soft rock began to fall.

"Cathy?"

I gave a swift glance upward. In the twilight of the cave I could see that the high vault above me seemed to be moving as if infested with startled bats. But the things that fell were rocks, and as I dived to avoid them, dust came like a cloud, so that for a moment or two I was blinded by it.

"For heaven's sake—come out." Harriet raised her voice. "There are probably masses of tunnels and—you could—get—lost." She spoke with pauses between the words, so that there was time for any echo to die away, and her words reached me clearly. Immediately after she had spoken there was a sound like distant thunder and, looking upward again, I went headlong into a rock.

I picked myself up, my knees and shins grazed, and the sound of thunder came again. It was directly above me, hollow and grating, and with it came another rain of small pieces of stone and dust that made me duck my head and momentarily close my eyes. I thought I could hear Harriet's frantic voice, but I couldn't answer her, for I had covered my head with my arms against an onslaught of small rocks. My throat, my nose, my eyes were full of the terrible dry, ancient dust. I tried to run but the movement I made seemed to increase the vibrations of the cave roof. In my dazed state I realized that my danger lay in any sound. I must move cautiously. I crept along, keeping close to the wall, feeling it with my elbow. Whatever happened I would shield my head from rock blows; my hands and my arms and my shoulders must bear the brunt.

"Cathy . . ."

Oh, God, you fool, don't shout at me. You're only making things worse . . .

Inching my way along the cave wall, I saw that the ceiling was still vibrating. I wondered with a kind of panicked irrelevance what strange menace existed in that terrible million-year-old dust—germs, viruses, bacteria—I thought of them all. And then, my mind distracted, I forgot to keep my elbow against the rock face and went slap into a jutting piece that broke and scattered about me, gushing dust into my mouth as I gave an involuntary cry.

Gasping for breath, I dropped to my knees. I could no longer see the entrance to the cave. *Dust hath closed dark Catherine's eye . . .*

What had seemed a matter of two or three hundred yards when I had entered the cave was now like a world, a universe away from safety. The terror-stricken thought came to me that, in my bewilderment and semiblindness, I was going the wrong way.

"Harriet . . . Help me, Harriet . . ." The words were scarcely more than whispered thoughts. She would never hear me through that persistent rumbling over my head, and I dared not shout even if my rasped throat could have managed the sound.

A great slab of rock fell with a dull thud right in my path. I edged around it somehow, tearing at the earth that seemed now to be blocking every inch of my way. In my effort to crawl forward, I had to leave my head unprotected, and every moment I dreaded an attack from that terrible, crumbling rock roof that could hit me into unconsciousness.

"Cathy . . ."

Suddenly something darker than the cave was in front of me; someone with weaving arms that caught me and pulled forward, dragging me half to my feet, so that, more than three quarters blinded, my toes struck more hazards of fallen rock.

"For God's sake . . ."

For God's sake, what? I heard Harriet choke over the last word

121

and knew she was as incapable as I of speaking. I thanked heaven that dust had silenced her, for I felt that even a whisper held danger for us both. It seemed to me in my moment of terrified light-headedness that the whole rock formation was strung on threads as fine as cobwebs, trembling over my head.

As Harriet pulled at my arms, the sounds behind us seemed to corroborate my own wild imagining that little more than spun silk upheld the cave roof. There was a sudden curious beating sound, like millions of wings. Gasping, I paused, looking back. Harriet gave a hoarse shriek and heaved me violently over the tortured ground. In that frantic moment, ignoring the pain her efforts were obviously causing me, she saved my life. For, almost simultaneously with that heave to safety, the cave disintegrated.

"Damn this bloody place!" A fit of coughing followed Harriet's words.

But we were safe; we were outside. We lay together exhausted and helpless at the edge of the great left-hand flap of cave which had hidden the northwest from us. And now, free of the rock shadow, our sore and burning eyes blinked at the last moment of sunset, bronze and vermilion. I forced my eyes to stay open, and it was as if the sky were painted with the fiery pain that racked my throat and my bruised body. Dust, pouring out of the cave, caught the glow and became motes of copper flame. The vague thought that I was too late to catch the sunset crossed my mind and fled. I was alive.

Even as my dust-rimmed eyes watched, the colors faded, and I began coughing and could not stop. Harriet crouched beside me, her breath rasping as she said, "Stay still. I'm . . . going . . . to the car . . . There's water . . . and some orange drink in there."

I couldn't answer but I watched her, in the speeding darkness, stagger toward the invisible Fiat. If Harriet hadn't come along when she had, I could not have lived much longer and would have choked to death before I could have been rescued. And after that, the falling roof would have buried me.

She saved my life. Harriet, hard, cynical, bitter, was suddenly a new person to me. How could I repay so much? But even to think of repayment was an insult to that unselfish achievement. For Harriet herself could have been killed in trying to rescue me.

I lay on my stomach with my eyes closed until I heard the crunch of her sandals.

"Here," she said, "take these," and handed me some tissues and a cup of water. "Bathe your eyes and wash your mouth out."

"I'm . . . all right . . ."

"Don't be so bloody silly."

I knew that she swore at me to rouse me from my exhaustion. I took the cup and the tissues and did what she told me, rinsing my mouth out with water and then swallowing some fresh orange juice from a bottle she had brought. I wondered if I would ever again enjoy the taste of it.

Harriet had brought a second cup and was doing the same, and as we gargled and rinsed, I started to laugh in sheer relief. But the effort was too much, and Harriet thumped me on the back as I choked.

At last I took one glorious long relieving breath and, in the slanting edge of the flashlight's glow, saw that she looked frightened. "I'm fine now. Don't worry," I said. But as I started to walk toward the car, I swayed.

"Hey!" She took my arm. "I think we ought to get back as quickly as we can. You sit in the car while I collect our painting things."

"I can help."

"Don't try to be so noble. You'll come to the car and wait for me there."

Dumb obedience was not my way, but fright had mesmerized me into inactivity, and from the car I watched her dark figure and the flashlight beam move away. The desert was now almost black with just the stars for distant relief. The Caves were out of sight, around the great jutting corner.

I had no idea what impelled me, but while Harriet was collecting our painting paraphernalia, I got out of the car and went to the corner and could just see the road Mark and I had taken. I walked to it and turned and looked back at the Caves. Then I knew. The boarded-up cave which had on our first visit been on my left, *was now on the right*. I had approached them from a different direction and, because of that, had not realized what was now so alarmingly evident. At some time between my visit with Mark and this evening, the planks had been changed and the dangerous cave opened up.

The jerking light of Harriet's flashlight beamed on me. "I asked you to stay in the car."

"Look," I said.

"Thanks, I've seen enough of this place."

"When I came with Mark, the boarded-up cave was on the left. Now, do you see? It's on the right. Harriet, *I went into the one that was dangerous.*"

123

"But you couldn't have. I—can't—quite—remember." Her voice slowed down, and then she cried, "I came out here about two weeks ago to paint and—oh, dear heaven, you're right!—it was that left one that had the boards across it. The utter, perfidious idiots!"

"Who?" I whispered.

"Well—whoever did this," she snapped. "Don't you see what happened? Because *I* do. The boards were badly propped up and they must have fallen down. Someone passed by and set them up again, but against the wrong cave. It's exactly the sort of thing that could happen out here."

I said slowly, "Or perhaps someone from that village I saw over in the distance—or from Bou Hammagan—deliberately moved the planks and then used some magic to try to will his enemy to go into the wrong cave. Only, whoever his enemy was, he didn't go near the caves. I did." An involuntary shudder tore through me. I could be the enemy. *Someone could have taken a chance that I might enter the wrong cave* . . .

Harriet patted my hand. "Calm down, dear. This is North Africa, not witch country."

I didn't believe in witchcraft either. Yet I sat in the car stunned by suspicion, waiting while Harriet collected the rest of our painting materials and settled herself behind the wheel of the car.

"Who knew we were coming here?"

She said easily, "Alexandra and you and I. And Justin, of course. Oh, and Mark, if he heard what I shouted at him as we passed in the street. But get a grip on yourself. None of us would play dangerous tricks."

She turned the car onto the track, sinking a back tire in a hollow and then lifting us as the ground rose into a hillock. When we had settled again, she said, "Of course, if we hadn't arrived back soon after dark, they would have sent a search party for us."

But by then it would have been too late . . .

We sat in silence. My tongue was dry and when I ran it around my teeth, I felt grains of dust still clinging inside my mouth. The first thing I would do when I returned was to have a bath and gargle until I had washed away the sand.

What I would not be able to wash away was a dreadful suspicion. Someone could have guessed that, coming to Kourifia, I would be attracted again by the Caves. Perhaps someone took a chance on my not being sufficiently observant on that first casual visit to know which one had been boarded up. Had we approached them from the same direction as last time, I might have known. But even then, the semicircle of rocks was like a giant's ring, and I might have trusted the position of the planks more than my memory.

Harriet turned her head and shot a quick look at me. "You know, when we get back, I think we both ought to see a doctor."

"For a mouthful of dust?"

She ignored my scorn. "You have no idea, nor have I, what peculiar things that eons-old sand was harboring. Or it might have a curse on it like that in the tomb of Tutankhamen." She spoke with a pretense of lightness. "Of course we'll have to report it to the police."

" 'Dust hath closed dark Catherine's eye.' "

The wheel jerked as Harriet turned and stared at me. "For heaven's sake, don't go linking that bloody verse with what's happened. It's just coincidence."

"I suppose so."

"Things happen—accidents that are the result of someone's sheer carelessness. You're a stranger here. You don't realize how casual people are—they would see two fallen planks and just put them up again anywhere. And nobody would think of reporting it. But don't worry. *I* will. What you must do is to see Abdullah Melilla—he's Alexandra's doctor and ours. We like him."

"I don't need a doctor. I'm a bit bruised and my knees are grazed but I'm not cut at all. The only thing that's really wrong with me is that I think I have sniffed up so much dust that I've probably lost my sense of smell." My voice had a heady lightness because the relief at my escape had trebled in retrospect.

When we arrived back at the house, I stood quite still in the center of the courtyard. "Harriet, I never thought I'd be able to smell roses again. But I can . . . I can . . . It's wonderful."

Alexandra paced the floor slowly, head down, seeming to study the pattern of every tile before she stepped on it.

We were in the great hall, and we had just told her what had happened at Kourifia. The lamps shone onto the squared pillars, turning them peony-pink.

"It's typical," she said. "Sometimes I think they make their mistakes deliberately, with a kind of demon fatalism. 'Whatever we do, if Allah wishes your life to be saved, it will be. *Inch' Allah.*' I only hope that when the New City is built and the Europeans come, there'll be some more stringent form of control over this sort of thing." She paused. "Let me look at you, Cathy." She put her hands on my shoulders, turning me around to the light. "You're very bruised." She touched my arms where the purplish red blemishes were beginning to show.

"I'm also full of dust, inside and out," I said.

"My dear, you must go and bathe at once. Take all the time you want, soak and relax—"

"I don't know about the relaxing part—"

"It was a frightening experience, but it's over. Of course we'll have to report it to the authorities—although that's a futile word to use for the Bou Hammagan police force. Run along and wash your hair, too. Then come down and I'll have a drink ready for you."

As I went upstairs I heard Alexandra talking to Harriet, who had sunk limply down on one of the two divans standing against the wall in the hall.

My bedroom felt stifling and the fans, whirring gently, did little to alleviate the heat of the evening. The shutters had been pushed back and the screen lowered over the open window. As I stood looking out over the darkness, voices came from below me and I heard my name.

I didn't like overhearing conversation that concerned me. It was not so much a point of principle as of embarrassment: a fear that I might hear something that would distress me—an adverse criticism, a comment on something rather stupid that I had done. I moved away from the window, but I could still hear the voices.

". . . let me know. What have you told her?"

"Nothing." Harriet's voice rose. "I've told her nothing that could possibly upset her. It's not my affair, anyway. But I'm scared. He has made a god of his freedom, and family life means nothing to him. You know that, don't you? I expect Louise used to say—"

"Do be quiet, Harriet. Your voice carries. Anyway, it's not for us to interfere."

"But if she is threatened—?"

"What can we do except guard her as best we can? We can't control her movements outside the house—if we always watched her, she would notice and feel like a prisoner."

I knew from the direction of the voices that they hadn't moved from the hall and that Harriet was probably still sitting on the divan. I realized, too, that the sound did not come through the open door to the hall or my window, but through the wall. I touched it, and it seemed solid enough, yet I knew there must be a flaw—a hollow place left when the house was being built.

Such things happened occasionally in modern apartment buildings in England. The hollow space created a vacuum, so that if people sat and talked near the wall, their voices rose as on a sounding board to the room above.

From nearby came the noise of hammering, and a cacophony of strange music broke out, both sounds merging and drowning the voices below.

I walked to the dressing table.

What have you told her? Alexandra had demanded.

What was there to tell? I had a sudden impulse to march down the stairs and face them. "I heard what you were saying. Tell me the rest. Tell me what I should know." But I couldn't do that. It was possible that they might even deny they were talking about me, and then there would be acute embarrassment for everyone. To admit overhearing what they had said required a courage—or an armor—that I did not possess.

There was obviously something they were keeping from me. In a small place such as Bou Hammagan rumors would circulate with the speed of lightning. It so often happened that the one most concerned was the last to know.

I felt a mixture of resentment that they were keeping some knowledge from me and gratitude that they were concerned. I undressed and went into the bathroom and—like a bright ghost as I turned on the taps—imagined an octagonal silver medallion dancing across the gush of water. A talisman for a beautiful girl.

There was a sound in the room behind me and, wrapping the huge pink towel around me, I went to the door.

"It is Lisette." She set a hair dryer on the dressing table. "Madame said you were washing your hair and I have brought this for you. If you like I will set your hair for you."

I told her that any set she might try on my hair would vanish in an hour. My fine hair was a hairdresser's nightmare, I said. "I have the sort of hair that can only be worn straight. But thank you."

The angular face with its long upper lip was turned my way. Her small eyes surveyed me and I knew she was comparing me in unfavorable silence with Alexandra, with her bronze pheasant's coloring. "It's just as you wish, of course, Mrs. Mountavon."

I tipped bubbles from a bottle into the bath, turning the water mauve, and lay soaking. Particles of Kourifia sand speckled the water. The tall mirrors showed me the mass of scarlet scrapes and bruises and gave back the reflection of my face, eyes reddened by the dusty irritant of the cave. At least, I thought vainly, my eyes would recover and my face was not marked.

After I had bathed, I washed my hair and partially dried it with the hand dryer. As I let the warm air blow on my head, I stood facing the hollow wall. The question nagged at me: What was it Harriet might have told me?

"You've washed your hair."

I leaped around. Pippa stood in the doorway coolly watching me.

"Hello, darling. Have you had a nice day?"

"Yes. Has Daddy come home?"

"I haven't seen him, but Harriet met him in the town earlier, so he's around somewhere."

Pippa crossed to her room, and through the open door I caught sight of her swimsuit and towel flying across and landing on the bed.

"Don't do that, Pippa, please. Those things are probably wet, and they might damage the divan cover. It's a very delicate silk, you know."

"They're not wet."

I said lightly, "I'll make a bet with you that the last thing you did before you came home was to have a final dip. That's so, isn't it? So your swim things must be damp."

"I dried them in the sun on the roof here. I've been home ages, but you didn't come and look for me."

"I'm sorry."

"I could have been lost, and you weren't even coming to look for me."

"I've been with Harriet at the Caves. If you were late home, Alexandra would have sent Ahmed to look for you, and she would have told me. So I knew you must be around somewhere."

"You didn't. You didn't even think of me."

There was a germ of truth in that. I was absorbed in my own shock. "Darling, I've said I'm sorry, but—"

"You could have *thought* about me and then *looked* for me. But you didn't."

"Pippa, don't be silly."

"I'm not. Alexandra says I'm clever. I know I am. Daddy thinks so, too."

"And so do I. But there are times when you behave rather like

128

someone much younger than you are. Now, please, don't let's start some idiotic quarrel."

She turned her back on me and swept up the swimsuit and the towel. "It's not a bit as I thought it would be."

"What isn't?" I was running my fingers through my hair, lifting it to let the warm air get through it. "Pippa," I insisted as patiently as I could, "what isn't at all as you hoped it would be?"

"Daddy."

"What do you mean?"

"Everything's like it was before." Her eyes, angry and luminous, flashed at me. "I thought it was going to be so lovely." She flung herself on her bed and lay quite still on her flat little stomach.

My narrow escape from death only a few hours ago had taken its toll of my energy, and my quiet voice was a dangerous sign of my own tension, had Pippa known it. "Just tell me in simple words what all this is about."

"You—you and Daddy, of course." Her face was thrust into the silken pillow. "You don't want me here."

"If I hadn't wanted you with me, I wouldn't have brought you. We had already planned for you to go to that camp in Dorset. We canceled it so that you could come with me to North Africa."

The pause was long, and when she spoke, she ignored my reassurance. "I like it best when Daddy's away."

I asked, shocked by what seemed a turnabout of her affections, "Why on earth do you say that?"

"Because then I can pretend he's coming back to me and not you. When he *does* come, it's *you*." She half lifted herself from the bed, and her cloud of dark hair veiled her face.

To have been badly frightened at the Caves was quite enough shock for one day. I was going to find it difficult to cope with Pippa's uncharacteristic mood. I didn't feel nicely adult and controlled. "You don't really believe a word of what you're saying," I told her, "because you know perfectly well your father loves you too."

She rolled over and stared at the ceiling, her arms over her head. "He did in England after Mummy died." Her eyes flicked sideways at me. She was implying "and before you became my stepmother."

I had a choice of laughing or losing my temper. I laughed. "You are rather a little idiot. The kind of love your father has for me is quite different from what he feels for you. We both have something that is entirely ours. Can't you understand that?"

She said angrily, "Love is love."

I thought with a small rush of despair: Oh, dear heaven, don't let her make pontifical statements like that when she grows up . . . But she was only a child, single-minded and using words wildly, out of her own wounded unreason.

It was useless to argue with her until her mood changed. I went back to my own room, and immediately Pippa sprang up and slammed the door between us. For a moment her violence stunned me. Then I wheeled around, opened the door again and seized her by the shoulders. "Let's get this quite straight once and for all, shall we? Something I have—or have not—done these past few days has upset you. Tell me frankly what it is and let's talk it out. I can't put it right until I know what it is."

"You don't want me; you only want that stained-glass window stuff you do and . . . and *all* Daddy's love."

"I've never neglected you for what you call 'that stained-glass window stuff,' and I've never taken any love that should be yours. Nor," I added for angry good measure, "have you ever questioned this before. So why now?"

Harriet? I asked myself in the moment of silence. Harriet, slipping in little snide remarks to amuse herself, indifferent to how a child would react? I was quite certain that she would never think of herself as a major troublemaker and that she used her tongue to inject a small spot of excitement into what she might consider to be a rather dull moment. Harriet had just saved my life, but that didn't prevent me from being perfectly aware that she could no more change her character than the leopard could change his spots.

I considered another possibility as Pippa wandered about the room, picking things up without interest and tossing them down again: Alexandra, never having had children of her own and admittedly not understanding them and their capacity for complete self-absorption, could have made some remark that Pippa had misinterpreted. The fact remained that, from whatever cause, Pippa was not the Pippa of our London life.

"I'm going downstairs," she said, breaking the silence, and walked past me, closing the door behind her with exaggerated quiet.

I sat before the mirror in the bedroom, and the memory of the first night in Bou Hammagan came back to me. I had suspected Harriet; I had suspected Alexandra. But it could have been Mark and I who had been the cause of the outburst which had perhaps smoldered for days and at last broken out. I remembered the look of lost, lonely shock on Pippa's face when she had burst into the room and seen Mark and me lying close.

Her sense of isolation from love must have begun early in her life when she had realized that her mother felt nothing but boredom toward her. I would tell Mark that, until Pippa felt secure in our love, we would have to be careful never to let her feel that we were complete in ourselves and that she was a mere appendage.

Throughout the frustrating skirmish with Pippa we had been hurling the word "love" at each other. Her concept of it had been a child's—natural and subjective. Mine? I knew what the word meant to me. I wondered whether it meant something quite different to Mark.

XV

WHILE I dressed and made up my face, I heard voices and laughter from downstairs. Alexandra's house was becoming the focal point of evenings, with the Mitchells and the Averys and even David all collecting like foreign residents at their special club.

When I arrived among them, I could hear children's voices in the courtyard. Clarissa and John Mitchell were with Pippa, and her laughter rang out more clearly even than theirs. It seemed that she had forgotten our quarrel.

The group of adults, which included Justin, was sitting in the patio, but Alexandra wasn't with them. After greetings, I chose the empty chair by Justin's side. Under cover of Frances's clear voice making some comment to Benedict about the roses, Justin said to me, "You know, Alexandra should have a notice on her door. 'You're welcome any night. Please come.' Because our glamorous Madame doesn't like being alone." He laughed softly and leaned toward me. "Your hair looks like crushed velvet."

"It feels like blotting paper. I haven't had time to dry it properly."

"What did you do, slide under your bath water?"

"I can't tell you now."

"Sweetie, they're so well away with their gossip, they won't even notice us."

Because I wanted to talk about it, I told him what had happened. He listened and then nodded. "Harriet said something about a gruesome adventure you'd had at the Caves. But she didn't stop to give me details; she was rushing off to get some more watercolors. I think she said something about going to the police, too."

"I should have gone with her."

"Oh, Harriet will cope." He paused and we both glanced toward the door.

Alexandra came straight up to me, tilted my chin and looked at me. "Are you sure I shouldn't call Doctor Melilla?"

"Oh, please don't. I'll be fine."

"Cathy has just had a horrible experience at Kourifia," she explained to her guests. "There are some rather fine primitive paintings on the walls. But don't go there until the whole affair has been gone into and sorted out. At the moment the wrong cave has been boarded up."

Interested eyes were turned on me, and I cut into the murmurs of sympathy, saying brightly, "In a few days' time I won't even have any bruises to show for what happened. And most people have some sort of accident once in their lives, don't they?"

Somewhere beyond the walls of the house a heavy object fell with a clatter to the ground. Durandal lifted his head, muscles stiffening. Alexandra bent and touched him, saying softly, "It's all right, Dura. Don't be silly."

He blinked up at her, lifted a paw and began licking it. Marian Avery was sitting on the edge of her chair, watching the cheetah with fascinated eyes. "You're not afraid to have him around?"

"Why should I be? No one here fears him; even Yussef, my doorman, who takes him for walks, loves him."

Benedict Avery, obviously fearing an animal conversation, asked what the roads were like out of Bou Hammagan.

"If you're meaning to civilization," Justin said, "then Algiers is nearest. But then you know that, don't you? You drove here from the airport. It's the only way to reach us."

"Oh, dear, I hope we've done the right thing in buying land here. I don't want to be bored." Marian looked to Benedict for reassurance.

I lost the trend of the conversation. I was remembering something my father had once said to me. "Never let yourself be bored, Cathy. It's a sign of one of two things—egotism or idleness."

By my side, Justin murmured, "Harriet—and escort. Good God, what a stage effect!"

Harriet came first through the arch, wearing yellow culottes and an embroidered bolero. I had never seen her dressed in bright colors before, and it was as if she were proclaiming herself as an artist to the future rich residents of Bou Hammagan.

Behind her was a dark young man who wore a kind of musical-comedy outfit—royal-blue suit, silver epaulets and a scarlet cummerbund.

The stranger bowed to Alexandra, and Harriet introduced us. He was Ibrahim el Hassan, an officer in the Bou Hammagan police force. And I, she said sternly to him, was the English visitor who almost lost her life at the Kourifia Caves.

Then she explained to me, "I went to the police and reported what happened. They want your story to corroborate mine." She turned and said airily to the assembled guests, "I'm sorry to disturb the party."

"Of course you must," Alexandra said. "If you hadn't gone to the police, Harriet, I would have. Please feel free, officer, to talk to Mrs. Mountavon." She waved a hand toward the house.

I had to forgive him, he said in fairly good English, for the questions he would ask me, but they were important. Had I, perhaps, removed the planks myself because I was curious to see what the boarded-up cave was like inside? Then, before I answered, he softened the obscure criticism. "The English are so venturesome." He smiled at me, proud of the big word he was able to use.

We sat on the silk-covered divan in the great hall where Harriet had sat earlier that evening when she carried on the conversation with Alexandra that I had overheard in the room above.

I assured him that I had not moved the boards. "I couldn't, anyway," I said. "They were too long and heavy."

"Ah, but no, that is really not so. They were light because they were rotting wood and could have fallen down easily. A child, even, could have dragged at them."

"Then perhaps a child did, out of mischief. I did notice a small village not far away."

"No, madame, the children would not dare to do that." His tone was severe. I had cast doubts upon the behavior of the young of his country. While he could punish the naughty and the destructive, a stranger must not do so.

"We have sent out some heavy boards," he said. "They will be fixed up tonight and made . . . how do you say?" He waved an eloquent hand. "Secure. I'm so happy, madame, that you are safe."

That makes two of us, I thought, and gave him a vague smile. Harriet came to the door from the patio. "By the way, Cathy, sorry to interrupt, but where is Mark?" She turned to the young inspector. "He is Mrs. Mountavon's husband. Did he call on you?"

"No. Only you came, madame." He rose, thanked me for talking to him, promised that he would investigate to see if children could possibly have been responsible, and left.

Harriet said, "And that will be the end of the affair."

"But he told me that they have already taken heavier boards out to Kourifia to block the cave," I said.

"Yes. I waited at their so-called police headquarters until I was sure of that. But they won't find out who did it."

Outside, in the courtyard, I could hear the scampering feet and laughter of the children. It mingled with the murmur of the conversation from the inner garden where the adults sat with their drinks.

I went toward the door leading to the patio. Harriet looked about her restlessly. "Why doesn't Mark come? I saw him around the town ages ago."

"Work doesn't end when the film crew returns to its base."

She bent down to take off one of her white sandals and shake it. "I changed everything when I came home, but I still feel as if sand is glued to my skin."

I suddenly felt that there were too many people around me, and instead of following Harriet to the patio, I went to the outer door of the house. I wanted to stand on the steps and be silent; I wanted to shake off the lethargy which I suppose was a reaction from too much tension. The door was ajar, and Yussef sat outside his hut, hands on his knees, an ecstatic expression on his face. I could hear only too well what was delighting him.

Mark and Justin were just outside the open door of the house, and they were not indulging in friendly gossip.

". . . and if you think I'm an untapped reservoir of ready cash, then you are a bigger fool than I thought."

"I'm no fool and you know it. But the sooner—" Justin broke off and looked over his shoulder.

Without realizing it I had leaned against the open door, and it creaked softly.

"Oh, hello, Cathy. We were just on our way in."

I turned and walked into the courtyard without a word. Yussef grinned at me. I doubted if he had understood many words of what he had overheard, but the low angry tones were sufficiently telling, and any diversion, particularly a heated one, must be a delight in his unexciting day.

I returned to the patio and a barrage of teasing. "What have you done, Cathy? Found ancient treasure and kept it? Or dared to enter a mosque?"

"She was probably propositioned by a Hammagarb and hit him over the head," Frances Mitchell said. "Pretty girls shouldn't go around on their own."

I was in no mood for even the most puerile banter, but before I could speak I saw their eyes go beyond me, and I looked over my shoulder.

Mark stood at the patio door.

Alexandra cried, "We're one drink up on you. Go and mix yourself a whiskey and soda."

"Thank you, but later. Cathy, come upstairs with me while I change."

I looked quickly at Alexandra to see the effect on her of his order, coldly, almost arrogantly given. But she just smiled and lifted her eyebrows.

Mark closed the bedroom door and faced me. His eyes, pinpoints of silver in the lamplight, were angry. "What the hell made you go into that cave?"

"Because it was the one—or so I thought—that you took us in the other day."

"Surely you were observant enough to realize that that was the one which was boarded up?"

I sat on the edge of the bed and dangled my shoe from my toes, watching the swing of the low white heel. "What were you and Justin quarreling about?"

I had taken Mark off guard and he looked momentarily startled. "Why should you think we quarreled?"

"You saw me at the door. It's obvious that I heard something of your conversation."

"How much did you hear?"

"How much are you afraid I heard?"

"Whatever it was, I suggest you forget it. Now, suppose we go back to our original conversation?"

There were always moments of irritation in friendship and in marriage. This was one of mine with Mark. I knew from experience that he was impervious to pressure; if he didn't wish to discuss something, nothing and no one could force him. The argument between his brother and him was their affair and on that score I was the outsider.

I conceded the victory to Mark and said, "About the Caves . . . Harriet and I went to Kourifia by a different route, and I'd been wandering over the rocks for some time, waiting for sunset, so when I arrived back at the Caves, the right might have been the left and the left, right, from where I was standing. They are all very alike."

"And when you were inside, what did you do?"

"Why, looked for the primitive paintings."

"It didn't occur to you that they were different drawings and in different places?"

"I didn't find any drawings—just carvings. That's what puzzled me."

"What did you do to dislodge the rocks?"

"Nothing."

He sat in the low chair opposite me, his eyes still cold. "You must have done something."

"Nothing happened until Harriet called to me that it was getting toward sunset. I wanted to paint the colors of it for Alexandra's window."

"And you answered her?"

"Of course. I said I was coming. And she didn't hear me because I was rather far back in the cave and so I shouted again and she shouted—"

"And your friendly shouting match caused the vibration which brought part of the cave ceiling down on you. Good God, even if you had been in the right cave, the one we visited, surely it must have occurred to you that if one was dangerous and had collapsed, the other should be treated with respect, since it is of the same soft sandstone. So, even had you been in the so-called safe cave, you should have walked quietly and not shouted."

"How was I to know? I don't go in for exploring caves, and when we were there the other day, you didn't warn me—or Pippa," I added.

"It didn't occur to me. I didn't expect either of you to burst into song."

We tried to outstare each other, both angry and irritated. Then simultaneously our expressions relaxed and we laughed together.

Mark reached for me. "I'm bloody-minded because what happened to you scared me."

"It scared me, too. It wasn't funny and I've got bruises to prove it."

He rose and pulled me to my feet, holding me close. "Never go taking risks like that again."

"I was taking no risk." I held my face against his coat. "I had no way of knowing the board had been changed."

"Vandals . . . hooligans."

"That note in Louise's box . . ."

"What about it?"

" 'Dust hath closed—' "

"Forget it."

"Like a fortuneteller's warning, sensibly ignored. But I can't, Mark, I can't."

"I don't pretend to know who sent that box or why. But I'm quite certain there's nothing for you to fear. Someone intent on harming you wouldn't send some damned silly warning—they'd go ahead and act. And, anyway, there's no reason to it. I'll make a bet you've never harmed anyone in your life."

"We all hurt people at times."

"So we're all quits," he said.

I looked away from him. "The reason, so far as I am concerned, could be just that I'm here in Bou Hammagan."

He laughed. "What does anyone think you can do? Put a black charm on the place?"

"Mark, it isn't funny."

"Oh, darling, I know. But what *can* anyone do?"

A lot, I thought. The police . . . But no one seemed to have much faith in them.

"I could go back to England."

"No."

I tried to will Mark to say he wanted me to stay for his sake. Instead, as if that uncompromising "no" were sufficient, he walked into the bathroom and turned on the taps.

"Thank God for baths," he said.

At that moment, the gong sounded from the hall below. The resonance rose, throbbed, lingered and died away slowly.

"Dinner," Mark called against the gushing water. "Go down and make my apologies. I'll skip the first course."

XVI

THE HOUSE was quiet, the guests gone. Alexandra's table had been a source of magic for the children because Lisette, who I learned with secret surprise adored the young, had planned her dishes with the maximum of color—green and red peppers, saffron tinting the meat dish, fruit piled in purple and orange splendor on one of the large, beautiful cloisonné plates. Embroidered silks and glowing tiles, great bronze lamps—a wonder-scene for the eyes of children. For me, the background for melodrama I had never believed would come my way.

We stayed a little while talking in the heavily starred night while Yussef took Durandal for his last run. Then, as the clock struck midnight, I got up from my chair.

Alexandra held out her hand to me. "Poor Cathy, you must be tired after that horrible time. You were wonderful to be so sociable to my guests. I doubt if I would have been in your place. Go to bed, my dear, you look tired."

For the first time, she kissed me—touching my cheek with her cool lips. I felt that this was as far as she would ever go to show affection.

Mark said, "I'll be up presently."

They had been happily reminiscing about mutual acquaintances, and as I left them, I heard Alexandra say, "I always enjoy meeting old friends and catching up with news."

"Always providing," Mark retorted, "that they don't stay too long and bore you. I suspect you only remained married to your two husbands because neither marriage lasted long enough to wear its interest out."

The last thing I heard as I went down the cool, hushed hall was Alexandra's laughter.

Pippa should have been asleep, for she had gone to bed immediately after the Mitchells' maid had come to collect the children. There was, however, a light under her door, and I heard the crashing of drawers being slammed shut.

I opened the communicating door. "For one thing, darling, you should be in bed. For another, you don't treat Alexandra's furniture as if you were told to break it up."

She swung around. She hadn't yet undressed, and her hair was wild about her shoulders. "Where did you put my diary, Cathy?"

"Nowhere."

"But you *have*. I can't find it." Her expression and her voice blamed me.

"You know that all I ever do is to slip it into a drawer if I see it around," I said.

"Then *which* drawer?"

"I've told you, I haven't seen it today. You had it last night."

"And now it isn't *anywhere* . . ."

"It can't vanish. You'd better have a thorough search."

"I have. And I know I put it in this drawer." She pointed an angry finger at the carved ebony bedside table. *"Where is it?"* The question was violently italicized.

"That's what we'll have to find out." I began opening the drawers of the ornate chest, looking in the cupboard, pushing aside the silken hangings to see if it had fallen on the floor. Standing in the center of the room, she watched me.

"Why are you barefoot?" I asked suddenly.

She didn't answer me but continued to level accusing silver-green eyes at me.

"Go and put some slippers on, Pippa, do you hear?"

She went languidly toward the bed and pushed her feet into the yellow babouches. The distress on her face made me say more gently, "Perhaps you left your diary in the garden. You do sometimes take it down there to write in it, don't you?"

"I wrote in bed last night and today I went to the swimming pool. I haven't been *home*—not all day. And *you*—" She broke off and tried to outstare me. She was questioning my honesty, and that was something I had no intention of being subjected to.

"When I tell you that I haven't touched your diary, I mean it. And I'm quite sure no one else has done so. Now, I'm going downstairs and I'll search the garden for you."

"It won't be any use." She turned away from me.

"Sometimes people mislay things and say 'I know where I put it.' And then find what they're looking for is in some entirely different place. Now get into bed and I'll look around and see if I can find it."

"Cathy . . ."

I hesitated at the door.

"Did you want to read what I wrote in my diary?"

"You should know me better than to ask such a question."

"I don't think I really know anyone." It was so like a remark a disillusioned adult might make that I had to remember that she was a child. And one who had been hurt long before I knew her.

"Oh, darling." I put my arms around her. "I want to find your diary as much as you do." I held her for a moment and felt my own dangerous comfort. I must not drown her in too much love, assuage my own hunger with a child. But I did not need to fear that Pippa would respond too readily. She drew away from me and I quickly released her—and went into my own room.

It was a distant possibility that Lisette, tidying up, had seen the book on the floor and thought it belonged to me, but I found nothing.

I went out onto the terrace and down the outside staircase to the courtyard. The fountain had been turned off, and the place was quiet except for the murmur of voices beyond the archway in the Women's Garden. I searched the seat under the orange tree where Pippa loved to curl up, but the diary wasn't there. Then I went through the archway to Alexandra and Mark. "Pippa is upset because she has lost her diary," I said.

143

"She has put it somewhere and forgotten where." Mark rose and looked at his watch. "Children are like squirrels, they hide things."

"We've looked everywhere."

"I think Lisette is still in the kitchen," Alexandra said. "I'll ask her if she has seen the book."

"I'd let her sleep on it." Mark said. "She'll remember in the morning what she has done with it. Tell her to stop thinking about it tonight, tuck her in and—"

"Suppose, just for once, *you* tucked her in?"

"Oh, no, she's like a clinging vine where I'm concerned. I'd never get away."

Alexandra left us to find Lisette, and Mark walked away from me and stood in front of the cheetah's cage. "We'll have to find something very original as a thank-you present for Alexandra, so you'd better start thinking." He flicked a finger across my cheek as I joined him. "Don't look so solemn. If it's Pippa you're worrying about, I'll get her some memo pads from the office. That'll solve her problem until the New Year. And I'll buy her two diaries next time in case she loses one again. I spoil her."

"I think what worries her is the thought that someone has read what she has written."

He said dryly, "You make her sound like Emily Brontë—she was neurotic about people reading her work. I don't want Pippa to be secretive. She must learn—"

"You don't keep diaries in order to show them around."

"Pepys did—" He laughed. "At any rate, we can't turn the place upside down at this time of night. And Cathy—" I was half turned away from him, and he pulled me around to face him. "Don't let her break your heart."

"Of course she won't. She's not hard."

"Don't you believe it! Children are self-absorbed young monsters where their interests are concerned, and Pippa's no exception. But I'd rather have her that way than play the 'hurt little darling' act."

"She's very vulnerable all the same."

"Oh, yes, but don't let that influence you, either."

"I haven't yet had a lot of experience at being a stepmother."

"You're doing pretty well, darling." His face, turned toward me, was heavily shadowed, so that I had no idea whether he was smiling or grave.

"Sometimes you're very casual toward her and I think it hurts her," I said.

"Shall I tell you a secret? I adore her. But I'm sufficiently awake and aware to know that she can be ruthless. So, Cathy, love her; but use your head as well as your heart. Now, will you go to bed?"

"It's such a beautiful night," I said, with my face raised to the moon.

"I know. And I'm going for a walk."

"Walk?" The word shot out of me more sharply than I had intended. "But, Mark, it's very late."

"I've had a hot and exhausting few days. Nothing went as right as it should have, and I want a few minutes' quiet."

"Of course."

"I won't be long."

Alexandra came out of the house, saying, "Lisette hasn't seen Pippa's diary. She knows what it looks like, of course, because it's so often on her bedside table. It can't be far and I'm sure we'll find it tomorrow." She put her hands up to her head and began to pull out the pins, so that her rich bronze hair fell about her shoulders. It was the first intimate, homey gesture I had ever seen her make in front of us.

Mark said, "I'm going for a short walk."

"You're tireless," Alexandra said, combing her hair with her fingers.

"I'm not, you know. But walking alone has always recharged my energy batteries. Cathy understands."

Alexandra said softly, "You're lucky this time, aren't you, Mark? I'm so glad."

"I'm lucky in my wife—and my friends—and my life." He lifted his hand in a half-salute and left us.

Alexandra leaned against a heavy stone urn, her head pressed against the massed red geranium blooms. "Do you *know* Mark, Cathy?"

It was a curious question, but I answered it without hesitation. "I think I know him as much as anyone can know another human being. But we all have times when we surprise other people."

"Louise always used to say that the longer she lived with Mark, the less she knew him. But then, you are far more intelligent than Louise, and she was incapable of knowing how to handle him. Instead of leaving him alone when he came back from his foreign assignments, she used to question him about his life and his friends abroad and, being Mark, he clammed up. That infuriated her and made her the possessive person she grew into. It was a pity, really, that Louise didn't have a career to keep her occupied. Or, since I don't think she was bright enough for that, she should have married a dull, sentimental man who would have come home to her every night and brought her flowers and told her how pretty she was. She needed a man who made her his whole world. Mark compartmental-izes his life."

She was right. In a way, he did. But his kind of work dictated his life.

We parted, and Alexandra went into the house. I climbed the out-side staircase, pausing once to look down into the empty courtyard. I heard Alexandra speak to Lisette in French. In a house nearby a baby began to cry, and two men, walking up the stepped street, talked in loud, excited voices.

The light was still on in Pippa's room, and I went in quietly. She lay curled up on the cold tiled floor, pulling at her lower lip and turning to stare at me with blank eyes.

I knelt by her side. "Darling, don't fret. We'll get some notebooks and you can write in those until we return to London. Then we'll see if we can find another diary like yours. Sometimes publishers have some left over."

She turned away from me and lay on her stomach, tracing the intricate pattern of a blue tile with an idle finger.

"This floor feels ice-cold," I said, "and after the heat of the day, I don't think it's very good for you to lie on it."

I put my hands underneath her arms and tried to lift her, but she resisted me and I gave up the struggle. Her eyes were closed, and I remembered how, when I was very young, I used to shut my eyes tightly to keep back the tears. She was not going to wail in front of me. But I knew the signs too well, and although I longed to be allowed to comfort her, prolonged sympathy would have worn us both out. Gentleness wasn't the way, and in any case Pippa didn't want it from me. She wanted only the practical matter of getting her diary back.

"Pippa, please get up." My voice was deliberately sharp. "You can do all the searching you need in the morning."

The unusual edge to my voice must have startled her, for she got up, and collapsed softly onto the bed in a light flurry of hair and limp arms and legs.

I bent over her and hoisted her up. "Go and wash, clean your teeth, undress and then get into bed. I'm staying here until you do."

She was rather too speedy in the bathroom, but I let that go. When she was in bed I tucked her in, kissed her and said, "Let's not worry too much tonight. There's some notepaper in my room. I'll get it and you can write about today on that and fill it into your diary when you find it—"

"I won't ever find it."

"Then we'll get some exercise books—"

"It won't help. I'll never remember what I put in in all those days. And even if I did, someone is reading *all* that's me." She let me hold her for a moment—thin, supine and dark-haired—and then, as if remembering some grudge she was holding against me, pushed me away and lay back on the pillows. "Why isn't Daddy home?"

"He's gone for a walk. He's been working since dawn for three days and he wanted to enjoy some night air."

"But he *knew* I'd lost my diary and he didn't care."

"Darling, he did. Only what more could he have done than I have?"

She lay cold and unresponsive, wrapped in the small tragedy of her lost diary, yet fiercely fighting a display of misery. I saw in her withdrawal from me something of Mark's remoteness. There was nothing to do but leave her. She averted her face as I tried to kiss her again, so I turned off the light and closed the communicating door firmly.

The telephone rang as I went down the stairs, and I heard Lisette's voice in the kitchen answering it. Her footsteps sounded across the floor and, as I reached the hall, the door opened and she said, "There is a call for you, madame. The man won't give his name."

I picked up the receiver in the little alcove behind the end column and nodded my thanks to Lisette. "Hello."

"Mrs. Mountavon?" His voice was deep and thick and slow. "Do you remember a car number?"

"I remember our own in London, of course. Why?"

"Not your husband's latest car, but the one before. A Rover, I think it was. The registration number was K.L.X. 13724."

"Really? What about it?" There was a tight feeling around my chest.

"It was the car that killed Louise Mountavon."

"Oh, of all the damned . . . the damned lies . . ." I stopped shouting. The line was dead.

I dropped the receiver into its cradle and stepped backward. My knees gave under me, and it was fortunate that there was a chair behind me. I knew the Rover; I knew the number. It had been Mark's car until the week he married me.

"It's monstrous . . ." I was shaking and talking to myself. If Mark had accidentally knocked Louise down, he would most certainly have stopped. And, after the accident, would have got rid of the car at once.

Or would he . . . would he? My demon, my alter ego, questioned me. To have sold the Rover immediately would be a proof of guilt. But Mark was not guilty. Evil was being inserted under my skin, into my brain, like the needles used in Chinese acupuncture. Someone wanted me to hate and fear Mark . . . A man? Or a man speaking on a woman's behalf?

I put my face in my hands. "Who drove the car at Louise?" Harriet had asked. And she had no reason to want me to suspect him; he was Justin's brother, and their lives and ours seldom touched.

When Mark came, would I tell him? *I can't, Mark . . . I can't drag up the past with this unspeakable suggestion.* Yet it hadn't been uttered as a suggestion, but as a fact. Someone in Bou Hammagan had been near Louise's house on the night of her death, had perhaps been coming to see her and was a witness to what had happened.

Oh, heaven help me, I couldn't say to Mark, "Someone here believes that you killed Louise . . . Please, don't come near me until I get this poison out of me . . . Because it isn't true and I must be able to face you without even a shadow of its horror showing."

I lifted my head and looked at the telephone. Then I reached out, took the receiver and waited for the operator. When she answered me in her charming broken English, I asked her if it would be possible to trace the call that had just come through to the House of the Fountains. It took her a moment or two to understand what I wanted —in that small African state I supposed it was miraculous that a telephone operator could speak even a little English.

She couldn't help me, however. All she could tell me was that it had come from the only public telephone booth in the whole of Bou Hammagan, in Isakila Square.

I replaced the receiver again and sat and looked at the wall. I felt neither shock nor anger, only a sense of weary dismay that someone had no intention of letting Mark and me alone.

"Why are you sitting in a corner like Cinderella?" Mark asked. He had entered the house so quietly that I hadn't heard him. Nor had I seen him coming toward me.

"Shall we go outside?" I got up and moved past him to the door leading to the courtyard.

I was glad of the length of the hall because it gave me time to control my face and my feelings. Whatever happened, I must keep the voice on the telephone a secret from him. I couldn't stand near him and say, "Someone has just accused you of killing Louise." The fact that I could add in all truth, "It's too monstrous!" wouldn't help. The words had been spoken, the accusation made.

We walked slowly, side by side, to the fountain. The water was lying still and luminous in the basin.

"Something odd happened last night," I said, "and it's just possible that it could be linked with the diary." I told about the disturbance that woke me, and the cigarette burning on the terrace near my room. "When I told Alexandra, she said that it must have been Yussef on his night round. It seemed possible, but now I doubt it. Someone could have come up the outside staircase and crept into Pippa's room."

"To take a child's diary?"

"It sounds ridiculous, doesn't it? But, for one thing, I can't believe that it was Yussef who disturbed me. There was an hour's difference between the time he said he had gone around the house and the time something woke me."

"Oh, hours are nothing out here."

I dismissed the easy explanation. "I believe someone managed to get into the house by way of the outside staircase last night. And if he can do it once, he can do it again."

"Alexandra risks a great deal by having so much that is valuable around."

"Whoever came took nothing of hers. That's why I'm frightened."

He looked at me strangely. "I don't see the connection."

I walked around the fountain basin, fighting an urge to tell him about the telephone call—and knowing that I could not. Revenge must be the reason for that accusation, and the plan must be that Mark should suffer through me. Yet why? Why not go straight to Mark? Was he so strong that whoever hounded us didn't dare attack directly?

"I'm frightened because it's I who have been threatened," I said.

"Was it a threat, or just someone showing off a piece of erudition? I don't know who wrote that verse, or even whether it is original, and until I get back to London and search the books of quotations, I won't know. But please leave it to me. Only, remember, I've got a demanding job, so give me time." He reached down and picked up a fallen leaf and smoothed it across his palm. "One thing puzzles me.

How could anyone enter Pippa's room while you were sleeping? They would have to pass right by your bed."

"I was only disturbed when it was too late. And Pippa sleeps very deeply."

Somewhere far away a dog howled, and in the silences between the strange, half-baying sounds, I heard the indistinct quarter tones of some stringed instrument.

"Surely it's possible to go through a list of Louise's friends and find out who might have taken the box? I'm sure there's a connection."

"If you could give me one good reason why . . ."

The voice on the telephone, Mark; the man who is here in Bou Hammagan and was there when Louise was killed. The dreadful thing I could not say to him . . .

"Perhaps the silver box got mixed up in some bequest, and if you could remember who might have received it—however outlandish the idea might be."

"I'm afraid she had dozens of acquaintances and not a few hangers-on. Any one of them could have taken the box at some time during their visits on those last few days before I closed the house for good. Any one of them could be touring along the North African coast and have paid a Hammagarb to deliver the box."

"Having brought it with them? But why?"

"They could have known through television that I was out here and, I've told you, perhaps the plan was to send it to me with some bloody silly threat. Then, hearing that you had joined me, they decided that you were more vulnerable. I'm sticking to that theory, Cathy."

"But the purpose behind it . . . ?"

"How the hell do I know?"

How could he, and what purpose was *I* serving by questioning a very tired man? "Let's go to bed," I said.

"And that," he answered, "is the best suggestion I've heard all day."

There was none of Mark's usual gentleness that night. He was harsh and violent with me as though trying to fight some devil inside himself.

I couldn't shake off the fears and complexities that overlay everything. They so haunted me that when we were lying still and quiet again, I said with my eyes closed, "Am I chasing shadows, Mark?"

"I don't know what you mean."

"I can't shake myself free of the things that have happened."

He remained silent, and I drew away and leaned on my elbows trying to see his face in the dark. "I'm not used to being hated," I said.

"Who is, except dictators? The rest of us get by with a few mild curses from those who envy us, and we learn to live with them."

"You mean, I must learn to live with the idea that someone wishes to harm me? Oh, Mark, I'm not *that* strong!"

"I've tried to explain that I believe *I* am the target, not you. Now, do you think we could let it ride for tonight? And, Cathy, trust me."

I did. I had to because I loved him. I buried my face in his pillow so near him that our foreheads touched.

In the distance the plaintive music played on; there seemed to be a slight breeze from somewhere, a stirring of air as if the garden breathed.

XVII

AFTER BREAKFAST the next day, Mark and Pippa sat under the orange tree. Durandal lay on his back, paws in the air. It had been one of the mornings when, instead of letting Yussef take the cheetah, Alexandra had gone down to the Kabenès Gate and got out her car, driving by a different route to the Phoenician Arch where Yussef had met her with the cheetah. She had taken him then and let him run by the side of the car, returning him after an hour to the waiting Yussef.

I stood at the bedroom window looking down at my husband and my stepdaughter. Mark was leaning forward, looking back over his shoulder, listening. And Pippa, curled up on the seat by his side, was pouring herself out to him, scarcely taking time for breath. It was barely eight o'clock, but already the garden lay in a kind of soporific dream of warm, golden light. The roses, grouped in their special colors of salmon-pink, yellow and orange, made a theatrical setting for my husband and my small, dark stepdaughter.

Suddenly, the happy, relaxed situation in the garden changed. The monologue became what looked to me like quick-fire question and answer. I saw Pippa put her hands around Mark's arm and lay her forehead against his shoulder in the characteristic cajoling manner she had when she wanted to win an argument.

He shook her off and swung around on her, seizing her shoulders, shaking her, so that her slim legs slid from under her and she was like a little yellow bundle harassed by violent hands.

I flew onto the terrace, down the outer steps into the courtyard. Pippa was crouching on the ground, her face tight with her attempt not to burst into tears.

Mark looked at his watch and then saw me. "Hello," he said cheerfully. "I'm just off. I'm meeting the architects of the new government building. We may show the plans and the model in one of our programs."

"Why is Pippa crying?"

"It's something to do with that blasted diary."

Her eyes opened and shone with rainbow tints as the sun caught the tears that she could not keep back. "It's not a b-blasted diary, and if you lost all your beastly tapes you talk about, you'd—"

"I'd swear, and hard. I'd say—oh, well, never mind what I'd say. But crying won't help. There's a shop near the Casbah where you can buy writing materials. Ask Harriet. I'd bring you some pads from the office, only knowing you, you'd need too many. I'll give you some money to buy exercise books."

She pressed herself into the bed of roses, her hands gripped like fists in her lap. "I don't want your money."

"Don't be silly. You always say you want to be called a person, not a child, so start behaving like one."

I bent forward and took hold of her unyielding fists and drew her to her feet. "Pippa, listen. I'll get you the books sometime today. But Ahmed will be taking you to the swimming pool soon, so why not go upstairs and get your swimsuit?"

"I want my diary. Where is it?" Her eyes were on me like the thrusts of green steel.

"For heaven's sake," Mark said angrily. "What would Cathy want with it? Don't be silly."

"But I wrote about *her,* and about you, Daddy—and about every-

154

one. Cathy took it because she guessed. People always want to know if you like them or not."

"I'd have thought that showed in their behavior," Mark said.

"Ahmed will be waiting for you if you don't hurry," I said quickly because I could see the conversation was getting out of control. Mark was not the most patient of men, and when Pippa decided to argue, she hated to give up. "You know, Clarissa and John will wonder what's happened to you."

"I'll go to the swimming pool if you'll come with me, Daddy." A smile quivered on her lips. Her forgiveness where Mark was concerned was always swift. Because she did not yet understand the quality of Mark's love for her, she was too afraid of losing it.

He rose from the long wrought-iron seat under the orange tree, and Pippa shot up and clung to him. "I didn't mean what I said just now, before . . . before . . ."

"All right. All right. But even if you think such thoughts, keep them to yourself until you've argued around the point and found out how wrong you are." He flicked at her hair. "I'll see you sometime later. I don't know exactly when. And, Cathy, the *souk* where you can buy those exercise books is just as you enter Isakila Square. You can't miss it. All the children get their schoolbooks there."

"I'll find it."

"Good." He touched my shoulder lightly. I felt that he had already left us in his thoughts.

Pippa ran after him. I could hear the flip-flop of her sandals as she disappeared through the archway. Whatever had moved him to be violent with her was over. Mark had dismissed both his anger and Pippa's hurt, and she was back in favor and happy in her wild love for him.

It was I who could not forget that small angry scene. I could not stop wondering what had caused it and why Mark had interrupted her explanation.

When Ahmed had taken Pippa to the hotel pool, I worked for an hour in the terrace room. Alexandra had approved the theme of the window, which was simply a figure not identifiable in feature as herself but bearing her poise and color. At her feet would be Durandal, and the background would be the tints of a desert sunset, which I had yet to catch on paper, made deeper and richer by their transformation into glass.

Since Bou Hammagan was on the rim of the Sahara, I knew that

I could capture the evening colors from the roof of the house. I hoped I would never again see the Caves of Kourifia either at dawn or sunset or any other time. It was one of my misfortunes that I could not easily shake off fearful memories.

From one corner of the roof I could see to the horizon and, well before sunset, I would set up my chair and drawing board there. During part of the next hour I went into the Women's Garden to draw Durandal. He watched me with indifference while I sketched the broad, blunt head and the supine body.

I was so absorbed in working that Alexandra's voice startled me. "Don't stay out in this heat too long, Cathy. Why don't you go to the hotel and swim? And then I'll meet you there later for drinks."

I sat back on my heels. "I'd love that. But I must go down and get those exercise books for Pippa first."

"You know what will happen, don't you? As soon as you get them, the diary will be found."

"I suppose so, but at least I'll have the satisfaction of knowing I tried to help."

It was much later than I intended when I went down to the *souks*. I was beginning to get used to the heat, and my skin was browning gently without burning. Physically, North Africa was good for me: the dry brilliant air a tonic after days spent in Chris Lanyard's great workshops. But I could not shake off a feeling that everyone was playing down the alarm they were admitting among themselves. I hoped I was imagining the anxiety that flashed in Harriet's and Alexandra's eyes when they thought I didn't see; I hoped also that I was being oversensitive about Mark's dismissal of my doubts about my own safety. I told myself that I must leave to him the question of who sent the silver box. But I was not reassured. I felt that I was being placated as if I were too young to have to face the possibilities my elders suspected, and that annoyed me.

Diverted by my irritation, I stumbled on a chipped step and put out my hand to save myself. The gray-white wall was already hot to my touch, and a beautiful little girl came out of a house and gave me a tired marigold. "Plis . . . Plis . . ." She held out the other hand.

The rich were settling in Bou Hammagan and the child beggars had also come to town.

I weakened, put a coin in the urgent little palm and returned her marigold. Then I went quickly into the muddle and noise of people, lean ginger dogs and she-asses, and merged into the crowd before the pretty beggar could summon her friends for their pickings.

I had noticed before when I had walked through the streets that my fair skin and my brief dress caused no one to turn and stare at me—the Hammagarbs had a natural dignity that allowed them to let strangers pass among them without embarrassment. I walked through the Square, keeping as near as I could to anything that gave shadow.

As Justin had explained, there was no plan about the siting of the *souks,* no romantic "Street of the Silversmiths," or "Street of the Carpetsellers." The Bou Hammagarbs had set down their stalls where they chose, and the first few booths I passed were taken up with men seated cross-legged on platforms making babouches and threading amber beads. But as I came to a corner, the herb smells became stronger and the street narrowed, so that it was like a crowded corridor, full of the commotion of hectic sounds and the monotonous hammering of metal by an old man making brass bowls.

I found the place where exercise books were sold together with slates and chalks and all the things that the native children would want at the schools. I bought four little exercise books of rough lined paper and paid for them without arguing the price, a fact which would have horrified Harriet. As I walked away, someone tugged at my arm. A small boy in a djellabah more gray than white was looking up at me with enormous eyes, grinning widely and nodding his head like a mechanical toy. "Lady, you from Beit el Faskieh?"

I said that I was.

"You want book. I know where to find book."

I waved my parcel at him.

He shook his head vigorously. "No, book—" He made weird signs with his hands. "You know . . ." He made more frantic signs as if writing on the air.

"I don't understand," I said in very slow English. "Look. I have what I want. And now I must hurry."

His expression tightened into desperation. "Lady. Book that lost. Lost, lady . . . Book lost . . ." He continued to repeat the words as if someone had taught him what to say in parrot fashion: it was obvious that he wasn't absolutely certain of the meaning of all the words.

I tried to shake him off, but his fingers clutched my arms, his nails filthy. "Book lost." His eyes, with their paradox of innocence and cunning, fixed on me. "Book lost . . ." It was the typical singsong of an Eastern beggar. "I show . . . I take . . ."

"To what?"

"Book . . ." Again he made wild passes in the air, pointing and gesticulating and making scrawls on his little grubby arms, and I knew what he was trying to say. The "book" was Pippa's diary and he could lead me to it. But it was impossible that this boy from the streets could have heard about it.

The boy, encouraged by my hesitation, began pulling at my arm again and pointing, his eyes huge and pleading, his words unintelligible to me.

"Book . . . *Sayeddati* . . ."

He was young—although I guessed not particularly innocent—and whatever place he might lead me to, he could not harm me. His persistence won. I gave in and followed him down a narrow alley leading off the Square. There were a few booths set between clay walls, but they were poor and their goods were mostly food infested with flies.

Here, unlike the more sophisticated Isakila Square, furtive eyes watched me, and when we reached the end of the alley, I stopped, liking neither the boy's clutching fingers nor his nervous energy. "How do you know anything about this diary?"

He looked at me blankly.

"Diary . . ." I insisted. "Book, then . . . ?" I did what he had done and made scribbling signs on my arm.

He grinned. "I take . . . I show . . ."

"Where to?"

He stared at me and again I tried sign language, but it was no use. My gestures were almost as untranslatable as my words. Standing at the place where narrow streets crisscrossed, I faced the challenge the boy offered me. Either I continued to follow him and took a chance that I would find Pippa's diary—or I refused and went back as quickly as I could to the comparative safety of Isakila Square. I didn't like these evil-smelling streets, nor was I happy that I couldn't speak Hammagarb. But stronger than these fears was the thought of Pippa's joy if I brought her diary back.

I wanted to believe the boy knew where it was, and I now began to doubt that it had been taken for any more sinister reason than a reward of money.

I took careful note of landmarks and memorized them. A broken arch; a cluster of gray-green cactus growing out of a wall; a door that lay on collapsed hinges across a dirty threshold.

The boy would probably not be taking me very far and, at the end, there would be a man demanding money. He must be very stupid, I decided, to think that I carried a large sum of Hammagarb currency around with me. But the thought that he might be stupid didn't help because such people were often the most dangerous. And it seemed senseless that a child's diary had been stolen from a house that held so many treasures, but that concern must be for later.

Harriet had been right about the old city. Except for Isakila Square, it was a maze of alleys where everyone wore the uniform garment of the djellabah and all men were swarthy and large-featured beneath their hoods and so, impossible for me to identify.

The boy sometimes looked over his shoulder and occasionally swung around and walked backward, watching me. He was obviously terrified of losing me. When we came to a covered market, I hesitated, but he ran back and tugged at my hand. With a sense of fatalism, I let him lead me through the crowds.

Strips of matting and metal sheeting were stretched on poles from stall to stall and held in the sounds of hammering on wood and beating on metal so that they were deafening. But the boy's high-pitched voice rose above the din. "I take . . . I show . . ."

It was his persistent, excited refrain as he pushed through the people, making a way for me. Beyond the noisy insalubrious market, three streets branched off. The boy led me down one so narrow that if I had spread out my arms I could have touched the dirty walls. Crooked balconies almost met overhead, so that the place was like a tunnel. People took a curious interest in me, eyes swiveling around as I passed. Children and lean dogs sat on dirty steps, and some of the doorways had only sacks hung across them.

The boy looked back at me, grinning, and said something in Hammagarb.

"Where are you taking me?" I sounded nervous and I was nervous. But the boy mustn't know it, and so I repeated my question, asking it the second time with angry authority. *"Where are you taking me?"*

I might have been talking gibberish, for he giggled and rushed on, his dirty heels kicking up the beige dust that had blown there from the desert. A laden donkey came toward us and I had to crouch against the wall to let it pass. At the end of the alley the boy turned into another even more sinister, its slits for windows like black masks staring with enmity at me.

Up to that point I thought I had memorized the turnings we had taken, but trying to see our route as a map in my mind, I knew I had lost my bearings. Turn left; turn right . . . I was in a part of Bou Hammagan where instinct told me no strange woman should ever go. I was there—and I had no idea how to get out again.

Although the passage was shaded from the sun by the dilapidated evil-smelling hovels, the airlessness and my own fear made my body sweat, so that my clothes stuck to me as if glued there; my hair clung to my neck, and my feet burned as if I had walked on red-hot coals. The haphazard alleys through which I followed the boy were a maze to those who did not live in them. I saw that I could walk for hours and find that all I had done was to move in circles. Suddenly some sixth sense warned me of a danger I hadn't defined. Was I being taken to a place where the diary awaited me, or was I walking into a trap? I stopped still. The boy, no longer able to hear my footsteps, turned. His thin, clawing little hand reached out and grabbed my arm again. I shook him off.

"I take . . . I take . . ."

"No, you do not. I'm going back."

He might not understand my words, but my meaning was plain. His eyes changed, grew dark with childish anger. He was seeing the bribe he must have been promised slipping away from him if he didn't bring me to the place where someone awaited me.

Pippa's diary, or someone waiting for me? I didn't dare think for what reason. Perhaps Mark had incurred a man's anger and I was walking toward the avenger.

"Lady—" He turned and pointed to the end of the alley and then did a little twist with his fingers to denote the way we would be going. So, there would be more alleys, more foul-smelling tunnels of streets strangely deserted and yet filled with invisible watching eyes.

I shook my head, turned on my heel and began to retrace my steps. The boy called to me, but I ignored him, and as I quickened my pace, my sandals made a hollow, echoing noise. The boy was following me and, as his unintelligible words rose to a shout, faces appeared under the cracked and broken arches that led into the stone hovels that seemed, in my sudden fear, to have acquired feet and be closing in on me.

I began to run, but the boy, sent to lead me like a small Lucifer out of the light into darkness, was as fleet of foot and was determined to drag me his way as I was to escape by mine. His little talons dug into my arm and his singsong whine began again. "You come. I take . . ."

After the flash of intuition that had stopped me following him, I no longer believed that I would find the diary at the end of the journey, or that money was the objective. No one would believe that I would be carrying a sufficient amount around with me. Only a few moments ago it had seemed a wild and unreal thought that I, and not money, was the objective. It was becoming only too feasible. The boy was obviously a street urchin and would not be paid much for me. Perhaps if I gave him money, he would be satisfied and stop pestering me. I opened my purse and got out some silver and tossed it to the ground. He flung himself down, groping for it.

A ginger dog ran out of a side alley and leaped in front of me, barking. I tried to avoid it, stumbled and fell against a wall. In those precious moments I lost the advantage of distance between us. The boy had collected the money and was racing after me again. I pushed myself away from the wall and felt fingers crawl around from behind my elbow and touch my purse. I snatched my arm away and, without looking back to see who had clawed at me from an open doorway, ran on. I felt that I was in some kind of nightmare, racing for my life through an oven. The backs of my heels were sore where my sandals had rubbed them, my hair fell in streaks over my face and I did not pause to push it back.

The alley led into another and at the end of that there were two. I had no time to stop and choose. I dashed down the left-hand one, past some men carrying straw. A man lay in the shadow of one of the houses, his djellabah wrapped about him, his sandals under his head for a pillow. He was fast asleep and didn't even stir as I rushed noisily past him. A strange, sickly sweet smell came out from behind the dirty sacking curtain over a door. I registered it vaguely as possibly some kind of drug being smoked.

I was reaching a state where I didn't care whether I could recognize a landmark or not so long as I could find human contact instead of these secret alleys where a child raced after me to stop my escape. I should have outdistanced him easily except that he was more used to the heat than I and probably geared to speed by frequent stealing from the *souks* and escaping.

The moment when I had no more breath left came too soon. I had to stop, and leaned against a wall, carefully avoiding any open doorway. The boy made one wild rush to reach me, stumbled and went sprawling, letting out a loud yowl. He had seemed to fall awkwardly and could have hurt himself. We were far enough away from where he had been taking me for me to go to him. My speedy move to his side was purely instinctive. My heart was still thudding and any moment I felt my knees would buckle underneath me. But he was, after all, a little boy and he needed help. For one moment, as I reached his side, I wondered if the fall was a ruse to attract my sympathy. But then I saw real tears coursing down his dark, dirty little face. "You've hurt yourself."

He lifted his robe and, weeping noisily and not very cleanly, showed me a grazed knee.

I put my arms around him and heaved him to his feet. "It's not a bad graze," I said. "Let me see you walk." I took his hand, as hot and sticky as mine, and made him walk a few steps with me. He neither limped nor cried in pain, and I realized that he had wept, not because of a grazed knee, but from sheer frustration and disappointment. By not following him I had deprived him of a small and precious bribe, and my handful of silver was merely a bonus.

I dropped his hand. "Go back." I pointed over his head. "Go on, and tell whoever wanted to see me that I've no intention of walking into a trap."

He stopped crying and, running the sleeve of his djellabah across his nose, stared hopefully at me.

"Finish!" I made a gesture of finality with my hands.

He looked swiftly over his shoulder and, following his glance, I saw a tall man striding along the alley. His hood shaded his face, so that I could see nothing to distinguish him. But my heightened sense of danger saw a link between them—the boy's sudden hesitation, his glance upward as if expecting the man to speak to him were proof enough to me. *The master has come after his servant because the servant has taken too long to collect his prey.*

I plunged down the nearest alley.

People, donkeys, hens and children scattered as I ran. At least I was entering a more populated area; the doorways no longer gaped emptily and the streets were not menacing and deserted. If I were manhandled, someone here would surely intervene. I paused as I turned another corner and looked behind me. The man was keeping a fair distance as if he were completely uninterested in me—or as if he knew he could spring forward and catch up with me at any moment.

Then suddenly, over the flat roofs I saw the blue dome of the mosque, and I knew that I was near the Square. I only had to try to find the breath and the effort to run straight on into that safe place where I could dodge my pursuers among the crowds. I even slowed down, turning to look over my shoulder.

The man had paused and a woman was speaking to him. She wore Western dress, but her skin was a pale coffee color and her black hair fanned out over her shoulders. I saw her make a swift, impatient movement with her hand as if stressing a point, and then she turned, apparently to look at me. For a moment before she walked away, I saw a great silver medallion glitter in the shaft of sunlight down the narrow street.

She was beautiful, she was young and I had seen her profile once before. Pippa had pointed her out to us when she was seated at the table where Pippa had seen Mark.

My attention had been too long on her. When I looked back at the man and the boy, they seemed to be arguing. I saw the man's arm go up as if giving some order to the boy. The sleeve of his djellabah fell away and there was something large and glittering at the man's wrist. As I turned and ran again, I had a single irrelevant thought. Strange that a Hammagarb living in a poor quarter of the city could afford so magnificent a piece of gold, for gold it must have been, since nothing tawdry would have shone so richly.

XVIII

THE ALLEY widened into a street and the street into Isakila Square. To my left, an old man I hadn't noticed before sat cross-legged, carving the figures for a chess set out of cedar wood.

The lamp hanging over the door of Harriet's house stood out clearly against the sky and spelled sanctuary. I had no need to cross the Square and climb the long stepped street alone. I took the last lap of my journey in long exhausted strides, like those of a sprinter barely making the finish line, and reached out and pulled the bell. The jangle it made mingled with the noises around me, but no one opened the pitted wooden door. I glanced quickly over my shoulder and could see neither the boy, nor the man, nor the girl. Breathless and sick with a paradox of relief and fear, I leaned against the door. At that moment it opened and I went headlong into the courtyard.

"What on earth are you doing?" Harriet's voice was like a choir of angels.

I leaned heavily against her and, thin though she was, she was like a rock. "Hey, hold up!"

"Shut the door. Shut the door."

"Don't tell me you've been running in this heat; you must be crazy. Come on in and have a drink. A brandy—or, no, we haven't any. Wine . . ."

"Something soft . . . A lemon drink, if you have it."

"Is that Cathy?" Alexandra's deep, low voice came from inside the house.

"It is," Harriet called, "and she looks like hell. Go on in." She propelled me with one hand in the small of my back. "My dear girl, you're wringing wet."

"I'm also scared," I said.

Alexandra, sitting in a rattan chair by the arched doorway leading to the courtyard, leaned forward, looking at me closely. "What happened?" Her voice was sharp.

I sat down in a second cane chair and ran the back of my hand over my forehead. "You could say that I've had an adventure and it wasn't very nice."

"Here, drink some of this." Harriet thrust a glass of something at me. "It's strong and it's not particularly thirst-quenching, but you look as if you'd had a shock and it'll do you good." As I hesitated, she added, "It's all right, you won't fall flat on your face. It's a Toulal wine—one of the new ones from that area, and the only North African wine Justin will deign to drink—though that's because he likes to feel he's a connoisseur, which of course he isn't."

Her irrelevant remarks gave me a chance to calm myself, which I suspected was her intention, but she was right. The ruby-dark wine didn't refresh me, and I would far rather have had a lemon drink.

They were both patient with me, waiting until I had finished the wine before they asked me again what had happened. I sat quietly and was grateful to them.

The shutters were closed over the windows and the living room was dim, but its characteristic untidiness gave me a sense of comfort. When I had drunk most of the wine, I told the two of them what had happened.

Harriet's reaction shook me. She burst into derisive laughter. "Oh, really, Cathy, how could you fall for that one? A wretched little urchin spins you a story about knowing who stole Pippa's diary. He wouldn't

166

know Ahmed—he's too grand—but the child probably knows Yussef or heard him talking about it and saw a way of making some easy money. So he watched you leave the house, followed you and got his story over to you. And you bit. Oh, ducky, how you bit!" She threw back her head, still laughing.

"Harriet, stop it!" Alexandra's voice cut across the laughter like a whip.

"But it's so obvious."

"I wonder?" Alexandra frowned. "You could be right, of course, but that doesn't alter the fact that it must have been a frightening experience for Cathy."

"Of course it was, but she doesn't know Africa yet. I do."

Alexandra's fingers drummed on the arms of her chair. "I don't pretend to understand the people here, but it's just possible that someone really meant to get Cathy away to some place where they could rob her. Nothing is so outrageous that someone in the world doesn't think of it. And robbery, unfortunately, is only too common."

"And then," I said, "there was the girl."

"What girl?"

"The one Pippa saw at the café table on our first morning. I recognized her by a huge medallion she wears."

Alexandra asked, "Who is she, Harriet?"

"How should I know?" she snapped back as if angry at being asked.

"Where does she come into your story, Cathy?" Alexandra asked.

"She spoke to the man. They were all three together, the girl, the boy and the man."

Alexandra got up and went into the courtyard. I saw her open the door to the street and look out.

After a few moments she closed the door and came back. "If the boy had really been sent to fetch Cathy—heaven knows why—and the girl and the man were following, I thought that they might have seen her come here and be waiting for her. But there's no one in sight."

I finished my drink, put down my glass and asked, "Why am I in danger?"

Neither of them answered me. I looked from Harriet in her pink shirt and dark cotton slacks to Alexandra, elegant in a brown and white dress.

I asked, unable to stop the belligerence in my voice, "Or do you still think there are perfectly simple explanations for everything that has happened?"

The hesitation was too long and Harriet's answer too bright and forced. "Oh, Cathy, really . . . As if anyone could wish to harm you. Try to realize that this is Africa, not London. You're a stranger here, so you haven't yet got used to the odd things that can happen."

"Like Louise's silver box," I said.

"Oh, that damned box!"

A dog in the nearby courtyard was giving short, sharp yelps of protest.

Alexandra said, "If Pippa saw the young woman with Mark, then it is he whom you should question, Cathy."

"Yes, I know."

"She may be someone who cleans for the television people, or shops for them."

"She may be." Suddenly I didn't want to talk about her.

Alexandra must have sensed this, for she said, "Shall we go home before the heat gets too fierce?"

I rose, thinking with relief of Alexandra's garden.

Harriet came to the door with us. "Don't ever again follow Hammagarb urchins, and if you are alone, always stay around Isakila Square."

Alexandra and I didn't talk much as we walked back to the House of the Fountains, and she seemed preoccupied. We were halfway up the stepped street when she suddenly took my hand. "Cathy, be happy here and don't worry. I'm quite certain everything will come right in the end. Things always do if people would only give themselves time. It's rushing into explanations and showdowns that spoil relationships."

"Relationships . . . you mean, between Mark and me?"

I had a feeling that she had not expected me to be so direct. Although she was my hostess, we could not really be called friends, since we knew so little about each other. In her circle, perhaps, one parried such a question, finding some sophisticated answer.

She said at last, "I mean, no relationship should be—well—too laid bare. There has to be subtlety."

And she was afraid that I would not be subtle in my dealings with Mark any more than a moment ago I had been with her.

"You think," I said, and reached the last step before the door of the house, "that I shouldn't ask Mark tonight about the girl. That's what you mean, isn't it?"

"My dear, how you behave toward your husband is your own affair. Let's not get profound."

I felt I had annoyed or embarrassed her by my bluntness, but as we entered the courtyard, she said easily, "I hope you need a long cool drink as much as I do. I can't drink Harriet's wine, and I doubt that it made you feel any better." She slid an arm around my shoulder as we entered the Women's Garden. "Now, Cathy, you can relax."

It was like a benediction, a forgiveness for my lack of savoir-faire. But behind it, I knew I had read a warning. *Don't demand too much of Mark. Leave him his freedom . . .* But freedom with me or without me?

One thing lifted Pippa's spirits that evening. Alexandra had bought her a child's embroidered caftan of pink silk. Pippa, who had lost her radiance since the disappearance of the diary, swiftly brightened as she undid Alexandra's parcel and then rushed to her bedroom.

A few minutes later she appeared at the door to the patio wearing the caftan. Her hair was released from its thin strip of ribbon and lay around her shoulders, and the pink silk of the robe highlighted her tanned skin. On her wrist she wore the silver bracelets Mark had given her.

"Look . . . look . . ." She paraded in front of us, trying to undulate like a model and managing to look what she was, a little girl dressed up. She went prancing through the archway, picking an olean-der flower as she went and wafting along like a pint-sized Ophelia going happily mad.

"It's very kind of you," I said, "but—"

Alexandra stopped me. "Oh, Cathy, don't protest. If I can do something to give Pippa pleasure and take her mind off her disappointment, then surely you can't object?"

It would have seemed ungracious to do so, yet I was afraid that if Alexandra intended to continue to give Pippa presents on such a lavish scale, the transition into our quiet, unpretentious London life would make her dissatisfied. One day she would be a little rich girl but, by then, I hoped she would be old enough to understand discrimination.

Mark and I sat together in the Women's Garden. Alexandra was having her hair washed by Lisette and we wouldn't see her again that night. Pippa was in bed. Throughout my wild escape from a dirty little boy that morning I had clung to the exercise books, and when I gave them to Pippa she thanked me without enthusiasm.

Whether she wrote in one that night or not I had no idea. For although I had hung around my bedroom watching for the strip of light under the door to remain on while she recorded her day, it had gone out almost as soon as I had left her.

From where Mark and I sat, I saw that her room stayed dark, and I hoped that she was asleep, tired out with a day at the pool and her own emotions.

The night around us was deep and rich, with the stars so low that they seemed to be suspended on invisible threads from the sapphire sky. The fountain had not yet been turned off and the sound of the water was like plucked strings.

I had already told Mark what had happened that morning. But when I came to the part about the man and the girl, I didn't describe her, nor did I mention the silver medallion. I knew I would have to tell him about that too, but cowardlike, I postponed the moment.

"It could very well be that the diary was stolen, because servants here, like servants everywhere, talk. And someone overheard a conversation and took a chance on you being prepared to pay for its return."

"That's what Harriet said."

"When the boy got you well and truly lost, he'd have snatched your purse and run. Don't do that again, Cathy. So far as Pippa is concerned, she'll have forgotten it all by the time she gets back to England. Now, what else is new?"

I told him about Alexandra's latest gift to Pippa.

"Well, if she wants to, let her. It gives her pleasure."

"I know, but in a way I feel there's a double snag to it. For one thing, it could spoil Pippa; for another, it makes us beholden to Alexandra."

He threw back his head and laughed. "Oh, Cathy, 'beholden' . . . because of a few gifts to a child?"

"Yes."

"That's silly. You know I shall repay Alexandra's kindness. We could have her to stay with us in London and give her a royal time at the theaters and art galleries. So, stop worrying."

"You don't stop worrying by just pressing a button inside you."

"But you can stop it by facing the fact that our being here is a diversion for Alexandra. She has nothing to do and no family to consider. She has always been easily bored. Don't imagine that when we get back to London she'll send Pippa costly presents—she'll probably forget all about her. Alexandra has no emotion, you know, no desire for love and no maternal instinct."

"Mark—"

"What is it?"

"I haven't told you all the story."

He sat very quietly, looking ahead into the banks of flowers drained of color by the night.

"When I found that I was almost back at Isakila Square, I relaxed —I felt that nobody would dare harm me with all those people looking on. That's when I turned around. Someone was talking to the boy and I've seen her before. She's beautiful and she wears a big silver medallion on a chain. When we walked through the Square on our first morning, she was sitting at a café table and . . . you remember, Pippa said you were sitting with her."

He leaned away from me to brush off an insect that had found its way into the screened patio. In my heightened, imaginative state, the withdrawal seemed symbolic, as if I had said something that had flung a barrier between us. But it was impossible to leave my words hanging upon a silence which I felt Mark had no intention of breaking. "Pippa is very observant," I said. "She didn't make a mistake, did she?"

"No."

"So you *do* know the girl."

"I know a great many people here. Why not? Before you came we used to spend any free evenings in the cafés. The walls of the house we've rented are bulging with us and our equipment. If we'd stayed in at night we'd have been at each other's throats. The rest of the crowd still sit in the cafés."

I brought the conversation back to the girl. "She was there, though, in that awful squalid street and she knew them, the man and the boy."

"If you live in a small town, you know everyone."

"Bou Hammagan isn't that small."

"Judged by most places I have to go to—"

"Mark, who is that girl?"

"Part Turkish and part Greek. And her name is Zaleida. Does that satisfy you?" There was a hint of impatience behind the light inconsequence of his voice.

"Can I meet her?"

"If I see her when we are together, yes, you can. But she's not intelligent and I doubt that you'd have anything in common."

I was putting too many questions, trying to tear information out of him. And in the end there would only be the essential question, "What is she to you?" And that I could not ask. For one thing, if there were women in Mark's life when he was away from me, I didn't want to know. Of all my memories, one would never leave me. Mark saying, "I can't be possessed, Cathy. I can only exist if I feel free in my work and my life."

Mark's arm brushed mine. I heard words pour out of me. "I love you—as I understand love. But I'm no martyr. My survival is the most important thing to me. My life. The present; the future. But if I stay here, in North Africa, I have a terrifying feeling that I shall have no future. I've told you this before, and you've said you wanted me to stay here—but I'm getting to a point where every time I go out, I feel I should look over my shoulder in case someone—or something—is there to harm me." Saying it aloud sounded melodramatic, but I couldn't help that. I was being honest with Mark.

"Then what do you want to do?"

"Go home. But I can't because I have undertaken a job. If I threw that chance up, I'd not only be letting myself down but Chris, too. I must wait for the church commissioners to make up their minds. I hate this waiting and I'll try to see David tomorrow about it. But whatever I feel about things, I *can't* just leave Africa."

"A matter of principle."

"And my own ambition. Mark, you love your work; I love mine."

"You also have the window to do for Alexandra, haven't you?"

"She has approved the design for that and I've only got to work on the color and get her to agree to that. Of course it will be completed in Chris's workshops."

Mark hadn't once looked my way. He sat a little distance from me on the long seat, and his profile, dimly outlined in light, was remote. "I want you to stay."

When I had first come to North Africa, it would have been wonderful to hear those words. Listening to them now, all I could ask was, "Why? Why, Mark?"

"That's an odd question. Because I'm here, of course."

"But most of the time you *can't* be here. You have to be away so much."

"You knew what my job entailed before you married me."

"I'm not complaining. Please, please understand. I'm just stating a fact. All right, so I'm scared; so I can't toss something off as being just the gesture of a sick mind . . ."

"I haven't yet discovered how Louise's box came to be here. That, I think, is what we are talking about."

And the girl? . . . But I held the words back, recognizing the edge that had crept into his voice as a danger signal.

"Now, shall we just go into the courtyard and take a look at the night before we go to bed? This patio is fine, but it's a bit enclosed. I like breathing space."

I was weak; I was bartering my unhappy curiosity for Mark's approval of me as a nondemanding wife. "Let's go," I said.

We stood together in the courtyard and looked up at the stars hanging glittering above our heads and smelled the smells of Africa.

"Do you know what I would like to do now?" Mark asked. "I'd like to drive out into the desert. It will be cool and vast and peaceful. But I won't. It will be more sensible to sleep."

On our way through the hall I paused and said, "Do you know that if anyone stands near that wall or sits on that divan and talks, someone standing by the same wall in our bedroom can hear everything that's being said?"

"I've heard of that happening in some new buildings, but I didn't know such flaws existed in old ones. The walls here are so thick. But there could be a small room that, for some reason or other, was sealed up. That sometimes happens, and if there's one here, then it would make the wall seem hollow." He picked up a strand of my hair, twisted it in a loose rope and laid it across my throat, his eyes amused. "So when you discovered it, you just blatantly eavesdropped. And what did you hear?"

I moved away from him without answering.

"What did you hear?" he asked again.

I lost my courage. "Oh. Casual conversation," I said, and thought in despair, *Once frankness is lost, all hope is gone*. Yet, paradoxically, by my evasion I was trying to hold on to harmony between us.

At that moment something moved at my feet and I gave a small scream.

"It's only a lizard caught out late at night and disturbed by the lights. It's gone. Oh, Cathy, would you scream at a mouse in London?"

We looked at each other and suddenly the tension broke.

"I love you when you laugh," Mark said. "Your whole face lights up."

"It was over such a silly thing."

"It's the small things we make or break our lives on, so go on laughing at them."

"And you want me to stay here?"

"Would I be wanting to make love to you tonight if I were wishing you'd go?"

Again, the non-answer; a question for question.

As we reached our room I looked down and saw, through the wrought-iron balustrade, Ahmed in the hall, padding silently to the wall switch. He gave us a long look and I had a feeling that he had been waiting to speak to one of us. To Mark? To me? But because we were together, he changed his mind. I could have been quite wrong. It was possible that he was only wanting to turn off the lights and go to bed. I wondered how much of the conversation of the house he heard as he waited, like an actor in the wings, to make his entry to serve, to attend, to ring down the curtain at the end of the day.

XIX

AFTER DINNER the following night Mark left to call briefly at the office. Alexandra and I sat in the patio drinking coffee, with the inevitable bowl of figs and apricots on the small ebony table in front of us. Pippa was hunched on her favorite hassock, hands clasped around her knees, leaning a little against Alexandra and watching the quiescent cheetah with adoring eyes.

"Choose." Alexandra held out both hands and Pippa looked up at her, hesitating. Then she said firmly, "I'll have *that* one."

In the palm of Alexandra's left hand lay a small garnet-and-pearl-cluster ring. "I used to wear that when I was a little girl," Alexandra said. "It's too small for my fingers now. I want you to have it."

"Oh, please—" I said quickly, "it's kind of you, but . . ."

Pippa swung around on me. "You don't want anyone to give me anything, do you, Cathy? But *you* couldn't wear it. Your hands are too big. It fits my middle finger." She held her hand up defiantly for me to see. "Oh, Alexandra, it's lovely. Thank you."

"You really mustn't mind, Cathy. I didn't even know I still had it. I have no sentiment, you see. But I found it at the bottom of my jewel case and, as I say, it's of no use to me."

Pippa gave me a look of shining triumph and waved her hand about so that the dark-red stones glowed.

From deep in the house the telephone rang, and when Ahmed came and announced that someone wished to speak to Pippa, she sprang to her feet, her eyes alight with excitement. "Someone—wants—me?" She cast a swift, questioning glance at Alexandra, who waved her toward the house.

"Go and answer it. It's probably one of your Mitchell friends. Did you ask the name?" She turned to Ahmed.

"He spoke in a very low voice, madame, and he sounded in a hurry."

Pippa had not waited for Ahmed's explanation, but had fled to the telephone. Her voice did not carry as far as the patio, but she came back with an even greater flurry of lean tanned legs and flying arms, flinging herself at the hassock and miraculously landing without overbalancing, her face radiant. "My diary. Someone has found my diary."

My heart gave a lurch. "Who was it on the telephone?"

"I don't know." She was impatient with unimportant questions. "He didn't tell me who he was, but he spoke funnily." She reached out for a fig, bit into it and said, her lips stained with the rich juice, "He said 'Is that Missa Mountavon?' and I knew he meant 'Miss' and so I said 'Yes,' and he said"—she paused and swallowed the last of the fig—"he said 'I will call you later this evening and tell you how you can get your diary back.' And I said, 'Tell me *now*,' and he just laughed and then there wasn't any more."

Alexandra frowned. "But how on earth did he get hold of it?"

"And," I asked, "why telephone?"

We each had questions the other couldn't answer, but I was seized with anger that whoever was playing games with us was involving a child. "Why call again?" I demanded. "Why not tell Pippa when she would have her diary back—and if he were going to demand payment, why not tell her—or one of us—what his price is?"

Pippa looked at me. "Suppose he asks thousands and thousands?"

"That," I said, "would be most unlikely. He probably thinks in small sums."

176

"Then I can pay," Pippa said grandly.

She could, of course, this little rich girl.

Much later that evening, after I had difficulty in getting an excited child to bed, I was halfway down the stairs when Alexandra called to me that there was someone on the telephone asking for Pippa. "A man who will give no name," she said. "But it's just possible I may recognize his voice, so if you like, I'll take the call."

I went through to the Women's Garden and waited at the door to the patio, my fingers stroking the petals of a yellow rose.

I could hear Alexandra's impatient voice trying to trick the man into giving himself away. "But how will we know you? Someone could be listening in . . . Oh, I see . . . Very well, I will go to the bank tomorrow . . . All right, then, no new notes . . . Yes, I understand perfectly."

A moment or two later, I heard Alexandra's footsteps behind me.

"That man," she said, "is still nameless. But he has the impertinence of Satan. Do you know what he said?"

I shook my head. I doubted that anything would surprise me.

"That the diary will be returned."

"But that's wonderful."

"You haven't heard the condition." She bent and caressed Durandal. "It is that we all leave this house tomorrow night at ten o'clock —even the servants. If we do that, the diary will be here when we return after midnight."

"But I don't understand. Why such cloak-and-dagger means?"

"There's money involved, of course. We are to leave it on a table in the hall," Alexandra said. "So you see, if you had followed the boy yesterday, someone would have been waiting to take your purse, as I thought."

"How much are they asking?"

"Curiously enough, the payment is to be in Moroccan money, fourteen hundred dirhams, which is equivalent to a hundred pounds."

"Mark will never agree."

"Whatever he says is unimportant. I am to leave the money on the first small table in the hall."

"You didn't recognize the voice?"

"Unfortunately, no. I can't think why I was so optimistic in imagining that I could—one Hammagarb voice speaking broken English sounds to me just like another. I doubt that even Harriet would have been able to help."

"You told him you would leave the money on a particular table, so whoever the man is, he must know the house."

"It wasn't quite like that. I told him where I would leave the notes. It's obvious that the reason for the theft of Pippa's diary is reward, though I'm afraid I don't understand why the whole thing has become such an elaborate affair."

If I accepted the matter at the level of the obvious, Alexandra was right. Yet the facile explanation of the boy's attempt to lead me to the diary was quite unacceptable. No one would imagine that I walked around a strange and as yet unenlightened African town with a hundred pounds in my purse. The telephone call didn't make sense to me either. Money could have been sent and the diary returned without anyone coming near the house. The whole plan was too elaborate for the simplicity of a small cash transaction. "But you can't leave your house completely empty. Mark would never agree—"

"What is it I won't agree to?" He came through the screen door.

Alexandra said, "You'd better go and get yourself a drink before we tell you. It's rather an odd story."

"Then I think I'd like to hear it with a clear head," he said and sat down in a chair in the shadows. Outside the screen, insects wheeled in drunken dances. Inside, we were all very still.

"Cathy"—Alexandra turned to me—"Mark won't refuse a drink if you put one in his hand. So would you like to get one for him while I tell him what happened? You see, I know that if you stay you'll try to dissuade him from letting me do what I fully intend to."

Glad of a chance for action, I went into the house and brought a whiskey back to Mark. He was saying, "I'll get the money tomorrow on my way to the garage. Cathy can come with me and bring it back."

"Oh, Mark, no. Don't expect Cathy to walk from the bank, of all places, on her own."

"She'll be all right. I'll see her as far as the steps. Bou Hammagan isn't a den of thieves."

"It seems to me," I said coldly, "that that's just what it is. But I'd come with you to get the money only, Mark, you just *can't* let Alexandra empty her house and lay it open for a possible pack of thieves you say don't exist here."

"I said that no one would attack you on the way from the bank," he said, "and I mean that. I'll be with you as far as the steps and this street is very safe."

"I don't understand you. You're letting Alexandra run this risk in a house full of treasures—"

"Just a minute, Cathy," Alexandra interrupted me. "You haven't waited to hear what I've already explained to Mark. Surely you give me credit for a little quick thinking. My house may be empty, but it will be watched. Pippa is my guest and she has a right to her diary and, at the same time, I have a right to protect my home." She looked at me through amused, half-closed eyes. "I have the perfect plan that will safeguard my possessions and reveal who it is who is demanding all that money for a child's diary. Yussef will be stationed on the adjoining roof—he knows the family who live there—and Ahmed will be hidden in a doorway across the street. He can stand so still that he could be taken for a shadow. And don't think that is all I shall be doing. There will also be concealed cameras just inside the doors leading to the courtyard and the Women's Garden. As soon as the man crosses either threshold, his photograph will be on the film for the police when I hand it over to them. What more precautions could I take, and what more certain way of catching whoever enters my house?"

"If you had the police here, too—"

"From what I know of them here, they'd botch it, anyway."

"Mark, please—" I appealed to him. "Don't let Alexandra agree to this."

"It looks as if we have no alternative. I know Alexandra of old. Once she had made up her mind to a thing"—he shrugged—"you can't move her."

I saw a look pass between them, the cool understanding of two people who regarded each other without emotion, with an acceptance that the years, and nothing deeper, had cemented their friendship.

"I'm going to tell Ahmed and Yussef what has happened and give them their instructions." Alexandra rose, and as she passed me she touched my shoulder lightly. "Don't worry." The silken caftan she wore gave little hissing sounds like a drowsy sea on a warm shore.

"You'll be here tomorrow night, won't you?" I said to Mark.

"I'm sorry, but I can't. We shall be driving to Bodaia so that we reach it just before dawn. I'll have to leave here before the crucial ten o'clock."

"But you must have some sleep."

"We'll snatch some at the office. We always arrange it that way when we have to do night driving. It's the only way of making certain that the whole crew is together and no one is whooping it up somewhere or other, or oversleeps. You'll be all right, Cathy. You'll have Alexandra and Harriet and Justin, as well as the servants. Whoever it is who is being so damned melodramatic over this is really only after the money. He obviously doesn't want trouble."

I so wanted Mark to be right that I ended the conversation there.

I could hear Alexandra returning, and I got up and went under the arch into the courtyard and sat on the seat under the orange tree. Between the leaves and the rich hanging fruit I could see the roofs of neighboring houses, and just as I could look up at that crumbling balustrade, so anyone on that roof could see down into this corner of Alexandra's garden.

Perhaps someone had stood on a roof nearby and watched us—watched a child writing in a book; watched me; watched Mark . . .

The fascination of Bou Hammagan, the flavor of it, was so much more Oriental than in the more famous North African cities which catered to tourists. It caught hold of the imagination and the emotions and cast its spell. Yet the fascination of the labyrinthine streets, the loveliness of Alexandra's garden, the exciting presence of the desert on the doorstep—all these were tainted with a shadow of the snake in Eden: the knowledge of evil.

XX

AHMED and Yussef had already gone to their watching posts, and Alexandra, who admitted that she disliked Harriet's house "which always smells of turpentine" was joining the Mitchells at the hotel. She told me that she hadn't explained to them what was happening. "I thought we'd better keep it to ourselves, for the moment, at any rate. I'm taking Lisette with me and telling the Mitchells that I want her to see something in one of the display cabinets there. It's a rather fine leather box tooled in gold which, if she likes it, I'll give her for her birthday. It's as good an excuse as I can think of to get her out of the house with me."

Alexandra showed me the cameras, both partially hidden behind pillars, which would function as soon as someone stepped on the rugs just inside the doors. She explained that someone in Paris had shown her how to set up such camera devices. "And with Yussef watching from the adjoining roof, and Ahmed waiting across the street to follow whoever comes, the man hasn't the remotest chance of escaping."

The evening dragged with desperate slowness. Mark left about nine o'clock and Pippa, overexcited at the drama of her diary, clung to him and upbraided him for leaving her. "You don't have to go out, Daddy, *please* . . . I want you to stay—"

"If I did," he said, disengaging her, "I'd be out of a job and you'd have to keep me."

"I could. I'm rich."

"I know. That's why I'm always so nice to you."

From the patio we could hear his banter continuing as Pippa went with him to the street door. We were all three of us restless for the next hour, and I kept wondering if Alexandra was regretting her generosity and the inconvenience to which the elaborate plan was putting her. But it was too late to protest.

We sat listening to music from some foreign station, watching the deep avenues of light thrust by the lamps through the shadows of the garden. Pippa was drawing the patterns of the tiles with her toe, her thin silver bracelets jangling, fretting and impatient for ten o'clock. She had been warned by Mark not to be a nuisance over the evening arrangements and was making a valiant attempt to hold herself in check.

I said, "Suppose it's all a hoax?"

Pippa lifted her head sharply, watching us.

"I don't think it is," Alexandra said. "And, anyway, we must take a chance on it. After all, the fact remains, Pippa's diary is missing." She glanced at her watch, a golden dial enclosed in small emeralds. "It's almost ten o'clock." She rose and went into the house, picked up a light peacock-blue cloak, and as she returned wearing it, Harriet and Justin arrived to collect Pippa and me. We all left together, parting in Isakila Square, Alexandra and Lisette crossing toward the hotel and the rest of us going past the mosque and the dark *souks* and the clusters of men carrying on their conversations in doorways.

Justin was complaining, "For heaven's sake, why has Alexandra agreed to such elaborate precaution just for—"

Harriet gave him an enormous nudge. Pippa, who was walking ahead of us, had obviously not heard, and Justin continued in a lower voice, "A child's scribble. It's absurd—"

"It would be," I said, "if that were entirely the reason, but it isn't."

"Then what is it?" he demanded.

"I don't know," I said unhappily.

"Oh, well, we'll all be wiser after midnight." Justin neatly avoided a dog sprawled asleep in a shadow and walked ahead and joined Pippa. I saw him take her hand and say something that made her glance up at him, giggling.

The street where Harriet and Justin lived was ill-lit and narrow. The shadows cast by the crusty walls with their heavy grilles were a thick, dead black, relieved only by the single light that burned over the door. The sounds of our footsteps and the door opening disturbed a dog which began to bark and, as we entered the house, there was a strong smell of the turpentine Alexandra hated.

Pippa, swiftly observant, crossed the room to a painting propped up on one of the rattan chairs. "What's that?"

Harriet said, "So, I don't paint good likenesses. Well, nobody does these days; realistic painting is out of fashion. *That,* my dear Pippa, is where I believe you went with Cathy and your father—the Kourifia Caves."

"Oh." She stared at it, pulling a strand of her hair across her mouth and biting on it. "I didn't see it like that."

Harriet said, "Trust a child to tell you the truth. Never mind, it's a commission and the man who wants it likes—as he put it—'a bit of the abstract, just to be up-to-date.' So, why should I mind that Pippa doesn't think much of it?"

"Oh, but I do." She swung around and flung out her arms, embracing the world. "I think lots about everything here, now . . . now . . . I *love* tonight."

I should be loving tonight, too, or rather be grateful for it, since, at the end of it, it was possible that the source of all the menace that seemed to encircle us would be made clear.

Justin said, "I think we'd better have a drink, don't you?"

"And can I go into your studio and use your paints and paint something?" Pippa asked.

I answered her. "No. Harriet says you can sleep in her bed for a few hours . . ."

"Oh, but—" Her eyes flashed resentment at me and then, obviously thinking better of it, she lapsed into silence.

"I'll wake you at midnight and we'll all go back to the house."

She let me take her up to Harriet's bedroom and, free of dress and sandals, lay down protesting only mildly, calling to me as I turned to go, "You *will* wake me, won't you? You won't let me stay here till morning?"

"I'll wake you, and that's a promise." I touched her cheek lightly and left her.

The stairs in the house were rough, uncarpeted wood, but my sandals made little sound. I could hear Harriet and Justin talking, but when I entered the room, the conversation ceased so abruptly that I knew they had been talking about me.

"Oh, Cathy." Harriet shot me an overbright smile. "Has Pippa been difficult?"

"I can't reasonably expect her to go straight off to sleep: she's too excited. But at least she's resting."

Harriet was leaning against the wall, her fingers beating a tattoo on a small table loaded with papers and English and French magazines. Her eyes were on me with a curious, speculative look. "We were talking about Mark."

And me, I thought, and said aloud, "What *about* Mark?"

"I do think he should have stayed with you until midnight. He could quite easily have driven himself to Bodaia afterward."

"He might not know the way," I said.

"There's nothing to worry about." Justin spoke reassuringly. "Either the diary is returned, or if it isn't, it won't be world-shattering."

Harriet got up and said that whether we wanted any or not, she was going to make coffee.

"I could do with a gallon." Justin stretched himself like an elegant cat and began to talk to me about native life in Bou Hammagan. I listened, amazed at the knowledge he had of North African life. Behind his lethargy was a good brain that worked well when it chose.

I could smell the rich scent of coffee as Justin said, "You should try to get Mark to take you to Tunisia while you're here. It's full of Roman ruins—a temple to Mercury, palaces, thermal baths."

"I sometimes think"—Harriet entered, carrying the coffee tray—"that Justin has an obsession with this place. I can't think why. It's hot and dry and dusty in summer and cold in winter."

"Every man, Harriet dear, must have a love affair with someone —or something."

"Like Mark with his work." Harriet poured coffee. "Though when he talks about it, it never seems to me that it's his absorbing passion. So I wonder . . ."

"Then stop wondering and hand over the coffee." There was a rare knife-edged sharpness to Justin's voice. He rose and turned on the radio. Harriet watched him, her mouth pulled down in an un-amused smile.

When eleven o'clock struck, Justin said, "I don't know why we're sitting here like victims before Doomsday. Let's do something."

Harriet yawned fully and noisily. "You do what you like. Cathy, come and look at my pictures."

She had been one of the most talented pupils at art school, and the draftsmanship was still there in the strange, torn landscapes that filled her studio. Savagery and color were her weapons, and she was living in just the kind of place where such things were presented to her every day of her life.

"Most of them," she explained, "are noncommercial. I can't sell them. The majority of tourists want charming, conventional pictures." She pointed to two lying on the table. "I work in that wild way when the devil rides me. Anger gushes out—anger mostly at the bloody unfairness of life."

They had a strange beauty and I told her so. "Harriet, you really can paint!"

"Oh, I know it. But these don't earn our daily bread." She walked over to the wall and turned a couple of canvases around to face me. "*These* do. The obvious Sahara—all nicely shaded, colors muted, polite pieces to hang on a drawing-room wall and to point to and say, 'I saw it just like that. We were there, you know, in Bou Hammagan last year.' What doesn't occur to them is that it wasn't like that—it was far more brutal. You know, I could have been really good and done well had I stayed in England. I've missed out on life, and it's my own damned fault. Oh, Justin is delightful—or so they say. But you can't eat delight; you can't exchange charm for bread and wine."

"Justin works."

"When the agents send him someone who demands a 'gentleman' for a guide. 'Watch the wall, my darling, while the Gentlemen go by.'" Her laugh was hollow, caught up by the smoke from the Egyptian cigarette she had lit. She coughed, swore softly and jabbed it out in a dusty green ashtray. "If money were all that counted, I'd have turned my face to the wall, but I had ideas about love. Stupid to look back on!"

"If you're so unhappy, why don't you leave Justin?"

"Have *you* walked out on Mark? Not on your life. They don't please us, the Mountavons, but they tie us."

"Mark doesn't tie me. He leaves me to my work and I never interfere with his. That way, we have our own lives—together and apart—and that's how we want it."

The question "Have *you* walked out on Mark?" had irritated me, as if Harriet were trying to enter into an alliance with me against the men we had married.

"You talk about your own lives 'together and apart.' Have you never questioned the 'apart' side of it?"

"Why should I?"

"No, while you've got Pippa on your side, why should you? She's the silver cord that binds you both. But watch her, sweetie. Children can be fickle and she's far too intelligent for her own good."

One sentence stuck in my mind. "While you've got Pippa on your side . . ." But Mark's daughter was no longer entirely on my side. Perhaps a little of the excitement of knowing—and Pippa was too bright not to know—that it was she who had set the seal of approval on Mark's marriage to me, had faded. I didn't want to think about it, and most certainly not in Harriet's studio with her knowing eyes watching me.

". . . so why did you?"

Harriet's voice brought me back with a jolt. I looked up from the painting I was staring at without seeing and asked, "Why did I what?"

"Come out here?"

"Because I had a commission. You know that."

She gave me her thin smile. "I'll make a guess you engineered that."

"I most certainly did not," I said indignantly. "You know that architects and engineers and the rest are converging on the New City. I was just one with a chance to come too."

"All right. But I thought perhaps someone could have given you just a little push."

Justin called to me from the courtyard, and I said, trying not to sound too eager and too relieved, "I wonder what he wants?"

"To look at the moon, perhaps," Harriet retorted. "He has a romantic streak."

She was right. Justin was standing watching the enormous moon caught in the topmost branches of the myrtle tree. "Just take a look at that," he said. "It's one of the things I prefer about England. The moon is the right size there—discreet and gentle, and that, by the way, is the way I wish all women were. Here, the moon is"—he shuddered—"like an Amazon's breastplate."

I said, "I'm sorry they've stripped it of all its glamour by landing on it, but I suppose you'd call that being sentimental."

As he turned and looked at me, his face became half luminous, and the light gave his features strange new planes, tilting them, so that he seemed pagan and alien. Yet when he spoke, his voice was gentle. "I wonder if women make the men they marry? Are you changing Mark? But don't answer me. Perhaps the Mountavons never change. I haven't—although I might have improved if I had met someone like you. That's one thing about the girls here in Bou Hammagan. Their men are their masters and they accept it. The only 'rights' they have are the rights men give them."

"They'll soon change that"—I laughed—"when they get Westernized."

"Oh, for heaven's sake." Harriet strode into the courtyard. "Instead of just standing there, Justin, dreaming at the stars, go down and see what's happening at the house. You may be able to help."

"Yussef is young and Ahmed is strong. Thanks, dear, but being noble in battle isn't my way."

"Go," she said. "Oh, go . . ." She was angry and on edge.

"If you like," Justin said, "I'll compromise, since my presence here annoys you. I'll slip down and get us some Turkish delight at Hashim el Krim's."

"Then you can walk a bit farther and—"

Justin grinned at her. "Turkish delight—but definitely no involvement. I have no intention of getting a broken nose." The heavy door banged behind him.

XXI

I REMAINED in the courtyard and listened to the cacophony of sounds beyond the gate. The real, pulsating Oriental city had seeped through the great wall and we were all caught up in it. Harriet confused me. She had saved my life at the Caves, but a few minutes ago in her studio she had seemed to be trying to destroy my faith in Mark. Yet I knew that there was really no confusion. In her strange, reluctant way she liked me and distrusted Mark.

"Coffee, strong and black again, I think, otherwise we won't have our wits about us when we need them," she called to me and then, as I joined her, she said, "If Alexandra hands the man over to the police, you'll have to testify, won't you?"

"To what?"

"Starting with Louise's box, I'd say." She poured coffee. "There could just be a link. And yet I can't see how—"

"If we talk about it," I said, "we'll only go around in circles. Let's get away from it."

"All right. Let's start with art school and you can help me catch up on everyone."

Masters and students were discussed, laughed over, admired and forgotten. We were both playing at being interested in a world far removed and almost unreal as we sat in the small room. I wished Justin would return. He had been gone too long for a short visit to the *souks*. Curiosity overcoming his hatred of involvement, he was probably also watching the House of the Fountains from some shadowed place.

At last it was midnight.

Harriet shot out of her chair. "For God's sake, Justin must know the time. What's he doing? He should be back to fetch us—*both* of us, because I'm going back with you. I've no intention of letting Justin take you and of being left out of the finale. On the other hand, we're not leaving without Justin. I'm not scared during the day, but I don't fancy two European women and a child walking around on their own at this time of night. Let's go and see if he's in sight. It's possible he has stopped to gossip with someone; he gets on well with the people here."

I followed her and when she opened the old, creaking door, I leaned around her shoulder and peered down the dark street.

A man came swiftly and silently out of the shadows almost opposite the house and walked toward us. His left hand went up to pull his hood more closely over his head, and as he did so, the light above Harriet's door caught him and I saw the glitter of gold at his wrist.

At the same moment Harriet clutched me and dragged me so violently back into the courtyard that I stumbled and nearly fell. Then she slammed the door and leaned against it, breathing hard. "Oh, God! Oh, damn all things to blazes!"

"That man . . . who was he?"

"Keep quiet," she hissed at me and her fingers drew the bolts across the door. Then she lifted the flap that hung over the grille set in the door and peered out. "Let's get inside and wait for Justin." She was shaking.

"He was coming here, wasn't he? He has been waiting—"

"God knows," she said wildly. "All *I* know is that he isn't someone two women and a child want to meet in the dark. I know his type. He's one of the local criminals. They come out at night like things that crawl from under stones."

190

"He was wearing something gold—a watch, I think. So did the man I saw the other day with the boy."

"Oh, probably a stolen one. You wouldn't be able to identify him by that. A lot of Hammagarbs wear wristwatches."

"But this one had a very wide band of gold." I put up my hands and pushed my hair back from my face. "He was watching this house, wasn't he, and waiting until we came out."

"There's no reason on earth why he should know that."

"Unless he's been here some time and saw Justin *and knew I would be going back to Alexandra's house at midnight . . . and hoped I might go alone . . .*"

"That's crazy . . ."

"Is it?"

She didn't answer me. Instead, when we had crossed the court-yard, she stood in the open doorway of the house and said, "That door, for all its age, is as strong as a fortress. We're quite safe."

I sat in a chair by the window. "That wasn't a watch on the man's wrist. It was more like a heavy gold bracelet."

"Where the hell has Justin got to?" She walked backward and forward across the room, her hands never still, picking things up and tossing them down again, tense and listening.

"I asked Mark about the girl; the one Pippa saw at Hashim's."

Harriet was bending down, pulling at the torn edge of a Persian rug that had once been very beautiful. "What did he say?"

"That he knew her; he knows a lot of people here."

"Was that all?"

"More or less."

"Who is she?"

"Her name is Zaleida." I waited, watching Harriet. "Do you know her?"

"On just the distinction of a first name? It's rather like asking me if I know a girl called Catherine in London." She had her back to me and was stacking used coffee cups onto the tray. Still clattering saucers and spoons, she said, "Why don't you go home to London, Cathy? Go and fill your life with work. You love it and it won't let you down."

"For the moment my work is here. It's a commission. I can't leave even if I wanted to."

"Since the churches haven't yet agreed on what kind of window they want, or even if they will have one at all, I can't see that they can force you to stay."

"Why do *you* want me to go?"

Her eyes swiveled around and met mine. I had never seen her really frightened before. "I don't like what's happening. I can't forget that damned silver box."

Suddenly she turned her back to me and her hands went up to her face, her shoulders shook and I knew she was crying. I had never seen Harriet in tears before and, for all her bitter amusement at life —or perhaps because she used it as a mask—I knew she hated me to see her weeping and would reject me if I went to her. I moved away, crossed the courtyard and, lifting the flap of the grille in the outer door, looked through it. There was no one directly outside, but I stood in the courtyard with my back to Harriet, waiting for her to find control again. I could think of no reason for her tears. If she were upset at Justin being away too long, she would have shown anger. If she felt that, being alone with me, she could relax and be herself— disappointed and unhappy with her life—she would have spat out her bitterness in words. But tears were not Harriet's way. They had to do with fear, and with the man with the gold at his wrist, and with me.

When she came out, she spoke almost jauntily. "Sorry about that, but I get a bit nervy here sometimes. Oh, I pretend to be tough, but—" She stopped.

There were footsteps in the street and, since Hammagarbs walked silently, I knew it must be Justin.

Harriet pushed past me and peered through the grille. Then she flung open the door. "Where the hell have you been?"

Justin dropped a box of Turkish delight onto the round garden table and said, "I've been doing just what you ordered me to. And after I'd done your errand, I wandered along to the top of the steps by the Phoenician Arch and looked down onto Alexandra's house. It was perfectly quiet and dark and peaceful. What are you looking at me like that for?"

"Nothing. Nothing except that I was getting anxious."

He shot her a grin. "That's the first time since we've been married that you've ever been so worried about my safety."

"It wasn't *your* safety, it was ours," she retorted. "We opened the door to look for you and a man came along—I think I recognized him. He was . . . he was one of those criminals they arrested for that attack on the Algerian some weeks ago. You remember? We saw him being arrested in the Square."

"I didn't."

"But you were with me."

"I haven't the faintest idea what you're talking about and, more-over, you know that I haven't. You're not a good liar, sweetie."

She leaned against the wall and watched him. "Why don't you want to remember, Justin?"

"Why do *you* want me to say I remember something I obviously know nothing about?"

I tried to make myself invisible. I didn't want to be a third party at someone else's quarrel. And yet I was involved and Harriet, at least, knew it.

She shot a swift look in my direction. "Justin has a bad memory," she said, "and we've quite enough to think about tonight without an argument on our hands. We'd better go back to Alexandra's, hadn't we? It's past midnight."

I said thankfully, "I'll fetch Pippa."

In spite of her excitement Pippa had fallen asleep, and I sat on the edge of the bed and laid my hand lightly over hers. "Wake up, darling."

She stirred and gave me a small, flickering smile. "Oh, Cathy . . ." Then, the sweetness of half-sleep vanished and her face became wary. "Where's Daddy?"

"He's driving out into the desert. He had to work. You remember he told you."

She pushed back the light blanket that covered her. "What did you do with my diary, Cathy?"

I picked up her dress and tossed it to her. "Wake up, and then you'll also remember that someone is returning it to you tonight. The man who took it. The one who spoke to you on the telephone."

She slid into her dress and pushed her tumbled hair back from her face. "I'm ready. Oh, please, let's hurry."

We walked through the midnight streets, past dark groups, shut-tered houses, music, quarreling and laughter, to the House of the Fountains.

Harriet pushed impatiently past Yussef. "What happened?"

He shook his head. "You will see Madame. Madame will tell you . . ."

Harriet said impatiently to me, "That's almost the extent of his vocabulary. Come on, we must find Alexandra."

Ahmed stood in the Women's Garden like a painting on a dark background, white uniform and mahogany head, upright and still;

the perfect servant, waiting. Alexandra had thrown off her light wrap and came toward us as we entered the hall.

Justin crossed to speak to Ahmed and Alexandra held out her hands to Pippa. "Go upstairs and see what is there for you."

Tiredness forgotten, Pippa went on wings. We heard her sandals making little clattering noises like birds on a tiled roof.

"No one came." Alexandra looked exhausted, and it struck me that for all her calmness as she emptied her house of people, she must have suffered two hours of anxiety for the treasures she had brought with her to the Turkish house.

She said, "When Ahmed and Yussef reported that they had seen no one and the cameras had not been set off, I thought it was some kind of hoax. I went up to Pippa's room, not for a moment believing that the book would be there, but it was. I never thought of it, but of course he must have used the outside staircase—that's one thing I didn't think of because I didn't dream he'd get past Ahmed and Yussef. The cameras were just an additional identification."

"But how did he get into the courtyard with two men watching?"

"I don't understand that, either. But the fact remains, nobody came through the door in the wall, and nobody crossed the courtyard."

"Is anything missing?"

"Nothing. I've searched. But now I must send Lisette to bed. Go to the patio, Cathy. We'll talk there, though I don't know what there is to say."

On the other side of the arch Justin and Ahmed were holding a rapid conversation in Hammagarb. I had often heard conversations between Bou Hammagarbs and thought them to be furious quarrels, only to hear them interrupted by a sudden burst of laughter. I listened as I went into the Women's Garden for laughter. None came. They were standing in the shadows, but Justin, who was facing my way, saw me. "Oh, Cathy. I just came to have a look at Durandal because if there had been an intruder I'm certain he would be agitated—he's as good as a watchdog. But he's completely calm. Look for yourself."

In the pause while I bent down and put my hand through the bars of the cage where the cheetah slept at night, and rubbed his head till he purred, Ahmed shot a single word at Justin. Then he went silently into the house.

"What did he say to us?" I asked.

"Oh, just 'good night.' "

But I knew the Hammagarbs used the ritual phrase *"Salem Alei-koum"*—"Peace be with you." Ahmed had not said that.

Alexandra came out of the house, and Harriet followed her carrying the drink tray.

"A lemon and soda—or brandy?" Alexandra asked.

Justin and Harriet chose brandy, Alexandra and I had lemon, fresh and tangy and beautifully thirst-quenching.

As we took our glasses, small quick footsteps rushed toward us. Pippa held her diary. "I've got it. I've got it. Oh, thank you, dear, *dear* Alexandra, for letting the man bring it back." Her arms went up, her small face nuzzled against the green silk of Alexandra's dress. Then she asked, "But *why* did he steal it?"

"That's a question we're all asking, Pippa."

"If Daddy had stayed, he'd know."

"The worker of miracles," Harriet murmured. "One day, Pippa, you'll grow up."

"I don't want to if it makes people look unhappy."

She had a point there. We must have seemed a small, gloomy frustrated group to Pippa who, having got back what she prized so highly, cared nothing for the plans and the failures of the night. But why should she? We were trying to probe a danger of which she was ignorant.

Justin was leaning against the screen door. "But how the hell did the man get in?"

"He dropped from the skies," Harriet flashed back. "Had you come here instead of mooning around the streets, you might have been the one to find out."

Pippa, clutching the diary, was fighting sleep.

"Go along," I said. "It's been a long night for you. Bed now. I'll come up soon and say good night."

She went with that sweet obedience that occasionally overcame her at moments when she felt a great gratitude. Bed to Pippa was a waste of glorious time; sleep was a nuisance. But whenever Mark or I had done something that had especially pleased her, her practical way of appreciation was not to cause us irritation by opposing us.

When Pippa was out of hearing, Alexandra said, "Yussef tells me he didn't take his eyes off the house during those two hours, and Ahmed only saw people come up the street and go right past the door. He says they were all people he knew."

"And there's no other way in." Justin glanced across at the high wall. "No one could scale that."

"Someone must have." Alexandra looked at us. "Of course . . . the wall. Why didn't I think of it?"

"What about the wall?"

"I don't know, for the moment. Let me think."

We waited, our eyes on Alexandra as she sat bolt upright, frowning. Scents from the garden drifted through the wire mesh of the screen, and somewhere not so far away the strange, wailing string music that was always a background to our evening conversation, ceased. Everything was suddenly hushed.

I looked up and saw through the tangle of jasmine leaves over our heads that Pippa's light was on. I would give her ten minutes to write about her night's adventure and then go up and switch off the lamp.

Justin was saying, in his light, inconsequential voice, "I might steal the *Book of Kells* or the original of *Pilgrim's Progress,* but not a kid's diary. If somebody could explain *that,* we might get somewhere."

"You're being rather obvious," Harriet retorted. "We all know—"

"Perhaps the diary was a means to get me away from the safety of this house," I said.

A stunned silence followed, and I was the focus of three lamplit faces.

"If you could give us one good reason why—"

"A reason, no. But a link—yes, I think so. Because when someone's attempt failed the other day to get me to some part of the town where I'd be in danger, they tried this method."

"But you were with us, Cathy. How could you come to any harm?"

"Justin went down to the *souks* to buy Turkish delight, so Harriet and I were alone with Pippa in the house, and the man we saw was strong. He could have got me away from you, Harriet, quite easily, had you not slammed and bolted your door so quickly."

Alexandra asked sharply, "What man?"

Harriet and I looked at one another, each waiting for the other to speak.

"Well, what man?" she repeated.

Harriet explained and then added, "He was just one of those men who lurk in the shadows here at night waiting to snatch at anything they can and make off with it. I'm sure it couldn't have had anything to do with . . . what happened here tonight. It was a coincidence. I was afraid, though, because he would know Cathy was a foreign visitor and guess that she had money on her."

"And you wanted to protect Cathy?" Justin gave his lazy laugh. "Harriet, dear, your heart is softening with age."

She shot him a blank, catlike look of cold dislike.

I said quickly, "So Harriet saved me again—as she did at the Caves."

"Saved your money, you mean. I hope you don't carry much about with you."

"No, I don't." I knew perfectly well that it had been unimportant how much money I carried with me. Fear of theft of my purse had not been the reason Harriet had been so upset, and I wondered if Alexandra believed that easy explanation either.

"Suppose we see if we can find out how someone got into my house without being seen," she said and picked up her glass and a flashlight from the table and went through the screen door into the courtyard. We watched her stand looking up at the high wall that ran around three sides and ended at the fourth where it joined that of the next house.

She sipped her drink slowly, deep in thought. Then she called, "Come here . . ." and when we joined her she said, "I think I see how it was done. It was the one thing that never occurred to me and so I didn't plan for it. Let's go outside."

We filed past an intrigued Yussef and into the street. The wall of the house ran around a deep bend in the street, and Alexandra shone her flashlight onto it. "Now, do you see?"

Missing stones in the pitted wall made little niches where a man could pull himself up and get a fair foothold.

I said, "And when he got to the top?"

She waved the flashlight up at the orange trees. "He could catch hold of one of those branches and swing himself down." The wide sleeve of her green gown fell away as she reached out. "I hadn't realized that the wall is in such a bad state around this corner. I must tell my landlord."

"But Ahmed would have seen whoever came past him."

"Past him, yes. But once the man rounded the bend, Ahmed wouldn't have known whether the man had gone up the hill or, as I'm now certain happened, climbed the wall. I'm afraid it wouldn't have occurred to Ahmed, as it didn't occur to us, that anyone would do that. And Yussef could only see the courtyard path."

"Even so"—Justin had wandered to the curve of the wall—"when he left, the man would have to climb up the courtyard side of the wall and that, if I remember rightly, is smooth."

"The trees again," Alexandra said. "The branches are strong and would bear even a man's weight. Let's go back and look."

We trooped into the courtyard, and Alexandra told Yussef to bolt the door and go to bed. "There's nothing more he can do tonight."

We followed her to where the orange trees grew. Their branches were low, and if the man were agile, he could have leaped up and grasped one and then swung himself onto the wall.

"But Yussef was watching from the roof of the next house. He would have seen if that was how it was done."

"Not with the line of trees in between. They were grown deliberately to form a screen to hide this courtyard from the eyes of those on neighboring roofs. Anyone using the wall and this end tree as a kind of ladder to get into the courtyard would not be seen. Yussef had a clear view of the entrance to the house and the front door. If the man came by way of the wall and then crawled on hands and knees up the outer steps, keeping to the shadows, he would have been perfectly screened and could have got into the house by the terrace and through your room, Cathy, to Pippa's bedroom. Why didn't I think of it? *Why?*"

"Or why didn't any of us?" Harriet said.

"Because our minds aren't trained in criminology," Justin said matter-of-factly.

"So he came, returned the diary, and went." Harriet turned to Alexandra. "Did he take the money?"

"Yes."

"And there's not a single fact we can offer to the police," Justin said.

Harriet said, "Not to Bou Hammagan police, anyway. Even if we could have given them help and they caught him, they might take him to trial, but again, they would be more likely to ignore it all if someone's palm was crossed with silver. Come back in five years' time and law and order will prevail. But now—" She shrugged and drained her glass. "Oh, God, Alexandra, your brandy is strong."

"We needed it."

Back in the patio I said to Harriet, "The man outside your door tonight . . . I still believe he must have known what was going to happen."

"Sweetie, you're imagining again. He was just a casual criminal out to collect whatever he could grab from purses."

Alexandra looked at her watch. "It's nearly one o'clock and time to end this rather abortive discussion. I think we should go to bed before we start seeing ghosts in the orange trees."

198

Pippa's light was out. I tiptoed to her room and she didn't stir. Tiredness had overcome her excitement and she was asleep.

But sleep wasn't easy for me. My mind was too tired to make sense of Alexandra's explanation of how an intruder could have got into the house. I lay in bed and longed for Mark.

XXII

I KNEW that I had to see David the following day and try to force a decision over the church window. The design for the one Alexandra wanted now only needed her approval of the detail.

In the morning, while Alexandra was in her suite, I tried to telephone David, and found that he had already left for one of the villas in the New City. I was told that he would probably be back at the hotel at lunchtime.

Alexandra had an excellent selection of books I could read and there were letters to be written to friends, but I wanted to do neither. I wandered restlessly up the steps to the roof and stood looking onto the roofs of the houses that cascaded down the hillside. Hens ran about, their feathers bronze in the sunlight, washing hung limply on lines and, on one roof, a woman was combing her long black hair, every slow sensual movement a delight to her.

In Bou Hammagan the rich and the poor lived side by side, neither resenting the other, enjoying their wealth behind their high walls or accepting, with placid fatalism, their poverty.

I looked over the roofs to the old city burning steadily under the ravenous sun and wondered where, in all that maze, the girl Zaleida lived. Harriet and Alexandra had not known who she was, but I had a feeling that, between themselves, they were guessing hard. Justin must also be wondering—or knowing—for Harriet was not given to secrets. And Mark? How well did he know Zaleida?

The sudden memory of all those walks he took in the early morning or late at night came back to me. *I need to be alone,* he had said. Alone? I could not stop asking myself—nor could I stop my self-hatred at my thoughts.

Late that afternoon, I collected my design for Alexandra's window, picked up my brushes and went onto the roof to paint the colors of the sunset. I took my chair to a place near the parapet where Ahmed had set up a sun umbrella to shade my painting from the slanting glare.

Once I got up and went to the roof edge. Bou Hammagan lay like a white dream touched with the green of trees, orange and palm. The sinister alleys, the crowded footpaths, the noise, did not seem to belong to the city I looked down upon, yet they were there, absorbed and glamorized by height and distance.

It would have been wonderful to see the sunset from the desert, to watch the violent rays change the lion-tints of hardened sand and deepen on the distant hills of Djebel Thamadi where Mark said streams ran and roses bloomed.

I turned and, leaning over the parapet, looked up the street beyond the Phoenician Arch where the desert began.

She was there. Almost as though she were part of a stage set, she had the columns of the great Arch for a background, and her face was turned toward the house as if she were watching or waiting for someone. She wore a white dress and I could not possibly have recognized her but for the glitter of the sun on the medallion resting between her neat, high breasts—unusual for an Eastern woman. But then, she was very young. Sixteen, perhaps even younger. I moved away from the roof edge, acutely sensitive of being seen watching her. The sky was already deepening, warning me that I had only a short time in which to catch the swift, important moment I was waiting for. I had to concentrate on that and forget the girl who watched Alexandra's house.

Suddenly, it came, those last moments that tore the sky into ribbons of vermilion and violet and copper and then fell back before the oncoming darkness. I painted frantically, enriching the colors that I had already mixed, catching, I hoped, the mood of that violent visitation of light yet remembering Chris's teaching about tones that would complement one another. I had already made a note of the color and texture of the stonework to be used for the church interior, but I was having to work "blind" where Alexandra's window was concerned, for her hall, when it was finished, was to be entirely covered in green and gold mosaics. She had shown me a sample of what was to be used and I worked with that in mind.

In the brief time that the sunset lasted, I was absorbed. Then the darkness fell, and I cleaned my brushes quickly in the last moments of light and pushed my chair back from the drawing board.

There was a resistance. Someone was behind me.

"Alexandra—" I turned sharply as I spoke her name.

Mark laughed.

"You scared me." I backed away from him and said more sharply than I meant to, "Please don't do that again—at least, not here. I'm too much on edge."

"I'm sorry, darling. It's always a stupid trick to startle people, but I really didn't mean to. I've just arrived back and came looking for you, and then I couldn't resist watching you work. You use such swift, sure strokes and I, who can't draw a straight line, find it fascinating."

"The house is so quiet," I said.

"I know. I've seen no one except the eternal Keeper of the Gate who always grins to show his splendid teeth." Mark went to the roof edge and looked down. I saw by the direction of his head that if the girl Zaleida had been standing there, she could have seen him against the ring of lights from the house. My acceptance of the fact that she must have been watching for Mark shook me so badly that I picked up my drawing board clumsily and dropped it with a clatter. "Oh, damn, and now I suppose I've smudged the painting."

Mark picked the board up for me. "Unless you have x-ray eyes, you won't be able to see if you have or not. Let's go inside into the light. And you can also tell me what happened last night."

"There's nothing to tell you. Pippa has her diary, but no one saw who put it back." We had reached my studio room, and after I had made sure that the painting was not damaged, I leaned against one of the columns that separated the room from the terrace and told Mark about what had happened on the previous night.

"But why would a diary be stolen from a house full of valuable things?"

"Yes, why?"

"And it's odd that nobody saw him climbing up the street or when he went back down it. If Ahmed was hidden in some doorway—"

A sudden, scalding pain hit me. "How . . . do you know . . . the man came . . . up the street and then *down* it?"

"It's hardly likely he would go into the desert. He would be far too likely to be chased and caught up there in open country. Whereas if he went down into the Square, he would immediately be lost in the crowds."

It was obvious, of course, and my overstimulated imagination was becoming too quick to seize on words or actions that could be translated into suspicion. I was silent for too long, and Mark came and put his arms on my shoulders. "The box still worries you, doesn't it, Cathy? All right . . . But, darling, don't let's exaggerate this diary business. Someone wanted to extract money from us and has done so in a way he knew would touch us most deeply—through Pippa."

I slid from under the light pressure of his hands and crossed the room. Below, voices mingled and laughed. Frances Mitchell had brought Pippa back and something was amusing them all.

I felt isolated in my suspicions, like someone suffering from hallucinations. Sometimes, working on one of the small stained-glass designs which had hitherto been all I was allowed to do on my own, I had found myself floundering in a welter of too many ideas. Then, just as I felt I would never find order out of the chaos, my mind would clear and the solution would stare me in the face.

It was exactly that which happened as I went down the stone staircase. I stopped quite still and, in the quiet, I could hear Mark lighting a cigarette; I looked over my shoulder and saw him standing, thin and dark, in the columned room. The stone balustrade was warm to my fingers; the rich night was like a black page on which my thoughts were written.

Pippa—too rich, too vulnerable—could be the reason behind all that had happened. If I lost my trust in Mark; if I believed what was hinted at and whispered about and flung at me over the telephone, and left him in fear, then there would be just the two of them. And which of those two would be defenseless?

I checked my soaring imagination, but it was pointless to argue that danger did not stalk certain people. It happened all the time: people plotting against others, families torn apart with hatred or greed or desire . . . Somewhere in the world there was always a man wanting to rid himself of a woman or a woman to rid herself of a man . . .

I heard Mark say something to me, but I had no idea what it was. In panic at what now seemed suddenly obvious, I turned and ran down the outside steps and plunged through the arch into the Women's Garden.

I had to find people, to hear conversation, for my need to escape my own thoughts was as desperate as if an assassin were rushing at me with knives.

The screens had been drawn in place, and as I joined Alexandra's guests, Frances Mitchell was saying, "That probably makes it the most expensive child's diary in the world today. How extraordinary —and rather frightening. It seems Clive and I will have to sleep with a shotgun at hand every night."

"I've been safe enough so far," Alexandra said, "and I'm not in the least afraid. What happened to us was an exception. The man, whoever he was, made no effort to find my jewelry, and even the collection of Georgian snuffboxes I keep in my own room wasn't touched. He just wanted the diary."

"But why?"

"That's what we would all like to know—" She looked around and saw me. "Oh, Cathy, I've just been telling Frances and Clive what happened last night. I've been thinking, and I feel that it might help for everyone to know about it. There's just a chance someone might hear something that could be important."

"It was a very elaborate plan for the extortion of a hundred pounds," I said.

"That's what it must have been. And perhaps whoever walked off with that money will throw it around in the *souks*. I've told Ahmed and Yussef to keep their eyes and ears open—" She broke off, gave a start and turned. "Oh, Mark, you must have been a jungle animal in your previous incarnation, you walk so silently."

He came toward us, saying lightly, "I had a mother who hated noise. I think my trying to play the piano started her fetish for quiet. I used to put my foot down on the loud pedal and belt out any tune that took my roving fancy."

"Where's Pippa?" Alexandra asked.

"Here I am." She came out of the shadows of the garden and through the screen door.

"You see?" Alexandra laughed. "You never have any need to ask where she is once she hears Mark's voice."

He picked her up and swung her around. "If you get much more sun tan you'll have to be rechristened with a Bou Hammagarb name because nobody will believe you are English."

"Zaleida."

From somewhere in the group half in the shadows came a sharply caught breath. I had shocked someone and shocked myself, too, and my heart thudded as if I had been running fast.

From my chair half facing the lights streaming from the house into the patio, I wondered who had been so startled at the mention of the girl's name. Whoever it was remained as silent as the rest who sat, eyes on me. I glanced around the group, watching each face—the only one I couldn't look at was Mark.

Alexandra spoke first. "It's strange how many women's names here begin with the letter 'Z.' 'Zaleida' is, I believe, quite common in Bou Hammagan."

Conversation flowed easily again, names and preferences were discussed. Frances asked me what my favorite name was and I couldn't think.

Justin said gallantly, "Oddly enough Cathy and Harriet have the same middle name—Elizabeth. That's my favorite. You see what exquisite tact I have—I neither offend my wife nor my sister-in-law."

Pippa said, "I have a funny middle name—Anne-Marie. No one ever calls me by it. I wish they would."

"Anne-Marie," said Frances from the shadows and everyone laughed.

XXIII

THAT NIGHT I was in that state beyond sleep when everything took longer than usual. I undressed in slow motion, sat in front of the mother-of-pearl dressing table and brushed my hair until the movement became so automatic that I stopped only when Mark quoted at me: " 'Nymph with long disheveled hair . . .' "

"That's what being so literary does for you," I said, trying to match his gaiety. "You have a quote for all occasions—" I stopped abruptly. I was about to ask, "What comes next?" But I didn't want to know. A thought entered my mind and spoiled the beauty of the words. Mark, I had said, had a quote for all occasions. *Dust hath closed dark Catherine's eye . . .*

Heaven, how much more deeply must I love Mark to stop this lurking suspicion from taking root?

The hairbrush fell to the floor. I picked it up and laid it on the table, slid the strap of my nightdress into place and looked over my shoulder at Mark's reflection. "Anyway, your quotation isn't apt. My hair is straight, and surely nymphs are virgins."

He gave a soft chuckle and flung himself onto the low divan, bunching up the pillows. "You're being very slow coming to bed."

I went to him, and he slid his arm between the pillow and my shoulders, holding me very quietly for some minutes. But I knew he only needed my closeness, and when he turned from me, I didn't try to hold him.

He pummeled the pillow, saying, "The desert must be the world's most exhausting place. I want to sleep around the clock and yet I want to make love to you. If I wake you in the night, will you want me or will I be a bore?"

"You could never be a bore, Mark, and I'll always want you."

"Wild words, darling. I'm not certain that passion lives that long. I have a feeling that only friendship is eternal. But we'll prove it one way or the other."

Something moved just beyond my line of vision. I lifted my head and looked toward Pippa's room. The door was open and she stood there. She had slid her arms into her sky-blue robe and had left it untied, so that her naked, immature body glowed a golden tan in the single light of the room. She was holding her diary in her arms like some beloved animal. "Daddy . . ."

Mark closed his eyes and I felt him stiffen with impatience. "I'm not listening to anything at half past twelve. Go back to bed."

"But, Daddy, you must. *Please.* This is important."

"Nothing is, after midnight, except—" His fingers touched me under the light yellow blanket.

Pippa hadn't taken her eyes off us. I knew she had seen Mark's face laid against my hair; she could even have seen that slight movement of his hand toward me. I edged away from him and asked, "Darling, what is it?"

"Someone has torn a page from my diary. I was writing in it and—"

"At this time of night? Dear Lord, how do we bring you up?"

"I'd been to sleep but *you* woke me. You banged something against my wall and then I heard you and Cathy talking. *Then* I remembered something else I wanted to write about."

"I'm sorry I woke you. That door springs open with a leap like a kangaroo, but never mind that. What do you mean, someone has torn a page from your diary?"

"They have. I was writing in it and I yawned and the diary fell on the ground. It opened where there wasn't any June sixteenth—or not much."

Mark heaved himself up in bed, held out his hand for the diary and flipped through it. "What did you write on that day?" The drowsy tone in his voice was gone; he was reading the top half of the torn page. "Well?" He glanced at her. "What came after this?"

"I don't remember."

"Oh, come, you must. Look at those lines and try to remember what came next." He thrust the book at her. "June the fifteenth was the day you left England to come here, so what did you write on the sixteenth?"

She stood in front of him, the blue robe trailing, her fingers playing with the loose cord, her dark hair a cloud about her shoulders, tense and a little frightened by this insistent father. But her eyes did not waver. "I just wrote about saying goodbye to people. Then I packed and got in a muddle and Cathy helped me and I went and saw the kittens in the house next door. They were black with white faces and—"

"All that's here," he said impatiently. "What came next?"

"There was such lots to write about. It was fun going up in the plane, like being free. Only I wished I was alone in it and didn't have all those people around me. I'd like to fly alone, Daddy." She waited. Then, when Mark made no comment, she continued, "When we landed, Uncle Justin met us and drove us here—and it took *hours* and it was awfully hot. I wrote about how I felt, with my hair sticking to my neck until Cathy put it up for me and tied it with a piece of yellow cord that we'd taken off a box of candies. And I felt much better then."

"You've told me nothing relevant."

"Rele—rele—?" She frowned at him.

"Skip it," he said. "There must have been something in that page that was important. *What else did you write?*"

"I d-don't know. It's so long—"

"*Try* to remember. Do you hear? You've got a brain and a memory. Use them."

She pressed her lips together as though afraid to yawn.

"Leave her alone tonight, please, Mark. Come, Pippa, let's get you back to bed."

I doubted that she heard me. Sensitive to every look and mood of her father, she was edging away from him, her eyes empty of the adoration she kept solely for him.

He reached out and gripped her wrist. *"You must remember what else you wrote . . ."*

"Mark, let her go."

He ignored me, his eyes not moving from her face.

She pulled out of his grasp. "Daddy, I can't *think*. I keep *telling* you."

"Remember!"

"Mark, I've told you. Leave her alone." I heard my voice again rip angrily across her next plaintive protest. I got out of bed and put my arm around her. "Don't cry, darling. It's all right. Everything is all right."

"Like hell it is," Mark exploded. "There was something in that diary that someone thought worth tearing out and keeping. For what?"

For money? Oh, no, Mark, you don't believe that . . .

Pippa had written down an observation that was too revealing to be safe to someone and so, a man and a boy—and heaven knew who else—had been recruited to get the diary and deal with me. *Because I was involved.*

"Come here." He held out both hands to her. "Come on, I'm not going to jump at you." He drew her close. "I'm sorry I shouted, but perhaps you'll remember in the morning. If you do, promise me something."

"What?" she asked suspiciously.

"That you'll tell me and no one else."

"I'll never remember."

"Sometimes we do if we stop trying to think too hard. Now, run along."

She walked back to her room, trailing her blue robe and carrying the diary. I followed her, sat on her bed and laid my cheek against her bent head. "Don't take it all so seriously, Pippa, please don't. People sometimes seem cross when all they really are is very worried."

"Why is Daddy worried?"

"Because he wants to know who stole your diary and why."

"But I've got it back."

Pippa had to be taught that something that was resolved for her could cause ripples that affected others; she had to learn that all was not well just because she was content.

I said, "Yes, you've got your diary back, darling. But it's been at a price for all of us."

"Price?" Unshed tears made her eyes silver-green in the lamplight.

"I don't just mean money. There are other things—like trying to find out why someone tore that page out. It's a little worrying for us not to know the whole truth."

It was an understatement, but it would serve for the moment. Her face in the light from the silk-shaded table lamp was bruised with tiredness and hurt. Unlike other times when something upset her, she didn't turn to me for comfort. I was alien. But she couldn't resist repeating the words that, to her, had seemed to anger her father. "I won't ever remember what I wrote." Her voice came small and sad from the hollow her head made in the pillow. "I write things down and when I've done it, they go out of my head. It's like writing an essay at school on something in history. It's all over."

"All right, don't worry about it now."

She let me hold her for a moment, and I hoped desperately that she would remember what she had written on that page. Had Mark the same reason as I for wanting to know? Or, if Pippa remembered, would Mark share her memory with me? I had to believe that he would. I told myself as I held his daughter close what I had been certain of up until now—that trust went hand in hand with love. But now I questioned it. Love had no qualifications. It was a complete and rounded thing.

I didn't love Mark for his virtues. Nor, I was sure, did Pippa. If he forced a promise from her never to tell me what she remembered she had written in her diary, nothing would pry it from her. I might never know.

Suddenly Pippa broke away from me as if ashamed of her need for my comfort. And, jolted out of her sleepiness by a thought, she sat upright and stared at her toes. "There's a horrid smudge right across the picture, the one opposite the torn page. And it's the loveliest in the book."

"Show me. I may be able to get it off for you."

She eyed me doubtfully and reached for the diary, opened it and showed me the illustration that preceded the summer season. The artist had painted the scene from *A Midsummer Night's Dream* where Titania lay in the moonlit grove fondling the ass's head. A heavy black smear streaked right across her silver dress and the lush dark green of the wood where the wild thyme grew. Titania's summer was marred by a thief's detestable hand.

A sudden thought came to me that this could prove to be a finger-print. But when I looked at it more closely in the lamplight, I saw that it had been made by a blackened brush or the line of a felt-tipped pen and had been deliberately smudged. "I'll try to get it off in the morning, but I can't promise."

"No." The few moments of confidence in me vanished. "I don't want you to touch my diary."

"I'll only try to clean that picture. You can watch me all the time. I promise I won't read what is written—"

She snatched the book from me and thrust it under the blanket. I was learning how swiftly children's moods changed and how flimsy was the base upon which their trust lay.

I was doing neither of us any good by staying. "You've got your diary and if you want to, we'll talk more about it in the morning."

I left her and closed the door firmly between us.

Mark was lying on his back.

"You frightened Pippa," I said.

"Oh, she's not easily scared, and I want to know what she wrote on that missing half page."

"And when she remembers, where will it lead us?" I waited. "Mark, *where?*" When he still didn't answer me, I cried, "Why won't you be frank with me?"

"You think I'm not?"

"Well, are you?"

"I think so. I can't tell you things I don't know myself, now can I? I'm sorry—"

I lay back on the bed, staring so hard at the ceiling that my eyes hurt. "Sorry for what? For not knowing anything? Or for not telling me what you suspect?"

"Cathy, stop playing my accuser."

I leaped up, crossed the ice-cold tiles and pushed open the screen, defying the night insects. "I'm involving you in a situation you hate? I can understand that. You have a job to do out here and I'm . . . I'm extraneous. But I *did* ask you if you minded my coming to North Africa, and I have tried to keep my life out here as separate as I can. Involving you was not my doing; I didn't send Louise's box to myself—"

"And so—?" His voice came quietly from the bed.

"And so," I said, not wanting to look at him, my body shaking with anger and fear and exhaustion, "and so . . . *help me, Mark.* Because if you don't, I'm throwing up this commission for the window and flying home with Pippa. I'm neither particularly courageous nor a fool."

"I thought we'd already talked this out."

"We did, and then something else happened that's disturbing and frightens me, even if it doesn't you. We need to talk it all out again."

"And each time I tell you the same thing. You are safer here than in London."

"Safer? When someone watches this house and knows every movement you make and acts when you aren't here?"

He dropped his arms and turned from me. "Damn it to hell . . . what am I supposed to do?"

"Go to the police."

"Here, in Bou Hammagan? You must be joking. And anyway, to tell them what? That some petty crook stole a child's diary for a hundred pounds' ransom. Do you think they'd ever find him in this devil's maze of a place?"

Mark had an answer every time and each was logical. Yet he floored me, and every question I put to him and every answer he gave me drove a deeper wedge between us. It was as if, out of our normal environment, we were comparative strangers with only our physical attraction for one another. I loved Mark, but I no longer had the measure of understanding which had once been mine. And its lack was a desolation.

I heard myself say in a flat, dead voice, "It isn't working, is it, Mark?"

He let the silence lie between us: a slow, beating hush that did not contain a denial.

"Mark"—I swung around—"answer me."

He tilted back onto the bed, lying with his arms stretched out on either side of him, his face turned to the ceiling. "If you want to be free, there's nothing I can do about it."

It was the worst answer he could give me. He was flinging the choice back at me and I couldn't bear that. I didn't want to be the strong one, to have to take the initiative to keep or break our marriage. I put my hands to my face, my fingertips digging into my cheekbones, deliberately hurting myself physically in order to subdue emotional pain. "It isn't what I want; it's what could be inevitable."

Mark lay in the pool of lamplight, unmoving, every line of his body passive. "Is there someone else?"

"No."

"But there's not just freedom from me to be considered, is there? There's Pippa," he said.

"At one time I believed I mattered to her. Now, I'm not sure."

"You're good for her."

"Oh, no, Mark. When trust between a child and an adult is lost, nothing good can come of the relationship."

"I think you underestimate her capacity for affection and discernment."

I sat down on the edge of the bed. "We're making Pippa the issue between us. She mustn't be. It's our lives, yours and mine, we have to resolve."

Again, the pause was long. Then he said, without any apparent emotion, "I'm not asking you to stay if you don't want to. You could be right. Perhaps the whole of our marriage has been a failure, because *I'm* a failure to a woman. Perhaps not a house but the world is my home and no woman can be expected to stand that. But Pippa . . . You're right there, too. She mustn't come into this argument."

Except for the movement of his lips, he hadn't stirred, and his arms still lay heavy and outspread across the bed. For all the pain his words inflicted, there was a quality of unreality about him.

I cried in anger, "Stop behaving as if we were having a kind of dream conversation. We're living, feeling people . . ." The bed swung gently with my shaking limbs. "Mark, come alive, for God's sake . . ."

He moved so suddenly that he toppled me and I fell onto the bed. He pinned me down with taut arms on either side of me. "What holds a marriage together, Cathy?"

"Trust," I said, "and a gift of laughter and . . ."

"And in the last analysis, neither of those." He dropped his arms and the sudden weight of his body took the breath out of me. "This," he said and kissed me.

He gave me no chance to protest that he was wrong and that he knew it and was deliberately evading an issue. He made love to me as if it were the last desperate thing he would ever do.

XXIV

I WOKE many times during that night, in between ridiculous, impossible dreams, and then toward dawn I must have slept very heavily, for when I opened my eyes to the light, Mark was no longer with me.

I knew he had to leave early for Tunis for some meeting with a television program chief, William Shelton, a man I had met and liked, who was passing through on his way to Tripoli. Mark told me that there was talk of a possible television program on the proposed movement to preserve the ruins of Carthage which were in danger of being lost by the expansion of the city of Tunis. The idea was that the shooting might be done while the crew was in North Africa.

Mark was up and dressed while I was still stirring out of a heavy sleep, and I heard him leave the house while I was in my bath.

Breakfast was laid for Pippa and me in the patio. She was being exaggeratedly polite and, had I not been so painfully involved, her perfect takeoff on a remote angel-child would have amused me. As it was, while we ate crisp bread and Lisette's marmalade, I felt caught in a web. *I can no longer do anything right in her eyes.*

Immediately after she had eaten Pippa asked if she might get up from the table. Her voice was so full of formal dignity that I burst out laughing. She gave me a cool stare and then spoiled it all by taking to her heels and running through the patio to where Durandal sat in a patch of shade.

By leaning forward I could just see him, head lifted, alert to the sound of her footsteps. Then, recognizing her, he went back to his own occupation, watching something that was crawling on the ground. For a few moments he crouched motionless. Then, like a streak of lightning, his paw shot out and a small insect died.

I was drinking my third cup of coffee when Pippa went into the house and appeared with her swimsuit and towel. She called a distant "goodbye" to me and with a clatter of sandals was away.

Left alone, I went to the terrace room and put a few finishing touches to the design for Alexandra's window, checking the width of space between the bars which would be the supports that must withstand stress. Large stained-glass windows usually had a fillet of white glass around the contour of the window which enabled it to be removed without damage to the actual design, but Alexandra had not wanted this. "After all, my window will never be moved," she said.

I wished I could feel a greater interest in the project, but it was the church window that I longed to start work on. I was beginning to see my great solo opportunity to be known as the designer of a relatively important stained-glass window fading because a few men sitting in conference could not agree.

I had already gone over the penciled outlines of my design in sepia ink, and as I looked at it in the golden daylight that beamed between the angular columns of the terrace, the colors that had seemed so natural the evening before looked almost garish. But they would be given depth by the jewel tints of the glass we used. What was now like the overcolored post-card reproduction of a sunset would glow more deeply and gently in stained glass.

Alexandra entered and, looking over my shoulder, said, "You draw beautifully, Cathy."

"It's a pity the window has to be made in England where you can't see it and approve it in its later stages."

She said, walking away from me, "Oh, I trust your taste. I know I shall love it. I'm waiting, by the way, for my architect to take me to the villa to meet a landscape gardener. I believe they are delivering mounds of earth today. I want a mass of flowers around me, and after we've discussed my garden, I shall go to the hotel. Frances tells me that another couple—quite young, I believe—have come out to supervise the building of their villa. So our circle is growing." Her voice held weary amusement. "Wherever one goes, nothing really changes. The cocktail parties continue; the discotheques rise up; the women fly to Italy or Paris for their clothes. It's a giddy world." She lifted her arms with a small, resigned movement.

Before she left me I asked if I might use the telephone. I wanted, I explained, to catch David before he left the hotel. I had to know if there was any more news of the church project.

Telephoning in Bou Hammagan was a lesson in patience. But when I finally heard the hotel receptionist's voice, she told me that I had missed David, but that he had left word that he would be back at midday if anyone wanted him. Alexandra offered to get him to call me from the hotel. "I expect I'll see him when I go there. All the hotel guests find their way eventually onto the terrace at drink time," she said. "And by the way"—she nodded toward the arch—"if you look through there, you'll see my gardener, Ibrahim. He has been cutting the dead heads off the roses. He usually waters the flowers while we are at dinner—he's a very unobtrusive little man."

He was also, I decided a very happy one, for he was singing as he worked, absorbed and entirely unaware that I was watching him.

I didn't know how to spend my day. There was nothing more I could do to Alexandra's window design; I had written all the letters I had promised to friends, and, although I knew I could join the Mitchells and Pippa at the swimming pool, I had no wish for people.

Yussef crossed the courtyard and went into the house. I guessed that there would be tiny, sickly sweet cups of Turkish coffee for him and for Ahmed in the kitchen. I went down and through the columned hall into the courtyard and sat on the seat under the orange trees. I closed my eyes and tried not to think of anything.

"I thought you'd be out, either at Alexandra's villa or the church," Mark said.

"And I thought *you* would be on your way to Tunis."

"There was a message for me at the office. Something important came up in London and Shelton had to catch a later plane. We're going to discuss it some other time, perhaps in London. So, today is a free day for us. The others have gone to the hotel to swim. I suppose Pippa is there."

"Yes."

"I'm glad I found you. Shall we have some coffee?" Without waiting for my answer he went into the house. When I heard Lisette's laughter and a burst of swift French, I envied Mark his gift for languages which made him supremely at home in so many countries.

He came out into the garden carrying a lacquer tray on which Alexandra's own Crown Derby china glowed crimson and green in the strong light. The coffee smelled good.

Mark set the tray down on the small garden table and said so quietly that his voice was almost lost in the street sounds beyond the wall, "I am going to take Pippa away."

I sat without moving, my hands in my lap. The rich scent of coffee steamed toward me. I felt no more emotion than if Mark had said, "It's a fine day," and when he touched my hand I made no response. I was like someone sitting for her portrait told to keep still and think of nothing.

"Cathy—?"

Next, he will ask for my understanding. Oh, but I understand. Someone wants him; hates me. She has won. I came suddenly alive and my heart began to beat rapidly. "Go on," I said, because I knew it would come, anyway, and it had better be quickly over. "Where are you taking her?"

"To some friends I have who live in Tunis. You've heard me speak of the Margetsons, Lila and Jack. He's attached to the Pasteur Institute there. Pippa will be fine—"

"You once told me . . . The Margetsons have four children. And now . . . they want . . . Pippa."

"For God's sake, do you imagine I'm giving my daughter away?" Irritation flared up and then as swiftly died down. "It's temporary, until we sort things out—"

"Don't stop. I'd better know everything, hadn't I?" My voice struck on my own ears with a brittle fatalism, demanding more hurt.

"I think it's best for her."

"To be away from me."

"No, not that. Or yes, perhaps to be away from both of us until—"

"You don't usually leave sentences unfinished," I said in the icy

218

voice that was all I could manage. I felt frozen and yet I was sweating in the hot morning.

Mark ran his hand over his head, a typical nervous trick I had seen in other men but never before in Mark. "Very well, I'll give you the truth. I'm afraid for Pippa's safety."

I turned slowly and stared at him. "Why should you think she's in danger?"

"I don't know. I wish I did. At the moment it's only a suspicion."

"*I* have a suspicion, too," I said in my new tight, hard voice. "My suspicion is that Harriet and Alexandra and even, perhaps, Justin know something that concerns me that I don't know. Why is everyone whispering and hinting and telling me nothing? And now, why are you pretending that you are afraid for Pippa without knowing *why?* Of course, you know. But you won't tell me. Mark, where did we lose our trust in each other?"

"For Christ's sake." He rose and his hand pulled me roughly around to face him. "I'm telling you what I suspect, not what I know, because I know nothing for certain. Pippa could be in danger."

"Oh, no, she isn't. *I* am."

The ground beneath me seemed to stir and shudder. I lost my balance and teetered forward but, as Mark's hand went out to me, I steadied myself.

"That," he said, "was an earth tremor."

"You're so wrong," I said in my new harsh voice. "It was my knees giving way. But let's forget that. You seem to be planning Pippa's life as if it were a television script, with no thought as to her wishes or interests. Mark, are you listening to me? If—"

He pushed past me. "I've got to find out where the seat of that earth disturbance was. It could be anywhere, but if it's at Bodaia, then God help them. There are a hundred men working—"

"Pippa . . ." He had interrupted me; now it was my turn. "Pippa," I said again, "and—us."

But Mark, whose ears were attuned to the slightest sound, turned. I looked too.

Ahmed was coming toward us. "Monsieur, the telephone for you."

"Tell them to leave their number and I'll call back."

"It's very urgent, your office . . ."

"Then go and keep them on the line; I'm coming."

As Ahmed disappeared, Mark said curtly, "Wait here."

"For what?" I called after him. "Explanations? Pleadings for my understanding? *Your* self-hate? 'You know, Cathy, men are so bloody unfaithful.' Thank you, you can spare me the self-analysis."

But Mark was already out of hearing and my anger and bitterness were wasted. I wanted to rush after him, to say, "Damn that call. Finish what you were saying; try to convince me that Pippa isn't the thin end of the wedge which is the beginning of a split between us."

I had no idea whether, when Mark returned to the garden, I would say that to him or not. I turned and fled. Yussef opened the outer door for me and I rushed through. I didn't hear it close, and it was possible that he was standing watching a crazed Englishwoman racing in the blaze of the African morning up the stepped street. *Allah be praised . . . the English are mad . . .*

My flight excited the dogs and the children, but, taking two paces for each of the wide worn steps, I reached the top of the street where the Arch stood.

Panting for breath, I leaned against one of the great pitted pillars and looked about me. I was on the outskirts of the town and beyond the few remaining clay houses were date palms and rifts of coarse gravel dotted with boulders. I could see the foothills of the Djebel Thamadi shimmering in the burning distance. It was odd that, torn by emotion, I should stand there and notice small things like the coloring of the desert—terra cotta and ocher and russet. It was a fragment of comfort that I could still see outside things, that despair had not swept away my eye for color. Nature was offering me relief.

But behind it all was Mark. *I am taking Pippa away . . .*

I was standing quite still, yet the earth trembled beneath me. I braced myself. This was ridiculous. Whatever shock I had received, my body at least should be able to withstand it; bone and muscle must not be affected by my emotional state. To test myself, I pushed away from the supporting stone and looked about me, wondering which way to go.

As if I had a choice. There was none. All I could do was to retrace my steps, go down and across the Square to Harriet and her salutary matter-of-factness. I had to tell someone or Mark's brief, cold statement would tear me apart—it would, anyway. But at least I would have Harriet to put me together again.

I took a few steps and then, looking up, I saw that a group of palms to my right were waving as if a strong wind had struck them. Simultaneously someone screamed. In one of the houses, I heard a loud and prolonged crash as though pots and pans had fallen, and as I began to walk down the stepped street, people came running out of their houses. A woman clutching two children shouted at me as she made for the open country beyond the Phoenician Arch. Others came after her, running past me, also shouting. One woman even tried to clutch me. Her grip was so hard that she bruised my skin. The long, narrow street was suddenly suffused with a fear I didn't understand. Nor did I try to. I was going to Harriet.

I got no further than the door to the House of the Fountains. Yussef was outside. "You come . . . you come in . . ."

"No, I'm going—"

"Come, please." He began speaking in the Bou Hammagarb patois, his hands weaving in an effort to make me understand. But I knew. My legs had not trembled and nearly given way from my own emotion. The cause was far outside myself. The city had suffered two earth tremors. The first had been so slight that most people would not have noticed it. But Mark had. And just now, the second one had been more severe. The earth had shifted, risen and settled again. In single words of English interspersed with wide explanatory gestures, Yussef made me understand that somewhere to the south there had been an earthquake. What we had felt was the edge of the disturbance.

Alexandra, hearing my voice, called me. I found her standing with Ahmed in the hall, and she had a transistor radio in her hand. "It's being broadcast," she said. "From Algeria. The news is coming through with a terrible amount of interference, but I can just manage to understand. The earthquake is thirty miles away. We're told that we are in no danger here and that the shock isn't a very bad one. They think a town on the way to Djebel Thamadi may have been destroyed, but at the moment it's all very vague. Don't worry. The fault in the earth's crust doesn't run through Bou Hammagan."

"Mark . . ." I said.

"What about him? He's on his way to Tunis to discuss the program on the ruins of Carthage."

"Oh, no, he isn't. His plans were changed; he came back to tell me so."

"But there was a telephone call, madame," Ahmed said in his careful deep-voiced English, "and he left quick. He tell me he have to go. It was the earthquake. They say he go and see—"

"They," the gods who directed him. And where there was danger, there was a story.

Alexandra said, "The nearest one they ever had before was at

Agadir, which is hundreds of miles away. I'm sure the scare is all past now. Thank you, Ahmed."

"Pippa . . ." I said, "I must go to her."

"Leave her where she is. I should imagine the children were having too good a time to notice the earth tremors; they were such slight ones, anyway. Pippa probably thought the swaying of the water in the swimming pool was caused by their play."

"Pippa won't be at the hotel."

"Of course she will." Alexandra looked at me sharply. "Why do you say that?"

"Because wherever Mark is, Pippa will be with him. They'll have to report on the earthquake without him because, Alexandra, he won't be there. I know . . ." My voice rose, so that the last word quivered and broke.

"Cathy, what are you talking about?"

The moment of panic died. I said more quietly, "Mark is on his way to Tunis—with Pippa. He has probably packed her things—her clothes . . ." I broke off and made for the stairs, leaping up them and into Pippa's room. I tore open the fretwork door of the wardrobe. Her few clothes were still there, her little embroidered slippers were by the bed, her brush and comb on the table with a rainbow medley of colored hair ribbons. But Mark could still have taken her, and I had to be certain. I ran back down the stairs.

Alexandra was standing quite still, and I knew I owed her an explanation. Anyway, she had to know . . . everyone had to know.

"Mark is planning to take Pippa away; he's sending her to people I don't believe she even knows, here in North Africa."

"Of course he's not planning to do anything of the kind. Or—if he is . . . why?" Something of her serenity had left her. "Why is he taking her away? Cathy, have you quarreled?"

I shook my head. "May I use your telephone, please?"

"Of course. But before you do anything rash, you must tell me what happened because I may be able to help."

"There's nothing I know for certain except what I've told you. And please, there's no time to waste. I must call the Mitchells and find out if Pippa is at the hotel."

"The number is in my address book by the telephone."

Pippa was most certainly there. Frances Mitchell reassured me that they had scarcely felt the tremors and that Clive had said the hill on which the House of the Fountains stood could have formed a barrier between the edge of the troubled seam and Bou Hammagan itself. That was why there was no panic.

I didn't explain that I had seen panic at the top of the street. I rang off quickly and returned to Alexandra.

She was sitting in the patio listening to the radio. "The first report is that there's little damage to human life, but that houses have collapsed. I expect they are the mud-brick places most of the people out in the desert towns live in, but I don't know. The newscaster promises more information later, and that may mean that reporters and television men are on their way. Have you telephoned the office?"

"No—"

"Then, Cathy, do it at once."

I ran back down the hall and picked up the gilt receiver. But when at last I was understood by the operator and connected, there was no reply. I telephoned the hotel again, and this time spoke to the receptionist. The film people had been there, she said, but they had been called to Zacnador. "That is the place of the earthquake," she said in her gentle, broken English.

So Mark must have gone with them, and through a terrible chance —the devastation of a town—Pippa was still in Bou Hammagan.

Alexandra was in the garden. "Someone just rang the bell. This is the last moment when we want social interruptions . . ." She gave an impatient exclamation. "I should have known. It's Harriet and Justin, coming, I suppose, for any details I might have heard and they haven't."

They strode toward us, asking together, "You know, of course . . ."

"Yes," Alexandra said shortly.

Harriet sat down on the rim on the fountain basin and stuck out her legs. She looked tired and strained and more tense with nerves than usual. "I suppose Mark has gone?"

I nodded.

"One of these days he'll get caught. You can't go on playing the brave man and laughing at fate."

I didn't bother to answer her. I was trying to remember accounts of previous earthquakes. Lightning, they said, did not strike the same place twice; earthquakes did. There could be another and another. Out at Zacnador Mark was in danger.

Alexandra said, "Perhaps Ahmed has more news. It could be on the local station." She pressed the bell in the wall.

Lisette, with her long gray face and black eyes, came into the patio. "I rang for Ahmed," Alexandra said.

"I know, madame, but he has gone to his family."

"Without my permission?"

"Something upset him. I think he did not want to talk about it. It could be to do with his daughter; Yussef, who knows everything, tells me that he was worried about her. She is beautiful and the beautiful"—she waved her hands expressively—"stray."

Alexandra was not interested in the psychology of beautiful girls and cut her short. "When he comes back, please tell him to see me."

I had no idea whether Ahmed returned or what Alexandra said to him. I was waiting for guidance from someone or something to give me a lead to my next move. A clock in a house nearby was striking midday when Alexandra, who sat in the patio with her transistor radio turned on, said, "Cathy, listen. There's more news."

". . . the British television correspondent, Mark Mountavon, has been reported missing in the earthquake area of Zacnador. He was last seen walking past a group of houses which collapsed on him. Rescue operations have already been started and troops and workmen are already digging among the wreckage; planes are flying in supplies of vaccine and blankets to the stricken area—"

Alexandra cried above the sound of the newscaster's voice, "Oh, dear God . . ."

"I said it would happen one day." Harriet put her hands to her face.

I shot up out of my chair and raced to the telephone, beyond the small courtesies of guest to hostess. I called the office, but I knew even before I heard the persistent empty ringing that there still would be no one there who could answer me.

Back in the patio, I said to the silent group, "I never believe rumors. It must all be such a muddle there that no one can be certain of anything."

Their eyes went meaningfully past me. I turned to see what they saw. Pippa was crouched on one of the embroidered hassocks, making herself small, shrunk by shock.

Alexandra said, "She knows. The Mitchells brought her to the door a few moments ago, while you were on the telephone. But they didn't stay. They wanted to get back to their children in case there were other tremors."

I went and knelt by Pippa. "I don't think we should worry too much yet, darling. Everything out there must be so muddled that I'm sure no one can be certain of the facts."

She looked at me with the unblinking stare of a little cat, her face small and pinched under the golden tan. I put my arms around her. "Pippa, *he's all right.*"

She stiffened and leaned away from me. "How do you know? You aren't there."

The practical question came from a child grown suddenly older by shock and no longer believing the facile reassurance of adults.

Harriet said in her dry, sharp voice, "You can't fool her, Cathy, so don't try."

Alexandra held out her hand. "Pippa, come here."

She went with a small, grateful rush and hid her face in the softness of the silk at Alexandra's shoulder. "I can't bear it. I can't. I can't. Daddy out there . . ."

Alexandra stroked the long cascade of hair. "You must understand that we all care and are worried. But we can't do anything; we are so helpless. That is what is so often terrible about these things. You just have to wait—and have all the hope you can possibly find in yourself. Do you understand?"

"No." Pippa broke away from the consoling hands and faced us, her features made plain by the bruised look I had seen before when pain hit her. "There *is* something you could do. There *is*. *I'd* do something, only . . ." She paused, surveying us as if we were her enemies. "Only none of you would let me. You'd lock me in—"

"Don't be absurd," Harriet said.

Pippa gave her a tight, angry look.

"What *would* you do?" I asked.

She turned on me. "I'd go to that place and look for Daddy. *I'd* go. *I really . . . would . . . go . . .*" She paused, took a deep breath and poured her anger out onto me. "You took all his love. Before you came, *I* had it . . ." Her eyes were like two green flames, but the anger was an outlet for her immeasurable despair. She was young, and she believed that her sense of rejection and loss was unique.

I said helplessly, "If I could only try to make you understand."

"Oh, I understand. *You* don't want to save my father."

My own unhappiness and my effort at patience were both becoming like raw wounds into which this desperate child was rubbing salt. "Now you are talking rubbish and you know it. There are doctors and ambulances already at Zacnador. They can do far more than I can, even if they'd let me go."

"I wouldn't wait for anyone to *let* me."

"No one would take you. It's a very long way."

"If I were older no one could stop me."

"Oh, Pippa, shut up," Harriet said wearily. I had almost forgotten she was there. "You're just being the center of attraction and enjoying your drama."

Pippa swung around on her, her arms flailing. Durandal, watching us out of alert golden eyes, quivered and moved very slightly.

Alexandra cried, "Be careful!" and caught at his collar.

Harriet held Pippa's wildly resisting arms. "There's one lesson you'd better learn, and quickly, my child. Never get violent in front of a cheetah. He'd sense danger and tear you apart."

"He wouldn't."

"He would, you know."

Alexandra said sharply, "Don't talk like that, Harriet. You know it's not true. He wouldn't attack, but he might spring at you. And he's heavy, he'd knock you down."

Pippa went limp and lifted her face, and I saw her eyes shining with tears. "Let her go, Harriet," I said.

Free of the restraining grip, Pippa turned and fled.

Justin said wearily, "Thank God she hasn't an ambition to be a dancer. She's so heavy-footed, she'd flop through the floor."

"Don't go after her," Harriet said to me. "She'll howl her eyes out and probably hate you for seeing her do it."

"All right, she can hate me," I said, "but she's too young to bear this shock alone."

I found her crouched by the oleanders, her face thrust into the heavy blossoms, not howling at all; seemingly not even crying. I knelt by her side, aware of the faint musty smell of overblown roses mingling with the scent of the oleanders. "They seemed hard because they didn't understand," I said. "I do. You see, I love your father, too." Her face remained hidden, but I knew she was listening to me and I went on, "If it would do any good I would drive out to Zacnador myself, but I know it wouldn't. I would just be in the way of all the people who have gone to help and who know exactly what has to be done."

She put her hands over her ears. "Go away." Then, before I could obey her muffled command, she got up from the ground and edged around me, careful not to touch me as if contact would hurt her physically. I let her go because I saw that Harriet was right. I couldn't reach my grieving stepdaughter by gentleness and reason. Nor could I bear my own solitude. I went back to the group.

Harriet and Justin needed little persuasion from Alexandra to stay to lunch. For all her grief, Pippa ate what was put before her. Either she was being very polite or, more likely, her natural healthy appetite overcame her grief. But no one could get a word out of her. Eating was one thing; talking was beyond her.

After lunch we separated, Harriet and Justin going home, Alexandra disappearing to her room and Pippa scuffing slowly around the garden, wanting none of us.

I lay on my bed tormented by the need for activity, yet not knowing what to do. I clung to the desperate assumption that Mark was alive and that the first news out of a stricken area was often garbled and hysterical. I could not believe that I would never see him again. It might only be across a lawyer's table where the miserable arrangements for a separation or a divorce would take place, but from that confrontation I would at least know that he was alive. Strange how we thought of those we loved as immortal.

When I next saw him, I would get one thing straight. Rather than that he should send Pippa away to stay with people she did not know in an alien land, I would return to England on my own. So far as the window was concerned, I was beginning to wonder if the members of the churches had realized that the sharing of a building had been a pipe dream. There was still obviously no agreement, and it could be that, even if I stayed, I would only be wasting more time and suffering more frustration. Facing Mark with my decision would simplify everything for him.

But there was Pippa to be considered. It could be that my growing suspicion was correct and there was a secret woman in Mark's life and that when I freed him, he would go to her. It could be her impatience to have him that lay behind everything—even the theft of the diary. For on that day, June the sixteenth, had Pippa heard something, seen something? I would know the answer to that when it was all over. I would know, too, why one part of the page had had to be destroyed.

I was so tense that I had lain stiffly, without moving. But I was suddenly aware that someone had entered the room. I opened my eyes and saw Pippa slipping toward the door on tiptoe. I had thought she was downstairs, but while I was absorbed in my own thoughts, she must have crept in, not wanting me to see her or speak to her, relieved to see my tightly closed eyes, and hoping that I was asleep.

I had been wrong to leave her on her own with nothing but her frightened fears for her father. The only thing I could think of doing that would help her was to take her back to the hotel where her love of swimming would be a diversion.

When I looked out of the door, I saw her far down the passage, going, not to the garden, but along toward Alexandra's suite of rooms. I was on the point of calling to her, but before I could do so, she tapped on a door, and someone must have called to her to enter, for she disappeared.

There was nothing I could do but wait. Alexandra was perfectly capable of sending Pippa away if she didn't want to be disturbed.

XXV

A QUARTER of an hour; half an hour passed and Pippa had not returned. I planned to pretend to be asleep when she did. Instead, I sat up the instant the door opened, and she started and stared at me as if she hadn't remembered that I was in my room. Her face was flushed and I knew that she had been crying.

"Where have you been?"

"Do you care?"

"That's a silly question. But please answer mine."

"I went to Alexandra."

"You disturbed her rest."

"She wasn't asleep and she was kind. *She* wouldn't have left my father to die."

"My *father*" . . . sliding out of affectionate childhood into cooler adolescence long before her time.

"Come here, Pippa."

She remained stubbornly where she was.

"Very well, then, you must listen to me while you stand there."

She began to trace the delicate carving of the ebony table.

"If we have no news by tonight, I will find someone to take me to Zacnador tomorrow morning. I'll go to the garage and hire a driver—"

"You only *say* that just to make me like you."

If I hadn't been moved by that drenched little face I would have felt like slapping her. Instead I held on to what vestige of discipline I had left after the tensions of the day. "I didn't say it to please you or myself. I said it because I have decided that that is the only thing I can do for all our sakes."

She was studying her feet, and her hair fell like a curtain over her cheek. I might not have changed Pippa's attitude toward me by my sudden decision, but I had certainly surprised myself. Before I had spoken, I could see no reason for going, for if Mark were alive, he would return soon enough. If he had been found injured, I would be informed. If he were dead . . . I stopped my thoughts. "I've promised you I'll do all I can to get to Zacnador tomorrow," I persisted.

She raised her head and looked at me through skeins of her hair. If I had had one moment's thought that my decision would buy back her affection, I had been mistaken. I knew only too well that small, cold withdrawal.

"Darling, please understand. We are together in this unhappiness."

"No, we're not."

"If you think that, then I don't know what to say to you."

"I don't want you ever to talk to me again," she burst out, fists tight against her body.

I had to hold on to the fact that Pippa was a child in a state of shock and that I must not expect reason. There was only one thing I could do, and although it was a desperate and unpractical measure, I heard myself say, "Very well. I will go to Zacnador this afternoon. In fact, I'll go now."

She looked at me for a long, considering moment. Then without a word she turned, went into her room, and the door closed. She hadn't believed me. I got up, opened my purse and checked my money. For good measure, I also took some travelers' checks.

Yussef, unprepared for someone to be around during the heat of the day, was stretched out in his hut fast asleep. I dragged at the heavy door and closed it as quietly as I could. I was acting on impulse and

I had no idea whether I could keep my promise. It could well be that I would find it impossible to bribe any driver to take me to Zacnador, and by the time I had reached the bottom of the stepped street, I was so certain of failure that I nearly turned back.

"And what in the name of goodness do you think you're doing, wandering about in this heat?" Justin stood in my way.

"I'm going to Zacnador."

"Or flying to the moon. I know, sweetie, one gets strange illusions in times of shock. Now, go back to Alexandra's cool house like a good girl. I couldn't rest, either, and I've been to Mark's office. There's no one there. I've also been to the police, who are in a state of utmost confusion and could tell me nothing."

"I'm going to find someone who will drive me to Zacnador."

"You'd be hopelessly in the way."

"I've got to know what has happened to Mark."

Justin said patiently, "If he'd been found he'd have been rushed to Tunis by ambulance and the hospital would have telephoned you. If you go to Zacnador you'll just be a maddening nuisance."

"Then I'll have to *be* a maddening nuisance."

"For sweet heaven's sake—" He was roused to rare irritation. "What's the matter with you? Do you enjoy risking your life? It's quite possible there'll be other earth tremors, and how do we know that the road near Zacnador hasn't collapsed, and driving along it, you'll go headlong into a gulley and that'll be the end of you, sweetie."

"I'll risk that."

He leaned against a shadowed wall and looked at me as if I were some strange animal. "What has Mark ever done for you that you can be so blindly devoted?"

"Loved me."

"Oh, come off it. Mark is married to a camera's eye. Or hasn't that dawned on you yet? So, suppose you just wait at the house for news. It will come."

"I'm going to Zacnador and I'm going now. The garage owner can find me someone who'll take me; I'll pay well."

"Since when have you believed that money is the Open Sesame that will induce someone to risk his neck for you?"

"Justin, go home. This is my business and I must cope."

"You're being an awful little fool."

"I know. But it won't be the last time in my life."

"If you go, it could be, at that!"

"I'll risk it."

"But no Hammagarb is going to risk *his* life for your pretty neck."

"The earthquake is over. He'll only have to drive me there—and the road could be perfectly all right."

"Well, then, we'll see."

"*We* . . . ?"

"That makes two fools, doesn't it? I'll take you."

"No, Justin . . ."

"Oh, let's not stand here arguing."

"It's wonderfully kind of you, but I'm sure I'll find someone. I couldn't let you—"

"Don't be so charmingly polite. I said I'd take you."

"After all your arguments?"

"Surely you don't resent a bit of a fight when in the end I concede victory to you? But whether you do or not, I'm taking you to Zacnador."

"But Harriet—"

"To hell with Harriet."

I began to walk away from the stepped street, but Justin stopped me. "Alexandra's house is nearer than mine. Let's go and collect some lemonade and fruit for the journey. Thirty miles is nothing in England, but out here and in the heat of the day—oh, well, let's not think of it. Let's act."

We climbed the interminable steps and were let in by a surprised and drowsy Yussef.

Justin went in search of food, and I went to Alexandra's suite and listened. But I needn't have hesitated to wake her. She was talking to Lisette. I knocked on the door and she called to me to enter.

She was sitting at her dressing table wearing a robe of green silk. Lisette had washed her hair and was combing it with slow, careful strokes. "Oh, Cathy," she greeted me. "Twice a week I have to endure this boring process. If I tried to escape, Lisette would be quite capable of finding me and dragging me to the washbasin."

Lisette drew down her long upper lip in protest. "Madame, you know your hair is so beautiful that it has to be looked after carefully, and in this climate—hot and with sand that gets in your throat and your nose—"

"Lisette, you exaggerate."

I said, "I'm going to Zacnador. Justin has offered to drive me."

Alexandra turned so quickly that the comb in Lisette's hand scraped her scalp and she winced. "I doubt that you will be allowed near the place."

232

"At least I can try. What I *can't* do is to stay inactive."

Alexandra leaned her head back and closed her eyes. "Oh, what can I say to you?"

"Just wish me . . . peace of mind."

She jerked her head away from Lisette's hands. "You're hurting me. Leave my hair and let it dry . . . Lisette, I said *leave* it. Thank you, I can manage now."

Lisette looked indignantly at me as if I had been the cause of the summary dismissal. When she had left us, Alexandra frowned at her reflection and, elbows on the dressing table, smoothed the flesh over her strong cheekbones. "It will be terrible in this heat, but I suppose if I were in your place, I'd go. At least Justin is a good driver and he knows the roads almost like a native."

"Do you mind if we take some lemonade and some fruit?"

"Take anything you wish." For the second time since I had known her, she bent and kissed my cheek.

I waited in the courtyard for Justin. If Mark were really dead, something of me would have died too. *But if Mark were dead, I would no longer be in danger.* For whoever wanted him would have no more reason to hound me out of his life.

"Hey, you'd better get a move on if we're going." Justin appeared in the distant doorway. "Or have you got second thoughts about it?"

"No . . . No . . ." Not second thoughts, just new ones, so frightening that I was glad of action, even of the long hot journey into the desert. I anticipated the discomfort as something that, by its extreme, would take my mind off the thoughts that had frozen me as I waited in that dreadful and beautiful African afternoon.

At first we drove through villages scattered over the hard dry earth. "I'm keeping away from the roads that the ambulances and the bulldozers will use," Justin said, "and this one is really just a track. So sit tight or you'll find yourself hitting the car roof in places. And, come to that, those who are already at Zacnador will hit the sky when they see us arrive. We'll be as unpopular as a flashlight on a courting couple."

"I don't care."

"Well, neither do I. Maybe Mark and I don't speak the same language, but he *is* my brother, and I've got a large stake in anxiety over him." He touched my cheek lightly. "Cheer up, they could have dug him out whole by now. Mark has more lives than a cat."

Even with the sweat gleaming on his forehead and his arms bare and brown, Justin managed to look elegant. "You're good for me," I said gratefully.

We passed plantations of eucalyptus trees with their dappled trunks and sage-green leaves, and date palms which sprang up haphazardly as if they, of all things on this hot earth, were free to choose the place in which to grow.

I forced myself to take an interest in everything. I even said, at one point, "We're climbing, aren't we?"

"Ahead of us is a small massif nobody has ever bothered to name. There's a rather uninteresting town built on it; you can see the minaret from here."

It pointed, pencil-thin, into the burning blue. A short way past the town, Justin pointed out the domed shrines of marabouts, the holy men of Islam. Ancient sandstone arches rose out of the baked earth.

"They say there's probably a city, two thousand years old, buried beneath here, but as yet nobody has excavated." Justin's voice was casual, his manner seemingly relaxed, but that, I felt, was a mask behind which he hid anxiety. "Up there"—he nodded toward a ridge of mountains to our left—"it's very beautiful, with juniper forests and small streams and flowers."

Mark had told me about that place, Djebel Thamadi . . . My heart began to thud with the heat around me and the fear inside me.

Thorn bushes made natural fences around the little villages, and here and there were the tawny walls of old buildings already forgotten, Justin said, when England was basking in the golden age of Elizabeth the First.

We followed the track for miles through the country of honey-colored dunes and clumps of prickly pear. Once, passing a caravan of camels, Justin told me they were nomads from the interior beyond the Sefra Atlas which lay to the east of Morocco.

A helicopter passed overhead, flying low, and away to our right, lines of trucks and ambulances appeared from the other side of the small massif.

"That's the road we should have taken," Justin said. "But we'd have been shunted off. Those trucks are carrying aid to Zacnador."

We passed great sand hills and wind-rippled plains.

"Underneath all that," Justin said, "there's probably an incredible wealth in manganese and gold and wolfram."

I didn't know what wolfram was and I didn't ask. I felt that Justin was talking as much to keep his own mind off the fear of what we might find at Zacnador as to divert my thoughts.

XXVI

FOR TWO HOURS Justin nursed the little car over the ruts and boulders. Once we passed a strange flat place, white and shimmering, in which robed men and women seemed to move like gauzy shadows, and mud domes rose up and became lost at the edge of the quivering light.

"That was once a salt lake. Now it is just a place of mirage."

Here and there were deep ditches which Justin told me were dug to hold back the sand. I listened, only half attentive, fretting for speed. Justin ignored my obvious impatience, and we stopped once for long cool drinks from the huge thermos and to eat fruit. I was startled to see what I thought to be a rock rise in the great silence with a grunting protest. Its head was raised with the proud carriage as though it wore an uncertain crown, but the swaying of its spindly legs as it rose was in comical contrast.

235

I watched the man who had climbed onto its back drive the animal over the rolls of sand that were near purple in the shadow-waves. Although the fruit and the drink we were having were thirst-quenching, I fretted at each wasted moment, but Justin was obviously as anxious as I and we were quickly on our way again.

After we had driven for a few more miles, Justin said, "Now you can see it."

Hope and despair fought like enemies underneath my sharp interest. "It's a straggling place."

"That's what the earthquake does. It heaves and spreads, throws up and swallows. Are you all right?"

"Of course." I wasn't; I felt more than a little sick with fear.

He patted my knee. "Good girl."

People appeared on the track-side, women wearing tentlike haiks, children wandering vague and dazed, dogs scavenging. The car edged forward until suddenly we could go no farther, for great fissures of upthrust earth blocked us. The rents in the sandstone crust were yards wide, piled on each other as if tossed by giants.

A pall of dust was rising like a yellow cloud toward the sun, veiling it, so that it was like a red balloon through the patches of cinnamon-colored gloom. There must, I supposed, have been another more recent earth tremor for the dust to be there.

Trucks were dotted like gray-black beetles in the flat spaces left by the upheaved earth; another helicopter passed noisily overhead, and in front of us was a mound of rubble that I knew had, only that morning, been mud-brick homes, because rough and broken furniture and pots and pans lay in the wreckage. Robed men and women were clawing at the piles of earth and rock, salvaging what they could of their possessions. And all the time a terrible wailing went on, rising and falling, as the people, bereft of their homes, tore the earth to search for what they could find, calling on Allah.

Children were weeping and clinging to their mothers' robes; dogs howled and the helicopter droned on.

Justin said, "I suggest you just sit quiet and let me investigate."

But I was already out of the car. The heat struck like a furnace and I felt that my clothes, already sticking to me, would melt and my skin would sear and burn up.

"Why don't you do what you're told?" Justin said.

"You know why—"

"Hey, Cathy, come back. I'm not at all certain how far we'll be allowed to go. It will depend on the authorities. We'll try to find the camera crew."

I was already out of earshot, climbing over the rifts and dodging two yawning chasms that cut straight through the stricken town. Children running after parents slithered down the sloping walls of earth. A woman crouched over a child, blowing on his face to give him air, too terrified to realize that he was alive and the danger was over.

As Justin and I clambered farther over the wreckage of the small town, I saw that quite a few of the houses still stood, and the mosque appeared to be undamaged. The earthquake had struck the edge of the town and then by-passed it.

"First, we've got to find the police, the relief teams or the Red Cross. I'm not certain about the first. They'll probably give us no news and throw us out. We're in the way."

A massive rescue operation had begun. Helpers were everywhere: men capped against the sun, shoveling rubble, hurling pickaxes at demolished walls; women dragging at bundles of possessions, helped by children and impeded by howling dogs and scattering hens. The air was still thick with dust and the sky looked like beige silk dusted with pepper. But I saw no casualties except for men and women being treated for cuts and shock.

"I'll make a guess the people will take to Tassourit, an oasis a few miles away," Justin said. "They'll camp there until their homes are rebuilt."

"Even building a small town like this will take ages."

"Oh, I don't know. The authorities will have to make this first priority and move builders from the New City. There's an officer of Bou Hammagan's almost nonexistent army over there." Justin made for him.

At the same time I saw a Red Cross ambulance. I left Justin and went over to the young man leaning against the hood, a strange straw sun hat tilted over his eyes. "Are you English?"

He answered me with only a slight accent. He was French and his ambulance unit had been lent to Bou Hammagan until it formed its own. "But what are you doing here"—his eyes flicked to my left hand —"madame? This is no place for you. They should have stopped you at the edge of the town. It's wrong to send women."

"No one sent me."

"So you are not a journalist?"

"My husband is working with a film crew and I believe they were sent here when the earthquake hit the town."

"That's right, they were."

"Then where are they? You must have seen them."

He stood still leaning against the truck. "I wouldn't try to look if I were you. It's been chaos here; it still is, as you'll find out if you go down there." He jerked his head toward a mass of half-ruined buildings.

"Perhaps the television crew is somewhere down there."

"Or they've been thrown out. Nobody who isn't essential is allowed here for the moment." His manner implied: "And that includes you, madame."

"We came by a little-known route," I said, "so we didn't pass anyone who might have stopped us."

"And now you'd better go back down that road, hadn't you?"

I said again, shouting at him as if he were deaf, "My husband is here and I'm not leaving until I have news of him."

He shook his head. "You are foolish. The earthquake lasted only a few seconds, but look what it has done. There has been a third tremor and the quake itself could strike again."

"I'll risk that."

"Then you're *very* foolish and I'm quite sure your husband will tell you so. You're just in the way."

"I'm sorry, but I must get news of Mark—my husband. Someone must have seen—"

"Good afternoon," Justin said from behind me. "Have you seen a film crew?"

"Monsieur," said the young man, "I suggest you take this lady out of here as quickly as you can. I've explained it all to her. The television people have probably left of their own accord or been thrown out. Sightseers—"

"I am *not* a sightseer," Justin said haughtily. "I'm a resident of Bou Hammagan and my brother is here with a television film crew and has been reported injured."

"Then he will have been taken to the hospital." The young man was unaffected. He was probably hot and tired and had seen too many accidents. "Please go." He pointed. "I have to keep my eyes on the men digging over there. Through those collapsed buildings cries have been heard."

Mark, was that the spot? . . .

"The rest of our fleet are over in the area to the right. That's another bad place."

"If there are foreigners among the casualties—"

"Then the hospital will tell you." He made a swift, sweeping gesture of Latin impatience. He didn't like us and his long, lean French face showed it. We should have stayed in Bou Hammagan and waited for news; we were a damned nuisance.

The yellow dust cloud was moving slowly upward and dispersing. A shadow, dark as an eagle, towered over us and a voice spoke in Hammagarb. We swung around and saw a uniformed man, his dark face streaked with dust and sweat.

I said quickly, "Tell him I am here to find my husband. Ask if there is anyone filming."

"That's precisely what I am doing. Now, let me take over and don't interrupt. We'll get on better that way," Justin ordered.

I pushed back untidy strands of my damp, limp hair, rubbed the palms of my hands down my slacks and watched the men's faces. Swift, alien words flowed half-angrily between them and I guessed the policeman was no more pleased to see us than the ambulance driver had been.

"At least," I pleaded, "let me know what you're saying."

Justin made a gesture of thanks to the policeman and turned to me. "We've been on a wild-goose chase," he said. "The birds have flown, the whole lot of them."

"I don't believe it. They'd stay—"

"Not if they were refused permission, they wouldn't. They apparently raced here, took a few shots and then were ordered out because there was danger of another earthquake and anybody who isn't essential is in the way. We are. They want rescuers who know their job, not amateurs looking for someone who isn't even here."

"But Mark . . ."

"I'm coming to that. You don't have to worry. News came that he was a casualty simply because when the camera team packed up, they couldn't find Mark—"

"But they must have searched."

"Just keep quiet and listen." Justin took my arm. "I'm trying to tell you what happened as near as anyone knows it. The policeman has just told me that he saw one of the cars—and it turned out to be Mark's—parked some way away from the rest of the crew. At some time while they were being ordered out, a group of houses collapsed, hiding the car in a cloud of dust and rubble. In the confusion nobody could see exactly what happened, but the policeman tells me that he saw Mark struggling out of the wreckage and spoke to him. Mark answered in what I'm quite sure was very bad Hammagarb, saying that he had to get back to the city; that there was something important he had to do."

Something important. Pippa . . . Mark wasted no time. By now he would be well on the way to Bou Hammagan, and however hard he drove, Justin would never catch up with him.

Mark was not dead.

But he had to be hard, to cut cleanly through the ties of love and emotion by which he felt I had held him. He had to be ruthless to all of us except Pippa.

Justin was leading me across the upheaval of rocks and sand. Men and women had stopped wailing and were stumbling in their long, dusty robes toward the truck load of food and tents and blankets. Justin and I could, of course, stay and help. But everything seemed to be so organized, so expert, that I knew we were expendable.

Also, I had to get to Mark and to Pippa. I had to know the truth. I no longer cared that Mark hated being questioned, that he guarded his freedom to act as he chose. I was involved and I intended to know how and why.

I followed Justin's leaps and bounds over the crumbled earth, and my thoughts frightened me. It could have been the havoc wrought in the little desert town that stimulated me to thinking of a more personal disaster, but the thought was there, blinding my actions, so that Justin kept having to turn and hoist me up over the rocks which tipped and rolled as I trod on them.

Although Mark had said that the delivery of Louise's box and the verse inside it could be a way of hurting him through me, I didn't believe it, and I wondered if he did, either. Mark knew more than he told . . .

The question that nagged and tore at me as I staggered through that blazing afternoon was the persistent mystery of who wanted to see him free of me. There were two people who, I felt, could give me a lead, but who—possibly out of a mutual ill-advised kindness—were keeping the truth from me.

I had come to Zacnador in fear for Mark. I was returning to Bou Hammagan with deepening suspicions that shamed me because of my love for him.

I had slid my hand out of Justin's and, unaware of where my feet were taking me, fell headlong into a heap of loose rock. "Damn, oh, damn . . ."

"Say worse, sweetie, I don't mind." Justin picked me up. "Are you hurt?"

"No."

"Look." He put an arm around me. "I know it's all too much for you—and in this heat. Go on, yell if you want to. I've had women weeping on my shoulder before and I hold no grudge against them for it."

With his arm around me we walked the few remaining yards to the car, and Justin drove across the trackless outskirts of the little town.

Even a few miles out of Zacnador the sky still wore a pale-bronzed skin and the plaintive wailing of the women was still in my ears; the shattered buildings, the upthrust earth and the cracked walls of houses that still managed to stay upright were like photographic transparencies hung between me and the desert. A helicopter droned over our heads, and on the road to our left I saw more trucks racing to Zacnador.

We had driven for only half an hour when Justin stopped near an oasis village and reached for the thermos of lemonade. I protested that I wasn't thirsty.

"But I am."

"Of course. I'm sorry."

"It upset you, didn't it, seeing what was left of Zacnador. But, you know, those people have few possessions to lose and homes will be rebuilt for them. In no time at all they will be kneeling facing the East and thanking Allah for their escape."

"I'm afraid I was thinking of Mark." I couldn't yet tell Justin why; I couldn't say, "He is taking Pippa out of my care." I couldn't say, "*She*—whoever *she* is—has won."

"Drink, sweetie." Justin pushed a plastic cup of lemonade at me and I drank, quietly grateful.

Justin took a deep draft from the bottle and let out a long, satisfied "Ah-h-h," put the bottle away and drove on.

The journey out had been too slow; the journey back was even worse. We were driving through the late heat of the day.

"Noel Coward had words for what we're doing," Justin said. "We're the crazy British who think it's clever to suffer heat and cold where others take siestas or hibernate. Oh, well, the things I do for the girls I love!" He flicked a hand at my cheek. The car swerved and hit a stone, bucked, and then as Justin swung the wheel, we were jogging along on the earth track again.

I sat fighting the urge to tell him why I was in a panic to get back to Bou Hammagan. I had never been quite certain what Justin's reactions would be to anything I considered serious. He could be sympathetic or he could disbelieve and mock. "The Mountavons," Harriet had said, "are not easy to know." Nor were they easy to talk to. So, too exhausted by heat to talk of inconsequential things, we drove in silence along the road that was no road, back past small oases and the hills of windblown sand. We saw again the straggling little town with its beaten-earth towers and the shrines of the holy men. I forced myself to look about me at camels taking dust baths and then rising on knobbled knees—their skins in wrinkled folds—and loping into the great distance. Native women walked like queens; hooded men rode asses; the palm tips quivered in a breeze I couldn't feel.

Nothing held my attention for more than a few moments. *Please, God, don't let Mark take Pippa away from me* . . . The words sounded in my mind like a child's naïve plea. But there was nothing naïve about the way I willed Justin to get me back to Bou Hammagan. *Go faster. Get on . . . Get on . . .*

I knew, though, that if Justin accelerated, he would probably plunge us into the disaster of a shattered car engine in this place of deep ruts and villainous rocks, and then we would have to wait hours to be rescued. Patience always involved a fight with myself.

A plane passed over our heads, coming in to land at some makeshift airstrip near Zacnador. I watched it, aware of my fingers working and fidgeting in my lap.

Justin said, "You should be riding a chariot through the streets of Rome with a whip in your hand and wild horses in the shafts."

"I didn't think it showed."

"Your impatience is shrieking at me. But you learn to treat the desert with respect."

I had always been a bad actress and I wore my thoughts like printed ribbons flying out of my head. "I'm sorry, Justin, and I'm grateful for what you've done."

"Think nothing of it. When there are no tourists to take around, I'm as idle as a lizard in the sun. Harriet despises me for it. But then, she's the lean, energetic type." He glanced sideways at me. "You're crazy about Mark, aren't you?"

"He's your brother, so perhaps you can't see what I see to be crazy about."

"No, I don't. I'm quite certain Harriet wouldn't put herself out for me as you are doing for him—as far as that goes, neither would I for her. Perhaps we're cold fish and our lack of emotion is the only thing we have in common. We were 'ill met by moonlight' if ever a couple were. But let's not be profound in this heat."

I closed my eyes and rocked in my seat as the car dipped through potholes. In spite of the anxiety and discomfort, I fell into a light sleep. My mind became a jumble of tiny pictures, each one a nightmare having for its theme the manipulation of two people rejecting a third. Pippa and Mark escaping from me—one of them in innocence, the other motivated by a determination that had yet to be explained to me.

The car suddenly tipped me forward, and I heard the end of Justin's sentence. ". . . damned ludicrous, but even in the desert we need seat belts."

XXVII

FROM THE DISTANCE Bou Hammagan was rimmed with tangerine light. A quiver of hope ran thinly through my fear. There had been a disaster and so Mark would not be free to make the long journey with Pippa to Tunis. He would have to remain with the rest of the film crew working on the report of the earthquake. He might even have returned to the House of the Fountains. But wherever he was, he would have to be near a telephone and not in a car racing across empty land to take Pippa from me.

I couldn't understand why he had left Zacnador so hastily. Of course, with this disaster out in the little town, he could not go off on a long journey.

And then the fear came back. How did I know what Mark would do if he were desperate? He could have taken a wild chance on driving Pippa to Tunis and returning in time to pick up the threads of whatever had to be done to get the tapes to England. After all, he had done his part already in his commentary. So, fear and hope jostled for a place as Justin parked the car and we climbed the stepped street together, each stone still burning with the day's heat, chipped and broken so that one had to walk up them with bowed head as if doing a penance.

Mark had had a long start and I would be too late. Thinking of it like that made it seem as if he were a criminal and I represented the avenging law. All he was doing was taking his own daughter out of my care for her safety.

When Alexandra's house was at last in sight, I saw that the great door in the wall was open and Ahmed was watching us approach. He was no longer in his servant's uniform but wore an immaculate white djellabah. One huge hand gripped the arm of a frightened girl who crouched by his side. Her black hair fell in a thick fan around her shoulders and the engraved silver medallion I had seen three times before swung like a pendulum as she tried to fight herself free of Ahmed's grasp.

"Zaleida!" I whispered.

Ahmed's usually impassive face was contorted; his fingers dug into the girl's soft arm as he swung her around roughly.

I might not have been there at all; he had eyes only for Justin, and as we came within hearing distance, he broke into furious Hammagarb.

For a few moments sentences shot like bullets from the two men, and then the girl, wrenching free, flung herself between them. Ahmed's hand rose as if to strike her, and I made an instinctive move to thrust her away. At the same moment I saw, as the sleeve of Ahmed's djellabah fell away, the gold at his wrist.

Gold watches were fairly common in Bou Hammagan, but now that I was near to it, I saw that it was not a watch but a wide, elaborate band of gold. The girl, Zaleida, clung to me. She was taller and plumper than I and the scent of sandalwood hung around her.

She was weeping and protesting in pained English to me, "Do not . . . let them . . . Please, madame . . . Stop my father—" But at that point her English let her down and she slipped into her own language. "My father; Ahmed . . ."

I cut the three of them short. "I'd be grateful if you'd let me in on all this. *I mean, talk in English,*" I shouted at them.

Ahmed turned flashing jet eyes on me. "Ah-h-h." I had an uncomfortable feeling that he saw me as less than a beetle crawling across his path. "You, madame, you do not know." His French-accented English was not easy to follow. "You are a woman and you choose to be blind."

"I don't, but tell me why you think I do."

"Your husband . . . like him . . ." He pointed a thick, dark finger at Justin. "Like him . . . They both shamed my daughter. They make it hard now for her to find a husband. And for that . . . *flous* . . . *flous* . . ."

Justin said, "He means money—silver. But he has plenty and there isn't going to be any more. She's still a virgin so far as I'm concerned, anyway. She'll find a husband."

Zaleida reached out a smooth, tanned hand to Justin, but he drew back. "It's over, sweetie. *Finis*. You know that." He turned to me. "Zaleida is beautiful, isn't she? I took her out a few times when Harriet thought I was dancing attendance on casual tourists spending a day in the city. But I drove Zaleida to Djebel Thamadi and I kissed her there among the roses. All pretty and romantic, but that's all that happened. It's over for me, though I'm afraid she doesn't see it that way. She began making herself a nuisance, so I asked Mark to help. I didn't want her coming around to the house and making a scene with Harriet. Mark saw her and tried to make her understand that a kiss isn't a signed contract for a wedding."

"Oh, Justin, you idiot!" I cried.

"You pay; you pay," Ahmed hissed at him.

"Oh, do shut up," Justin said wearily. "I've paid. And plenty. You've had enough out of me now for a nice rich wedding for her."

"There is your brother. He must pay too."

"My brother did nothing but try to talk Zaleida out of following me around. And, since I have no money, he paid what you demanded. Now are you satisfied?"

"No."

The girl fell on her father, hands clutching him, pleading. He thrust her away with such force that she was flung across the step.

Justin caught her just before she fell. "Now look," he said to Ahmed, "she's a girl and she's gentle and I'm not going to see you roughing her up. Have you got that? You're a pretty good giant of a man, but I've got a punch like an ass's kick when I choose to use it." He waited. "You may not have understood all those words, but you've got the meaning. Zaleida became a bit of a nuisance, but what she wants is a husband. Get her married and stop her following European men around or heaven help you when the New City is built."

"She was there in the alley when I followed the boy," I said. "Why were you watching me, Zaleida?"

Her father answered for her. "My daughter was there because that is where she live. You were a stranger and so she watch you. She is simple, my Zaleida, but she is also curious."

"A boy was sent to lead me deep into a strange part of the city. I sensed danger and so I turned back. You were there."

"Of course. I tell you, we live in that street. It is not a good place, but we are poor—"

"Like hell!" muttered Justin.

"You knew the boy I was following."

"This is my city. I know everyone." He spoke as if he were boasting of a virtue.

"Did you ask the boy why he wanted me to follow him?"

"I did not notice that he was, madame."

"Oh, yes, you did."

"You are questioning my word?"

"I am."

"Then what have I to say, madame?"

"The truth."

"That I knew that little"—his English failed him—"*gamin?*"

I gave up the argument, and Justin took my arm. "Go inside, Cathy. We're getting nowhere with this."

But I had to make one more attempt. "You were outside Mrs. Mountavon's house on the night the diary was returned. I recognized that gold band on your wrist."

"It is a small city, madame."

"But my sister-in-law was frightened. Why?"

"Sister-in-law" puzzled him.

"My wife," Justin said impatiently. "And now let's stop talking. I know the Hammagarbs too well. If they don't want to give explanations, they'll skirt around them and there's nothing you can do. Zaleida, for heaven's sake get off that dusty ground and go home. You're all right now, Cathy. Go on in and have a nice cool bath. I'm off."

Ahmed made no effort to stop him, but as he watched Justin walk swiftly away, he said to me, "Madame is not here. She is at her villa in the New City, and I have a message that you must go there quick."

"Why?"

"She tells me to tell you that she has taken the little girl there for safety."

"Safety from whom?"

"I don't know."

Safety from Mark . . .

"Have you seen my husband, Ahmed?"

"No. But I will. I must. He took Zaleida, also."

"That is something I refuse to believe," I said impatiently, "but there is no time to argue the point now. I must go to the villa. Will you please take me?"

"I go with my daughter back to our family."

I guessed that Zaleida's wildly waving hands were a protest. But I was certain that Ahmed, with his eyes on Justin's swiftly retreating figure, had no intention of letting his beautiful daughter go free.

"Then I suppose I must ask Yussef to take me."

"He has gone to the villa with Madame."

Of course. Alexandra would take a man, and a young and strong one at that, to guard herself and Pippa from whatever or whomever she feared.

I knew the way to the New City, but I dreaded walking so far on my own, and in the dark. I had no intention of letting Ahmed know that, though, and so I said, "But I haven't a car and I can't walk all that way."

He shrugged. "I cannot help you."

"Nor can you leave this house unattended while you take your daughter home."

"Lisette . . ."

Of course, Lisette, the shadowy woman I had forgotten.

In the light of the lamp which shone over the door as the swift darkness hit us, Ahmed's eyes flicked over me. The insolence and arrogance of that glance angered me and I asked, "Has Madame given you permission to leave the house with only Lisette to guard it?"

"I no longer ask permission. I do not stay here. The New City will have rich people—very rich. I shall work there." He reached out to Zaleida who, drained of energy, was leaning against the wall. "Come" —he jerked forward—"we go." And before I could push past him, he had slammed the great door and was nudging Zaleida in front of him down the stepped street.

I put out my hand to touch the bell and then stopped. Lisette, left to guard the house, could not come with me to the villa, and Justin was gone, slipping away from unpleasantness with a characteristic speed. There was only one place to which I could go for help. Harriet had a car and she would take me to Alexandra's villa.

I had no fear of the stepped street. I had become used to it, and I had seen the children and the dogs many times before. The men who hung around in groups did not even turn as I went by. The Europeans living at the House of the Fountains were of no interest to them.

I ran across Isakila Square, winding my way through the crouching groups of men and the ginger dogs. The old man, still carving his intricate chessmen, looked up as I passed and said something. But I had no idea whether he was speaking to me or to someone at the back of the booth outside which he sat.

Harriet answered the bell almost immediately and gave me a long, blank look. "Oh, I thought Justin had forgotten his key. But what news have you? Come in. Come in."

I told her that Mark was safe and asked if I could call the office and find out if he was there. But he wasn't, and John Mayne, who spoke to me, had no idea where he was. "I gather he beat it out of Zacnador," he said. "We thought at first that he had been buried under a collapsed building, but when they dug, they found no one. One of the ambulance drivers said that he saw a man get into a small car and race off. He was going so quickly that he thought the car would overturn on the chaotic road."

Harriet had been watching me, and as I crashed down the receiver, she said, "I gather Mark isn't there. Then where?"

"I don't know. Harriet, I just don't know. But I have to get to Alexandra's villa in the New City. *I have to* . . . When we returned from Zacnador, Justin saw me as far as the house and then he left me. And so I don't know where he is and so I can't ask him to take me."

"Why go to the villa?"

"Because Alexandra is there with Pippa. Ahmed told me."

"For God's sake . . ." Harriet stared at me. "Cathy, you can't waste time. Go there . . ." She ran to a table and opened her purse. "Here are the car keys." She threw them at me.

"But I've never driven your car."

"It's like any other; it has gears and a brake. And for the love of heaven, don't stand there arguing."

"I have no license to drive abroad." The tension had tightened in the room. "Suppose someone asks for it? Harriet, *I* can't take your car without a license."

"Who the hell cares? You can drive and no one will be around in the New City to stop you. There's only an old night watchman, and he won't care if you've got a license to drive in this place or not."

"Harriet, please take me."

"I can't. I must wait for Justin." She looked at me with frightened eyes, her head turning quickly left and then right as if expecting someone to leap out of the wall at us. "Go *on,* Cathy. You know the way. You drive around the back of the Square and onto the road to the New City. Alexandra's villa is just beyond where they're building the church."

I knew I could find the way, but I wanted Harriet with me. "Why don't you leave a note and come too?"

"Oh, don't argue. Go . . ."

Harriet's agitation sparked off a deeper fear in me, but as I ran to the car, I couldn't name it. It was like the black wing of a gigantic, unknown bird bearing down on me.

The car stood against the wall. I got into it and started the motor. Only when I was away from the crowds in the Square and onto the road to the New City did I really think about what my undefined fear had been.

Harriet didn't trust Mark. The conversation I had overheard through the hollow wall at the House of the Fountains had proved that. What I had just told her verified it. She understood my urgency and had matched it with her own. I was certain she was already on her way to find Justin at one of his café haunts. And when she found him, she would tell him what she knew and I, as yet, did not know.

XXVIII

THE LITTLE CAR was not the easiest to drive. I doubted that
it would pass any of the stringent British mechanical tests. But it got
me to the New City, past the watchman's hut, across the open space
in front of the church to the oleanders that formed an arc around the
back of Alexandra's unfinished villa.

I parked the car by the bushes and ran to the house. No light
showed, and for a moment a new fear hit me. Suppose Alexandra
and Pippa weren't there, had never been there—but someone had laid
a trap for me? A dark house in an area as yet undeveloped meant
that there would be no one around to help me. It was a perfect setting. Had Ahmed known? Perhaps it was he who had thought up the
message he had said had come from Alexandra.

It was too late for questions, and I handed myself a crumb of comfort. Harriet knew where I was. She would find Justin and they

would both follow me to the New City because she had seen I was afraid, and she was afraid for me.

I could not see a car, so, if Mark had come, he had already left and taken Pippa with him. Alexandra would know. She had to be there to tell me what had happened, to explain, to help me.

I called her name loudly and listened. There was no sound. An instinctive sense of self-preservation made me stand still. I had no intention of walking through the gaping blackness where the door would be and perhaps into the trap set for me. I was staying well outside and within easy running distance to the car.

As I looked up at the two-storied house, black against the sapphire-blue of the sky, a half-moon glimmered above a group of date palms and lit up a shadow that moved at the top of the outside steps.

Someone was waiting.

"Pippa?"

If she had been there, she would have answered and, in spite of her new distrust of me, would have come running, for the one thing she still hated was the dark.

"Pippa?"

Again there was no reply, but I thought the shadow, which moved again, was much too tall for a child. Sending me to the villa now seemed even more of a trap, but I was reasonably safe outside. The little car gave me courage . . . I could run, and run fast, and I had taken the precaution of leaving the door ajar so that I need not waste time opening it. "Whoever is up there, say something."

"Cathy."

I drew a great breath of relief and ran halfway up the steps. The flimsy temporary rail trembled in my hands. "Alexandra. Oh, thank heaven. Where is Pippa?"

"She's quite safe here with me. Pippa, call Cathy."

"No . . . No . . ." The cry came small and scared. "Please, don't let her come."

"You'll have to learn never to be frightened, won't you, Pippa? Courage and self-possession and poise. Those are the most important things you will have to be taught."

"It's d-dark—" she wailed.

"You should have stopped being afraid of the dark long ago."

"I don't wonder she's scared," I said, "in a strange place. Pippa, I'm here and—"

"Don't come any nearer, Cathy," Alexandra called. "Durandal is with me."

"I'm not afraid of him. He knows me."

"Oh, he won't mean to harm you, but he might spring at you if you startle him. He is already restless because Pippa is upset. He senses agitation and it makes him nervous. He's heavy and he could knock you down those steps without meaning to be vicious. So just stay where you are."

"Why did you ask me to come here? Where is Mark? And why is Pippa upset?"

Alexandra's soft laughter came at me through the darkness. "Your questions are like darts; you take my breath away. I sent for you because this is the safest place in which to talk."

"Talk about what? . . ." I waited, leaning cautiously against the rail and felt it give a little with my weight. "Alexandra, why is Pippa here?"

"You told me Mark was going to take her away."

"Yes, but she could surely have been guarded more easily at your house. Or, of course, that's probably why you brought Yussef."

"He only came with us because Durandal is too strong for me. I have sent him home. Later, he'll come and get us."

"Later?"

"When it's all arranged and there is no more danger for Pippa. She's my main concern."

"And mine," I said and took a step nearer the tall shadow on the terrace. "You think Mark will come?"

"He'll do anything in the world to find Pippa. But I can't allow him to take her."

"This is *my* problem . . ."

"Oh, no. It's out of your hands, Cathy. You knew that, surely, when you heard Harriet and me talking after your experience at the Kourifia Caves. One wall on that side of the house is hollow. You were in your bedroom and so you couldn't help hearing."

"You intended that I should?"

"Of course. We were trying to warn you without having to say it directly to you. You must have guessed then who had changed the boards at Kourifia, taking a chance that, as you were going there with Harriet, you would go into the cave again and perhaps not notice that a different one was blocked up. It's a muddled kind of place, or so I've been told. At any rate, if it went wrong, there were other ways—"

"Of . . . ?"

"Of losing you—shall we put it more gently that way?"

"I don't believe you."

"Mark knew you were going there—Harriet flung that bonus at him as she passed him in the city, and he seized the opportunity to get to the Caves first."

"I still don't believe a word of it. I won't . . ." My protest should have been defiant. Instead it came from my shattered, constricted throat in a hollow sound as if I had no breath left.

"And who had the opportunity to take Pippa's diary?" Alexandra asked. "Who was conveniently absent when it was returned? Surely you can't be that blind with love, Cathy."

A shadow, smaller than Alexandra, moved.

"Don't you dare s-say that Daddy t-took—" Words failed Pippa as they had failed me. She gave a little wail and slumped against the wall. I could not see her face in the darkness, but I felt that her eyes would have the dead look of someone too hurt and shocked to find any more words.

Only the faint, high whine of a mosquito disturbed the absolute silence. Even Durandal was still.

I brushed the insect away and said scornfully, "You really believe that Mark would read a little girl's diary? Why, in heaven's name?"

"Because there was something in it he wanted no one to know. So he destroyed it."

"What?"

"That's for us to find out, isn't it? It's the key to everything."

"Daddy would n-never, never read anything I wrote unless I—I asked him to. I know he w-wouldn't."

"The young have such trust . . ." Alexandra said.

"Oh, please." Pippa was weeping. "Please, someone turn on a light."

"Lights attract people. Cathy, tell me, do you want Mark to come and find Pippa here?"

"Yes. I want to speak to him."

"I want to go home . . ." Pippa sobbed.

"It's all right," Alexandra said softly. "You're safe with me. Once we have talked—" She stopped and listened. A car was racing with tires screaming across the unmade track that led to the house.

I turned quickly, dazzled by the headlights, and the slender balustrade shook again. "Mark . . ." I barely whispered his name, but Alexandra heard.

"Don't be afraid. He'll have to come up the outside staircase because it's the only one here as yet. When he does, I'll set Dura free. He'll never kill, but as I told you, his weight is sufficient to knock a man down. And steps are treacherous things. Mark could fall . . ."

"Cathy. Cathy." The voice was Harriet's. "Are you all right?"

"Yes, of course."

"I can't see you. Where are you?"

Before I could speak, Alexandra's voice lashed out. "You fool . . . you utter fool. Don't come near us. This is my affair now. You've lost your chance."

But Harriet ignored her and raced up the steps and past me. The car's headlights didn't beam our way, but we were just within their periphery. I saw Harriet fling herself at Alexandra, heard a scream and then Pippa cried, "Oh, don't . . . please don't . . ."

I flew up the rest of the steps, but before I got to them, the scuffling ended and someone fell. I couldn't see if it was Harriet or Alexandra; all I knew, and thanked God for, was that Pippa was safe. She was pressed into the wall as if desperate for invisibility. "You hit her . . . Alexandra . . . you hit Aunt Harriet . . ."

I dragged Pippa to me and she clung, sobbing, not caring that I was Cathy but wanting only the relief of arms holding her safe from the two women's wild, shadowed fighting.

"Get out of here, Cathy. Go on . . ." Harriet gasped. "Run for your life, or you won't have any life left . . ." She choked on the words.

I saw Alexandra's arm go out. Durandal fretted around her.

"Run, Pippa," I said. "Run down the steps and to one of the cars. Quick . . . quick . . ."

"Oh, no, she doesn't." Alexandra swung around on me. "She stays with *me*. I've told you—"

"Don't listen. For God's sake, don't listen," Harriet cried. "It was she . . . and . . . and . . ."

A rush of footsteps muffled the rest of Harriet's sentence, and the two shadowy women, locked together in hatred, disappeared into the house. I reached for Pippa, but she crouched away from me and pressed into the wall. Again there was the sound of a struggle, then a crash and another scream.

I darted toward the room, but Alexandra was standing in my way. She was breathing heavily and she was having difficulty controlling the cheetah.

"Where's Harriet?"

Alexandra's voice was devoid of emotion. "The young fool jumped from the window space, and she has probably broken her neck."

"We must get help."

"Stay where you are, Cathy. Harriet jumped because she's a coward. Now let's leave her."

"We can't." I put out both hands to push past Alexandra, but she was stronger than I and she repelled me as if I had no more resistance than a windflower.

"Now, let's talk."

"Not before I've seen if Harriet is hurt or not."

"It's too late, so stop worrying about her. Pippa, don't hold on to Dura's chain like that. Let go . . ."

I said softly, "Come here to me, Pippa."

I saw her little dim figure try to break out of Alexandra's encircling arm. "Oh, please, can't we go home?"

"Just stay quiet," Alexandra said. "It won't be long now."

"What do you mean by 'long'?" I asked.

"Our talk, Catherine."

Catherine . . . My blood ran cold. *Dust hath closed dark Catherine's eye.*

"I have a question to ask you." Alexandra's voice came softly out of the darkness. "You wouldn't want to die for Mark, would you? You're not that stupidly brave."

"Die—for—Mark?"

"That's the leading question. Would you?"

"I won't die."

Her silence was an assertion of what I was denying.

"I don't understand," I said clearly, hiding my fear.

"Do you really think Mark cares for you?"

"What makes you ask a question that I doubt *you* can answer?"

"Because I know. Mark is no woman's man. But many women want him."

"You?"

I heard her laughter echo faintly through the empty building behind her. "Mark—and me? Oh, don't be so stupid. I don't want him; but I shall have to have him. Because, you see, I want Pippa."

Anyone . . . anyone might say that. But not Alexandra.

"You have no maternal instinct," I said. "You told me that yourself."

"I haven't. I want a child that is over its first stage of life so that I have the material ready to be molded. When I saw Louise's daughter, I knew that she was the one I wanted more than any other. She is such eminently promising material and I need the stimulus of a career. Pippa will be that career. A living being created according to my dream."

She was—she must be—quite mad. Shock made me inarticulate. I looked about me. Below, nothing stirred. The wooden rail I was gripping was rough and slightly warm; the scent of the Orient—musk and oleander and camel—breathed around me.

I could still see the hood of Harriet's car, which I had parked close to the bushes. I had no idea whether she had driven away, terrified or unhurt, in whatever car she had borrowed. As I had fought to get past Alexandra and into the house after that dreadful scream, the noise we had made could have drowned the sound of a retreating car. Or she could be lying injured somewhere in or beyond the dark house. I was powerless to find out. Alexandra, strong as a lion, barred one way. And if I turned to go down the steps, the cheetah would be set on me.

XXIX

IN THE MOMENTS of carefully hidden panic, I had to think, not only of my own safety, but of Pippa's. For both our sakes I didn't dare risk breaking my neck by a fall from the wooden staircase or a cheetah's spring. But, even as I was planning to play for time and for safety, my reflexes acted on their own and I shot forward, grabbed Pippa and raced to the steps.

Dura sprang and Pippa kept crying, "No . . . No . . . No," as Alexandra seized her and dragged her from me.

The cheetah's paw was on my arm, but he didn't hurt me. Very gently, like a soft mountain bearing down on me, he floored me. I lay gasping on the steps.

"I warned you," Alexandra said and caught at Durandal's chain. "Now get up and don't do a silly thing like that until I let you go."

261

Alexandra had drawn back into the room behind the arch, but I knew that it would be dangerous to follow her.

"I didn't want anyone's child," she was saying, "just Mark's. You know why, don't you? One must have good material to work with, like an artist with the best equipment money can buy. In Pippa's case it is her brain, her intelligence—when she's not being a baby and crying as she is now—"

"You hit . . ."

"Oh, not that again. You must learn to stop being repetitive. And also, Catherine—"

"Catherine . . ."

"I like the thought of the distinguished heritage behind Mark's child. Beauty she never will have. It doesn't matter. She will have wealth of her own and—in the meantime—so have I. With that I can mold her. The breeding and the intelligence will do the rest. I have what I want—my great and final hobby—to watch Pippa's growth from a child to a magnificent young woman. *Now,* do you see?"

"It wasn't Mark . . . who planned the things that happened to me."

"Of course it wasn't. But if you had been sensible and believed me and left Bou Hammagan—left Mark for me to tell him: 'Cathy wants her freedom,' and had gone out of his life, then I could have taken over without all this fuss and unpleasantness." She waited. "There's still time. My car is outside and I could drive you to Algiers and put you on a plane for London."

"It doesn't occur to you that Mark might come after me?"

"Oh, my dear, you are only a subsidiary in his world. When I made it clear to him that you didn't want him to follow you, he would leave you alone. If you liked, we could even invent a lover. As for Pippa, she no longer trusts you. You lost her love when you were determined to have Mark completely to yourself and shut her out, just as Louise did."

"That's a most damnable lie."

"Is it? Pippa, didn't you come to me because you were unhappy? You came more than once and I comforted you."

"You hurt Aunt Harriet. I hate people hitting other people . . ."

"Oh, do stop saying the same thing over and over in that silly way."

"It's not silly." I was shouting. "She's shocked . . . She doesn't fully understand."

"Of course she does. You know quite well, don't you, Pippa, that when you and I are together you will have what you want—*all* your father's love. I will make you clever and admired and successful."

"Don't listen. It's evil, Pippa. You must grow up to be yourself, not the way someone else wants for you."

"Why don't you turn on the light?"

I reached toward the frightened child.

"Oh, do keep back," Alexandra said crossly. "You're exciting Durandal."

I stood my ground. I didn't feel in the least courageous, but I had to hear everything that Alexandra could tell me. It would be useless, if I survived, to be able to tell only half the story. At the same time, I had to watch every move the tall, cheetah-guarded woman made because I valued two lives—Pippa's and my own. "Everything you told me Mark had been guilty of was your doing . . . *You* planned it all to try to scare me into suspecting him and leaving him."

"That's right." She was standing very still.

"You sent Louise's silver box to me."

"Yes."

I clung to the wild hope that if I kept her talking, she would relax a little of her sharp vigil. If that moment came, I would seize it and take a chance, lunge for Pippa and run. "How did you get hold of the box?" I asked.

"By the simple means of taking it."

"But you weren't in England when Louise died. You told me you were in South America."

"Why shouldn't I have lied to you? I did. I was passing through London on my way to Paris and I called on Louise on the night she died. Until now, only I have known what happened—not that knowing will do you, or Mark, any good. The shadow will hang over him for the rest of his life."

I knew only too well what the shadow was, but I asked because I had to prompt her to tell all her story. There was a kind of hypnotic compulsion that made me ask, "What shadow?"

"That he killed Louise; that he was the driver of the car that didn't stop, of course. All that happened out here was just fuel added to the fire of your suspicion—and don't tell me that behind your blind feeling for him, you didn't ask yourself more than once whether he was guilty."

"The telephone call, giving the number of Mark's old car—"

"Ahmed always does what I tell him. I pay well."

"Never again, Alexandra," I said. "He's gone to even richer pickings in the New City."

She brushed aside my words, obviously not believing me. "What a pity you didn't listen to those suspicions of Mark and escape while you still had a chance. But you didn't."

"What happened—on that night?"

"I went to see Louise, as I've told you, and I trapped her into admitting that she had a lover. Some of his letters, she said, were kept in the silver box. She was such a little fool, but then Mark wasn't sufficiently interested or suspicious to wonder if she were behaving herself in his absences. I picked up the box and told her that unless she left Mark, I would show him the letters. We had a fight about it—in spite of Louise's nagging, she didn't want to lose Mark. His professional position mattered to her; she liked being a television wife."

There was a small, hurt protest from the deep darkness behind Alexandra. Pippa, listening, was understanding too much. But she kept away from us both; her only prop was the cold, inanimate wall against which she leaned.

"So," I prompted, "you kept the box?"

"Louise hadn't a chance against me. I was stronger and I got to the door. She flung herself at me and I hit the doorpost. In my purse was a flask of the special scent that is made for me in France. The bottle broke and the perfume poured out. I ran from the house holding on hard to the silver box, and I knew that the hall of the house must reek with the oozing scent. As I got halfway up the drive, I looked back and saw Pippa on the staircase. I'm sure she didn't see me because it was a very dark night and the trees threw heavy shadows across the drive. I ran fast across the road to where I had parked my car . . . I had purposely not driven up to the house; I hoped I might surprise Louise with some man. I did better than that; I learned about the love letters in the box." She gave one of the low throaty laughs I had heard so often. "Louise dashed after me, screaming at me. It was then that the car came and hit her. Just like that."

"It didn't stop?"

"No."

"And you . . . didn't go to her . . ."

"Why should I? She was stupid; she didn't deserve this child with all her potentialities; she wouldn't know how to channel them into magnificence. I do."

"You talk in big words, but heaven forbid that you should ever try to mold Pippa. She is intelligent, but so are thousands of other children; she is also fiercely emotional and highly sensitive. Your influence would never work; you'd destroy her. Pippa is no abstract phenomenon."

"The act of making her one would be my triumph."

She was like a terrible architect working on the foundation of a child's body and heart and spirit. Her search was for a glory of which she must be the perpetrator. Beneath my apparent calm, I was scared to death of this tall, mad woman I had thought I had come to know so well. As she watched me, her head was held high as if she felt herself a queen, and Louise's emerald burned at her throat.

"The diary . . ." I began.

"Surely you realize now that since I had looked back and seen Pippa on the stairs the night her mother died, the diary worried me. There was very little risk that Mark, who arrived home I believe much later, might smell my spilled perfume—the scent would have faded with all the coming and going after Louise's death. In spite of that, I decided not to risk using it while he was staying here with me. But as Pippa was on the stairs when it all happened, she must have smelled it, and with her perceptiveness and her memory . . ." Alexandra drew a long, hissing breath.

"And so?" I urged.

She lifted her hands to her forehead as if her head ached.

"On your first evening here, I found Pippa coming out of my dressing room, and when I went in, there was a heavy smell of spilled scent. She must have been curious to know what was in the bottle and, being clumsy, upset it. That's when I became afraid that it might ring a bell in her memory—she has a prodigious one in some ways—so I had to find her diary. It was quite likely that she might confess to it that she had had an accident with the perfume and have written that she had recognized it. Anyone could have got hold of her diary, out of curiosity, and read what she had written and what she might have remembered. I didn't dare have the case reopened."

"Why not? What was your part in all that, Alexandra?"

"One of the witnesses saw a woman running away—it's all down in the police records. He thought she was just escaping from seeing an accident . . ."

Pippa moved. She fought wildly to free herself from Alexandra's grasp. "*You* took it. You read my diary."

"Oh, do be quiet."

"I won't. I won't . . ."

Alexandra laid a firm hand over her mouth, and her strong arm held the struggling child.

Behind the listening and the watching, a thought—irrelevant in the tenseness of the dark villa—crept into my mind. The stained-glass window Alexandra had told me she wanted had been suggested in order to keep me in Bou Hammagan. That way, she would build up fear and suspicion until I could bear no more.

When I had come to measure for the window, I had seen some electric-light switches by the gaps where the doors would be. I groped first with one hand and then the other and felt, on my left, the small, square fitting set in the wall. I flicked the knob and the naked light sprang on.

Alexandra flung her arm up to her face. Pippa cried out, "Cathy . . ."

I darted forward and seized her and pushed her behind me so that I stood between the child and the fretting cheetah.

"Run," I said. "Go on, *run*. Get to the car. It's by the bushes, and wait for me there. *Run . . .*"

She darted behind me and clattered down the wooden stairs. I didn't dare turn my head to watch her; I held my breath and my eyes outstared the cheetah. His alert, golden gaze watched me and then looked away. I breathed again. For some reason which possibly only his animal brain understood, Pippa's lean little scampering body didn't agitate him, perhaps because she was small, or because some trust had been built up between them.

"Now," I said to Alexandra, "I'm going too. And if you want to set Durandal on me, you can." I would hold on hard to the rail, and it would be he who would leap past me and hurtle down the steps. Durandal wouldn't be hurt; cats landed on their feet.

Alexandra was laughing. "Pippa won't get far; she can't drive a car. You do understand, don't you?"

"Oh, perfectly. Even had I been a moron, you've made it plain enough for me to grasp. It was a wonderful chance for you to work on me when you heard I was coming out to North Africa—I suppose if I hadn't, you'd have turned up in London. I wouldn't have escaped you, would I?"

"No."

"You spread suspicion about Mark. I suppose Zaleida was a bonus thrown in for good measure. Only I was there tonight when Justin and Ahmed came face to face, and so I know the truth about her."

Alexandra might or might not know. In case she didn't, I was not going to tell her any more. As if she read my thoughts, she said, "But there's Harriet—"

266

"If she's dead, God help you!"

"When I tell you the truth, perhaps you won't be so wildly compassionate. Harriet was working for me, against you. She needed money and I promised her a great deal."

"I don't believe you."

"Who do you think changed the boards at Kourifia and put into your mind that you should have another look at them? Who opened the door at midnight for Ahmed to come and take you where you might never be found? The mastermind is seldom in the foreground, my dear. I made plans—others carried them out. Ahmed likes money too. But Harriet spoiled every plan because each time she lost her nerve at the last minute, the poor coward. I gave her a few chances. Then tonight I knew I had to take over."

"And the boy in the marketplace?"

"Oh, Ahmed found him. But that was *my* failure. You weren't stupid enough to follow deeply into Bou Hammagan's back alleys."

"If I had, Ahmed would have been there."

She sighed heavily. "The desert loses its victims very successfully."

"I nearly came to know that." There was still a faint tinge of courage left in me that made me snap back, "But in all your plans, you seem to have forgotten Mark."

"Oh, no. I understand him. His work and his child are his loves. I will leave him free in the one and will please him in my devotion to the other."

Devotion and Alexandra were an eternity apart, but that was nothing about which there was time to argue.

We stood in the harsh light of the single bulb. The smell on the threshold of the house was of stone and dust and wood chippings. It was as if, with the change of tenor, there was also a change of atmosphere and sound. There *was* a sound . . . I listened, willing it to come closer, but it seemed to drift away.

"Thomas Nashe wrote the lines I sent with the box," Alexandra said conversationally. "He lived over three hundred years ago and the name he used in the poem was 'Helen.' But yours scanned beautifully, didn't it? Harriet, of course, wrote the illuminated script."

"So, after Louise died, you hoped Mark would marry you."

"Yes."

"When you saw Louise being knocked down by a car that didn't stop—*not Mark's car; whatever you say, not Mark's*—you left her lying there."

"I pushed her."

It was spoken so quietly that it was almost a whisper. But I shuddered as though I had been startled by a tremendous noise. I saw then why she was desperate not to have Pippa even remotely recall the perfume that had been spilled in the hall that night. "I hoped—that I could begin to understand you. But I can't. Dear heaven, I can't."

"I was too strong for you. Ahmed was useful, but Harriet ruined every plan I made. The fool . . ."

"You have no conscience."

"No, I haven't. It makes one's actions much easier."

So, I had had a triangle of enemies. It wasn't Mark who was hated; nor, for that matter, was he loved. Pippa was the goal—the glorious, stupendous, insane dream of a woman who would destroy Mark's daughter. For Pippa could never live up to the pinnacle upon which Alexandra would have her climb.

I heard the sound again, out in the open spaces beyond the villa. I recognized the throb of a car's engine.

"Harriet." I shot across to the terrace steps. She hadn't been badly hurt after all, and now she was escaping from Alexandra. Perhaps even the denouncement and the scuffle meant nothing and there was another way out of the villa. If so, then Harriet had fulfilled the final part of Alexandra's plan and taken Pippa away.

I called once more, in case I had been mistaken. "Harriet . . ."

"Stay where you are," a voice shouted up at me.

Wild, frenzied relief sent me racing down the staircase. The wooden baluster quivered and rocked. Behind me Alexandra cried, "Go on, Dura. *Vite . . . Vite . . .*" It flashed across my mind as I stumbled on the last few steps that of course he would understand French commands rather than English. Alexandra had bought him in Paris.

I fell at the bottom step. Someone came across the glare of the headlights toward me. Mark said my name, "Cathy . . . Cathy . . ." But the voice became lost in the violence of the rush of sound behind me.

Durandal was hurtling down the steps with Alexandra screaming behind him. Mark's hands picked me up roughly and threw me to one side. "Get in the car."

The scream from the steps swelled and hung on a terrible frenzied note.

Helpless and momentarily stunned with horror, I saw the lovely green gown ripple around Alexandra, the rich bronze hair loosen as it became caught in the splitting wooden rail. Durandal's chain was stretched taut as he dragged Alexandra after him across the ground beneath the broken wooden staircase.

Mark and I collided as we dashed forward.

"Call Justin. He's in the other car with Harriet. We came together, the three of us . . . Cathy, do as I tell you." He turned his back on me and crouched down and spoke to the cheetah. His voice was soft, and I saw that the sudden quiet had steadied the agitated animal. Alexandra lay still, her head twisted, no longer fighting to free her wrist from the chain that was wound around it. Mark was doing that very gently, but he said harshly to me, "You're doing no good here. Do what I tell you, get Justin."

If Mark had intended his quiet, cold voice to be therapeutic, he succeeded. The frozen feeling left me and all my limbs sprang back into mobility. Mark needed more powerful help than I could give him, but for all its urgency, I did not dare run and excite Durandal again.

Justin met me at the far corner of the house. "What's going on?"

"Mark wants you, quickly. Alexandra has had an accident."

XXX

IN THE SINKING moonlight the unfinished house was like a white ruin. As we crossed to the pillared front, Justin cried, "Good God Almighty. Cathy, get in the car. Leave this to us. But not Mark's car because Harriet is in there and she's unconscious on the back seat. Pippa is in ours. Go to her. Keep her away from here."

"Take care," I said. "Durandal is there. Don't run or you'll excite him."

But Justin was already out of hearing. I stood hesitating, torn between going back to help and staying with Pippa. Her need won, because if she were left alone in the car, she would most certainly dash out and find us.

I crossed the rough ground where Alexandra's garden would have glowed and saw the little Fiat. As I got in, Pippa's small voice came from the deepest shadow of the side seat. "Cathy, it was horrible . . . tonight is horrible."

"It's all right. Everything is going to be all right now." I reached for her, but there was no response, so I left her crouched in her corner.

Almost at once Justin returned, came to the car window and said, "I'm going to get the night watchman to call the police. Mark can't leave Alexandra."

"She's conscious?"

"She's dead," he said. "The staircase was flimsy and it crashed under her weight. The fall broke her neck."

"Durandal was dragging her, and his chain got caught around her wrist."

"That's what finally killed her," he said.

I could find nothing to say that didn't sound like an anticlimax after the horror of the night.

"Harriet told us everything she knew as we drove here. The rest we heard for ourselves after we had carried her to the car. She injured herself quite badly when she jumped from the window gap."

"And then you came back to the house?"

"Yes, but we couldn't show ourselves. If Alexandra had known we were around, we would never have got to the truth, and God knows what would have happened to you. So we waited, near enough to see that no harm came to you. We were in the shadow at the side of the steps. And now," he flung his orders at me, "get Pippa away. Go to our house and wait for us. Here are the door keys. This is no place for either of you. Mark and I will cope."

Alexandra is dead, he had said. And as I started the car, I could not see her as ever dead. She had seemed to possess a terrible immortality. But the chain by which she controlled her golden pet had proved her to be mortal.

"I saw . . . her . . . h-hit Aunt H-Harriet," Pippa whispered. "I hate people hurting each other. Is she r-really dead?"

"I don't know, darling. Let's not think about it any more now. Everything is all right," I said for the second time.

"No, it isn't. She read my diary. Cathy, I thought it was you. But *she* d-did—and she said she l-loved me more than anyone. She said . . ." Overtired, overstimulated and frightened, Pippa burst into tears. This time she let me hold her.

"I've got to get us to Justin's house," I said. "Then we can talk. But before we start, please believe one thing. The feeling your father has for me has nothing to do with what he feels for you. Never, never think that I shall take from you anything that is yours."

I didn't expect a miracle; I didn't hope for arms to go around me and to receive small, impetuous kisses. And I didn't get them. There was no sweet asking for forgiveness, no "Cathy, I do love you." Only time would heal the years of hurt for Pippa, and I must be patient.

Justin sat in a big, fan-shaped rattan chair with pieces of broken bamboo sticking out like giant rat's hairs. I was on the settee with Mark next to me, and Pippa, sleepy and the least perturbed of any of us, leaned against his knees. She had wept herself free of terror.

"Don't you think," Mark said to Justin, "you're old enough not to go on being a bloody fool?"

"Are we masters of our characters?"

"If you continue, one of these days you'll get a knife in your back. Just keep away from the girls of Bou Hammagan unless, that is, you are in a position to marry one—and you can only do that if you and Harriet break up."

"After what's happened, I think she'll need me. She has no one else."

He surprised me. Somewhere deeper than their heckling of each other was a certain affection, a loyalty, perhaps, between the ill-matched couple.

Mark said, "I think you'd better go and fetch Harriet. Dr. Melilla must have finished patching her up by now."

Justin got up, stretched himself, turned slowly around and looked at us. "What in heaven's name must she have felt like to have thrown herself out of that hole in the wall? She told me on the way to the doctor's house that even if there had been glass in the window, she'd have plunged through it. I can't think—"

"I can. The alternative was the cheetah, and however much Alexandra argued about his being so tame, fear brings out the primitive instincts. You can never entirely control the big cats. He could have mauled Harriet to death, and she knew it. I suppose she is being given a tetanus injection?"

"That was the first thing the doctor did," Justin said. "The mound of earth the gardener had dumped near the wall for Alexandra's garden saved Harriet's life. She fell softly. But a twisted shoulder, a broken wrist and a banged head were secondary to the fact that she had a few cuts. Tetanus was the primary danger, and I think she was injected in time."

"She's lucky," Mark snapped.

"Look, let's get this quite clear before I go to get her." I had never seen severity on Justin's face before. "Harriet would never have harmed Cathy. She kept saying that when she regained consciousness at Dr. Melilla's. And I know she was speaking the truth. Money means a lot to her, and she was seeming to do what Alexandra wanted and then deliberately failing. The Kourifia Caves incident gave her her worst fright. She had to bring you back a little tattered, Cathy, or Alexandra would have made her pay in some terrible subtle way for failing. But she never dreamed the cave would disintegrate so fast."

"And she imagined she would get paid by Alexandra for no results?" Mark demanded in absolute disbelief.

"I think she hoped for a miracle."

"Oh, not Harriet. She would never believe in them."

"She wanted to ward off any real danger to Cathy until the design for the church window was finished and Cathy had left Africa. Then, Harriet felt she would at least be rewarded for trying."

"How naïve! As if you can serve two masters—God and the devil. One always wins."

"The devil certainly didn't," I said. "Harriet saved my life more than once. That's how I want to remember it all—that is, if I find I can't forget."

Pippa said, "Won't I ever see Durandal again?"

"I doubt it." Mark ruffled her hair. "We took him back to the house for Yussef to look after. Someone out here will have him; some rich Hammagarb who will perhaps look on him as a status symbol."

"What's that?"

"I'll tell you in the morning."

"Ahmed was involved," I said. "The cigarette left burning, the telephone calls—all things that were meant to take suspicion away from anyone in the house—except you, Mark."

He nodded. "Harriet told it all when she came to get me. We almost met on the office doorstep. We needed Justin too. Harriet guessed that he would be at Hashim's and he was. The three of us drove like hell to get to you."

"Zaleida was Ahmed's daughter. But you knew that, Mark, didn't you?"

"Yes. He was collecting a nice dowry for her and something more for his own comfortable nest."

Mark gave his brother a cool look. "I can't think why I shielded you from Cathy. There was no need. She can keep secrets. She wouldn't have gone to Harriet telling her you were running around with Ahmed's daughter. But in our growing up together, we seemed to have acquired a respect for each other's confidences. Well, so I met the girl, lost my argument that you owed her nothing in hard cash, and paid—for your job's sake, Justin."

"Pippa *did* see you at Hashim's café?"

"Yes, but I assure you I didn't see her. I left quickly because John arrived—we were meeting there—and it was a longer job than he thought to get his car put right. We were in a hurry."

"And . . . Pippa? You were taking her to Tunis."

"Daddy, you never told me." She brightened. "Is it a gorgeous long journey?"

"You're not going." He looked at me. "If you hadn't dashed off this morning when we were in the garden and I was called to the telephone, you'd have heard why I was planning to take her away. But when I came back, you were gone and there was no time to look for you. We had to get immediately to Zacnador."

"Why were you going to take Pippa away?"

"I had a feeling that behind everything was a plan to kidnap her. I could think of nothing else to account for it all. I thought someone was laying false trails to put us off the truth. And when he thought we were well and truly fooled, guarding you, he would strike where he had intended—at Pippa. God help me for my abysmal ignorance."

"There was no reason to suspect Alexandra. She was an old friend and so you naturally trusted her."

He refused to exonerate himself. "I'm experienced enough to know that people wear masks and that evil can lie like an underground stream beneath the face of charm."

"Mark, what are we going to do?"

"Sleep at the hotel; the three of us."

"We'll meet," Justin said to me. "I'm not letting you out of my life, my weary little sister-in-law."

I said nothing, marveling again at the revelations of his character: in this case the seeming swift recovery from shock. But then I had learned something about Justin that night. He, too, wore a mask. The face of insouciance.

I wondered if we would ever see Harriet again. That she had saved my life, after risking it, was not restitution enough. Harriet, with her tanned skin and her pale fawn hair, had never been deeply in our lives, and it would be a long time before she entered our world again, if she ever did. But Justin was Mark's younger brother, and there would be other involvements and other tangles to unravel for him, because that was the way he was made.

When we went to the car to take Pippa first of all to the hotel, Mark got in the back seat with us. "Now," he said and put an arm around Pippa, "we're going to have a little talk. You were reminded tonight, weren't you, about what you had written on that page of your diary."

I had expected a shrinking from the terrifying memory of Alexandra, and a refusal to speak.

Pippa was made of sterner stuff. "Yes, I was." She leaned her head against her father's arm.

"Why did you go into Alexandra's room on that first night?"

I tensed, dreading her answer.

"Because I hadn't seen you for ages but you didn't want me. You just wanted Cathy. Mummy used to say I was in the way and when I saw you and Cathy, it was like everything the same all over again, and I thought it was going to be so different." She drew a breath and then ran on, rather as she wrote, without any apparent punctuation, absorbed in her story. "So I ran and hid in a room and someone was coming so I went to a door and opened it. Something flew in—a moth, I think, it had green wings like the one we saw in the garden. And it hit me in the face and I put up my arm and—I couldn't help it, I really couldn't—I knocked over a scent bottle. And then I was scared and I ran. There wasn't anybody around and I didn't say anything and nobody said anything. So, I just wrote about it in my diary."

"What did you write?"

"Oh, that I was sorry I spilled the perfume because it was lovely."

"And—?"

She looked at Mark.

"Didn't you write something else about it?"

"No."

"That you remembered smelling it once before?"

"Oh . . . oh, I just *thought* I did, and I put that bit in my diary. But I don't think it was really true because you can't remember scents, can you?"

Of roses and apricots, oleander and camel. Oh, yes, you could. But a year and a half was a long time in a child's world for accurate memory.

Mark explained it with more reason than I could. "I think some-

276

where deep down, in what we rather grandly call our subconscious, you did remember that scent."

Pippa had had sufficient shock for one night and I willed Mark not to try to remind her of the night Louise had died. He didn't disappoint me.

"Come along, my little love," he said. "Come and sit by me while I drive to the hotel."

She must have been tired, for she made no attempt to ask him what "subconscious" was. Instead, she curled up on the front seat, making herself so small that all I could see from my corner in the back of the car was the top of her dark head.

"When we get to the hotel we'll take you to Mrs. Mitchell. She'll look after you until Cathy and I have packed our things and can join you."

"Daddy, you haven't told me everything that happened tonight. Cathy made me run to the car and I did, because Alexandra was angry with Harriet and hit her and I thought she would get angry and hit me. But after I ran away, what happened?"

"Nothing for you to write about in your diary."

"Why not?" She was stifling a yawn.

"You ask too many questions."

"But I want to know. Alexandra frightened me."

"She frightened me, too," I said.

Pippa sighed heavily. "Being scared makes me tired."

"And that's an understatement," Mark said. "It would exhaust everyone else."

Yussef let us into the courtyard of the House of the Fountains.

I said awkwardly, "I'm sorry . . . it's terrible . . . about Madame."

"It is the will of Allah." He smiled at me.

Mark was going to see Lisette. "This will be a shock for her, and I want her to know she can come to me for help. She'll probably want to go back to France."

I sat in the patio and watched one of Bou Hammagan's unique moths flutter green-fringed wings at the screen. I poured some lemonade from a covered carafe on the table into one of the tall crystal tumblers. Then I lifted my glass and made a libation to the tiny midnight dancer.

I heard Mark's voice talking to Lisette. Mark . . . People with dignity could not be forced to be taken completely into one's life, to be unreservedly possessed. Nor did Mark expect to dominate me.

277

Just as he would give me a great freedom, so I must give him his in order to retain his love.

Somewhere a clock chimed. It was midnight. The little green moth knocked itself out and fell to the ground. Mark came into the patio as I opened the screen door and picked a leaf and lifted the moth onto it. I laid the leaf on a thick oleander branch and turned and was immediately in Mark's arms.

"Lisette will go back to Paris," he said. "I'm arranging it for her. And as for us—Cathy, does time bring forgetfulness?"

"Seldom. But it softens memory."

He looked about him at the dark garden. "It is so beautiful, and it housed the tragedy of a corroding evil, the terrible ennui of a cultured mind that tipped over into madness when it became frustrated. Now, shall we go?"

He bent toward me. "Your lips taste of lemonade," he said.

About the Author

ANNE MAYBURY lives in an apartment high over London. At night she can see far out over the roofs and trees to the towers of Westminster Abbey, St. Paul's, and the Houses of Parliament.

She has worked in a film agency, on a magazine and as secretary to a peeress, but any job she took was only a break from writing, which, Miss Maybury says, "was and always will be my first love."